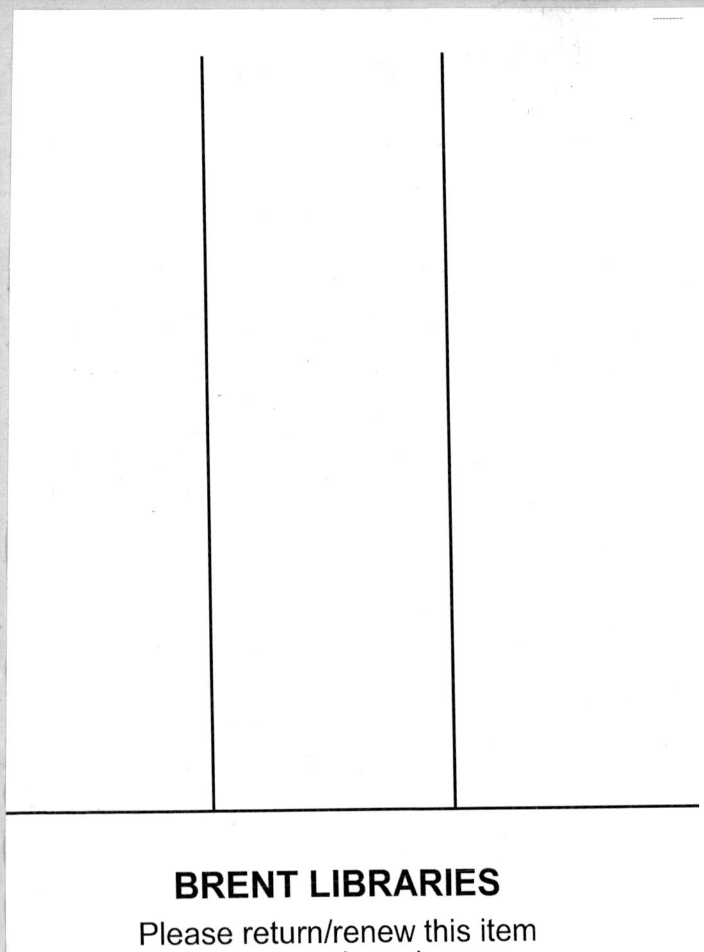

D0785786

Also by Elle James

Marine Force Recon
Show of Force
Full Force
One Intrepid SEAL
Two Dauntless Hearts
Three Courageous Words
Four Relentless Days
Five Ways to Surrender
Six Minutes to Midnight
Hot Combat

Also by Barb Han

Sudden Setup
Endangered Heiress
Texas Grit
Kidnapped at Christmas
Murder and Mistletoe
Bulletproof Christmas
Stockyard Snatching
Delivering Justice
One Tough Texan
Texas-Sized Trouble

DRIVING FORCE

ELLE JAMES

CORNERED AT CHRISTMAS

BARB HAN

MILLS & BOON

First Published in Great Britain 2019
by Mills & Boon, an imprint of HarperCollins*Publishers*
1 London Bridge Street, London, SE1 9GF

ISBN: 978-0-263-27440-0

1019

DRIVING FORCE

ELLE JAMES

I dedicate this book to Sweetpea, a good dog who gave me lots of love and companionship for thirteen years. For one so small, you were a big part of my life and heart. I hope you're running free and eating all the good treats across the rainbow bridge. I will miss you so very much.

Chapter One

She struggled to surface from the black hole trying to suck her back down. Her head hurt and she could barely open her eyes. Every part of her body ached so badly she began to think death would be a relief. But her heart, buried behind bruised and broken ribs, beat strong, pushing blood through her veins. And with the blood, the desire to live.

Willing her eyes to open, she blinked and gazed through narrow slits at the dirty mud-and-stick wall in front of her. Why couldn't she open her eyes more? She raised her hand to her face and felt the puffy, blood-crusted skin around her eyes and mouth. When she tried to move her lips, they cracked and warm liquid oozed out onto her chin.

Her fingernails were split, some ripped down to the quick and the backs of her knuckles looked like pounded hamburger meat. Bruises, scratches and cuts covered her arms.

She felt along her torso, wincing when she touched a bruised rib. As she shifted her search lower, her hands shook and she held her breath, feeling for bruises, wondering if she'd been assaulted in other ways. When she felt no tenderness between her legs, she let go of the breath she'd held in a rush of relief.

She pushed into a sitting position and winced at the pain knifing through her head. Running her hand over her scalp, she felt a couple of goose-egg-sized lumps. One behind her left ear, the other at the base of her skull.

A glance around the small, cell-like room gave her little information about where she was. The floor was hard-packed dirt and smelled of urine and feces. She wore a torn shirt and the dark pants women wore beneath their burkas.

Voices outside the rough wooden door made her tense and her body cringe.

She wasn't sure why she was there, but those voices inspired an automatic response of drawing deep within, preparing for additional beatings and torture.

What she had done to deserve it, she couldn't remember. Everything about her life was a gaping, useless void.

The door jerked open. A man wearing the camouflage uniform of a Syrian fighter and a black hood covering his head and face stood in the doorway with a Russian AK-47 slung over his shoulder and a steel pipe in his hand.

Her body knew that pipe. Every bruise, every broken rib screamed in pain. She bit down hard on her tongue to keep from letting those screams out. Scrambling across the floor, she moved to the farthest corner of the stinking room and crouched, ready to fight back. "What do you want?" she said, her voice husky, her throat dry.

The man shouted, but strangely, not in Syrian Arabic. He shouted in Russian. "Who are you? Why are you here? Who sent you?"

Her mind easily switched to the Russian language, though she couldn't remember how she knew it. In her gut, she knew her native language was English. Where had she learned to understand Russian? "I don't know," she responded in that language.

"Lies!" the man yelled and started toward her, brandishing the steel rod. "You will tell me who you are or die."

She bunched her legs beneath her, ready to spring.

Before he made it halfway across the room an explosion sounded so close, the ground shook, the walls swayed and dust filled the air. Another explosion, even closer, shook the building again.

The man cursed, spun and ran from the room, slamming the door shut behind him.

Her strength sapped, she slumped against the wall, willing the explosions to hit dead-on where she stood to put her out of her misery. She didn't think she would live through another beating, which was sure to come, because she didn't have the answers the man wanted. No matter how hard she tried to think, she couldn't remember anything beyond waking up in her tiny cell, lying facedown in the dirt.

Another explosion split the air. The wall beside her erupted, caving into the room. She was thrown forward, rubble falling on and around her. Dusty light spilled into the room through a huge hole in the wall.

Pushing the stones, sticks and dirt away from her body, she scrambled to her feet and edged toward the gap. The explosion had destroyed the back of the building in which she'd been incarcerated. No one moved behind it.

Climbing over the rubble, she stuck her head through the hole and looked right and left at a narrow alley down below.

At the end of the alley was a dirt street. Men, covered in dust and carrying weapons, ran along the street, yelling. Some carried others who had been injured in the explosions. The sound of gunfire echoed through the alley and the men threw themselves to the ground.

She ducked back inside the hole, afraid she'd be hit by the bullets. But then she realized she'd rather be shot than take another beating. Instead of waiting around for her attacker to return, she pulled herself through the gap and dropped to the ground. A shout sounded on the street at the other end of the alley. She didn't wait to find out if the man was shouting at her; she turned the opposite direction and ran.

At the other end of the alley, a canvas-covered truck stood, the back overflowing with some kind of cut vegetation, dried leaves and stalks. With men shouting and brandishing weapons all around her, she wouldn't last long out in the open. She dove into the back of the truck and buried herself beneath the stems and leaves.

A metal door opened and slammed shut, the truck's engine roared to life and the vehicle rolled along the street. With no way to see where they were headed, she resigned herself to going along for the ride. Anywhere had to be better than where she'd been.

As she lay beneath the sticks and leaves, she realized they were drying stalks of marijuana, a lucrative crop for Syrian farmers. Where they were taking their crop, she didn't know. Hopefully, far enough away from the people who'd held her hostage. She touched her wrist where the skin had been rubbed raw, probably from having been tied with abrasive rope. In the meager light penetrating her hiding place, she noticed a tattoo on the underside of her wrist below the raw skin. She pushed the leaves aside to allow more light to shine in on what she recognized as a three-sided Trinity knot. Below the knot were a series of lines and shapes.

The more she tried to decipher the symbols, the more her head ached, and her eyes blurred. The tattoo wouldn't rub off. Since it was permanent, she should know what the knot and the symbols stood for. No matter how hard she tried to remember, she couldn't.

The rumble of the engine and the rocking motion of the truck lulled her into a fitful sleep, broken up by sudden jolts when the truck encountered a particularly deep pothole.

What felt like hours later, the vehicle rolled into what appeared to be the edge of a town.

If she planned on leaving the truck, she needed

to do it before they stopped and found her hiding in the marijuana.

She dug her way out of the sticks and leaves, crawled to the tailgate and peered out between slitted, swollen eyelids.

The truck had slowed at an intersection in a dirty, dingy area of the town. With a dark alley to either side, this might be her only chance to get out unnoticed.

As the truck lurched forward, she rolled over the tailgate, dropped to the ground and ducked into a shadowy alley. With her face bruised and bleeding, she wouldn't get far without attracting attention. But she had to get away from the truck and figure out where to go from there.

Turning left at the end of a stucco tenement building, she crossed a street and ducked back into a residential area. Between apartment buildings, lines were hung with various items of clothing, including a black abaya cloak. Glancing left, then right, she slowed, then walked up to the clothesline, pulled off the black abaya and walked away as if she owned it.

A shout behind her made her take off running. She turned at the end of the building and shot a glance over her shoulder. An older woman stood beneath the space where the abaya had been. She wore another abaya and shook her fist.

"Sorry," she murmured, but she had to do something. With no money, no identification and a face full of bruises, she couldn't afford to be seen or stop to ask for help.

The salty scent of sea air and the cry of gulls gave her hope. If she were at a port town, she might find a way to stow away on a ship. But where should she go? She didn't know who she was, or where she belonged, but one thing she was very certain about, despite the fact she could understand Syrian Arabic and Russian, was that she was American. If she could get back to America, she'd have a better chance of reconstructing her identity, her health and her life.

Dressed in the abaya, she pulled the hood well over her head to shadow her battered face and wandered through neighborhoods and markets. Her stomach rumbled, the incessant gnawing reminding her she hadn't eaten since the last meal the guards had fed her in her little prison two days ago. Moldy flat bread and some kind of mashed chickpeas. She'd eaten what she could, not knowing when her next meal might come. She needed to keep up her strength in the event she could escape. And she had.

Walking through the thriving markets of a coastal town, everything seemed surreal after having been in a war-damaged village, trapped in a tiny cell with a dirt floor.

As she walked by a fruit stand in a market, she brushed up against the stand and slipped an orange beneath her black robe. No one noticed. She moved on. When she came to a dried-fruit-and-nuts stand, she palmed some nuts. With her meager fare in her hands, she left the market and found a quiet alley, hunkered down and ate her meal.

Her broken lips burned from the orange juice, but

it slid down her throat, so refreshing and good, she didn't care. The nuts would give her the protein she needed for energy.

What she really wanted was a bath.

Drawn to the water, she walked her way through the town to the coastline, learning as she went that she was in Latakia, Syria, a thriving party town on the eastern Mediterranean Sea. People from all over Syria came to this town to escape the war-torn areas, if only for a few days.

The markets were full of fresh produce and meats, unlike some of the villages where fighting had devastated homes and businesses.

Women dressed in a variety of ways from abayas that covered everything but the eyes to miniskirts and bikinis. No one noticed her or stopped her to ask why her face was swollen and bruised. She kept her head lowered and didn't make eye contact with anyone else. When she finally made it to the coastline, she followed the beach until it ran into the shipyards where cargo was unloaded for sale in Syria and loaded for export to other countries.

By eavesdropping, she was able to ascertain which ship was headed to the US later that night. All she had to do was stow away on board. She wasn't sure how long it would take to cross the ocean, so she'd need a stash of food to see her through.

Back out to the markets, she stole a cloth bag and slowly filled it, one item at a time, with fruit, nuts and anything else she could hide beneath her abaya.

At one fruit stand, the proprietor must have seen

her palm a pomegranate. He yelled at her in Arabic and grabbed her shoulder.

She side-kicked the man, sending him flying back into a display of oranges. The wooden stand collapsed beneath his weight, scattering the fruit into the walkway.

Not knowing how severe punishment was for stealing in Syria, she ran until she was far enough away, and she was certain no one followed.

With a small collection of food in her bag, she made her way back to the ship sailing later that evening to the US. Containers were being loaded by huge cranes. She found one that she was able to get inside and thought better of it. She could get in but couldn't secure the door. And if someone else secured it, she'd be locked in until the outer door was opened at the destination. Some containers weren't unloaded until they reached their final destinations…months later.

A container like that wasn't worth dying in. She'd have to find another way. The gangway onto the ship was her only other choice, and it was out in the open. She would never make it aboard in an abaya.

Waiting in the shadows of the containers she watched the men going aboard and leaving the ship. Some wore hats to shade their eyes. Others wore uniforms of the ship line or dock workers' company.

In the late afternoon, some of the men took time to eat dinner. One in particular found a shady spot to open the bag containing his meal. He sat by himself, out of view of the others in his own little patch of shade, seeming grateful for some relief from the baking afternoon sun. He wore a uniform shirt embroidered with the logo of the ship line and a hat emblazoned with the same. As he settled with his dinner, he shed his outer shirt and hat, preferring to sit in the cool spot in a tee, soaked in sweat.

Another man called out for assistance getting a container door shut.

The guy eating his dinner lumbered to his feet, leaving his shirt, hat and food in the shade. He trudged toward the other man, without looking back.

Providence.

She gave a silent prayer of thanks as she sneaked up, took the shirt, hat, chunk of bread and a plastic water bottle, disappearing before the man had a chance to return.

Though the shirt was sweaty and too big for her, it would hide any female assets and help her to look more like a man. She shoved her hair up into the baseball cap and pulled it down over her forehead enough to shadow her swollen eye.

Now, all she had to do was wait for it to get a little darker. Not too long, or they'd pull up the gangway and set sail without her. She had to get back to the US soon. If the people who'd captured her discovered where she was, she would not be safe in Syria.

Shadows lengthened with the sun angling toward the sea. The crane continued loading containers all through the day and into the evening. Men boarded and left the ship.

She waited until there was a gap in people coming and going. Pulling the cap down low over her

eyes, she tucked the cloth bag full of food beneath the baggy shirt and walked across the gangway as if she belonged, hoping she appeared to be an older, slightly heavyset man getting back to work aboard the ship.

No one stopped her on the gangway.

Once aboard, she found a stairwell and descended below deck. As she went down, a man came out of a hallway several steps below.

Her heart jumped into her throat as the guy took the steps two at a time. Fortunately, he was in a hurry and ran past her without commenting. She looked away hoping he wouldn't notice she was a female with a battered face. Once she'd passed him, she let out the breath she'd been holding and hurried downward to the lowest deck she could go. Then she dodged between containers in the hull until she found a dark corner near the back. Hunkering low and pressing her body against a container, she prayed they would finish loading soon and leave port.

She must have fallen asleep while waiting. When she woke, the ship rocked gently beneath her, the rumble of an engine letting her know they were underway.

For more than a week, she rationed her food, sneaked into the galley in the middle of the night and scrounged for food and water. Like a rat lining her nest, she found a blanket and a pillow in a closet near to the crew's quarters. In the middle of the night, she used the facilities, and though she didn't feel she could linger long enough for a shower, she did manage to clean up, using a washrag and a towel.

The long journey across the water took ten long

days. She filled her days trying to learn more about the ship and where it was going. Remaining undetected became a game she got very good at.

When she ventured out of her dark hole into some light, she studied the tattoo on her wrist, recognizing the squiggly lines as numbers in Hebrew. The more she contemplated them, the more her gut told her they were a set of coordinates.

When the ship finally pulled into port, she'd determined they were docking at one near Norfolk, Virginia.

As soon as she was able to sneak away, she walked into town and bought a T-shirt from a tourist vendor and jeans from a used clothing consignment store, using money she'd pilfered from workers on the ship. She ditched her uniform in a trash can and tugged on the tee and jeans in an alley. From there, she quickly found a library with computers and keyed in the numbers to find the coordinates. She learned the street address and searched county tax records to discover who lived at that street address.

A Charlotte Halverson lived there, and from the satellite street view of the location, the Halverson estate was a veritable fortress. If she wanted to get to Charlotte Halverson, she'd have to scale a wall, fight her way past security and possibly guard dogs. And for what? To tell a woman who likely didn't know her that she'd found her because of the GPS coordinates tattooed to her wrist?

A quick check on who exactly Charlotte Halverson was didn't make her feel any better about tres-

passing on the woman's property. She was a very wealthy widow, who employed a number of bodyguards, based on the photos of her attending various events in the DC area.

In fact, one news article reported she was scheduled to attend an upcoming charity ball at one of the swanky hotels in DC.

Getting past a stone wall and guard dogs might be extremely difficult, but she damn well could get past the security at a hotel. The event was the next night. That gave her a day and a half to get from Norfolk to DC and find her way into that hotel to get an audience with Ms. Halverson.

She prayed the woman could help her solve the mystery of just who the heck she was.

Chapter Two

"I don't need more than two bodyguards inside the hotel at the Hope for Children Gala." Charlotte Halverson, the wealthy widow of a renowned philanthropist, settled a white faux-fur shrug over her shoulders and straightened the diamond necklace around her throat. "The hotel is providing tight security. Apparently, there will be a number of celebrities in attendance for the tenth anniversary of the organization."

"What does Hope for Children do?" Augustus "Gus" Walsh asked as he fought with the bow tie that matched the tuxedoes Charlie insisted both her bodyguards wear for the event.

"They raise awareness and help combat human trafficking of children."

Gus was all for putting a stop to selling children into slavery. He'd seen too many atrocities toward children during his deployments as a Force Reconnaissance marine in the Middle East where little girls of six and seven years of age were married off to grown men.

His stomach clenched at the thought of what those

little girls endured. But tonight was about glitz and glamour. Yeah, he would be completely out of his element. Give him an M4A1 rifle, camouflage paint and a mission to take out some terrorists and he would be more comfortable. Dressed in a black tuxedo that made him look like a really tall penguin with his face shaved to within an inch of his life, he wasn't feeling it. And the damned tie…

"Here, let me." The team's benefactor, Charlotte Halverson, didn't ask them to play bodyguard to her very often, but when she did, she wanted them to blend in, not stick out. Thus, the tuxedo at a black-tie event. The older woman tugged and pulled at the bow tie until she was satisfied. Then she patted his cheek with a smile. "You look magnificent." She turned her smile to the team leader, Declan O'Neill. "Both of you look wonderful. I'll be the envy of the ball. The gossiping old biddies will be jealous that I have two very handsome men escorting me." She winked. "We don't have to tell anyone that you're my bodyguards. Although, I'm sure they'll figure that out." Charlie chuckled. "I haven't gone to many galas since my husband's death, but this is one I can't miss. This organization meant a lot to John. He would want me to continue to support their efforts."

"We don't mind going. You've done so much for our group we can't begin to repay you," Declan said. He hadn't had any difficulties at all with his tie. He stood straight and tall in his tuxedo like he owned it, though it was rented.

"Oh, shush. You and your men are helping me realize a dream. One my husband had, as well. What you've done so far to help others is phenomenal. Declan's Defenders is exactly what I'd hoped for. I'm just sorry I'm using you for bodyguard duty tonight."

"Since we aren't otherwise assigned, we're glad to do it. Heck, we're glad to do it anytime." Declan lifted her hand and stood back. "You look stunning."

Charlie's cheeks reddened. "Thank you. We should get going. Arnold is chauffeuring us tonight. I don't want to keep him waiting."

Gus followed Charlie and Declan out of the widow's mansion to the waiting limousine. Mack Balkman would lead in a dark SUV and Jack Snow would follow to make sure nothing happened on their way to the Mayflower Hotel.

Charlie had already been the target of a kidnapping attempt in DC. Declan had been there when it happened and saved her from being taken. That incident had led to all six of the former Force Recon team being employed, forming Declan's Defenders.

The timing could not have been better. After being processed out of the marines with dishonorable discharges for disobeying a direct order, they'd been basically unemployable and out on the streets. Charlie had given them jobs and hope.

Gus would do anything for that woman. Including dressing up in a tuxedo to go to a black-tie gala in DC. She'd saved them all from being homeless veterans living on the streets.

Forty minutes later, after navigating traffic into the downtown district, they arrived at the Mayflower and handed off their vehicles to the valet. Gus and Declan would go inside with Charlie, while Mack, Snow and Arnold guarded the outside perimeter.

Gus counted four guards at the entrance to the hotel. A red carpet had been rolled out for the arriving guests. Ahead of them, reporters leaned over the cordon ribbon to snap pictures of a pop rock singing sensation who'd brought her latest boyfriend to the event.

Charlie waited for the young woman and her date to move on before she moved closer.

As before, the reporters leaned over the tape and snapped photos of Charlie, one of the city's leading benefactors. Gus understood that in DC, Charlie was as much of a celebrity as the singer. She and her husband had given so much to many of the nonprofits and helped hospitals and communities with their generosity.

Gus stood beside her, trying not to blink at every camera flash, watching the crowds for anyone who might pose a threat to his boss.

Behind them, another limousine pulled up. The reporters abandoned Charlie for the latest celebrity sighting.

Finally, they were able to move into the building. Just inside the door stood two more security guards and a woman with an electronic tablet checking names against those on her list.

"Good evening, Mrs. Halverson. We're so very glad you could make it to the gala this year." The woman glanced up from her tablet and smiled. She looked from Declan to Gus. "Which one of you is Mr. O'Neill?"

Declan nodded. "I am."

"Thank you." She turned to Gus. "And you must be Mr. Walsh."

"Yes, ma'am," Gus said.

The woman chuckled. "Please, don't call me ma'am. I'm not that old."

"Yes, ma'am," Gus said again. "Miss."

She smiled again and backed up a step. "We hope you enjoy the evening, and thank you for supporting the children who need it the most."

Mrs. Halverson swept past the woman and the guards.

Gus and Declan had to hustle to keep up with her. Once they cleared the spacious foyer, hotel staff directed them into the grand ballroom.

Already, there were hundreds of guests mingling and visiting with each other, all dressed in their finest. Men in black tuxedoes and women wearing sparkling dresses in silver, gold, blue, red and more.

The crush of people made Gus nervous. How were they supposed to keep Charlie safe when any one of the guests could easily get close enough to jab a knife into the widow?

Gus found himself stepping in front of Charlie every time someone approached.

"Gus," Charlie said. "It's okay. These people are harmless. They were all screened by the event coordinator. Now, scoot back and let me mingle with the people who paid a lot of money to support the charity. It's the least I can do to ensure this organization gets the funding needed to help the children." Charlie marched forward to a group of men and women, smiling and greeting every one of them by name.

Declan touched Gus's arm. "She should be okay," he said, though his attention continued to be directed at Charlie and the people surrounding her.

The widow laughed at what someone in the group said. Another man with a black tuxedo and a crooked bow tie approached Charlie.

The hairs on the back of Gus's neck spiked. He started forward, expecting Declan's arm to shoot out.

His leader didn't slow him down a bit. Instead, he stepped out with Gus and swung wide around the man heading for Charlie.

Gus headed straight for the man and clamped a hand on his shoulder.

Declan stepped in front of him at the same time.

The man frowned. "Excuse me—is there something you want?"

"We're here with Mrs. Halverson," Declan said.

"Exactly who I wanted to speak with." The man looked past Declan. "If you'll excuse me, I'll just have a word with her."

Gus didn't loosen his hold on the man's shoulder. "You won't mind if we check you for weapons, will you?"

The gentleman's eyes rounded. "What?"

Gus ran his hands down the man's sides, patting his tuxedo jacket for bulges.

"I beg your pardon." The guy backed out of Gus's reach. "I do mind being treated like a criminal."

"Gus, Declan, what are you doing?" Charlie's voice sounded behind Declan.

"The man was converging on you at a high rate of speed," Gus explained. "We're making sure he isn't carrying a weapon."

"Good Lord." Charlie stepped between Gus and the man. "This is Joseph Morley, the event reporter. He always features me in his account of this gala." She turned to Joseph. "Please excuse my overzealous bodyguards. They don't know everyone."

Morley straightened his jacket and gave Charlie a tight smile. "At least they have your best interests at heart."

"Yes, they do. I can't fault them for that." She gave Declan and Gus each a narrow-eyed glare. "But they can stand back and let me have a little space while we're here."

Heat rushed into Gus's cheeks. How was he supposed to know who was friend and who was foe?

Declan and Gus took the clue and stepped back, allowing Charlie a chance to visit with Morley.

"I don't like how close everyone is to Charlie," Gus admitted.

"I know what you mean." Declan pressed his lips in a tight line. "But we can't smother her. She's already angry with us for assaulting the reporter."

"I didn't assault him," Gus said. "I only patted him down."

Declan's lips twitched. "Find anything?"

"No," Gus admitted.

"Then we should just stand back and let Charlie do her thing. As long as we keep an eye on her, she should be all right."

Gus nodded. "Sounds like a plan that will work for her."

For the next hour, they followed Charlie around the ballroom as she spoke with everyone, laughed, joked and talked about the need for funds to help keep children from being sold and trafficked in the US as well as abroad.

"Gentlemen, I shall be retiring to the ladies' room for a few minutes." She held up her hand. "I will not need your services in that area. Feel free to get a beverage and some of the appetizers. I don't plan on being here more than another hour."

Gus clamped down on his tongue to keep from saying *thank God.* He'd read that the gala started around 6:00 p.m. and didn't end until well into the wee hours of the morning.

At least Charlie didn't feel the need to dance into the night. She'd made that clear up front. They'd stay for a couple hours and then head home.

One hour down, one to go.

The patent-leather shoes he'd rented with the tuxedo were chafing at his ankles. He'd love it if he could kick off the shoes and walk barefoot through the crowd.

Gus and Declan followed Charlie through the throng of beautifully dressed people toward the hallway where the facilities were located. They gave her just enough room that she wouldn't feel crowded but stayed sufficiently close to get to her should someone try to jump her.

Out of the corner of his eye, Gus noticed a woman dressed in a long figure-hugging black gown standing near a giant potted tree. She had hair as black and silky as her dress and deep, dark eyes almost as black as her outfit. *Striking* was the word Gus would use to describe her. But what drew his attention to her was that her gaze never left Charlie. It followed her all the way into the ladies' room.

"Wanna go for that drink or appetizers while I stay and guard the door?" Declan asked.

"No," Gus said, his attention on the woman in black.

Declan must have heard something in Gus's voice. He frowned, glancing around. "Something bothering you?"

"My gut is sending up warning flags," Gus murmured.

Declan stiffened. "About?"

With barely a lift of his chin, Gus motioned toward the woman in black. "Her."

"Wow. She screams black widow in that killer dress," Declan said. "You *are* talking about the black-haired beauty near the potted tree, right?"

"I am."

The woman looked left, then right. She spotted Declan and Gus and the slightest frown appeared and then disappeared on her brow.

"Did you see that?" Gus asked. "She frowned when she noticed us watching her."

"I thought I imagined it, but yes. I saw it." Declan turned his attention to Gus and smiled. "I'll pretend we're having a manly discussion about sports or something while you continue to watch." His grin broadened, and he spoke a little louder. "How about those Patriots?"

"You know I'm an Alabama fan," Gus said, also in a conversational volume. In a whisper, he added, "She's moving."

"Which way?" Declan asked. "Alabama is college football. The Patriots are a real team."

"Toward us," Gus muttered without moving his lips. Then he snorted. "I guess we'll have to agree to disagree."

"Yeah. You watch your team. I'll watch mine."

The woman in black sailed past them, her head held high, her silky black hair flowing around her shoulders, her chin tilted upward, displaying a long, regal neck.

Damn she was beautiful. But something about her didn't fit in with the other women in the room. She was thin, but athletic, and she walked with confidence and purpose.

Perhaps it was the purpose that made her different than the other women in the room. Most were content to socialize and mingle. Not the woman in black. She appeared to have something on her mind and was in a hurry to get it off.

"Passing you now," Gus said, his gaze remaining on the ladies' restroom as the woman in black walked away.

"Got her in sight," Declan affirmed. "Appears to be in a hurry."

"Unlike every other woman in the room."

"Maybe she forgot to let the dog out at home."

"Yeah." Gus relaxed a little, since the woman in black appeared to be leaving and, as such, no longer seemed a threat.

Charlie emerged from the ladies' room laughing and talking to another guest similar in age to the wealthy widow. When she spotted Gus and Declan, she nodded, letting them know she was okay. Then she walked away with the other woman, rejoining the crowd in the ballroom.

Gus and Declan followed, not too far behind.

Several men came between Charlie, Gus and Declan.

Before Gus or Declan could work their way around the group of men, the woman in black appeared beside Charlie and hooked her elbow in her grip.

"She's back, and she's got Charlie," Gus said to Declan.

Gus shoved his way through the men, without excusing himself. He didn't have time for pleasantries when someone had Charlie and was leading her toward an exit door.

Caught in the group of men, Declan fell behind.

Trying not to stir up panic, Gus half walked, half ran after the two women who disappeared through the exit door into another part of the grand hotel.

His heart beating faster, Gus gave up trying to keep it cool and broke into a sprint, hitting the exit door hard, just seconds behind the two women.

The woman in black was hustling Charlie toward another door at the end of the hallway, talking in a low tone as they moved.

Charlie skipped to keep up.

Her abductor shot a glance over her shoulder, spotted Gus and glared.

"Stop!" Gus shouted.

The woman didn't follow his command, just kept moving, dragging Charlie along with her.

Unencumbered by another person, Gus caught up to the two women as they reached the exit door to the outside.

"Gus," Charlie looked over her shoulder. "I'm glad you're here."

"Let go of Mrs. Halverson," he demanded.

"Not until I have some answers," she said. "She's the only one who can help."

Gus pulled the gun from beneath his jacket and pointed it at the woman. "Let go of Mrs. Halverson."

The black-haired woman released her hold on Charlie and raised her hands. "I don't want to hurt her. I need to talk to her."

"Then set up an appointment when she's not at an event and when we can properly vet you," Gus said. "For all we know, you could be a criminal. Perhaps you should come with me and talk to the security guards. Are you even a registered guest?"

The woman's eyes widened briefly. Then as if a

shutter slid down over her face, she became completely expressionless. "No."

"No, you're not a guest?"

"No, I won't go with you to the security guards." She backed up a step, then another.

"Charlie, get behind me," Gus warned.

"It's okay. She said she wouldn't hurt me."

"Please, do as I say," Gus insisted.

Charlie frowned, but moved behind him.

"Now, either you come with me willingly, or my partner and I will take you there unwillingly. Your choice."

She shook her head. "I can't." In a flash, she turned and slammed against the door, pushing it outward enough to slip through and out into the night.

Declan came running down the hallway. "Charlie, are you all right?"

"I'm fine, but I don't think that woman is." Charlie shook her head.

"Stay with Charlie," Gus said. "I'm going after her."

"I've got her," Declan said. "Go."

Gus raced through the door and out into the night. Two guards caught him before he'd gone three steps. They pulled his arms up behind him and disarmed him. "What the hell. Let me go. There's a woman I need to catch."

"She said you'd come flying out the door after her," the guard holding his right arm said.

"She also said you had a gun and you were going to kill her." The man on the left held his pistol.

"I have a conceal carry license. I'm here as bodyguard to Charlotte Halverson. That woman tried to abduct her. You should have captured her, not me."

"Right. And I'm Santa Claus." The guard on the right snickered.

Two men raced around the side of the building and ground to a stop, silhouettes in the darkness.

"Gus?" one of them said. "Did you find her?"

"Mack? Snow?" Gus called out.

"Yeah," Mack responded. "What's the problem?"

"She got away, thanks to these guards."

"Don't come any closer, or I'll shoot," said the guard holding Gus's Glock.

Mack and Snow held up their hands. "Don't shoot. We're here as bodyguards to Charlotte Halverson."

"I told them the same, but they're not buying it," Gus said. "Call Declan. Tell him to notify the man in charge of security that their guards are holding up the wrong person."

The guard holding his arm up between his shoulder blades pushed it up higher.

"Hey, you don't have to break it," Gus said. "I'm not fighting you."

Gus could hear Mack talking to Declan through his headset. A moment later, the radios clipped to the belts of the guards holding him hostage both squawked.

"Peterson, Rawlings, check the identification of the man you're holding," the voice said. "If his name is Augustus Walsh, you can release him. He's here with Charlotte Halverson and needs to get back to her."

The man holding his arm gave it one last shove up between his shoulder blades before he released it. "Sorry," he said, though he really didn't sound sorry at all. "Just doing our jobs."

"I get it," Gus said. "I was, too." He rubbed his sore arm. "If you see that woman again, detain her. She tried to take off with Mrs. Halverson."

"We will." The guard holding his weapon handed it back. "No harm, no foul."

"Yeah." Gus holstered his Glock and straightened his tuxedo jacket. "Now if you'll excuse us, we have to get back to work."

"By all means." The guard who'd jacked up his arm waved him by. "You'll have to go back around to the front of the building. The door you came through doesn't open from this side."

Gus took off, jogging. He met up with Mack and Snow.

"Did you see a black-haired woman in a long black dress?"

Mack and Snow both shook their heads.

"If you do, keep an eye on her. She tried to take off with Charlie." Gus moved past his teammates, hurrying back to the entrance of the hotel. Declan was capable of handling Charlie's safety on his own, but Gus wanted to be there in case the woman in black returned for a second attempt.

Chapter Three

She should have known Charlotte Halverson would have multiple bodyguards protecting her. A woman of her wealth and status might as well have a target on her back at all times. A person could collect a significant amount of ransom money if he successfully abducted her.

Money wasn't her goal with the Halverson woman. Answers were worth much more to her. Why did she have those coordinates on her wrist? Why did she have a Trinity-knot tattoo? Why had she been detained and tortured in Syria? Why had she been there in the first place?

More than anything…who was she?

All the effort she'd gone to in order to gain access to the gala had been a bust. All she needed was to talk to the Halverson woman and no one else. At this point, she wasn't going to risk interaction with a single soul other than Halverson. If the woman's bodyguard hadn't been so attentive she might have gotten her alone long enough to figure out the puzzle of her existence. Now she was back to square one. Not even square one. The bodyguards would think she had tried to abscond with the rich widow. They wouldn't let her anywhere near her now, and she still didn't know if she could trust anyone other than Halverson.

Once she'd made it past the guards, she'd circled the entire building, counting the number of security personnel on the outside at every entry or exit point. The only reason she'd gotten through the first time was she'd gone in as one of the housekeeping staff, with her dress and shoes tucked beneath the uniform she'd pilfered from the back of a laundry van. She'd helped clean rooms, stating she was new.

Eventually, she slipped out of sight and hid in one of the unoccupied rooms until close to time for the gala to begin. She'd showered, dressed and applied the makeup she'd borrowed from one of the rooms. The shoes had belonged to one of the guests at the hotel. Appropriately dressed, she'd found her way down a staff elevator to the kitchen and from there into the ballroom after a majority of the people had already arrived. She'd mixed and mingled as if she belonged until she'd spotted Charlotte Halverson.

Thankfully, by the time she'd made it to DC, her bruises had faded enough that makeup covered them. The swelling around her eye had all but disappeared.

Now, standing outside the Mayflower Hotel, frustration ate a hole in her gut. The only keys she had to her identity were the tattoo on her wrist and the woman inside, and she was stuck outside. Without a coat, the cool air wrapped around her, raising goose-flesh on her skin. She wrapped her arms around her middle and stared at the Mayflower Hotel wishing she had one more chance. Just one more chance was all she needed with Charlotte Halverson.

THE WOMAN IN the black dress haunted Gus. All the way around the massive hotel he searched the shadows for her. Damn the security guard for stopping him from capturing her and getting answers about why she'd tried to take Charlie.

Did she want to take Charlie away and hold her for ransom? Had the Halversons wronged her or someone in her family, requiring retribution? Was there another reason she'd tried to get close to Charlie, to give her something, tell her something?

Mostly, he couldn't forget the brown-black eyes filled with mystery and a touch of sadness.

Who was she?

Once again, he had to run the gauntlet of the security personnel at the front door and the woman holding the tablet with the list of names of persons who were allowed inside.

Gus wondered if the woman in black was on that list. If not, how had she managed to get past the security personnel? And if she was able to get past them, who else had done the same?

That thought made him worry that much more. Once his ID had been compared to the names on the roster, he hurried to find Declan and Charlie.

Making a beeline for the ballroom, he searched the faces, finally finding Declan, who stood with Charlie at the far end of the ballroom. Declan was easy to spot. He was a good head taller than most of the women and many of the men in attendance.

Gus worked his way around the side of the room, refusing to make eye contact with anyone, in case they waylaid him and tried to strike up a conversation. He wasn't in the mood to talk to strangers. Except maybe the woman in the black dress.

Ten minutes had passed since he'd left Charlie and Declan inside the hotel to chase after the woman who got away.

"Everything okay?" he asked when he finally reached them.

Charlie frowned. "I can't get that woman out of my mind."

Gus caught himself short of saying, *you and me both, sister.* Instead, he nodded. "Did she hurt you in any way?"

"No," Charlie said, shaking her head. "She kept saying she just needed to talk to me. Something about being the key to who she was." The older woman's frown deepened. "There was a certain desperation in her eyes. I should have gone with her."

Declan touched Charlie's arm. "We don't know who she is, or why she felt the need to drag you out of the hotel. For all we know, she could have been on a mission to kidnap you and hold you for ransom."

Charlie looked up into Gus's eyes. "I don't think so. She didn't hold a gun or knife to my head. I could have shaken free of her grip had I tried hard enough. I truly believe she only wanted to get me alone to talk to me. About what, I can't imagine. I've never seen her before in my life."

"Do you think she might claim to be a secret daughter of your late husband?" Declan asked.

Charlie snorted. "I don't think so. We didn't have children. John was infertile." Her lips curled into a sad smile. "He wanted children, but he never could have fathered them. No, the woman couldn't have been his daughter." She pinched the bridge of her nose. "I'm getting a headache. Perhaps it's time for us to leave and let the younger people stay and dance the night away." She straightened her shoulders and placed her hand on Declan's arm.

Gus fell in step at her other side.

They'd only gone a few feet when a loud, whining sound penetrated the roar of voices in the ballroom.

Gus tilted his head and listened as the noise continued. "Fire alarm."

The hotel concierge appeared at the opposite end of the ballroom, carrying a bullhorn. "Ladies and gentlemen. We're sorry to disturb your evening, but what you are hearing is the fire alarm. We need everyone to leave the building through the closest exit to you."

Declan pointed to one of the signs to the outside. "This way." He cupped Charlie's elbow and led her toward the exit. Gus cupped her other elbow and the two men escorted her out of the ballroom, into a long hallway with a bright red exit sign over the door at the end. In the hallway, the alarm was even louder.

The door at the end of the hallway, like the one

he'd chased the woman in the black dress through, opened to the outside.

"Should we go out a door closer to the bulk of the crowd?" Gus suggested.

"No," Charlie said. "They wanted everyone out in case there really is a fire."

Gus pushed open the door. Before he stepped out, he looked for the security personnel first. No one stood outside. In fact, the back of the building appeared deserted.

Gus held open the door while Declan led Charlie out of the building.

"Are you guys evacuating?" Mack said into Gus's earpiece.

"We are," Declan responded. "We just stepped out of the building at the southeastern corner. We'll make our way around to the front, coming up the eastern side."

"We're on our way to rendezvous with you," Mack said.

As they rounded the corner of the building, men jumped out of the shadows and surrounded them.

Declan and Gus stepped in front of Charlie.

"We've got trouble," Gus said into his microphone.

"How much trouble?" Mack asked.

"Six deep," Gus said. Six big burly men, none of whom wore the uniforms of the paid security guards.

Gus braced himself as the men rushed them.

The first one to Gus swung a meaty fist at his head. Gus ducked and slammed his fist into the man's gut.

The man doubled over but was replaced by the next man behind him.

Gus didn't let the fact they were outnumbered slow him down. He had to keep even one of them from getting to Charlie.

Declan had his hands full, throwing punches, ducking some and taking a couple to the jaw. The men they were fighting were trained combatants. For every punch Gus threw, they hit back with equal aim and dexterity.

While Gus and Declan fought off two each, the fifth and sixth men circled around them and grabbed Charlie's arm.

She screamed, kicked and cursed, doing her best to protect herself. But she was one woman. The two men were bigger, stronger and meaner than anything she could offer in the way of a fight.

Gus punched and kicked like a madman, but he couldn't free himself from the two men fast enough to help Charlie and neither could Declan.

Then, out of the shadows, came a whirling dervish in a black dress. She attacked the men holding Charlie, landing a side kick in one guy's kidney. She spun and swept her other foot around, hitting the other guy in the temple.

Both men staggered and loosened their holds on Charlie long enough for her to get away.

The woman in the black dress didn't stop there.

When the men reached out for Charlie again, the woman grabbed one man's arm and, using his own momentum, flipped him. He landed hard on his back, the wind knocked out of his lungs.

The other guy, seeing his partner laid low, went after the woman in the black dress. He grabbed her from behind around the middle and lifted her off the ground.

Gus had his own hands full taking care of the two who had him cornered. One pulled a knife and lunged at him. Gus grabbed the wrist of the hand holding the knife, twisted it around and slammed the knife into the second man's ribs. The man went down with the knife still stuck inside him.

An elbow to the nose of the man still standing got his attention. Gus brought up his knee at the same time he slammed the man's head down. He lay still on the pavement.

Gus went after the guy holding the woman in black.

Before he could reach him, the woman doubled over, her feet hit the ground and she flipped with the man holding her around her waist. Twisting free, she rolled out of range and came up in a ready stance.

The two men who'd fought with the woman took off, running for the shadows.

Declan's two attackers broke free, grabbed the man on the ground by the arms and hauled him to his feet. Then they ran after the others.

The man with the knife in his ribs lay groaning on the pavement, his voice trailing off as blood spilled onto the ground.

Declan ran for Charlie who stood nearby.

Gus approached the woman in the black dress.

She raised her hands. "I'm not here to hurt Mrs. Halverson. I only need to talk to her. Nothing more."

Security guards ran toward them.

"I can't stay," the strange woman said, her eyes wide as the guards came closer. "I can't let them question me."

"Meet us at the corner three blocks in that direction." Charlie pointed. "We'll pick you up in my car."

The woman hesitated.

Charlie reached out and touched her arm. "Trust me. We'll be there."

After a solemn nod to Charlie and a glance over her shoulder at the people headed toward them, the woman ran.

"What were you thinking?" Declan asked. "You don't know who she is or what she wants. She could be after the same thing those men wanted. You for ransom."

"If she hadn't shown up when she did, I might not be standing here," Charlie said. "You two were outnumbered."

Gus nodded. Charlie was right. The men they'd fought had been trained in hand-to-hand combat. They hadn't been easy to overcome. If the mystery woman hadn't come along when she had, Charlie could have been taken or killed.

"Now, let's get past all the police questions and on the road home. I want to know more about our mystery helper." Charlie started for the front of the hotel. "First off, where did she learn to fight like that? I need her to teach me a few tricks so I don't get into another situation like that. I don't like feeling helpless."

Gus would like to know more about the woman, as well. She'd impressed the hell out of him with her fighting skills. He had questions for her, too. And he wasn't so sure they could trust her. Obviously, she could take care of herself, but would she use those skills on them to overtake the team and the driver and abscond with Charlie?

THREE BLOCKS DOWN the road from the Mayflower Hotel, she waited in the shadows, watching for a limousine. Had the Halverson woman told her she'd collect her to get her to leave her alone?

Wearing only the dress and the high heels she'd worn to the party, it wasn't long before the chill night air set in. She rubbed her bare arms and stamped her feet, praying a limousine would drive up, she'd get in and the heater would be on full blast.

She'd ask all the questions after she'd thawed her cold hands and quit shaking like a blender on full speed. And she'd thought the heat intolerable in Syria.

At that moment, she could stand a good reason to sweat. If she weren't wearing the heels, she'd jog up and down the alley to get her blood moving. Alas, the straps were digging into her skin and making blisters. Running was only an option if her life depended on it.

Without a watch, she couldn't tell how much time had passed since Charlotte Halverson had promised to pick her up. Several vehicles had gone by, but none had been a limousine.

Giving up wasn't an option. She had nowhere else to go. No money, no home, no extra clothing. The jeans and T-shirt she'd arrived at the hotel in were where she'd left them when she'd changed into the staff's uniform.

She didn't think she was the kind of person who stole items on a regular basis. When she had, it had been purely a matter of desperation. Until she knew who she was, she didn't know whether she'd had a job, a bank account or a home. Surely someone missed her somewhere. Someone who knew her life history. Her name.

One thing she'd learned about herself in her journey to that corner in DC was that she knew how to fight. Her moves were instinctive. Though she'd bet they were learned. The kind of learning that required lots of practice and repetition. Training.

Had she been in the military? Perhaps she was a member of the CIA. That would explain why she had been captured and tortured. It would also explain why she had no identification papers on her.

If the Halverson woman didn't know who she was, perhaps she'd go to the CIA and ask if they were missing an agent.

Unless…she was wanted by the CIA. In which case, she would be trading one prison cell for another. And she couldn't go back into captivity. She'd die fighting before she would allow anyone to capture and torture her again.

A dark SUV slowed at the corner Charlotte Halverson had indicated. Since it wasn't a limousine, she had no intention of stepping out into the open. What if the men she'd fought with that night had come back to seek revenge on the woman who'd foiled their attempt to abduct the rich widow? She'd overpowered them once. What were the chances they'd let her get away with it again? Slim to none.

The SUV continued a little farther down the road, inching along until it came to a full stop. A man got out and stood waiting.

Headlights indicated the approach of another vehicle.

She watched from the shadows of the alley, shivering in the cold.

Hope blossomed in her chest as a smooth black limousine pulled to a stop against the curb.

Still, she waited, not willing to expose herself to trouble when there was already one man waiting nearby. He could be there to make another attempt to nab the Halverson woman.

Another SUV pulled in behind the limousine. A second man emerged. The two men standing guard were big, muscular and held themselves with the confidence and bearing of those who'd known military service.

The limousine driver got out of the vehicle and opened the back door.

The same man who'd chased her out of the hotel in the first place emerged from the vehicle and bent to assist the rich widow out, as well. She was followed by the other bodyguard who'd been inside the hotel with her.

They stood for a moment, all looking around.

"I don't like this. You're far too exposed out here on the street," said the bodyguard who'd forced her out of the hotel.

"Gus, we promised we'd come to pick her up," Mrs. Halverson said. "I keep my promises." She turned to her other bodyguard. "Declan, have your men look for her."

The one called Declan nodded. "I will, Charlie, after you get back into the limousine with Arnold." He nodded to the driver. "If anything happens, I want you to drive. Get Charlie out of here as fast as you can."

Arnold, the driver, nodded. "I will." He held the limousine's back door open. "Mrs. Halverson, please. Let Declan's Defenders do their job. If the woman is here, they'll find her."

The widow frowned. "Fine. I'll get into the limousine…in a moment." She turned a full circle, staring into the shadows in all directions. "Young lady, don't be afraid," she called out. "I only want to thank you for helping us. Please, let me return the favor." After a long moment, she sighed and slid into the limousine.

Afraid Charlotte Halverson would leave before she told her who she was, she stepped out of the shadows into the dull yellow glow of a streetlight. "Wait. I'm here."

If it was a setup to grab her and take her to the police, so be it. With no better options and nowhere to go, she figured it was worth the risk.

Mrs. Halverson started to get back out of the limousine. "Oh, thank God. I was worried you'd been hurt in the fight. Please, get in." The older woman changed directions and scooted across the seat, making room for her in the limousine.

The man called Gus stepped in between the Halverson woman and her. "Perhaps it would be better if she rode in one of the SUVs."

"Nonsense, Gus. She's riding with me," Charlotte said. "I'll be safe with you, Declan and Arnold to protect me." She patted the seat beside her. "Come on. Let us take you where you need to go."

"I understand your hesitation to trust me." She stared into Gus's eyes and raised her arms. "If you want to frisk me, you can. I'm not carrying any kind of concealed weapon."

Gus snorted. "You don't need to. Your hands and feet are lethal by themselves."

She held her wrists together in front of her. "If it will make you feel better, you can bind my wrists and feet to keep Mrs. Halverson safe." The thought of being held captive made her quiver inside. But she reassured herself that she could escape if she had to.

Gus glanced toward Declan. "Did you bring zip ties?"

Declan nodded. "I did." He reached into the front of the limousine and pulled out a handful of plastic zip ties.

"Oh, don't be ridiculous," Mrs. Halverson said.

"No, really. I don't mind," she said. "They are only doing their jobs and keeping you safe from me. I would expect no less." Again, she held out her wrists.

Declan slipped a zip tie around them and pulled it snug. “I’m sorry, but we don’t know you, or what you want from Charlie.”

Gus frowned. “Aren’t you going to secure her legs?”

“Absolutely not.” Mrs. Halverson glared at her bodyguards. “This woman is my guest. I won’t have you treating her like a criminal. Now, let her get into the vehicle before I fire all of you.”

Gus frowned heavily before he finally moved out of the way and allowed her to get in beside Mrs. Halverson.

He slid in next to her and Declan sat across from them.

“Make one wrong move,” Gus said, “and I’ll make sure you regret it.”

The woman nodded. “I’m not here to hurt Mrs. Halverson. I only want information.”

Arnold closed the back door, slid into the driver’s seat and pulled in behind the lead SUV.

“Okay, now that you have my undivided attention,” Mrs. Halverson said. “Who are you, and what is it you want from me?”

“That’s just it,” she said, her heart sinking. “I don’t know who I am. I was hoping you could tell me that.”

Chapter Four

Gus frowned. "Wait. What? You don't know who you are?"

The woman shook her head. "No. All I know is what I have tattooed on my wrist." She held out her hand, palm up.

Charlie gasped and grabbed her wrist. "That's the Trinity knot." She shot a glance at Declan. "What are the chances that this is a coincidence?"

"I don't believe in coincidence," Declan said, his voice tight, his jaw even tighter. "You don't know who you are? How did you know to come to Mrs. Halverson?"

The woman nodded toward the tattoo. "The coordinates below the symbol."

"What coordinates?" Gus stared at the tattoo. "All I see are squiggly lines."

"They're numbers in Hebrew," she said.

Gus wasn't buying her story. Who tattooed coordinates on her own body? And in Hebrew? Highly unlikely. "How do you know they aren't a telephone number or someone's birth date?"

"I had ten days in the hull of a ship to think about it. As you can see, there are two rows of numbers. When I reached the US, I gave the telephone theory a shot. When I called the first one, it played a recording that it was out of service. I got a day care facility on the second one. Given the numbers, I figured they were longitude and latitude. The coordinates pointed to the Halverson Estate in Virginia." She stared into Charlie's eyes. "I don't have any other ideas. If you don't know who I am, I don't know where to go from here."

Charlie studied her for a long time and then shook her head. "I'm sorry, but I don't recognize you at all." Her brow furrowed. "But then I wasn't always privy to all of my late husband's activities. Perhaps he knew you?"

The woman's shoulders sagged.

Charlie reached out to her. "I'm sorry. I wish I could help you. It must be very distressful not knowing your own name. In the meantime, we have to call you something."

"Jane Doe," Gus said.

"That's so impersonal," Charlie protested.

"It's temporary until we figure out who she is," Declan said.

The woman in the black dress shrugged. "It's as good a name as any." She nodded toward Gus. "And like he said, it's temporary. Or at least I hope it's temporary. Until I figure out who I am, I have no home, no identification and no job that I know of."

"In other words, you're broke and homeless,"

Gus said. "Can't blame you for chasing down a rich widow. I guess I would, too, in your circumstances."

Jane Doe's eyes narrowed. "I don't want Mrs. Halverson's money. I want to know who I am. Right now, I have no history, memories or family that I know of. If I had a job, I'm sure, by now, I've been fired for not showing up."

"You said you spent ten days in the hull of a ship," Declan's eyes narrowed. "Is that where you were when you came to or discovered you'd lost your memory?"

She shook her head, her jaw hardening. "No."

Gus leaned forward. "Where were you?"

She didn't look at him, but stared into Charlie's face. "I was locked inside a tiny cell in a small village in Syria."

Charlie's eyes widened. "Syria?"

"Yes, ma'am. Syria."

"What were you doing in Syria?" Charlie asked.

Glancing away, Jane shook her head. "I don't know. All I know is I was held captive. That's where I woke up without my memory."

"Why were they holding you captive?" Declan asked.

"They wanted information from me." A shiver shook her slender frame. "I couldn't give them the answers they wanted."

"So, they tortured you?" Gus didn't trust the woman, but the look in her eyes was so haunting, he could almost feel her pain.

She nodded, raised both hands to touch the corner of her eye.

That's when Gus saw the faded bruise, barely visible beneath the makeup she wore. His hands clenched into fists. He didn't like seeing bruised and battered women. Men who hit them deserved to die.

"Oh, dear." Charlie touched Jane's arm. "I'm sorry you had to go through that."

"How did you escape?" Declan asked.

"There was an explosion close to the building. It blew a hole in the wall of my cell. I got out by crawling over the rubble and hiding in the back of a truck full of unprocessed marijuana."

"And the ship?" Gus prompted, amazed at the woman's tenacity and determination to be free.

"I found my way to the port town of Latakia. I didn't know where I belonged, but it wasn't Syria. Based on the language I felt most comfortable speaking and my accent, I assumed I was from the US and needed to get back there to discover who I am."

"And I failed you." Charlie sighed. "I'm so sorry."

"It's not your fault. If you don't know me, you don't know me. I'll have to keep looking until I find another clue as to my identity." Jane glanced out the windows of the limousine. "Please, let me out at the next convenience store. I won't hold you up any longer."

Silence reigned for all of three full seconds before Charlie exclaimed, "I won't hear of it. You're coming to stay with me."

Gus wanted to stop Charlie before she promised the stranger the world. But he couldn't.

Charlie was on a roll. "I have loads of room. You'll stay in one of my spare bedrooms." The older woman's eyes widened and she clapped her hands. "I'll have my men help you find the answers to your mystery." She turned to Declan. "Between you and your team and my husband's connections, we should be able to help out this poor woman."

Gus held up a hand. "Charlie, you don't know her."

"Exactly," Charlie shook her head as if speaking to a slow child. "That's why we need to help her."

"She could be a wacko out to steal from you, or hurt you," Gus said. He glared at Jane. "We know nothing about her."

"I'm usually a good judge of character," Charlie said. "I took a chance on Declan and his recommendation for a team, based on his willingness to help me and my gut feeling that he was a good guy."

"But you knew who he was when you hired him," Gus argued.

Charlie's lips thinned. "I didn't know who he was when he pulled me out of the kidnapper's van. When I did learn who he was, I still hired him, despite the black mark on his military record."

"This is different," Gus said.

Charlie crossed her arms over her chest. "I don't think so."

"Without any identification, you can't look her up and tell if she's a convicted felon. She could have escaped from prison where she'd been serving life for murder."

"Gus has a point." Declan shrugged. "Having just escaped from prison would explain her lack of identification."

"I escaped from a prison in Syria," Jane said. "Not here in the US."

"And there's a difference?" Gus challenged.

"I was being held for the information they wanted out of me." Jane sighed heavily. "Not that it makes a difference, but they never charged me with a crime or tried me in a court. That I know of."

"The point is, my instinct is telling me to trust Jane," Charlie said. Her jaw firmed. "She's coming to stay with me. Gus, since you're so worried about her, Declan can assign you to watch out for her." Charlie smiled at Jane. "Don't let these men bother you. They're only looking out for my well-being."

"I understand," Jane said. "If I were them, I too would have great difficulty trusting a stranger. Actually, I wouldn't have let me inside the vehicle in the first place."

Gus nodded. "What she said."

"Gus, are you up for the assignment?" Declan asked. "If not, I can assign one of the other guys."

"After seeing Jane in action, I know what she's capable of." He gave the woman a narrow-eyed stare. "I'll watch her."

Jane gave as good as she got with an equally narrowed glance. "You'll be bored when you discover that I'm no threat to Mrs. Halverson."

"Charlie," the widow said with a smile. "Call me Charlie. And, Declan, please remove her restraints."

Declan frowned, but cut the zip tie binding Jane's wrists.

She rubbed at the red marks the ties had made on her skin and nodded toward Charlie. "Thank you."

"I get the feeling that being around you will be anything but boring," Gus said.

Declan chuckled. "Yes, sir. You're the right man for this job."

Gus wasn't quite certain why Declan thought it was funny that he was the right man for the job. He took protecting Charlie seriously. If that meant sticking with the black-haired beauty like a fly on flypaper then yes, he was the right man for the job.

Where Charlie's instinct was to trust Jane, Gus's was telling him where Jane went, trouble would follow.

Jane Doe.

She knew it wasn't her name, but it gave her hope that it was only temporary.

When they arrived at the entrance to the Halverson estate, Jane studied the impressive stone fence and wrought iron gate. Yes, she was almost certain she could have gotten in, but she didn't know what kind of security system the Halversons had in place. She might only have gone two steps before a guard dog ripped her to shreds or a dozen heavily muscled men converged on her, aiming automatic rifles and fully loaded handguns.

Invading a person's private residence might not have gotten her invited in like meeting the wealthy widow at a gala. Not that her execution had gone exactly according to her original plan. In the long run, she was here, going in under the watchful eye of her assigned guard.

Charlie had no idea who Jane was, but her promise to help her find answers was better than being turned back out on the streets where she'd had to steal to survive.

"I don't like taking charity," Jane said. And she didn't like stealing. "If there is something I can do to repay you, I'm more than happy to earn my way until I'm able to return home." Assuming she had a home. Hell, for all she knew, she might live in Syria, not the US.

Deep inside, she didn't think so. But her memory only went back as far as the beatings she'd endured at the hands of her captors. Anything before that was a complete blank. Why she knew how to speak Russian and Arabic was just as much a mystery to her as her fighting skills.

The caravan of vehicles drove on the curving road through an archway of ancient oaks. When they emerged from the wooded acres, Jane's breath caught in her throat at the three-story mansion ahead. They pulled into a circular drive and stopped at a marble staircase leading up to a massive double door.

A woman and two men emerged and came down the steps.

Arnold, the driver, parked the limousine and hurried around to open the door. Gus got out and offered his hand to Jane.

She felt certain she wasn't used to having a man help her out of a vehicle. Given the dress and high heels, she accepted the hand.

He pulled her to her feet with enough force she bumped against him.

Jane planted her hands on his rock-hard chest and looked up into his deep brown eyes, reflecting the light from the front entrance.

"I'm watching you," he whispered and then held her until she was steady on her feet before stepping back to offer his hand to Charlie.

He was gentle helping the older woman out of the vehicle.

Jane had the urge to plant her foot in his backside. She resisted, knowing it would only buy her a little satisfaction for a short time and make her look bad to her benefactor. Until she got the answers she needed, she had to play nice with the cranky guard assigned to look after her.

"Charlie, are you all right?" The woman who'd exited the house hurried forward to engulf Charlie in a hug.

"Grace, of course, I am." Charlie glanced around at the other men exiting the SUVs. "I take it good news travels fast?"

"Mack called ahead and let me know what happened," Grace said. "I knew I should have gone with you to the gala."

Charlie shook her head. "I'm fine. I had sufficient

backup and a little help from my new friend Jane." She turned to Jane. "Jane Doe, this is my personal assistant Grace Lawrence. Grace, this is Jane. At least until we figure out who she really is."

Grace shook Jane's hand. As soon as she released it, she frowned, her gaze shooting to Declan. "I don't understand."

"I'll explain later," he said. "Right now, let's go inside. We didn't get a chance to eat at the gala and I'm hungry enough to eat a side of beef."

Grace stepped back, allowing Charlie to move ahead.

Charlie led the way into the house, not stopping until she arrived in a large, modern kitchen. "Carl," she called out, looking around.

A barrel-chested man wearing a white chef's smock and carrying a canister emerged from what appeared to be a walk-in pantry. "Yes, ma'am."

"We have a lot of hungry people converging on your kitchen," Charlie said. "What have you got?"

Carl grinned. "I'm about to pull a ham out of the oven. I'd planned on having ham and eggs for breakfast tomorrow, but we can eat it now. I can steam some vegetables in just a few minutes and toast some baguettes."

"Perfect. What about wine?"

"I'll get the wine," Grace offered and headed for a door on the far end of the kitchen.

"I'll help." Declan followed. They descended a staircase that led downward, possibly into a wine cellar.

Carl grabbed mitts and turned to one of the two

ovens. When he pulled the door open, steam rushed out along with the heavenly scent of baked ham.

Jane's knees wobbled and her stomach gave a loud rumble. How long had it been since she'd eaten a good meal? She'd scrounged for everything she'd eaten over the past two weeks since her escape from her cell in Syria. While held captive, her meals had been few and inadequate. She'd probably lost ten or fifteen pounds she couldn't afford to lose.

While the men shrugged out of their jackets, Carl set the ham on the counter and carved off a stack of slices. "If you're too hungry to wait for vegetables, you can make sandwiches." He pulled out a loaf of fresh bread and sliced the entire thing, laying it on a plate beside the ham.

"That's what I'm talking about," one of the men said.

Charlie laughed. "Don't worry about the steamed vegetables. Lettuce and tomatoes will suffice. I think we're all ready to eat now, not twenty minutes from now."

"Done." Carl hurried to the refrigerator, extracted the requisite lettuce, tomatoes and condiments and returned to the island. In less than a minute he had everything sliced and ready.

Grace and Declan emerged from the wine cellar, carrying two bottles each of red wine. Gus reached into a cabinet and retrieved wine glasses, handing several to Jane before loading his hands with more. They carried them to a huge table in the corner of the kitchen.

Carl made sandwiches to order one by one, starting with Charlie. Once they had their plates, the men and women moved to the table and claimed seats. Carl brought his own plate and several bags of potato chips and joined them.

Once everyone had a chance to eat several bites, Charlie went around the table, introducing everyone.

She nodded toward the brown-haired, blue-eyed man who'd ridden along with them in the limousine. "You met Declan O'Neill at the gala. He's the leader of my team of former Force Recon marines."

Declan gave her a chin lift.

Charlie nodded to Gus who'd taken the seat next to Jane. "And you met Augustus Walsh who has been assigned to protect you."

Jane almost snorted, but held back. Protect her? The hell he was. He was going to keep an eye on her to keep her from hurting Charlie or any of his band of brothers. Jane nodded politely. "Do I call you Augustus?"

"Just Gus," he said in more of a grunt than polite conversation.

Her lips twitched. "Okay, Just Gus."

His glare was worth the teasing, making Jane's smile broaden.

"Next to Gus is Mack Balkman," Charlie continued. "He was at the Mayflower Hotel tonight pulling outside guard duty."

A man with black hair and blue eyes lifted a hand. "We got caught up in the evacuation of the ballroom and missed the fight."

"Jack Snow was outside the hotel as well," Charlie said.

A tall man with dark blond hair and gray eyes winked. "Declan says you held your own with two attackers." He nodded. "I'm impressed."

Jane shrugged. "I did what I had to."

"For which I'm extremely grateful," Charlie said. "You met Grace." She nodded to her assistant and then tipped her head toward a man with brown hair and brown eyes. "Frank Ford was security backup here at the estate, along with Cole McCastlain who works with my computer tech Jonah Spradlin, who isn't here tonight."

The man she'd called Frank Ford gave a chin lift. "You can call me Mustang."

The man with the close-cropped hair and hazel eyes Charlie had introduced as Cole nodded.

"Do you have a different name you go by?" Jane asked.

"Cole is it," he answered.

"Gentlemen and Grace," Charlie announced, "this is, for all intents and purposes, Jane Doe. Our mission is to discover who she is and help her find her way home."

Home. The word filled Jane with warmth and hope. She prayed she had such a place and that a family was there to welcome her.

Chapter Five

"You don't know who you are?" Mack asked.

Jane shook her head. These former military men had every right to be suspicious of a woman claiming she didn't know her own identity.

"How did you end up with Charlie?" Grace asked.

Jane showed them the tattoo on her arm and explained about the numbers in Hebrew. She ended her life history with, "Now you know as much as I do."

"I'm amazed you knew how to read Hebrew," Grace said.

"I've discovered I can understand and speak Russian and Arabic and that I know how to fight."

"I'm even more impressed," Grace said. "My friend Emily is a Russian instructor and translator. It's not an easy language to learn. And I can imagine Arabic is even harder."

"The question is why she had the longitude and latitude of the Halverson estate tattooed on her wrist," Declan said.

"All I can think is that it might have had something to do with my late husband's secret activities." Charlie lifted her glass of wine and sipped. “It might be worth a trip to his corporate office to see if he left any files. As for that matter, we can tear apart his home office and see if we can find anything that will help. It’s about time I figured out what he was up to. He kept secrets from me, telling me it was better that I not know some of the things he was doing. He assured me it was all for the good. The good of what, I don’t know. But I trusted him. John was a good man. He only wanted to help people.”

“Mack and I can go through the home office tomorrow,” Declan said. “I can have Cole go through your husband’s computer.”

Charlie frowned. “Jonah already has, and he couldn’t find anything.”

“A second set of eyes might help,” Declan said.

“I’ll work with Jonah and see if we can find anything,” Cole said.

“Would it help if I went to your husband’s office?” Jane asked. “Maybe somebody there will recognize me.”

Charlie tilted her head, as if considering Jane’s request. “That’s not a bad idea. With nothing else to go on, it won’t hurt to try.”

“Then Jane and I’ll go tomorrow,” Gus said.

“I’ll go with them,” Jack Snow added.

“And I will, too,” Charlie said. “You’ll need my permission to get in.”

“Thank you all,” Jane said. “I don’t know what else to do. For now, I’m completely at your mercy.”

Grace ran an assessing gaze from Jane’s head to

her toes. "I think between Charlie and I, we can come up with some clothes for you to wear until we can get you to a store."

"If I can get back to the Mayflower, I left some jeans and a T-shirt in one of the broom closets."

"I'm sure by now, they have been discovered and tossed." Charlie patted Jane's shoulder. "We'll take care of you."

"As long as I can repay you when I can," Jane insisted.

"Sweetheart," Charlie said, "as far as I'm concerned, I should repay you. Between you, Declan and Gus, you saved me from those men tonight."

Heat rose up Jane's neck into her cheeks. "You don't owe me anything. I would have done that for anyone under attack."

"But it was me, and I'm thankful. The least you could do is let me help you."

Though she wanted to refuse, Jane couldn't. The truth was she needed Charlie's help. "Okay, but any clothes you purchase, I'm keeping receipts. I'll pay you back as soon as I can."

"Deal." Charlie smiled. "Now, if you'll excuse me, it's way past my bedtime. Good night, all."

As soon as she left the kitchen, the others came to the same conclusion.

"Cole and I are headed out," Mack said. "We shared a ride earlier."

"I'll be back early tomorrow morning to start sifting through Mr. Halverson's computer files," Cole said. "We'll see if we can find information about his secret operations and our mystery lady, Jane."

"I'm out of here," Jack said. "Let me know when you leave the estate. I'll meet you at the Halverson corporate offices."

"What do you want me to do?" Mustang asked.

"You can ride along with us and help protect Charlie," Gus said.

"Then I'll be back bright and early." Mustang gave a mock salute and headed for the door.

"I moved the vehicles around to the side of the house," Arnold said.

"Do you have any clothes with you, Gus?" Grace asked.

"Fortunately, I brought something to put on besides this rented tuxedo. I didn't want to wear this penguin suit any longer than I had to. I also have a bag with my workout clothes in it."

"Good," Grace said. "As Jane's bodyguard, you'll be here for the night."

By the look on Gus's face, he'd already made up his mind to stay wherever Jane would be.

Jane shivered at the intensity of his determination to protect Charlie and his team from her. She admired that in the man. He was loyal and true to his friends.

"Jane, if you'll come with me, I'll show you to your room," Grace said.

"If Charlie has a suite, that would be ideal," Gus said. "Since I'm staying with Jane."

A shiver of awareness rippled across Jane's skin.

She raised her eyebrows, pretending a cool reserve she wasn't feeling. "Is that necessary?"

"Absolutely." Gus crossed his arms over his chest. "I can't keep an eye on you if you're in another room."

She lifted her chin. "You're not sleeping with me." Her belly tightened. Holy hell. What would it be like to sleep with this man whose broad chest and thickly muscled arms could sweep any woman off her feet? Even one as tough as she.

"Not to worry. I have just the suite you'll need." Grace led the way up a sweeping, curved staircase to the third floor. "Charlie keeps these rooms for special guests."

"Ones who can climb all these stairs, I hope," Gus said.

"Of course." Grace chuckled. "You and Jane will have the Rumba Suite."

Grace opened the door. Inside was a large sitting area at the center and two bedrooms, one on either side of the sitting room.

"Will this do?" Grace asked.

"Yes," Gus said.

"No," Jane said. "I'm not comfortable having a strange man in my bedroom."

"Oh, he won't be in your bedroom," Grace said. "You'll have one of the bedrooms, and Gus will have the other. You'll have to share a bathroom and a sitting area. I think this will work out just fine."

Jane wasn't so sure. Considering her situation, and the fact she had no home, no money and no identity, though, she could deal with sharing a suite.

"It'll work," Gus said.

Apparently, whether she liked it or not, they were going to share the space.

After a glance around the posh interior, Jane couldn't complain. It beat the hell out of the filthy dirt floor of the cell she'd been confined to in Syria.

Jane eyed her guard. If the man tried anything, she had the fighting skills to defend herself. What she couldn't understand was why she'd ended up locked in a cell, if she could fight like she had outside the Mayflower hotel? Then again, she'd been weak from hunger and beaten pretty badly. For a moment, she closed her eyes and tried to remember anything past the day she'd woken up in that cell. No matter how hard she tried, she couldn't drag even a shred of a memory from the depths of her mind.

"Jane? Are you okay?" Grace asked.

Jane opened her eyes and gave a weak smile. "I'm fine."

"I'll be back in a few minutes with clothing you can use until we can get you to a store."

"Thank you." Jane walked around the sitting room and into the bedroom on the right.

Gus did the same, entering the bedroom on the left. He walked out of that room and passed her as she emerged into the sitting room.

"Was the other room not satisfactory?" she asked, standing in the room's doorway.

He entered the bedchamber on the right and walked across to the window. After opening the window and poking his head out, he closed it again. He came to a stop in front of her. “This room will do for you. The other has a trellis up to the window.”

“Why is that important?” Jane asked.

“It could either be a good way to escape or be attacked. Take your pick. I prefer to be the one manning that room with that drawback.”

“Are you afraid I will attempt an escape?” She snorted. “Where would I go? I have no money, no family that I know of and no job—again, that I know of.”

“You could be lying and setting us up to slit our throats in our sleep.”

“Or I could be telling the truth.” Jane heaved a heavy sigh. “Look, I don’t expect you to trust me. I’ll have to earn your trust, if I want it.”

He nodded. “That sums it up.”

“I found some jeans and a top that might fit you, and a nightgown.” Grace’s voice sounded from the door to the suite.

Jane spun to face her, heat climbing her neck into her cheeks. “Okay. Thank you.”

Grace’s eyes widened as she stared from Jane to Gus. “Did I interrupt something?”

Gus pushed past Jane. “Not at all. While you sort through clothes, I’ll go grab my stuff from my truck.” He paused on his way out, a frown furrowing his brow. “That is, if you’re okay being alone with her.”

Grace smiled. “I’m sure I’ll be just fine. It will give us a chance to do some girl talk.”

Gus shot a glance at Jane, his eyes narrowing. “I’ll have Declan come check on you.”

"No need," Grace assured him.

Jane bet her life Gus would have Declan come up anyway.

He left the room, albeit reluctantly.

"I trust my instincts. And my instincts say you won't hurt me." Grace handed Jane the stack of clothing she'd brought with her. "The jeans might be a little big on you. You're so thin, compared to me."

That's what happens when you don't get nourishing meals on a regular basis, Jane thought, but didn't voice. "I'm sure they'll be fine. Anything, at this point, is better than nothing."

"I also provided a bra and some panties. Everything is fresh and clean. We can shop tomorrow for things that will fit you better." Grace tipped her head toward the bathroom. "There's plenty of shampoo, conditioner and body wash in the cabinets in the bathroom. If you need anything else, just let me or Arnold know. We probably have some of just about everything in the storeroom." She stood for a moment, her arms empty, her brow dipping. "It must be frightening not to know who you are."

Jane wouldn't say frightening. Waiting for the next beating in a dirty cell in Syria was what nightmares were made of. "More frustrating than frightening," she admitted.

"If anyone can help you, it's Charlie and Declan's Defenders." She smiled a friendly smile. "They helped me when my roommate went missing. And they helped my roommate through some troubling times.

Trust them—they'll do everything in their power to get you the answers you so desperately need."

"Thank you," Jane said. Grace seemed like a really nice person. Genuinely caring and trusting of these people who'd taken Jane in despite her questionable background. "And thank you for the clothes."

Declan showed up in the doorway, a smile on his face.

Just as Jane expected. A smile curled her lips. Gus was predictable if nothing else.

"Are you finding everything you need?" he asked.

"Yes, thanks to Grace," Jane said.

"Don't worry," Declan said. "We're going to get to the bottom of our mystery guest."

"I hope you don't regret what you find," Jane said. She really did like these people. What if they learned she was some kind of criminal with a checkered past? Or worse, a serial killer? Her breath caught in her throat and lodged there. What if she was a terrible person? Maybe she couldn't remember because she didn't like who she was. What if the men who'd beaten her did so because she'd deserved it?

GUS HAD HURRIED DOWNSTAIRS, found Declan and asked for someone to keep an eye on Jane while he gathered his things. Declan hadn't hesitated, climbing the stairs two at a time to the third floor.

With Declan as backup, Gus hastened out to his truck, grabbed his gym bag and the clothes he'd brought to change into after the gala. The sooner he got out of the tuxedo, the better he'd feel. He hoped he hadn't damaged the suit in the fight outside the Mayflower. The tuxedo rental company would probably charge full price to replace it.

He had no doubt Charlie would reimburse the cost, but she already did so much for him and the rest of the team.

Gus made his way back up the staircase to the third floor, feeling a sense of urgency to get back to the job of watching Jane.

When he arrived at the suite he'd share with her, he found Grace and Declan standing in the doorway.

"I'm sure whatever we find will be good. You seem too nice to be anything but good," Grace assured the woman.

"Everyone who knew Ted Bundy thought he was a charming, nice man," Gus said. "Except the girls he murdered."

Grace gasped. "Gus, surely you don't think Jane is another Ted Bundy."

Jane's gaze met his, her face devoid of expression, but her dark eyes widened slightly, as if in fear. That look lasted a split second and then was gone.

What was she afraid of? That he was too close to the truth, and too close to revealing the criminal she was? He couldn't help but feel that she feared the truth about herself.

Was the woman who could take on two men at a time in a street fight really vulnerable? Was she being honest? Had she lost her memory?

Gus shook away the thought. He couldn't let himself go soft on Jane. Until he knew everything there was to know about her, he couldn't let his guard down for a minute. Too many of the people he cared about most could be at risk with her living amongst them. Charlie's generosity toward a stranger could get them all in trouble.

Declan clapped a hand on Gus's shoulder. "Holler if you need anything. We're only a floor away." He took Grace's hand in his.

"That goes for you, too, Jane," Grace said. "Have a good night's sleep."

Finally left alone, Gus tipped his head toward the bathroom. "You can go first in the shower."

"Thanks," she said. "I don't think I normally wear high heels. If I ever wear them again, it'll be too soon." She gathered the pile of clothing Grace had brought and carried all of it into the bathroom, closing the door behind her.

Once alone in the suite, Gus did another pass through. Though there were two bedrooms, Gus wouldn't be sleeping in his. He wouldn't hear her movements. She could sneak out of the suite in the middle of the night without him knowing.

He tested the couch in the sitting room. It was firm, but manageable. Though a little short for his tall frame. It would have to do. He'd hang his feet over the edge if he had to.

While the shower was going, he pulled the comforter off the bed in his room and carried it and a pillow to the couch. The sitting room had a set of French doors leading out onto a small balcony. It was high enough up, it would be a stretch to think someone could jump to the ground and not end up with a broken neck. Still, if Jane decided to leave that way, she'd have to pass him on the couch. He'd have to sleep with one eye open.

He walked to the suite door and studied it. How would he keep her in the room? The couch was close enough he would know if she tried to go through the French doors. Being on the third floor, he was almost certain she wouldn't attempt the drop.

At the very least, he needed a way to rig the door to make a noise if she tried to leave.

"Why don't you just move the couch in front of the door and sleep there?"

Gus turned to find Jane standing in the doorway of the bathroom, a terrycloth robe cinched around her narrow waist.

"What if you try to go out the French doors?" he asked.

"Then I deserve the broken neck I would get from that foolish a move." She carried the stack of clothing Grace had brought, the black dress folded neatly on top, the high-heeled shoes dangling from her fingertips.

Barefoot and makeup-free, her wet black hair slicked back from her forehead, she appeared to be not much older than a teenager. And the bruise around her eye was more pronounced.

Gus's chest tightened. He knew how cruel some men in Arab countries could be toward women. Hell, toward anyone. If what she said was true and she'd escaped a place where she'd been beaten, she was a brave woman with a whole lot of gumption.

He wanted to admire her, but he couldn't let himself. Not until they knew more about her. Mostly, he wanted to rip apart the men who'd beaten her.

Jane entered the bedroom and placed the clothing on top of the dresser.

She turned back to him. "Come on. You won't get any rest if you're worried about me taking off." Jane crossed the sitting room to the couch. She gave it a good shove, but it didn't move. "It's heavier than it looks."

Gus joined her at the other end and leaned all of his weight into it while she pulled it toward the door. It moved, but only a few inches at a time.

She gave him a crooked smile. "At least you'll know I won't be able to move it, if you're not helping me." Jane dug her bare feet into the carpet and leaned back, pulling at the arm.

Little by little, they shoved the couch toward the door.

"We can stop short of the door. As long as it's close, I'll hear if anyone tries to get in or out. I don't want to create a fire hazard by blocking our only safe exit."

"Nice of you to think of me." Her lips twisted. "But for now, go ahead and move it up against the door."

"Why?"

Jane propped her fists on her hips. "If you want to get a shower, you won't feel comfortable leaving me alone in here by myself."

She was right. He wanted that shower after wrestling with the attackers at the hotel. He leaned into the couch and, with Jane's help, shoved it against the door.

"And you can leave the door to the bathroom open. I'll even sit on the couch so you can keep an eye on me." Jane raised both hands, palms up. "See? I'm trying to make it easy for you."

His eyes narrowed.

Jane rolled her eyes. "I know. You still don't trust me any further than you can throw me."

His lips twitched. "I could probably throw you pretty far. You don't look like you weigh very much."

"You don't get much to eat when you're held captive by Syrians who don't like you very much." The words came out like a statement of fact. She didn't appear to be fishing for pity.

Still, his gut clenched. Jane was too thin. She could use a hamburger a day for the next month to put some meat back on her bones.

Gus rummaged in his gym bag for shorts, ready to get the hell out of the fancy clothes and into something less constricting. He glanced at Jane.

Jane held up a hand. "I do so solemnly swear to be right here when you get out of your shower." Then she sat on the couch, tucking her legs beneath her.

She'd been beautiful in the figure-hugging black dress, but seeing her in the white robe, her dark hair a stark contrast to the white terrycloth, she took his breath away.

Whoa, dude, he counseled himself. He couldn't

get all wrapped up in this woman. Even if she awakened in him a desire he hadn't felt toward a woman in a long time.

He hurried into the bathroom and closed the door just enough to allow him to strip with a little privacy, but open enough he could look out and check to see she was as she said she'd be…on the couch.

Once naked, he peered around the edge of the door.

Jane smiled and waved. "Still here."

Gus stepped in the shower, turning on the water to a lukewarm setting. He was far too aware of his nakedness with a half-open door the only thing standing between him and the woman who'd taken on two attackers without breaking a fingernail. She wasn't wearing much beneath the robe and she had long, sexy legs that seemed to go on forever, disappearing beneath the robe's hem.

Once beneath the spray, he turned the water cooler, hoping to chill the rise of heat in his loins.

Jane was the job. Nothing else.

Hell, her name wasn't even Jane. What was it? He focused on a name that suited her to keep from thinking about those long, bare legs.

Salina? No. Jezebel? Maybe. She talked all innocent, but he suspected she had a fire burning deep inside. He could imagine how passionate she'd be in bed. A fierce fighter, she had to be no less fierce in bed.

And there he was back to thinking about her in a purely unprofessional manner. He turned the water cooler. By now it was so cold, gooseflesh rose on his skin.

In quick, efficient movements, he washed his hair and body and switched off the cold water. When he reached for the towel, he realized he'd forgotten to get one out of the cabinet.

A hand reached around the curtain extending a towel toward him. "Take it," Jane's voice said from the other side.

He snatched the towel from her and held it low in front of him. "What the hell are you doing in here?"

She stood on the other side of the opaque white curtain, her body silhouetted in hazy gray. "Getting a towel for you. When I got into the shower, I forgot a towel and had to get out to get one. I figured you might have done the same. I was right?"

"Yes," he said, hating to admit it. "But I could have gotten it myself."

"With the door open?" She snorted softly. "I figured you were a little more modest than some."

He wrapped the towel around his waist, praying he wouldn't make a tent out of it. Then he flung the curtain aside. "Thank you."

She stepped back, her gaze running the length of him from head to toe. "Glad I could help." Her lips curled and she pointed at his torso, just about his belly button. "You missed a spot." Then she turned and left the bathroom and Gus, getting aroused to the point his towel tented.

Sweet hell, the woman was going to make him crazy. Thankfully, she'd sleep in the bedroom. The couch would be sufficiently uncomfortable to take his mind off the woman in the other room.

He closed the door just enough she couldn't see him. Gus slipped into the shorts and opened the door again.

Jane wasn't on the couch where she'd been when he'd gotten into the shower.

Gus's heartbeat galloped ahead. The couch was still in front of the door where he'd left it and the French doors were closed.

"I'm in the bedroom, in case you're wondering," Jane called out.

The breath he hadn't realized he'd been holding whooshed out of his lungs and he remembered to draw in a fresh one.

She leaned out the door, her smile twisted. "You thought I'd left, didn't you?"

By not answering, he gave her his answer.

Jane shook her head. "I told you, I don't have anywhere else to go. I'm homeless and I can't even get a job because I don't have an identity. No social security number, no driver's license and no car. How am I supposed to live?"

"You made it this far in two weeks from Syria?"

She pressed a hand to her flat belly. "Hungry, stealing to survive and hitchhiking on a container ship isn't my idea of a good time. If the authorities randomly stop me, I'll go straight to jail. They might even deport me, claiming I'm an illegal alien. Hell, I might be." She sighed heavily. "So, you see, I'm staying here until I figure out who the hell I am. I won't hurt Charlie or anyone working for her. Why would I bite the hand that's feeding me?"

Gus held up his hands. "Okay. I'll give you the benefit of a doubt for now. But I'm still sleeping on the couch."

Jane shrugged. "It's your back. I can't tell you the last time I slept in a real bed." She yawned, pressing a hand over her mouth. "I'm looking forward to clean sheets and a comforter to keep me warm. You do what you have to. I'm going to bed." She turned away, slipped the robe from her shoulders and laid it on the end of the bed.

The nightgown she wore was icy blue and barely covered her bottom. She pulled back the comforter and sheet and slipped into the bed. "Good night, Gus. I really do hope you sleep well. I plan on it." Then she pulled the comforter up to her neck and reached over to turn off the light.

For a long moment, Gus stared at the darkened room.

"Go to sleep, Gus," she called out softly.

Gus moved the couch a little away from the door, enough they could get out if needed, but not enough Jane could slip by without him noticing. Then he stretched out on the comforter, his gaze on the bedroom door.

He lay awake for a long time, a dozen questions racing through his mind, all centering on the woman in the other room. Frustrated that he didn't have any more answers than he did, he could only imagine how Jane felt, not knowing who she was.

If she really didn't know.

Chapter Six

When Jane lay on the soft bed, in the clean sheets, with her head snuggled against a feather pillow, she fell asleep as soon as she closed her eyes, thinking heaven couldn't be more comfortable.

How long she slept, she couldn't tell. But the heaven she'd fallen asleep in soon turned to hell. She was back in the cell in Syria, waiting for the next visit from the men who'd beaten her.

The smell of urine burned her nostrils and the cold hard ground pressed into her bones. She'd lost track of how many days she'd been there and couldn't remember how she'd gotten there in the first place. Her captors kept asking her questions she couldn't answer. They asked the same questions and she gave them the same answers. She couldn't remember. No matter how many times they hit her, she still couldn't tell them what they wanted to know.

She lay on the dirt, dried blood crusting on her lip and nose, her eye nearly swollen shut, and prayed for a miracle.

The door opened and a man yelled at her to get up.

When she couldn't, he stalked into her cell and kicked her hard in the ribs.

She cried out, loud enough to wake herself out of her dream.

Still shaking, her rib still hurting from the dream kick, she sat up in the nice, soft bed and wrapped her arms around her legs. Going back to sleep was not an option. If she did, she'd be right back in that cell, suffering from the latest abuse.

She tried to think about anything other than Syria and the stench of her cell.

Jane. They call me Jane Doe. Whispering softly to herself, she tried to talk herself down from the nightmare. "You're not in Syria. You're in Virginia. You're not being beaten. You're okay." Her eyelids drifted downward. Once…twice…

As soon as they closed, she was right back in that cell, her captor yelling down at her. Again, she opened her eyes, forcing herself back to consciousness.

When she thought she might fall asleep again, she pushed aside the comforter and left the bed, padding barefoot to the open door.

In the pale light from the stars outside the window, she could see Gus lying on the couch, his arms crossed behind his head, his eyes closed.

She wanted to wake him to talk to her and ground her in Virginia. But he looked so peaceful and asleep.

Jane sat on the carpet in front of the French door, determined to sit up all night. If she didn't go to sleep, she couldn't dream. If she didn't dream, she wouldn't end up back in Syria, wishing she could just die and get it over with.

Through the window, the stars shone, filling the sky like so many diamonds brilliantly sparkling. When she'd been in her cell, she hadn't had a window to see outside. She'd gone days without fresh air or sunshine. Days passed, but she didn't know how many or how long she'd been in her cell.

Now, sitting on a comfortable carpet, she should be grateful and happy that she was clean, well-fed and pain-free. But she couldn't relax, couldn't settle until she knew.

Who was she? Why had they captured her? What had they wanted from her?

Sitting in a plush house with all the food she could possibly eat, an endless amount of hot water for showers and people who could help her, she felt anxious, restless and worried.

If she could, she'd do her own sleuthing. By herself. That way if she learned anything about herself that was unfortunate or heinous, only she would know. She could live with that. But if Charlie and her team of former military men, Declan's Defenders, learned that Jane Doe was a horrible person, she would feel that she'd let them down. All of their help would have been for naught. She'd have to leave, if they didn't turn her over to the police, FBI or CIA first. A shiver rippled through her, shaking her entire body. She couldn't bear to see the hate and disappointment in their faces after all they'd already done for her. And Gus would have been right to be suspicious.

She looked back at the couch and her heart stood still.

Gus was gone.

Jane sat up straight, her body tense, her pulse now pounding, shooting adrenaline through her system.

"I didn't mean to sneak up on you." Gus appeared from behind her, carrying the blanket from her bed. "I thought you could use this." He draped it over her shoulders. "I would have said something, but you were pretty caught up in whatever you were thinking about."

Jane wrapped the blanket around her shoulders and pulled it close. "Thank you."

"Couldn't sleep?"

"Didn't want to," she replied.

He went back to the couch, grabbed the comforter and returned, spreading it out on the floor beside her. "Bad dreams?"

She pulled her knees up under her chin and wrapped her arms around her legs. "Yes."

"Sometimes it helps to talk about them." He lifted a shoulder and let it fall. "Or so my shrink said. I don't always buy into that crap."

She laughed softly. "In this case, I don't think talking about it would help. It would only reinforce the memory."

"Oh, so you have one?" He turned toward her, his eyes wide, questioning.

"Only from my captivity. And those are memories I'd rather forget."

"Right." He looked out the window. "If it helps, I thought some of my worst memories would never fade. I had nightmares for years about a mission gone incredibly bad. But the memories finally faded. They aren't gone, but their impact doesn't plague me nearly as much as it did in the beginning."

Jane crossed her arms over her knees and rested her chin on them. "I don't even have any good memories to think about to counteract the effects of the bad ones." She wasn't whining, only stating the facts. She didn't want pity from the man beside her. Only understanding.

"Yeah. That's gotta be tough."

She looked at him, her eyebrows raised. "So, you believe me about my memory loss?"

He gave a twisted smile, still staring out at the stars. "No, but I can imagine what it would be like not to remember the good times in life."

"What are some of your good memories?" Jane asked. "Maybe I can borrow yours to think about when I'm in a bad place."

He continued to stare out the window without speaking.

After a long moment, Jane didn't think he would respond.

"The day I left the foster care system and joined the military is one of my best memories."

"You were a foster child?"

He nodded. "Since I was seven and my parents

and little sister died in a car crash on their way to pick me up from school. That was one of the days I had nightmares about for years," he said, his voice so low, she barely caught his words.

"I'm sorry. It must have been hard for you."

He shrugged. "You learn to keep moving. If you sit too long, you get swallowed by sadness. I kept moving. I got shuffled from one foster family to another. The first family had a boy of their own about my age. He was a bully and made my life pretty miserable. I put up with it until one day he shoved me so hard, I hit my head on the concrete sidewalk. I came up dizzy but fighting mad, and bloodied his nose."

"The beast deserved it," Jane said, wishing she could have been there for the little boy who had it hard enough dealing with the deaths of his parents.

"The boy's parents blamed it all on me. I got placed with another family who had two other foster children. One was a teen with drug issues. The other was his brother, a kid just trying to survive in a world that had let him down. The teen ended up overdosing on meth. The foster parents were so distraught they quit the program and the two of us were farmed out to other homes. I had six different foster homes before I graduated high school. And I only graduated high school because I knew that's what my mother and father would have wanted. I joined the marines to get away from it all."

"I'm sorry you had to go through all that."

"I'm not. You don't know the good times unless you had the bad times to compare it with. I'd forgotten what it felt like to have a family who cared. Until I signed up for Force Reconnaissance."

"Your team is your family?"

He nodded. "I'd give my life for any one of them. And they'd do the same."

Jane sighed. "You're lucky."

"Who knows?" Gus said. "We might find out that you have a whole family waiting to hear from you."

"Or not. I feel like, deep in my gut, there isn't anyone out there waiting for me." She stared out the windows of the French door.

"Don't give up yet," Gus said. "Cole is pretty good at anything internet related."

Jane gave a weak smile. "How can anyone find information about a person who has no basis or starting point?"

"The FBI and CIA do it all the time. Charlie has contacts in both from dealings her husband had with them. We'll find out who you are soon enough."

"And if you don't like what you find?"

"We'll cross that bridge when we come to it."

Jane yawned and laid her cheek on her folded arms. "I'm so tired."

"Would it help if you leaned on me? Maybe having someone close will keep you from reliving your nightmare."

"Why would you do that?" She stared at him, her brow furrowing. "You don't even trust me."

"You know the saying... Keep your friends close but your enemies closer?" He gave her a crooked grin.

"Some say Sun Tzu was the originator of the

quote," Jane said. "But he said something like, 'know your enemy and know yourself and you will always be victorious.'"

"So, you've studied Sun Tzu?"

Her frown deepened and she stared at the ground. "I must have."

"Perhaps some of your memory is starting to come back."

"I hope so," she said.

"In the meantime, the offer still stands. You're welcome to lean on me."

She sighed. "I'm willing to try anything for a chance at dream-free sleep."

Gus scooted closer and held open his arm. "Come here."

She leaned into him and snuggled her cheek against his chest. "At least you won't have to worry about me sneaking out while you sleep," she said, her eyes drifting closed. Fully expecting the nightmares to continue, she waited.

Nothing. No images of angry men slapping her around, punching her and kicking her in the side. Just the arousing scent of male cologne and the reassuring feel of rock-hard muscles beneath her cheek. Gus, his military fighting skills and the backing of his band of brothers in arms would ward off the men who wished to hurt her in her dreams.

Jane drifted into a deep sleep. Her only dreams consisted of a man who held her gently, surrounding her with a feeling of family she was sure she'd never known.

GUS HELD JANE the rest of the night. At one point, he eased her down onto the comforter beside him and pulled her back against his front, spooning her body.

He told himself he only did it because it made it easier for him to keep track of her. If he were honest, he would admit he liked having her close.

Seeing her sitting on the floor in the borrowed nightgown, her long black hair hanging down her back and her narrow shoulders hunched, touched him somewhere he hated to admit existed. Because if it existed, it left him vulnerable in a way he hadn't been vulnerable since his parents had died.

In some ways, she reminded him of the little boy he'd been with his trash bag full of whatever he could carry from his home to his foster family. He'd arrived at a strange house where nobody knew him and they knew each other. Every house he had gone to, he'd been the outsider, the person who didn't really belong.

He saw that in Jane and it made his chest hurt.

Granted, she wasn't a grieving seven-year-old who'd lost her parents. But, if she was telling the truth, she had lost a lot more than her family. She'd lost the memories that made her who she was.

Gus had faded memories of the father and mother who'd loved him, and the little sister who'd idolized him from the time she could talk. He had those memories to pull out whenever he was in a bad place.

What did Jane have? Memories of being beaten and held in a dirty cell in Syria?

His arm tightened around her, pulling her closer.

He rested his cheek against her silky black hair and inhaled the scent of her skin. The first time he'd seen her he'd been impressed with her beauty. The long, sleek lines and raven-black hair had captured his attention, even before he realized she'd been watching Charlie's movements.

From the strength of her determination to get to Charlie and the answers she so desperately desired, to the vulnerability of a woman fighting horrific nightmares, she made Gus think. About her, about her story and about his own reaction to the way she felt in his arms.

The situation had *bad idea* written all over it.

Yet Gus couldn't let go. She felt right in his arms. Her body fit perfectly against his. She wasn't too tall or too short. Jane was just right.

Gus must have fallen asleep.

Sunlight filtered through his closed eyelids, forcing him to crack them open. He lay for a moment in the sunlight, letting the bright rays warm his body.

Jane lay with her head on his biceps and one leg slung across his thighs, making it impossible to rise without waking her. Her breathing was deep and steady. No signs of despair or nightmares.

Though he ached from lying against the hard floor, Gus couldn't regret having defended the woman against her bad dreams. Not when her warmth pressed up against him with only the thin fabric of her nightgown between them.

As he lay there, desire built from a spark to a

flame. The longer he held her the more he wanted. She was not someone he could make love to. She was an assignment, the job, his responsibility, not his lover.

Gus had to get up and move away.

He slipped his legs from beneath hers and was in the process of scooting his arm from beneath her head when she blinked her eyes open.

She stared into his face, a slight pucker forming on her forehead. "Who…what…" Then as if recognition dawned, she bolted to an upright sitting position. "I must have fallen asleep." She pushed the hair from her face and turned toward the sun shining through the window. Her eyes widened. "It's morning."

Gus chuckled and sat up, pulling the comforter across his lap to hide the evidence of his desire. "Yes, you slept and it's morning."

She shook her head. "I'm sorry I took advantage of you. It couldn't have been comfortable sleeping on the floor."

"I've slept on worse."

For a long moment, she stared out the window, the pulse at the base of her throat pounding hard. Finally, it slowed and she turned back to him. "Thank you. I don't think I've slept that well in…well, I don't really know how long."

With her hair mussed and her face pink from sleep, she was even more beautiful than she'd been in the black dress the night before. Despite the faint bruise near her eye. The soft morning sunlight added a certain vulnerability, making her no less mysterious, but more approachable.

The more he stared, the more he realized he was getting caught in something he wasn't ready to deal with.

Gus pushed to his feet, immediately turning away from Jane. "People are usually up pretty early around here. Carl will have breakfast ready before we get downstairs. You should probably get dressed." And he should take another cold shower. But he couldn't explain the need without revealing why. Instead, he grabbed his jeans and held them in front of himself, waiting to dress until Jane went to her bedroom.

"I won't be long," she said.

The sound of the door closing behind him gave Gus the chance to release the breath he'd been holding. He quickly slipped into his jeans and eased the zipper up over the hard ridge of his erection. He pulled on a T-shirt and let it hang loose over his waistband, hoping to hide the evidence long enough for his desire to abate.

Socks and shoes came next and then he shoved the couch back to where it belonged in the sitting room. He collected the comforters from the floor and draped them across the couch.

The bedroom door opened and Jane stood framed in the doorway, wearing dark slacks, a soft pink sweater and black shoes. She'd brushed her hair back from her face and tucked it behind her ears.

She lifted her chin and gave him a tight smile. "I'm ready when you are." The vulnerable woman of minutes before was safely hidden behind a poker face.

Gus couldn't imagine what this woman had gone

through and was currently going through. His gut was telling him to trust that she was telling the truth. But what if she wasn't? He worried that his desire made him soft and vowed to remain vigilant to protect his team and Charlie. "I'm ready." He was ready to bring on the day and all that it might reveal.

Chapter Seven

Jane must have imagined the gentleness in the way Gus had held her the night before. His look as he opened the door to the suite had shifted back to the professional military man on a mission. She couldn't blame him. He had a job to do. Knowing how he felt about his team, she would expect no less. They were his family and he had to protect them at all costs. From her.

Her chest tightened as all the horrible scenarios she'd come up with the day before resurfaced. Today could be the day that they learned who she was. Originally, she'd thought knowing was better than not knowing. Now she wondered.

Though he was all professional and cool, Gus held out a hand to her at the top of the staircase.

She laid her fingers in his palm.

He closed his hand around hers. Without a word, he started down the staircase to the ground floor.

They followed the voices coming from the kitchen. Before they reached it, Jane pulled her hand free of his. If she turned out to be a threat to his team, he didn't need to explain why he'd been holding the hand of the enemy.

Some of the team were already there. Jane went through the names she remembered. Cole, Declan, Arnold, Carl, Grace and Charlie were gathered, along with a man she didn't recognize.

"Oh good," Charlie turned to smile at them. "I was about to send Grace up to check on you two. Carl has breakfast ready. I trust you slept well?"

Jane nodded. "I did." She couldn't vouch for Gus, since he'd slept on the floor with her in his arms. This, she didn't share with her benefactor. In this case, less information was better.

"Cole and Jonah have been up and working the computer since six this morning." Declan nodded toward a man Jane hadn't met. "Jonah, Jane. Jane, Jonah Spradlin, Charlie's tech guy."

A younger man with blond hair and gray eyes nodded in her direction. "Hey."

"Nice to meet you." Jane's pulse quickened as she faced Cole and Jonah. "And? Did you find anything?"

Cole shook his head. "We've used all the passwords Jonah knew when he worked with Mr. Halverson, but haven't cracked the secret databases yet."

"We're working on it," Jonah said, "but it might take a little more time to hack in. He had it locked down pretty tight."

Jane didn't know whether to be frustrated or glad that they didn't know anything yet. She leaned toward frustrated. If the news was bad, she'd deal with it. Who she was in the past didn't set the course for who she could be in the future. Unless she ended up in jail. Jail put a damper on planning for a future. Still, she couldn't borrow trouble. She'd cross whatever bridge she came to, when she reached it.

Mustang arrived as they gathered around the table.

"Where's Snow and Mack?" Mustang asked as he set a plate on the table, pulled up a chair and sat.

"They're going to meet with one of my CIA contacts at Langley," Charlie said as she scooped scrambled eggs onto her plate. "They're going to check into Syria and see if they can find a connection to a woman fitting Jane's description."

"Do you happen to recall the name of the town you were held captive in?"

Jane shook her head. "I have no idea. I was too worried about getting out of it to stop and ask."

Charlie gave her a gentle smile. "Not to worry. They'll get whatever intel they can and bring it back here for us to sift through."

Jane found it difficult to breathe. Her chest was so tight, air didn't seem to want to move in or out. She stared down at the food on her plate for a long moment, vivid images of her cell, the explosion, the rubble and the back of the truck carrying marijuana all flashing through her mind at once. How long would it take for them to fade into dull memories?

A large hand settled on her left knee and squeezed.

She looked up into Gus's face, glad he was next to her. His strength and determination gave her hope for a future of her own choosing. If a seven-year-old boy could overcome a difficult upbringing, Jane would work through her flashbacks until they no longer consumed her.

Forcing a deep breath into her lungs, she resumed regular breathing and attacked the meal in front of her. If her situation got bad, she might be back out on the street. She'd need her strength to keep going.

"Charlie." Jane set her fork beside her plate, having eaten every last bite. "Do you mind if I ask, what happened to your husband?"

Charlie shook her head. "I don't mind your asking." She took a deep breath and let it out before answering. "He was murdered."

Jane's heart contracted. She'd known he was deceased, but murdered? "I'm so sorry. Did they get who did it?"

Charlie's eyes narrowed. "No. There was no evidence to go on. He was shot leaving his office building. There were no witnesses and the security cameras showed nothing. The police suspect a highly trained sniper pulled the trigger. I hired a private investigator to look for the man who killed John. We found nothing."

"So, the murderer is still running free."

Charlie nodded. "When someone tried to kidnap me, I was fortunate enough that Declan was nearby and saved me from my kidnappers. That's when I decided to employ Declan and his team of marines. Too much gets by the police. I wanted a way to help others so they didn't have to go through what I've endured."

"We're lucky to be here." Declan tipped his head toward Charlie.

"I'm lucky to have you and your team on my side." Her brow wrinkled. "Something that keeps surfacing in the situations we've encountered are references to Trinity." She tipped her head toward Jane. "Like the symbol on your wrist. We've seen it now several times. We aren't sure what it has to do with what's happening and why all these events seem to tie together."

Declan shook his head. "That's something I asked Mack and Snow to check into while they're visiting your contact at the CIA. Maybe they can come up with the connection or an explanation of what the Trinity symbol stands for in this situation."

Jane rubbed the tattoo on her wrist. It had been the only thing she'd had to go on when searching for her identity.

"I've been thinking we should bring Cole or Jonah with us to my husband's office," Charlie said. "If we need to get onto his desktop computer, we'll need someone who knows his way around."

"I can continue to work on getting into John's computer here at the house," Jonah said. "If I find anything, I'll notify you immediately."

"Thank you." Charlie's gaze swept the room. "I can be ready in ten minutes."

"I'll pull the vehicles around to the front," Arnold said.

Charlie turned and left the room.

"Ten minutes," Declan said. He and Grace rose and started to gather plates from the table.

"Don't worry about the dishes." Carl waved them

away. "I'll take care of them. You have more important things to do."

"Thanks, Carl," Declan said. "And thanks for breakfast. You always feed us well."

"Yes. Thanks, Carl," Jane said. "The meals are truly delicious."

Carl beamed. "I do my best. Can't ask for a better job."

Jane almost envied the chef. To know who he was and enjoy the job he performed had to be satisfying. What kind of job had she had before she lost her memory? What kinds of jobs took a woman to Syria? She spoke a few languages and she had fighting skills. Could she be a member of the CIA? Maybe she should be going to Langley with Mack and Snow. But if she were a double agent, working for the Russians or Syrian rebels, going to Langley could get her in hot water.

Letting Mack and Snow take on that task seemed to be the right answer for Jane. She didn't want to end up being interrogated by the US government any more than she had been interrogated by her Russian captors in a Syrian village.

She glanced toward Gus. He might be her guard to protect his team and Charlie from anything she might throw their way, but he'd actually become her protector, as well. She found comfort knowing he was there, and he was strong and a capable fighter. If she were attacked, he would help her to escape. At least, she hoped he would.

Just as Charlie had said, they met ten minutes later

in front of the mansion where three vehicles were lined up. Instead of the limousine, Arnold would be driving a luxurious town car.

"Grace and I will ride with Charlie and Arnold," Declan said. "Cole will take the lead SUV and Gus will follow in the SUV with Jane."

They climbed into their assigned vehicles and the convoy drove out of the Halverson estate and into DC.

"Does Charlie always have lead and trailing vehicles when she goes places?" Jane asked.

"She's been attacked twice since we've known her," Gus said. "It makes sense to provide her with as much security as we can."

"She's a generous woman." Jane frowned. "Why would anyone want to hurt her?"

"Her husband was equally generous from all accounts I've heard. Why would someone want to kill him?"

"Charlie said he had secret activities he was involved in. Perhaps that was what got him killed."

Gus nodded. "That's our bet. I hope we learn what those activities were sooner than later. I have a feeling they are the reason someone has tried to take Charlie twice now."

"They might think she knows more than she does."

"Could be. Let's hope Cole is more successful getting into her husband's computer at his office than he's been on John's home desktop."

Jane sat in the passenger seat, staring at the car ahead of them carrying the woman who'd opened her home to a stranger who could prove to be a danger to her. Charlie might have put her trust in the wrong person when she invited Jane into her home.

Jane clenched her hands into fists. No matter who she had been in her past, she refused to harm one hair on Charlie's head in the future. The woman had a heart of gold. She treated the people around her like family. Anyone would be lucky to be a part of Charlotte Halverson's family.

THEY ARRIVED AT Halverson International Headquarters in downtown DC. The five-story Georgian-style white building with its tall columns and huge entry doors stood on a corner and stretched for an entire block.

Gus was thankful they had no more problems than the usual stop-and-go traffic getting into downtown DC. No one tried to run them off the road or hijack Charlie's car. When they arrived, they drove right into the reserved parking lot beneath the Halverson building.

Charlie led the way inside.

Security guards snapped to attention and ushered her and her entourage through to the information desk where her guests were given lanyards with temporary passes attached. One by one they scanned their passes through the turnstiles and were finally through to the interior.

Charlie used her ID card inside the elevator, taking them to the top floor.

When she stepped out of the elevator, a mature woman in a gray skirt suit, with faded red hair combed into a neat French twist, met her there. "Mrs. Halverson. It's so nice to see you. Can I get you and your guests something to drink?"

Charlie turned to the group who'd followed her into her husband's office. "This is Margaret Rollins. If you want to know where anything is, ask her. She was my husband's assistant. She knows as much, if not more, than my husband did about this business."

Margaret nodded. "Thank you."

Charlie gave her a brief smile. "I'll be conducting a meeting with my guests in my husband's office. I'd appreciate it if we were not disturbed."

"Of course, Mrs. Halverson. Please, come this way." The woman led the way down a long hallway to a massive wooden door at the end. She pushed through into a spacious office suite with a reception desk guarding another office behind it.

"Would you prefer to be in Mr. Halverson's conference room, or his office?" Margaret asked.

"His office, please," Charlie said. "If I recall, he had sufficient seating for all of us."

"Yes, ma'am. Nothing's changed since…" She stumbled on her words for a moment and then seemed to get a grip. "Since your husband's passing."

Charlie touched the woman's arm. "That's nice to hear."

"It's really good to see you here," Margaret added.

"I should have come sooner. It's just hard to come here and not see John sitting at his desk." Charlie gave her husband's executive assistant a weak smile.

"I understand," Margaret said. "I had a hard time

coming back to work knowing he wouldn't be here." She sighed. "I'm thinking about retiring at the end of the month. But I'm glad I got to see you again before I leave."

Charlie took the woman's hands in hers. "I'll be sorry to see you go. I know I should have stepped in sooner to take over. I just couldn't. But I'm here now."

"I'm glad you are. You and Mr. Halverson will always have a place in my heart. You've been so good to me."

"He couldn't have done the job without you, Margaret." Charlie looked past her to her husband's office and her bottom lip trembled.

Margaret squeezed her hands. "Go on in. It's just as he left it."

Gus could see Charlie's hesitancy. Except for a few brief meetings in the office building, she never went there. He sensed it was too painful.

Grace hooked Charlie's elbow on one side and Declan on the other.

Charlie shot them a grateful smile, took a deep breath and moved forward into the office where her husband had successfully led his company for more than three decades.

Gus, Jane and Cole followed, giving the widow a little distance to come to grips again with her loss.

John Halverson's office took up the entire corner of the building, with floor-to-ceiling windows overlooking downtown DC and many historic buildings and landmarks. He even had a shiny brass telescope positioned to overlook the Washington Monument.

Charlie walked to his desk in the center of the room. It appeared to be only a desk without a computer or monitor.

Gus looked around for the computer. Had someone taken the desktop computer out of his office when he'd passed? The secretary had indicated his office was just as he'd left it.

Charlie gave a small smile. "He was so proud of the work he'd done, building his business in international trade to what it is today. I never begrudged him the time he spent late into the evenings working so hard. Often I'd bring dinner to him and we'd have a picnic here in his office with the night skyline shining through the windows."

No one said a word, allowing Charlie to remember the good times she shared with her husband.

She drew in a deep breath and pressed her finger into the desk. A computer monitor popped up from a panel in the surface.

Charlie looked up at Cole. "You'll want to sit at his desk to access his computer." She laid a slip of paper beside the monitor. "These are the passwords he used when he was alive. I don't know if they've been reset."

Cole grinned and hurried forward. "I was beginning to wonder where it was hiding." He sat in the leather executive office chair and pulled it forward. Within seconds, he had the computer booted and was keying away, using the passwords provided.

Charlie walked to a credenza against the far wall and pressed her thumb against a fingerprint scanner and a door slid open exposing a file cabinet. "We can go through these paper files while Cole looks through the digital ones." She moved over several feet to another fingerprint scanner and pressed her thumb there. Another door opened to reveal yet another file cabinet. "My husband kept a lot of records over the years. Before he died, he must have known he might meet an early demise. He had me come in one evening and gave me access to the files only he had access to. He had my thumbprint and my eye scanned. And he gave me a list of his passwords, telling me not to share them with anyone I didn't trust completely." She shot Cole a glance. "I trust Declan's Defenders with my life. I guess that's as completely as you can get. Until now, I didn't see a need for you to go through my husband's information."

Cole nodded. "Your secrets are safe with me, Charlie."

"And me," Declan echoed.

"As well as with me," Gus said.

"And me," Grace added.

Which left Jane. She held up her hand. "Charlie, I know it's too early for you to put full trust in me, but I swear on my life, your secrets are safe with me, too."

Charlie smiled. "Thank you."

They went to work going through every file in every cabinet, spreading them out on the small conference table in one corner of John's office. After an hour, a voice sounded over the phone intercom.

"Mrs. Halverson, Quincy Phishburn, the acting CEO, would like to have a word with you."

"Could you schedule him for an hour from now?" Charlie asked.

"He said he only has a small window of opportunity to meet with you between other meetings. He'd like to see you now."

Charlie glanced around at the file folders spread out over the conference table. "Where?"

"In John's office," Margaret said.

Charlie pressed a button on the phone. "I have it on mute."

"We can set things to rights in under a minute," Grace said. She nodded to Declan, who grabbed up a stack of files and carried them to the cabinet. Grace, Gus and Jane carried the files they'd been working through and placed them in the cabinets. Moments later, the cabinet doors were closed.

While they had restored the files to their proper places, Cole shut down the computer and the monitor disappeared into the slot on the desk.

Charlie looked around at the neat room and pressed a button on the phone. "Please, show Mr. Phishburn in, Margaret."

Cole joined Gus, Jane, Grace and Declan at the small conference table as the door opened and a man with graying temples, wearing a charcoal-gray pinstripe suit, entered the office and crossed the room quickly toward Charlie.

Gus, Cole and Declan were halfway out of their seats to intervene when Charlie raised a hand and gave a little shake of her head.

Phishburn took Charlie's hands in his. "Mrs. Halverson. What a pleasure it is to see you here."

She smiled at the man. "Thank you, Quincy. It's been too long."

"We understand. Losing a loved one is never easy." He released her hands and turned to the people gathered around the table and frowned. "I trust everything is all right?"

"Quite," Charlie said. "I'm only here because I needed a place to meet with my team on a project I'm working on."

"And what project is that?"

"Nothing that concerns the corporation," Charlie said. "And I'll be coming to the office more frequently. So, you can expect to see me more often."

Quincy's attention jumped back to Charlie. "Are you concerned about the corporation or my performance?"

"Not at all. I'm an owner in this business and I need to be as involved as my husband was."

"Mrs. Halverson, there's no need for you to feel as if you have to fill your husband's shoes. He hired a team of employees to run the business. We're all quite capable."

Gus's fists clenched at the patronizing tone in Quincy's voice. The man didn't understand Charlie at all.

He didn't have to worry about the widow. She was more than capable of defending herself. "Quincy, dear, I'm quite certain you are capable, but the corporation needs owner oversight to make certain it's headed in the intended direction." She tipped her head up, looking down her nose at the man. "I'll be in next week to start reviewing profit-and-loss reports, balance sheets, sales and marketing. Of course, I will take all the advice I can get, but I'm aware of how this organization runs, having worked with my husband more years than you've been with Halverson International." She walked toward the door and opened it. "Now, if you'll excuse us, we have work to do."

Gus swallowed hard to keep from laughing out loud.

"Yes, ma'am." Firmly put in his place and his cheeks a ruddy red, Quincy Phishburn left the office.

Charlie closed the door with a loud click and shook her head. "I really despise men who think they know more than me just because I'm a woman. I earned a bachelor's degree in international marketing at Harvard and my masters in operations management at Yale. I'm not an idiot." She went to the cabinets again and opened them with her thumbprint. "Let's get this done. Obviously, I need to come here more often. And I will."

Cole leaped to his feet and got to work pulling up the computer and digging into the files.

An hour later, they admitted defeat.

"I'm not finding anything on this computer, or in any of the corporate databases," Cole said. "I dug into Phishburn's files and noticed he has a Fantasy Football spreadsheet with tabs dating back several years."

"I don't care about his football bets," Charlie said. "But I will be checking into the job he's doing for the corporation. I might be making some management changes in the near future. Although, John hired him, so he must have seen something in his credentials." She snorted. "I threw my degrees at him, but they don't mean squat if you don't have the intelligence to find your way out of a paper bag."

"Charlie, we all know you've got paper bag navigation down pat," Grace said, with a smile tugging at the corners of her lips.

"It's a good thing you're pretty," Charlie said with a stern look. Then a smile broke free. "Most important, you have a big heart and a sense of humor. Those are key in my books." Charlie clapped her hands. "Let's head back to the house."

"I'd like to make a stop along the way, if we can," Gus said.

"Where?" Charlie asked.

"At a marine recruiter's office I know of." Gus locked gazes with Jane. "They have a fingerprint kit I'd like to borrow."

Declan grinned. "Good idea. They keep more than criminals' prints in the system."

"Perfect," Charlie agreed. "I hadn't thought about that, but Jonah has a friend in the FBI with access to the IAFIS system. For that matter, he might have direct access, via hacking. He can run Jane's prints. She might show up in the government employee or military database."

Jane grimaced and added softly, "Or the criminal database."

Chapter Eight

"Are you okay with that?" Gus asked.

She nodded. "I need to know who I am. No matter the outcome."

Gus's thoughts had run along the same lines, but it could be one of the fastest ways to get to the bottom of who Jane Doe really was.

Charlie touched her arm. "Don't worry. I don't think you're a criminal."

"But what if I turn up on that database as having committed a crime?"

"We'll worry about that *if* it happens. And I'm betting it won't." Charlie gave her a quick hug. "Come on—we might find out who you are sooner than we thought."

They left John Halverson's office.

Charlie stopped at Margaret's desk. "Have a nameplate made up to replace John's. I'm moving into the office next week."

Margaret smiled. "Thank God. I might even put off retirement, if you plan on staying a while."

"If you want to retire, go ahead. But I'd really like it if you stayed." She gave Margaret a hug.

"Mr. Phishburn won't be happy that you're going to take over where Mr. Halverson left off."

Charlie winked. "All the more reason for me to step in."

Margaret grinned and sat behind her desk. "I'll have that nameplate up before the end of this week."

Charlie led the way out of the suite to the elevator. "I've let grief keep me on the sidelines far too long. I have too many good years left in me before I sell the business." She stepped into the elevator, her lips firm, her head held high. "John would want me to do this."

"You're a smart woman," Grace said. "You'll do great things."

"You know that means you'll be coming to the office with me every day."

Grace smiled. "I know. I'm okay with that."

"We'll have to dedicate a space for Declan's Defenders."

Gus could almost see the wheels turning in Charlie's head.

"We're flexible," Declan said. "We don't need a dedicated space."

"You might not, but I do," Charlie argued. "I like having a war room to plan and strategize. There's a conference room next to my office. It will serve nicely as a war room for you."

"Like I said," Declan repeated, "we're flexible."

"Then it's settled," Charlie stood straighter. "I'll

have Margaret get corporate badges for you to enable you to get in and out of the building easily."

Declan gave her a mock salute. "Yes, ma'am."

They left through the garage and pulled out onto the street, Gus and Jane in the lead vehicle, Cole in the trailing SUV.

Gus led the convoy to the marine recruiting headquarters. A man he'd gone through marine basic training with had landed there as a recruiter. They agreed that only Jane and Gus would go into the office. The others would wait out in the parking lot in their vehicles.

Gus led the way into the office. Jane followed.

"Can I help you?" A young lance corporal manned the front desk.

"I'm looking for Staff Sergeant Haines."

"One moment, sir." The corporal punched a button on the desk phone in front of him. "Sergeant Haines, you have guests in the front office." He released the button and looked up. "He'll be right with you."

A black man wearing the Marine Corps dress blues walked out of a back office, grinning. "Walsh, you old son of a gun. What brings you to a recruiting office? Don't tell me you want to sign up again?"

Apparently, word hadn't gotten out about Gus's dishonorable discharge from the Marine Corps. Otherwise, Haines wouldn't have suggested signing up again, as that wasn't a possibility. Gus preferred to keep it that way.

"I need a favor," Gus said.

"Name it. I owe you a few from basic. I don't think

I'd have made it through without help from my old pal Walsh." He held out his hand.

Gus took it and was pulled into a bear hug that took his breath away. "Good to see you, Haines."

"You too, man." He clapped him on the back and stood back. "Now, what's this favor you need?"

"Do recruiting offices still have fingerprint kits?"

"I think we might have one around here somewhere. We rarely throw anything away. Come on back to my office. I have a supply cabinet back there. If I have one, it'll be there."

Gus stepped aside to allow Jane to pass.

"Who've you got here?" Haines grinned. "A recruit for us?"

"Not this time." He turned to her. "This is Jane Dole," he said, obviously forgoing the Doe surname so as not to trigger questions. "She's a new recruit to the company I've gone to work for. We need to run a background check on her."

"You know they have companies that do that kind of thing for you."

"I know, but my boss didn't want to spend the money." Gus hated lying to his friend, but the truth would take a lot longer to explain. "I was hoping to get the prints and have a buddy of mine run the check."

"Gotcha." Haines opened a metal cabinet full of office supplies and military gear. He dug around inside and came out with an ink pad and a couple blank fingerprint cards. "You know how to do this?"

Gus nodded. "I think we've got this."

"I'll give you a hand, just in case." Haines set out the ink pad and the card.

One by one, he rolled Jane's fingers in the ink and then into the corresponding block on the card.

When they were done, he showed her to the bathroom where she could wash up.

"It's good to see you," Haines said. "I'd heard you'd gotten out." He shook his head.

Gus stiffened. Just what had he heard?

"Whatever the charges were, I'm betting it was all bullshit," Haines said. "You were always straight up and gave one-hundred-percent. Not everyone makes it into Force Recon. I always knew you could. I have the utmost respect for you, man." He held out his hand. "Semper Fi."

Gus gripped the man's hand, his chest tight. "Semper Fi. Thanks." For helping him with the fingerprinting and for believing in him when the powers that be in the Marine Corps hadn't.

Jane joined him and they left with the card. Minutes later they were on the beltway, headed back to the Halverson estate. Gus and Jane took the trailing vehicle position.

"What was Haines talking about, charges?" Jane asked.

"I left the Marine Corps with a dishonorable discharge," he said, his tone flat, discouraging further conversation.

"I'm sorry to hear that," she said. "What happened?"

"We made a command decision to disobey an

order that would have had extreme consequences and collateral damage." Gus snorted. "Because of our decision, our team took the hit and we were shown the door."

Jane stared across the console at Gus. "I'm betting you and your team did the right thing. Politics can be harsh, even when you do the right thing."

He shot a glance her way. "And you know that because?"

She stared out the windshield at the vehicle ahead. "I don't know why I know that. I just do."

"It doesn't take a genius to figure it out, either, but then the higher ranks and politicians aren't always geniuses. But thank you for the vote of confidence."

She lifted a shoulder. "You're welcome."

Gus glanced in the rearview mirror and stiffened. They'd gotten off one major road onto another and the vehicle behind them was the same one that had been there for the past five miles. He handed his cell phone to Jane. "Call Declan—he should be the first number in my favorites. Give him a heads-up."

"Why?" Jane twisted in her seat.

He nodded toward the rearview mirror. "We might have some trouble."

JANE STARED AT the vehicle behind them, her pulse picking up.

"See that dark gray SUV back there?" Gus asked.

"Yes." The vehicle didn't appear to be dangerous.

It was following approximately ten car lengths behind them. A white sedan swerved in between them.

The SUV sped up, passed the white car and pulled back in behind them, now eight vehicle lengths back.

"It's been there through the last interchange and keeping pace. When we change lanes, he changes."

"You think he's following us?" Jane hadn't been watching the entire time but he sure appeared to be following them.

"We can find out easily enough," Gus said. "Call Declan."

Jane found Declan's number and sent the call, putting it on Speaker.

"What's up, Gus?" Declan's voice sounded loud and clear.

"Got a dark gray SUV following me for the past fifteen minutes. Wanna get off the next exit and back on to see if we shake him?"

"I'll have Grace notify Cole. Be ready to get off at the last minute."

"We'll stay on the line," Gus said.

Jane held the phone, turned sideways in the seat to better watch the vehicle behind them. She could hear voices from the interior of Declan's vehicle, Grace's voice, then Declan's and Charlie's.

"Getting off now," Declan said. Their vehicle took the next exit.

Gus waited until he'd almost passed the exit before he swerved to get off, no signal.

Jane held her breath. The dark gray SUV followed them on the off ramp. "He's sticking with us."

"We have a stoplight ahead," Declan said.

"Can you blow it without causing a wreck?" Gus asked.

More voices from Declan's vehicle.

"Blowing," Declan said.

Ahead of them, they could see Cole's SUV race through the red light, across the intersection and onto the ramp leading back onto the highway. Declan's vehicle followed.

A car coming from the other direction skidded to a stop, barely missing the rear end of the vehicle carrying Charlie and the others.

Jane gasped and held on as Gus hit his hazard lights and then his horn and followed Declan through the red light and the intersection, racing up the on-ramp leading back to the highway they'd just left.

The dark gray SUV started through the intersection and stopped when two other vehicles blocked his path.

"He got stuck at the intersection," Jane said, grinning. A moment later her grin died. "Damn."

"What?"

"He made it through the intersection and is coming up the ramp."

"We hear you," Declan said. "We'll try some evasive measures. Be ready to zip in and out of traffic."

"Following," Gus acknowledged. "Just go. We'll keep up and try to get a license plate number."

"You watch the front. I'll let you know what's

going on behind us." Jane twisted more in her seat and watched out the back window for the SUV.

Gus maneuvered through several lane changes, moving ahead in the heavy traffic, a little at time.

"I don't see our tail," Jane said, squinting to see in the distance around several cars blocking her view. "No, wait—he's back there. Three vehicles between us."

More lane changes and the dark gray SUV disappeared again. "I think we lost him."

"Good. But we can't let our guard down."

"I'm watching." Jane turned in her seat, looking all around for any other signs of being followed. They passed a ramp leading off the freeway, crossed a bridge and slowed as merging traffic clogged the rest of the vehicles moving through.

Out of the corner of her eye, Jane saw a flash of dark gray metal as an SUV darted out of the merging traffic from the on-ramp and crossed two lanes of traffic, heading for them.

"Look out to the right!" Jane cried. "He's back and coming straight for us."

The dark gray SUV slammed into the side of their vehicle, crushing Jane's door inward and shoving them into the fast lane.

The car on their left swerved onto the shoulder and slammed on the breaks to let them pass, the driver laying on the horn.

Gus gripped the steering wheel, his knuckles turning white as he fought to keep the SUV from running off the road into the concrete barriers.

The dark gray SUV didn't let up, pushing them closer and closer to the concrete.

"Hold on," Gus said.

Jane leaned toward the console, holding on to the handle over the door.

Gus jerked the steering wheel to the right, pushing back on the other vehicle. He couldn't slow and let him pass because that would leave Charlie's vehicle vulnerable.

Jane tried to see into the other SUV, but the windows were so darkly tinted she couldn't make out the driver, even though they were close enough she could have spit into his window.

Gus jammed his foot onto the accelerator, continuing to steer his vehicle into the SUV. The other drivers on the road slowed, giving them space.

"You okay back there?" Declan called out over the cell phone.

"Don't slow down. Get Charlie home," Gus said through clenched teeth, his arms straining as he maintained his hold on the steering wheel.

"Going," Declan acknowledged. "Grace is calling the highway patrol. Hang in there."

Suddenly the gray SUV jerked to the right, running parallel to their vehicle.

Jane had time only to take a breath before the glass in the window beside her exploded inward, showering her with small shards.

"Damn!" Gus hit the accelerator. "Get down!" he yelled and raced ahead of the other vehicle, ducking as low as he could.

Jane leaned low in her seat, staring up at the bullet hole in the passenger window. She followed its trajectory to Gus. Bright red blood dripped from his shoulder onto the seat.

"You're hit!" Jane cried out and started to sit up.

"Stay down, damn it!" he yelled.

The dark SUV raced up beside them again.

Gus didn't wait for the driver to start shooting again. He jerked the steering wheel to the right, slamming into the other vehicle. Then he goosed the accelerator and shot in front of the gray SUV, blocking the driver from coming up again on the side. When he tried to go around, Gus planted his vehicle in the way every time.

Jane risked a look over the back of the seat in time to see the driver stick a gun out the window, aimed at the back of their SUV. "Look out—he's going to shoot at the back."

Jane ducked low again, just in time. A bullet hit the back windshield and exited the vehicle through the front. If she hadn't ducked, it would have gone through her head.

"Brace yourself," Gus shouted.

Jane didn't know what to hold on to. She grabbed the armrest and gripped tight.

Gus jammed on the brakes, bringing the SUV to a skidding stop in the middle of the freeway.

The driver behind him hit his brakes, but too late to stop before slamming into the back of their SUV.

Jane was flung forward; her seat belt tightened,

keeping her from flying through the windshield and out onto the pavement.

Gus let off the brake and hit the accelerator, racing ahead of the gray SUV.

Jane glanced back to see steam rising from the hood of the other vehicle. It wasn't moving. As the distance increased between them, her heartbeat slowed and she took a breath. She stared across at Gus whose arm was bleeding. "Get to the nearest hospital. You've got a gunshot wound."

"I'm fine. It just grazed me."

"Grazing doesn't bleed that much." She searched the interior of the vehicle for napkins or tissues to use to stop the flow of blood. When she couldn't find any, she pressed her palm against the wound, applying pressure. "Seriously, you're bleeding like a stuck pig. At least go to a convenient care clinic and get some stitches."

"When we get to the estate, I'll ask for a Band-Aid."

She sighed. "You're hopeless."

He shot her a grin. "And you're doing great. Most women I've known would have fainted at the sight of blood."

"You've known the wrong women. I'm not most women," she grumbled.

His grin faded, but his look was intense. "No. You're not."

"I hope you didn't get blood on my fingerprint card. We still need to find out what kind of woman I am."

Chapter Nine

Gus made it back to Charlie's place without bleeding out. With Jane applying pressure all the way, she'd pretty much stopped the flow by the time they arrived.

The others were standing outside the mansion on the steps when Gus pulled in behind their vehicles.

Declan hurried forward. "Ho-ly… Gus. Are you okay?"

As soon as he shifted into Park, he took over from Jane and pressed his hand over the wound on his shoulder. "I'm fine."

"If you're so fine, why are you bleeding like a stuck pig?" Cole asked.

"What's with people and stuck pigs?" Gus shook his head. "All I need is a shower and a Band-Aid. It's just a flesh wound."

"I'm calling my doctor," Charlie announced. She had her cell phone out and was dialing before Gus could tell her he didn't need one.

"It's just a flesh wound," he insisted.

"Let the doctor be the judge of that," Charlie said as she ended the call. "He'll be here in ten minutes."

"Your doctor makes house calls?" Mustang asked.

"For me," Charlie said. "I set him up in his own practice just down the road. He returns the favor on occasion. I don't abuse the privilege, only when I think it's necessary. And I think it's necessary based on the amount of blood you have all over you and Jane. Come on—let's get you inside and cleaned up."

"I'll grab some clean towels and gauze." Arnold hurried up the steps ahead of them.

"I'll get the alcohol," Cole said.

"Shouldn't he wash the wound first?" Charlie asked.

Cole shot a grin back at the others as he stepped through the door. "I'll leave that to Gus. I'm getting the beer and whiskey."

Declan shook his head and turned to Gus. "You sure you're all right?"

"Seriously, it's just a flesh wound," Gus said.

Declan snorted. "You'd say that if half your arm was blown off."

Gus chuckled. "Probably. And you'd do the same."

"Yeah." Declan grinned. "And Cole would get the booze."

"While you guys are being guys, Gus is still bleeding." Jane wrapped her arm around Gus's waist and looped his arm over her shoulders.

"What are you doing?" Gus asked.

"You've lost a lot of blood, cowboy. I'm going to

make sure you get up the steps without passing out." Jane started up the stairs.

He frowned down at her. "I've never passed out a day in my life."

"Then do it yourself," she said and started to duck out from under his arm.

He held on tight. "No. I think you're right. I'm feeling a little fuzzy."

"Come on, cowboy," Declan said, shaking his head. "Let's get inside before you stain the concrete and marble."

Gus leaned a little more than he should have on Jane, but he liked her arm around his waist and that she cared enough to help him up the stairs. He didn't need the help and he didn't feel at all woozy. He wasn't going to tell her that. She wouldn't believe him anyway. It looked like he'd lost a lot of blood, but he really hadn't.

"Can you make it up to the second floor?" Charlie asked. "You can use the shower in my room."

"Not necessary. I can make it to the third floor just fine."

"Great," Jane said, already breathing hard.

He stopped leaning so heavily on her but let her keep her arm around his waist. "Better?"

"Much." She frowned up at him. "Faker."

"I told you I didn't need the help." He leaned close to her ear. "Don't blame me if I liked it."

"Jerk," she muttered and continued up the stairs with her arm around his waist.

Once they made it to the suite they shared, she

walked him straight to the bathroom before she ducked from beneath his arm to reach in and turn the knob on the shower.

When the water was nice and warm, she turned back to find him pulling his T-shirt over his head. The wound on his arm started bleeding again, dripping onto the floor.

"You could have waited for me to help," she groused.

"Why? It was going to bleed anyway." He pressed the T-shirt to the wound.

"Hold that thought while I untie your boots." She leaned down and loosened the laces on his boots.

He toed them off.

She helped him remove his socks and then straightened.

He touched her cheek with the hand on his injured arm, leaving a streak of blood. "You're pretty handy to have around when a guy is bleeding. Sorry, I just left some on your face."

"Shut up and let me maintain the pressure while you get out of those jeans."

"You sure you want to do that?"

"I'd rather hold the wound than have you slip and break your neck in your own blood." She held the shirt against the injury. "I'll even close my eyes."

Just the thought of getting naked with her made his blood pump faster and his desire swell in his groin. "I don't think it's a good idea."

She glared up at him. "I repeat. Shut up and do it." Then she closed her eyes.

While she held his arm, he slipped out of his jeans, pulled the shower curtain over to cover himself and then clamped his hand over the wound. "Okay, I've got this now. You can go."

"I'll stay long enough to help you out. Once you wash all the blood off, you'll need help getting dressed without messing up your clean clothes."

He hadn't thought of that, when all he could think about was the effect she was having on his libido. "You make a good point. But I'm not sure I want your help."

She frowned. "Do you want me to get one of your teammates? I can do that."

He didn't like that idea either. "No. I suppose you'll do."

Jane shook her head. "Ingrate. Move. The doctor will be here to sew you up any minute."

"Maybe we should have waited for him before doing the shower."

"You're a mess. Get in the shower before all the hot water is gone."

"Yes, ma'am." He stepped behind the curtain.

A hand came around the side of the curtain with a clean washcloth. "Use this to apply pressure to the wound and just let the water wash over your body. You can get a better shower after the doc sews you up."

He stopped short of asking her to wash the blood away from his body. If he weren't her guard and she weren't an unknown potential threat, he might have done it. He reached down and turned the shower cooler.

The woman was getting to him more than he cared to admit. His body had no problem demonstrating its desire for her.

"Are you okay in there?" Jane's voice sounded from the other side of the curtain.

"I'm fine," he said through gritted teeth. The water was damned cold, yet it did little to get his desire in check.

"I found some shorts in your gym bag. Where do you keep your underwear?"

He chuckled. "I don't."

"You don't what?" she asked.

"I don't keep them."

"Oh."

Gus smiled, imagining the look on her face when she understood that he went commando whenever he could. When he couldn't he wore boxer shorts.

Holding the cloth over his wound, he let the water sluice over his body, washing away as much of the blood as he could see. When he was clean, he turned off the water.

A towel flew over the curtain rod and slapped him in the face.

"Thanks," he said.

"You're welcome."

He could see the outline of her body standing near the curtain.

"Need help drying off?" she asked.

"No. I've got this." He managed to get to most of the water, patting himself dry.

"I'll step out and let you get into your shorts."

"Mighty decent of you, ma'am," he said in his best imitation of John Wayne.

"Don't give up your day job, Gus," she said and pulled the door closed as she left.

Gus tugged on his shorts while holding the cloth in place. He barely had them covering all the important parts when Jane stuck her head through the door. "The doctor's here."

Thankful for the distraction, Gus left the bathroom to find a young man carrying a black satchel. The guy barely looked old enough to be out of medical school.

"I'm thirty-five years old," the doctor said as he set his bag on an end table near an ottoman. "I happen to have a young face. But I'm good at what I do." He glanced toward Jane. "Can I get a towel or two to spread out over this seat?"

Jane nodded and hurried back into the bathroom, returning with a stack of clean towels. She spread two over the ottoman and stood back.

The doctor pointed. "Sit."

Gus did as he was told. The doctor might look young, but he worked quickly and efficiently, examining the wound and applying three sutures to close the edges.

"When was your last tetanus shot?" he asked.

"I don't know. Maybe five years ago," Gus said.

After the doctor applied gauze and tape to cover the wound, he gave Gus a shot, some antibiotics and then he closed his case. "As far as I'm concerned, you've suffered a bad abrasion." He gave instructions for wound care and left.

"Not much of a bedside manner," Jane said, as she inspected the doctor's handiwork. "But he did a good job."

"And he's not reporting it to the authorities as a gunshot wound. We don't have time for the red tape." Gus raised an eyebrow. "Satisfied? I'm sure I could have applied a couple of butterfly bandages and been just as effective."

Jane rolled her eyes and held out a T-shirt. "Want help getting into this?"

He sighed. "Is there no end to the humiliation?"

"Stop being a baby and put on the shirt. I'm sure you don't want to sit at the dinner table shirtless."

He didn't, so he let her help him into the shirt.

"You kinda need a shower. You have almost as much blood on you as I had on me."

She nodded toward the door. "If you want to go down and join the others, I'll get that shower."

"Have you forgotten that I'm supposed to be keeping an eye on you?"

Jane sighed. "Whatever. I'm getting a shower. Do what you want. I'm not going to make a run for it when Carl said he had a big pot of Hungarian goulash on the stove. I can smell it all the way up here." She inhaled deeply. "Nope. I won't make a run for it until I've had some of that."

She collected clothes from her bedroom, took them into the bathroom and closed the door between them.

Gus stood on the other side, every instinct telling him that she was one of the good guys and that he could trust her. In which case, he wouldn't have to treat her like a potential threat. He could explore this reaction he had to her nearness.

If she was willing.

He heard when she turned on the water.

His imagination pictured her naked, standing beneath the spray, water sluicing down over her shoulders and breasts. He could be in there, rubbing soap over her skin, sliding his hands over every inch of her body.

Gus groaned. Why was he torturing himself?

The water turned off, but Gus was still turned on.

"Gus?" Jane called out.

He thought he'd imagined it.

"Gus?" The second time, she was louder.

His pulse quickened and he hurried to the bathroom door, opening it a crack. "Yeah."

"I forgot to get a towel out of the cabinet. Would you hand me one?" Jane stood on the other side of the curtain, her naked body a hazy gray silhouette.

"Sure." He reached into the cabinet and pulled out a fluffy white towel. He slipped it around the side of the shower curtain and she took it from him.

"Thanks."

"You're welcome," he said, choking on his desire.

He made it to the door when the shower curtain whipped to the side.

He glanced back over his shoulder.

She stood, wrapped in the towel, water droplets gleaming off the swells of her breasts. "I'll be ready in a minute."

Gus dove for the door. He was ready now, but not for Hungarian goulash.

AFTER GUS LEFT her alone in the bathroom, Jane rubbed her body dry with the towel he'd given her.

The whole time she'd helped him undress and get into the shower she'd fought the overwhelming urge to get in with him. It would have been easier for him, if she had. But what purpose would it serve? The man made her blood burn hot through her veins. When he'd stripped down to get into the shower she'd done her best not to peek, but damn. He was one hell of a male specimen.

She'd slept in his arms the night before and felt the strength of his muscles and the heat of his skin against hers and wished for a lot more than being held. But she couldn't ask for more. It wouldn't be fair to him. Making love to her wasn't part of his job duties.

Oh, but what she wouldn't give to have his hands on her body, touching her from head to toe. How long had it been since she'd been with a man? Hell, she had no idea. Frustration burned a hole in her gut.

Jane finished drying her body and wrapped her hair in the towel to soak up the water. She slipped into the panties and bra Grace had loaned her. Then she pulled on a soft red jersey dress. It slipped down over her body, hugging every curve and swell, falling all the way to her ankles. She couldn't remember wearing a dress. Did she do it often? Or was it a new experience?

The shoes Grace had given her to wear with the

dress were high heels. After the day she'd had, Jane had no desire to wear spike heels, deciding instead to go barefoot.

She hung the towel on a rack and pulled a brush through her hair.

The thought of Gus waiting in the other room made her want to hurry to see his reaction to the red dress. It wasn't as fancy as the black one she'd worn to the gala, but it suited her more. She felt comfortable, yet feminine wearing it.

Once she'd smoothed all the tangles from her long hair she stepped out of the bathroom.

Gus stood by the French doors. He'd changed from the shorts into a pair of black jeans and a pair of leather boots. He still wore the T-shirt she'd helped him into and his hair was combed back from his forehead.

Dark stubble peppered his chin, giving him a more dangerous appearance.

He turned toward her, his eyes widening briefly as he took in her form in the dress.

"You clean up nicely," he said.

Her lips quirked. "You're not so bad yourself."

"And I managed to dress myself," he said, puffing out his chest.

"Now that you're not bleeding," she reminded him.

"Thanks to you," he said. He crossed the room to stand in front of her.

She stared up at his face, her gaze dropping to his full lips, curious to know if they were as soft as they looked. Was he a good kisser?

Her stomach rumbled, pulling her back to reality. Heat rose in her cheeks and she pressed a hand to her belly. "I suppose we should go downstairs."

He nodded and tipped her chin up. "Thank you for taking care of me when you didn't have to."

"You're welcome," she said, her voice barely more than a whisper.

Gus's head dipped lower. "I have an uncontrollable desire to kiss you."

Her breath caught and her heartbeat ratcheted up. "What's stopping you?"

"I can't think of a damned thing." He lowered his mouth to hers, brushing a feather-soft kiss across her lips.

She sighed, leaning up on her toes to deepen the connection.

Gus's arms wrapped around her, bringing her body flush up against his. When his tongue traced the seam of her lips, she opened to him and met him thrust for thrust.

The moment lasted forever and was over in a second.

He lifted his head and she wanted to cry for the loss of his lips on hers.

Leaning her forehead against his chest, she whispered, "We should go down."

"In a perfect world, I'd say to hell with that and keep you up here in our own little suite and kiss you again."

She lifted her head and stared up into eyes so dark

with passion they made her burn for him. "What's stopping you?"

He breathed in and out again as if steadying himself before answering. "We aren't alone in this house. The others will be expecting us to come down soon."

Jane nodded. "Then let's go."

He cupped her chin and lifted her face to his. "Tonight." He spoke the one word like a promise.

A shiver of excitement rippled through her. "Tonight," she repeated.

Gus extended his arm to her and she looped her hand through his elbow.

They walked all the way down the stairs before she let go and preceded him into the kitchen.

As they strode into the room every member of Declan's Defenders turned toward them, their gazes intense, all frowning.

A lead weight settled in the pit of Jane's belly.

"What?" Gus asked.

"Mack and Snow?" Declan turned to them.

Mack focused on Gus. "Our trip to Langley was enlightening."

Snow continued. "Apparently, the CIA has been tracking certain people who have had dealings with the Russians and the Syrian rebels." Snow's gaze shifted from Gus to Jane.

"And?" Gus raised a hand to the small of Jane's back.

She moved away from him so that his hand fell to his side. She didn't want his marine brothers to think he had anything to do with her, other than his responsibility to keep an eye on her. What they had to say wasn't going to be good. Gus didn't need to be associated with her if she was purely bad.

"What did you find out?" Gus prompted impatiently.

Declan looked to Snow. "We think we know who Jane is."

Jane's heart raced and her pulse pounded so hard against her eardrums she could barely hear.

"Spit it out, damn it," Gus said through gritted teeth.

"It's okay," Jane said. "Whatever you have to say, I need to hear." She stood with her shoulders back, her chin held high.

"The CIA has been tracking a secret agent who goes by the code name Indigo."

"Are you telling me our Jane Doe is Indigo?" Gus demanded.

"She fits the description," Mack said. "Dark hair, dark eyes."

"That could be any woman in Syria," Gus argued.

"Speaks several languages," Snow continued.

"Again, that could be a number of people in Syria," Gus said.

Jane touched his arm. "It's okay. I need to know."

"There's a reason she's a skilled fighter," Mack said, his eyes narrowing as his gaze shot to Jane. "She's a trained assassin."

Chapter Ten

Gus flinched as if he'd been punched in the gut.

Jane? His Jane? A trained assassin?

She stood beside him, her face pale, her eyes rounded.

"Any of this coming back to you?" Mack asked.

She shook her head. "No."

"I can't believe it," Gus said. "She can't be a trained assassin."

"I have my guy at Langley searching files for images." Mack shifted his gaze from Jane back to Gus. "They will contact me as soon as they have something."

Gus shoved a hand through his hair and stared at his friend and teammate. "How did you approach the subject of Jane? Did you tell them she was here? With us?"

"No. Actually, they don't know we have anyone. We went on a mission to find out more about what's going on in Syria. We asked if there were persons of interest they were following who could be a danger to the US."

Gus shook his head. "And they jumped right to this Indigo person?"

"No, they had a list of Russian spies, Syrian rebels and mercenaries for hire."

He wasn't buying into Jane being Indigo, but he had to know how the assassin fit in. "Which group does Indigo have allegiance to?"

Mack's lips pressed into a tight line. "That's just it—she doesn't claim any of the groups. They think someone is using her to orchestrate his own agenda."

"What agenda did the CIA come up with?" Gus crossed his arms over his chest.

Snow answered. "A high-ranking Russian military leader, Lieutenant General Mikhail Marouchevsky, was assassinated minutes before he was due to evacuate the Shayrat Airbase. All the Russian planes made it out before the US bombed the airfield. All the Russians survived, except the lieutenant general."

"If they thought I was this Indigo assassin, that would explain why the guards beating me spoke Russian," Jane said. "They were dressed like Syrian rebels, but they spoke Russian and carried Russian AK-47s."

Charlie's eyes rounded. "Your tattoo led you here." She pressed her hand to her mouth. "Could you be…" She shook her head. "No."

"Your husband's assassin?" Jane's face turned even another shade paler.

"This is all circumstantial," Gus said. "Jane might not even be this Indigo assassin."

"Does the CIA know of others like her?" Grace asked. "Are any of them marked with the Trinity knot?"

"Who do we know so far who has had a connection to the symbol?" Declan said.

Charlie's brow furrowed. "My husband had a ring with that symbol on it."

"My friend Riley's nanny had that symbol on a similar ring," Grace said. "And she was a Russian sleeper spy, living in the US."

"Now we have Jane, who speaks Russian and Arabic," Declan said. "Coincidence?" He shook his head. "I think not."

"But what would my husband have to do with an organization that employees Russian sleeper spies and trained assassins?" Charlie slipped into a chair at the kitchen table and buried her face in her hands. "Oh, John, what were you into?"

"All the more reason to break into his files." Cole stood. "He had to know something about what tied them all together. Maybe I can find some information on the Dark Web."

"Be careful. You open yourself up to all kinds of fanatics when you go there," Declan warned.

Cole nodded. "I'll be sure to set up a special IP address and mask it to maintain anonymity."

Charlie stared at Jane and finally shook her head. "No. I can't even conceive of the idea that Jane was the assassin behind my husband's murder. She wouldn't have done it. She's had ample opportunity to harm any one of us since staying here, and she's done nothing but help instead."

Gus felt the same way. But what if he was wrong?

"Mrs. Halverson, I pray I didn't," Jane said. "If your husband was anything like you, I couldn't have killed him. You are a good person, with a heart willing to take in the strays and help those in need. The world needs more people like you, not fewer."

Charlie gave her a weak smile. "Thank you, dear." She looked around the room at the others. "I'm not giving up on Jane. If she is Indigo, what proof do we have that she's assassinated anyone? If she's not Indigo, we still have to discover who she is. Don't stop searching yet."

Mack nodded, his gaze on Jane. "In the meantime, what do we do with Jane?"

"I won't promise not to hurt you, because you probably wouldn't believe me. If I am truly the assassin Indigo, even assassins can turn over a new leaf. I don't have to be an assassin, if I don't want to. And I really don't want to." She looked around at the doubting faces. "The other alternative is to kick me out."

Gus's gut clenched. Though he hadn't wanted to be her guard, now it seemed he didn't want the job to end.

When Charlie shook her head and opened her mouth to say something, Jane held up her hand. "It's okay if you do. I've probably overstayed my welcome, as it is." She looked around at the men of Declan's Defenders, their boss, Charlie, Arnold the butler, Carl the cook and Grace, Charlie's assistant. "You are a family. I'm the outsider."

Gus felt a hard tug at his heart. A family was all

he'd ever wanted. And quite possibly, it was all Jane wanted, too. He could hear the hollowness in her voice, the hopelessness of her situation.

"I don't suppose any of you want to eat after all that?" Carl asked softly.

Jane's stomach rumbled loudly. She pressed a hand to it. "I only ask that you don't kick me out until I've had at least a taste of Carl's goulash." She faked a laugh, though it sounded more like a sob.

Gus was almost certain assassins didn't cry.

Charlie drew in a shaky breath and crossed the floor to Jane, pulling her into a tight hug. "I don't believe you killed John. There has to be another reason that tattoo is on your wrist, and that it led you here. And we'll find it." She pushed Jane to arm's length and stared into her eyes. "I promise."

Gus let go of the breath he'd been holding. Charlie had every right to boot Jane out of her home. Hell, if they thought she was Indigo, they had an obligation to turn her over to the CIA for questioning. None of them stepped forward with that suggestion.

Instead, they gathered around the kitchen table and filled their bowls full of Carl's Hungarian goulash and ate a hearty meal.

Gus sat beside Jane. At one point, he laid his hand over hers where she rested it in her lap.

She glanced his way and then looked away, moving her hand from beneath his.

He'd meant to reassure her that he was there for her. Was she already letting go?

He hadn't known her long, but what he'd seen of

her was enough to make him want to spend more time with her. She was strong, determined and capable of taking care of herself. But it was the vulnerable side that drew him even more.

He hoped the CIA was wrong about Indigo being his Jane. But if she was in fact Indigo…hell, he wasn't sure what he'd do then.

Jane rolled the name Indigo over and over in her mind. It didn't kick off any bells or alarms. In fact, it didn't sound right to her ears. Perhaps it wasn't a name she used for herself. But if not Indigo or Jane, what name fit? She wanted to bury her face in her hands and weep.

An assassin?

She ate the goulash, savoring every last bite as if it might be her last meal. And the way things were shaping up, it just might.

When the platter of rolls was passed to her, she grabbed two, setting one on the table beside her plate. She'd wrap it in a napkin and take it with her when Charlie got smart and asked her to leave.

The usual lighthearted humor was absent from the table.

Snow shot a glance toward Declan. "What happened to the SUV out front?"

Gus told him about the run-in they had with another SUV on the freeway.

Mack tilted his head slightly. "The entire time he was after you, did he even try to get past your vehicle to Charlie's?"

Gus thought about it. The dark gray SUV had a

couple of opportunities to race past them and attack Charlie's car. "No. He never tried."

"Could it be whoever was attacking your vehicle might have been going after Jane?" Snow pointed out.

"Why would he?" Declan asked. "*We* don't even know who Jane is. How would anyone else? The only people who know she's here are in this room."

Gus shook his head. "That's not exactly true."

"Gus is right," Charlie said. "She was at the gala when Charlie was attacked. And we went by Halverson International Headquarters. She was seen by any number of people, from security guards to receptionists."

"Don't forget your husband's executive assistant, Margaret, and your CEO, Quincy Phishburn," Cole added.

"Do you think someone in the Halverson headquarters knows about Jane?" Charlie asked.

"Could be." Declan tapped his chin. "The question is why would they want to run her off the road?"

"Obviously, to kill her," Gus said, his food lodging halfway to his stomach.

"Yes, but why would they want to kill her?" Declan continued. "Who knows she's an assassin?" He gave Jane a crooked smile. "Assuming you are."

She shrugged.

"Someone who knows about her and what happened in Syria?" Mack suggested.

"Someone who doesn't want anyone to know what happened in Syria," Gus guessed.

"All the more reason to get to the bottom of who

Jane is and why someone is after her." Charlie shook her head. "I just assumed the vehicle following you was ultimately after me. That's what I get for assuming."

After the meal was complete, Jane approached Charlie. "Do you want me to leave?" she asked quietly so that no one else could hear. She wanted Charlie to have the opportunity to cut her losses and let her go without the pressure of everyone watching or judging.

Charlie shook her head adamantly. "Absolutely not."

"What if I'm the assassin who killed your husband?"

"You're not." Charlie patted her arm. "I'm completely convinced of that. You could have hurt us all by now, as I said, if you are an assassin. I doubt you would have wasted so much time just to gain our trust. It doesn't make sense. You didn't kill John."

"You won't hurt my feelings if you want me to go. I'd have kicked me out long ago if I were you."

Charlie smiled. "Then it's a good thing you're not me. I have a feeling John would have wanted us to help you. He was that kind of man. He helped people who needed it. Given all the information we have thus far, I'm sure he wouldn't have kicked you out, either."

"Thank you, Charlie. I hope you don't come to regret your decision."

"I won't. And we're going to figure out this mess. You'll see. Everything will turn out right in the end."

Jane wished that was so.

Until they reached the end, she vowed to walk a

very straight-and-narrow line so that her mere presence among Declan's Defenders didn't make the men nervous.

Charlie stared at Jane, her brow dipping low as she swept her gaze over the younger woman. "We need to get you to town and buy some clothes that fit."

"I'm fine with what Grace provided."

"The red dress is lovely, but you need other items of your own, like jeans. Two women can't wear the same pair of jeans. We're all built so differently." Charlie looked past Jane. "Arnold, tomorrow we'll need the car brought out around nine o'clock in the morning."

Arnold nodded. "Yes, ma'am."

Jane shook her head. "I don't want to bother you, Charlie."

"You're not a bother. It's settled—we're going shopping in the morning." She glanced toward Declan. "We'll need coverage to make the trip into town."

"We're on it," Declan assured her.

"Have you finished searching John's things?" Charlie asked.

"Not yet," Declan answered. "While Cole and Jonah work on digital data, we'll search the entire house."

"Not just the house," Charlie said. "We purchased this estate from a retired FBI agent. He had all kinds of secret hiding places and passages. I think he was a little paranoid."

"We'll search everywhere," Declan said. "I know

about the underground passageway to the garage. Are there more?"

"Yes. I believe there's one to the garden," Charlie said. "There might be some hidden rooms behind the walls here in the house and garage. I'm not certain I know where all of them are. John might have found some I didn't."

"Don't forget the fingerprint card we made with Jane's prints," Gus reminded Cole.

"Got it," Cole said. "We'll work on that first."

"What do you know about the IAFIS system?" Gus asked.

"Enough to find matching prints in the criminal, military and government databases. Why?" Cole asked.

"If you find a match, can someone be automatically notified if they're looking for that person?"

Cole's brow knit. "I'm not sure I follow."

"If someone is looking for that person and another investigator finds a match, will the original searcher get notification of that match? I don't want anyone to know where to find Jane, if we get a hit."

That Gus was concerned for her well-being made Jane's heart swell.

"Good point," Cole said. "I'll be sure to route it so that the inquiry doesn't show up any IP address associated with Halverson estate."

"Good," Declan said. "We don't need to bring any more trouble to Charlie's doorstep than we already have."

Was that it? The warmth Jane had experienced

over Gus's concern for her cooled. He was worried about bringing the bad guys here.

When had Jane started thinking everything was about her? She should know better. If she wanted to be protected, she had to take care of herself. She was already thinking of where she could go, if her location was compromised. Staying with Charlie wouldn't be an option. The woman didn't deserve to have more threats dropped at her door.

They split up, assigning different areas of the house and grounds for each person to search.

Gus and Jane took the third floor and attic since they were rooming up there anyway.

They felt their way around every wall in every room on the third floor; they touched wall sconces, moved furniture and checked beneath rugs. Nothing jumped out at them and no walls opened up magically to reveal a hidden room.

Narrow stairs led up into the attic. A fine layer of dust coated the contents of the space. Some of the items appeared to have been there from the previous owner. Cardboard boxes were stacked in several corners along with old furniture and lamps. A single yellow light bulb lit the space, albeit inadequately. As they moved around the attic, dust rose with every step, making it even murkier than before they entered. The light reflected off the particles of dust, giving it a hazy surreal atmosphere.

Jane shivered, not liking the feeling of the place. The dust reminded her of the dirt floor in her Syrian cell. The sooner she got out of there the better.

"I don't see anything up here," Gus said. "Let's go to the ground floor. Maybe there's a secret cupboard off the subterranean conference room below Mr. Halverson's office."

Glad to be out of the attic, Jane hurried downstairs.

Declan met them halfway down on the second floor. "Anything?"

Gus shook his head. "We even tapped on the walls and listened for anything that sounded hollow."

"Same here," Declan said. "We checked every room except Charlie's. Grace is helping her go through it now."

"We thought we might look in the subterranean conference room." Gus followed Jane down the steps, Declan close behind. "Perhaps there's a hidden door we haven't noticed."

Declan nodded. "It would make sense, since the conference room is more or less hidden beneath Halverson's old office." When they reached the ground floor, Declan fell in beside Gus. "I'm surprised Halverson didn't involve his wife more in what he was doing."

"He might not have wanted her to be so close to the truth of what he was doing that she'd become a target."

Jane snorted. "She lived with the man. Isn't that close enough? Don't you think the attacks could be continuations of the effort to end whatever John Halverson was doing? They might think Charlie is just as involved."

"True. All the more reason for full disclosure,"

Declan said. "We need to know just what John Halverson was dealing with."

"We could go through his office again," Jane said. "We might be missing something." She so desperately wanted to find anything that would help her to understand why she had been led to Halverson's estate. What did he have to do with the Trinity symbols? Was he involved with an organization that used the Trinity knot as a sign? Or was he investigating such an organization in an attempt to bring it down?

What was the Trinity organization and what was it involved with? Did they hire out like mercenaries to assassinate for a paycheck? Was that why she'd been in Syria?

God, she hoped not. She prayed she wasn't an assassin for hire. That the intel had been wrong. She wasn't a cold-blooded killer. She didn't feel like it was in her nature to kill unnecessarily.

"I'm going out to the garage via the access tunnel to help Snow search there." Declan nodded toward Halverson's study. "Good luck. We didn't find anything when we went through the files and drawers. But then a second pair of eyes is always a good thing."

Alone in the office with Gus, Jane couldn't help glancing his way. Before they'd discovered she could be a trained assassin, he'd kissed her and left her with a vague promise of more that night. Would he carry through with that promise, now that he knew she might be a ruthless assassin?

Jane didn't hold out any hope of that happening.

A man would have to be crazy to consort with someone like her.

She ran her fingers along the top of John Halverson's desk, searching for any recessed buttons or switches that would open the desk like the one at corporate headquarters. The desktop was all smooth mahogany, not a bump or crevice anywhere on its shiny surface.

Squatting in front of the desk, she tried to think like a man who had things to hide. She felt along the underside of the surface for any indentations that would fit a finger. Again, she found nothing. Studying the overall construction of the massive desk, she realized the drawers didn't start until a good six inches below the desktop. The wood above it was an intricate, inlaid panel of highly polished mahogany with carved designs that appeared to be a kind of latticework of vines crisscrossing over each other. She touched the pattern, feeling along the raised carving all the way to the corner. Her fingers pressed into the corner and it moved outward. When it moved, the rest of the inlaid design dropped forward on hinges and a thin shelflike drawer popped out.

Jane jerked up so fast, she bumped her head on the desktop.

Gus turned from the fireplace mantel he'd been running his fingers across. "Hey, are you okay over there?"

"I think I found something," she said, rubbing the top of her head. She rose up to stand, looking down at the shallow drawer. Inside was a journal, flat enough to fit in the small space. She lifted it out of the drawer and laid it on the desk's surface.

Gus joined her as she opened the journal and read the words on the first page.

"The Trinity Syndicate."

A cold chill rippled down the back of Jane's spine and a heavy feeling settled deep in her belly.

She turned the page and read what appeared to be a diary written by John Halverson about his investigation into the inner workings of the organization called The Trinity Syndicate.

He'd first learned of the group when a potential presidential candidate was killed in a freak hunting accident during the primaries. Though the police couldn't prove it was anything more than an accident, rumors spread that the candidate had been murdered, the murderer having staged it so it didn't appear deliberate.

John hadn't thought much of it then, but when a bombing occurred in a government building, everyone assumed it was a product of Taliban terrorism. True, the vehicle used to carry the bomb and left in the underground garage had been driven by a man associated with the Taliban, but the type of bomb was much too complicated and intricate to be something generally associated with the Taliban brand of terrorism.

A German delegate to the European Union who opposed lifting sanctions against Russia was believed to have committed suicide by jumping from a bridge onto a deserted stretch of the Autobahn in the middle of the night. Though an autopsy was conducted, there wasn't much left to look at after his body had been run over by several large delivery trucks before anyone realized it was a human body in the middle of the road.

One page after another detailed incidents deemed accidents or terrorist activities that John believed were in fact orchestrated by The Trinity Syndicate to cause different outcomes in political arenas.

Near the middle of the journal, John had sketched a diagram that caught and held Jane's attention and made her heart thud against her ribs.

In effect, the diagram was an organization chart with code names at each level. At the bottom of one of the tree branches was the name Indigo.

Chapter Eleven

Gus stared down at the name on the page. He could feel Jane stiffen and hear the sharp intake of breath.

"We don't know that you are that person," he reminded her.

"What if I am?"

"We deal with it. Until then, you can't worry about it."

"Oh, but I can," she whispered.

"Declan! Mack! Gus! Snow! Anyone!" Cole's voice came through the open door in the wall of the study that led down into the basement conference room. "You gotta see this!"

Declan appeared in the doorway to the study, Mack close behind him. "Is that Cole?"

Gus nodded, grabbed the journal and hurried down the stairs into the room below the study.

Cole sat at a desk with an array of six monitors arranged in two rows of three each attached to the wall.

Jonah Spradlin sat beside him, staring at the different screens, shaking his head. "Wow. Look at it all."

Gus, Jane and the others all crowded around behind Cole.

"What are we looking at?" Declan asked.

"I'm on the Dark Web. I got a tip to look in a certain location and found all of this." He waved a hand toward the monitors.

One screen played a video of children in their preteens and teens wearing tattered dirty-white martial arts shirts and pants. Their heads were shaved whether they were boys or girls and they were being yelled at by a man with an equally shaved head. He instructed them on the proper way to take a man down and snap his neck. The children were then paired off to practice the moves up to the snapping of the neck. When one failed to perform it properly, he or she was beaten with a horse-riding crop.

Jane tensed. With every blow, she winced, feeling the child's pain as if it were her own.

"And look at this." Jonah pointed at a screen of newspaper articles about children whose parents had passed away and how they were being placed in foster care. Then the foster parents were charged with child neglect when the children ran away or disappeared.

Pictures of the missing children were displayed on milk cartons and in newspapers. Beside the child's milk-carton photo was another of a similar child in appearance with the shaved head and white outfit of the Trinity recruits.

"They're stealing children," Grace said from behind Declan.

Cole nodded, his lips forming a tight line. "And forcing them into their training programs."

"John would never have been involved in something like that," Charlie said. "He loved children, even though we never had any. He would have done everything in his power to help them."

Gus held up the journal. "I think that's exactly what he was trying to do."

Charlie took the book from his hands and opened it to the first page. "Where did you find this?" she said, her voice cracking. "That's John's handwriting."

"It was in a secret drawer in his desk," Jane said.

As Charlie turned the pages, Declan and the others peered over her shoulders. When she got to the organization chart, she gasped and looked up at Jane.

Jane nodded in acknowledgement. "He knew about Indigo."

"We don't know if that's you or not," Charlie said.

"Based on the diagram, he was trying to determine the names of those in charge at each of the levels of the organization."

"Indigo is the bottom of the pyramid, a soldier on the front lines," Snow said. "She followed orders of the person above her."

"And that would be the guy with the code name Mule." Gus pointed to the next level on the diagram. "His handler is Wolf and the top of the food chain is Asp."

Charlie turned the page to the next journal entry. "He found Indigo." She looked up into Jane's eyes.

Jane moved closer to the book and read the words written in bold black ink.

I learned of the next operation Trinity had planned to initiate their operator Indigo. Buried in the Dark Web I understood this to be her first assignment, the one she needed to prove herself and her loyalty to the syndicate. Her tasking was to kill a Saudi crown prince. This particular prince was known for frequenting brothels where young girls were kept as sex slaves in the back alleys of the Bronx. This Saudi prince was also known for selling Russian secrets to the Chinese. Apparently, the Russians were willing to pay a hefty sum to have that information leak fixed.

I flew to NYC, dressed as a homeless man and lay in the alley near the entrance to the brothel waiting for the crown prince to show. He did, with three of his bodyguards, just as the informant on the Dark Web said he would. He was inside for over an hour when he finally emerged, with all three of his men surrounding him.

I never saw her slip into the alley, but suddenly Indigo was there. She wore a tight dress and spike heels with enough makeup to make her look like a street whore. When she walked up to the prince, he thought he was going to get a little more action. He made a grab for her breasts.

She barely blinked before she punched him in the throat, crushing his trachea. The prince clutched at his throat, unable to breathe past the blockage.

The three bodyguards, caught unawares, tried to capture her, but she was too fast. In some incredible martial arts moves, she had all three men flat out on the ground and unconscious in under a minute. Meanwhile the prince's face turned blue and he dropped to the ground, lying perfectly still.

Indigo bent to feel for a pulse. When she was satisfied there was none, she straightened and entered the brothel.

That's when I knew she was different. She wasn't just a trained assassin. She'd probably broken all the rules of her training by not leaving as soon as she'd completed her mission.

I waited, hoping her handler would appear and I'd have another link in the chain of command. If I wanted to stop the assembly line of child conscription, I had to find the leader.

Her handler never appeared. A few minutes later, Indigo emerged from the brothel, carrying one young unconscious girl over her shoulder and leading a dozen others. Indigo's face was bloodied, but the men inside hadn't stopped her. She got those girls out.

I followed her to the nearest hospital where she left the unconscious girl and the dozen others at the entrance to the ER. She stopped an

> older couple on their way in and asked them to send help outside for the girls. When they said they would, she waited a few moments longer with the girls. As nurses and orderlies emerged to help, Indigo disappeared into the shadows.
>
> I heard later that the men running the brothel had been critically injured and wouldn't be in the business of selling young girls for sex ever again. I made certain the girls had the care they needed to wean them off the drugs, and legal assistance to lead them through the red tape of immigration.

Charlie sniffed, a fat tear rolling down her cheek. "John had a good heart."

"Indigo murdered that crown prince," Mack pointed out.

Charlie glared. "He grabbed her first. She was defending herself. The prince didn't deserve to live after what he'd done to those poor girls."

"I think I recall the reports on television." Declan's lip twisted. "They said the Saudi crown prince had been killed in a mugging."

Charlie turned the page and kept reading. "I can hear John speaking these words." Another tear rolled down her cheek. "He only wanted to help."

Gus stared at all the images on the monitors and then turned to Jane. Had she been one of the young children who'd gone missing from foster care? Had they beaten her and trained her to be an assassin?

Jane stood back from the others, her face pale, her eyes wide. She stared at the images in front of her,

her eyes darting back and forth from one to the next. Her hands shook and her body trembled. Then she looked into Gus's eyes, her own dark with whatever was going through her mind.

"What's wrong?" Gus crossed to her and tried to take her into his arms.

She held up her hand and shook her head. "Don't touch me," she whispered.

Her entire body shook and she wrapped her arms around her middle as if in pain. "I remember," she said. "I *am* Indigo."

AS SHE'D STOOD staring at the videos and photos of the girls and boys being indoctrinated into the Trinity Syndicate, something had happened. The iron gate that had been closed for all those weeks due to her beatings and torture opened and a flood of memories washed in. She remembered being taken from the front yard of the foster home where she'd been placed only days after her parents had died in a plane crash. She hadn't even had time to get used to the family that had taken her in when she'd been thrown in the back of a van and taken far away to a training camp in the woods.

She couldn't even tell anyone where the camp was located. She hadn't been able to see out of the van as it traveled for miles along endless highways and then dirt roads, coming to a stop in a place with ramshackle huts and outhouses instead of toilets. All bathing and laundry was done in the nearby frigid stream. She wasn't allowed to speak to anyone without getting hit in the side of the head by some heavy-handed instructor.

The newest recruits slept on dirt floors with only scratchy and threadbare wool blankets to keep them warm. As they graduated from one section of training into another, and they proved themselves worthy, they got army cots or wooden bunks. If they didn't prove themselves strong, fast or smart enough, they were beaten.

The physical demands had been hard, but she'd managed to build her strength and stamina. Along with that, she'd learned never to show emotion.

From the beginning, she'd demonstrated an aptitude for languages. Her trainers sent her straight into Russian and Arabic language training. All of her instruction from then on out had been using these languages only.

Once she'd surpassed her instructors, they turned her to teaching the others until they deemed her ready to deploy.

Her first assignment had been as John's journal had depicted. She'd studied the Saudi crown prince's dossier. He was a piece of work. Not only did he rape young girls, he systematically eliminated anyone in his cabinet who dared to disagree with him. He'd married ten times. When he tired of a wife, he had her killed.

Thankfully, her first assignment was to kill a man who deserved to die.

She'd been given the information on when he would arrive and depart the brothel. She'd wanted to dispatch him before he entered, but he'd arrived earlier than expected. Forced to wait, she practiced her attempt at street girl seduction. Never having flirted in her life, she wasn't very good at it. It didn't matter to the prince. Anything with breasts was fair game. He'd grabbed, she'd punched and the bodyguards had gone down smoothly. Her orders had been to leave at that point. With the prince dead, she'd nailed her first kill.

But she couldn't leave, knowing there were young girls inside the brothel being held against their will. She'd known she'd catch grief if word got back to her handler that she'd gone in. She hadn't cared. This was something she had to do. It was easier to ask forgiveness than for permission.

Her stomach roiled at the memories of the inside of the brothel. The stench of fear and urine filled her nostrils. Images of angry men and screaming girls raced through her mind. She remembered going into that brothel. Remembered taking down the men who'd chained those women to the beds or dosed them heavily with drugs. Rage had burned through her when she'd found the girl who couldn't have been more than eleven years old, beaten and drugged into a coma.

How could these men do this to them? Why wasn't anyone stopping them?

So, she did.

"Jane?" Gus touched her arm. "Are you okay?"

She flinched. "Don't touch me," she said. "I'm exactly what I hoped I wasn't. An assassin. I shouldn't be here. With my kill record, I could spend the rest of my life in prison."

"How many?" Gus asked, then held up his hand. "I don't want to know. Like you said, who you were isn't who you are now."

"Do you remember how you knew my husband?" Charlie asked, clutching the journal close to her chest.

Jane closed her eyes, recalling the day John Halverson had come into her life. She'd been assigned the task of killing a man who'd turned in a Russian sleeper spy who was then sent back to Russia and executed for failing in his mission.

The Russian president had hired Trinity to find and kill the man who'd forced him to eliminate a spy in one of the best positions he could be, as an American government employee of the CIA. He'd had top secret clearances and access to all the data the Russians needed to know exactly what the US was up to almost before mission personnel knew what was going to happen.

Jane had been sent to kill the man who'd lived in the house next door. He was a history professor at a local university.

When Jane had arrived at the man's house, she had disguised herself as a jogger.

Her mark routinely arrived home at a specific hour and walked from where he parked his car on the street up the sidewalk to his front door.

Jane had faked a fall in front of him. All she had to do was stick the syringe of arsenic into his neck, get up and keep jogging.

But the sound of a little girl's voice made her hesitate.

The front door had opened on the man's house and a little girl of four or five years old smiled broadly and cried out, "Daddy!"

The professor helped Indigo to her feet and turned to scoop his little girl up into his arms. "Hi, sweetie pie. How's my best girl?"

Jane hadn't been able to breathe, much less jab the needle into his neck. He'd called his little girl the same thing her father had called her when he'd come home from work. After all those years of suppressing memories that hurt, they all came back to her, reminding her of how it had been before her parents passed.

She'd looked at the man and his little girl, thanked him for helping her and jogged away. She would have kept running, but a man stepped in her path.

"I met John Halverson after an aborted attempt at an assassination."

"Aborted?" Gus asked.

She nodded. "I couldn't pull the trigger. Or the plunger, in this case." She twisted her lips in a wry smile. "John was there. He'd seen what happened and offered me an alternative to working for Trinity."

"What was the alternative?" Gus asked.

She lifted her chin, her eyes narrowing. "He wanted me to help him bring Trinity down. He said that if I helped him, he'd help me to start over with a new identity, and a new life. I wouldn't have to kill anyone else. I could start over." She shook her head. "I should have known it wouldn't be that easy. But after I didn't hit my mark, I knew I would be in trouble with Trinity. My days would be numbered. He told me no matter what, whether I helped him or not, he'd set me up in my new life. He gave me the coordinates of his home as a measure of his trust in me. If I was ever in trouble, all I had to do was go to him and he'd help me out."

"What did he want you to do for him?" Charlie asked.

"He asked me if I'd be willing to go back to Trinity and find out who was in charge."

GUS CURSED. "And you agreed?"

She nodded. "It meant continuing to help them in their efforts to disrupt the world political arena. By the time I met John, I was ready to do whatever it took to stop Trinity from ruining young girls' and boys' lives."

"How did you end up in Syria?" Declan asked.

Jane closed her eyes for a moment. "I hadn't heard from John in a few weeks. He usually sent me encrypted texts from his burner phone to my burner phone. That way neither one of them could be traced back to the owner." She drew in a breath and continued. "It had been a couple of weeks. I had been out of the country in Germany doing some intel gathering for Trinity when I received a text from John."

Charlie frowned. "How long ago was this?"

"Four weeks, I think," Jane responded.

Charlie shook her head. "My husband was murdered four months ago."

Jane frowned. "I got the text from his burner phone number."

"Someone else sent it," Gus said, his gut knotting. There were too many twists and turns in Jane's tale for his comfort.

"He wanted me to get in on a mission to Syria. Trinity was going to assassinate a high-ranking Russian general. John…or whoever…wanted me there to get the general out. He said this would be the last time I'd appear to work for Trinity. After that mission, he'd insist on me leaving the syndicate." She gave a tight smile. "All I had to do was get the general out alive. I was in the right place at the right time with Trinity to be assigned to the mission in Syria. They tasked me to kill the very general I was to save."

"We all heard the news," Gus said. "If you're talking about Marouchevsky, he was supposedly killed when the US bombed the Shayrat airbase."

"That's what they reported." Jane shook her head. "I was there." She raised her hand. "I didn't kill him, but someone else did. Apparently, Trinity was onto me. The person who assassinated the general came after me. I got away from him. Unfortunately, I got too close to the bombing. I must have been knocked unconscious, because when I woke, I was in a cell being interrogated by Russians who'd been working with the Syrian rebels. They wanted to know who had called for the evacuation of the Russian planes but didn't call for *their* evacuation."

"I take it someone from the US gave the Russians a heads-up that Shayrat was about to be bombed,"

Declan said. "That gave them plenty of time to get their planes out."

Gus didn't like that Jane had been a major pawn in a deadly game. "Funny how our enemies know more about our secrets than we do."

"The general was a double agent for the US and Russia. I'm not sure what kind of deal he worked out with the US, but he was supposed to be evacuated out of Syria to the US. I was supposed to be on the transport with him." Jane sighed heavily. "Neither one of us caught our ride."

"The Senate is conducting an inquiry about that bombing," Cole said.

"When?"

Cole pressed his lips together and stared off into a corner. "I don't remember exactly. I saw it on the internet in passing when I was working at getting into the Dark Web. It's either tomorrow or the next day. Whichever, it's soon."

Charlie yawned, covering her mouth. "It's getting late. I fear I'm losing focus, and others might be, as well. We have what we need for now. Let's call it a night and pick up where we left off in the morning."

Gus started for the stairs leading out of the basement conference room. When Jane didn't follow, he turned back.

"Aren't you afraid I'll be a problem?" Jane asked.

Charlie smiled and yawned again. "If my husband trusted you, I trust you." She patted Jane's cheek. "However, I do want to find out who sent you on that last mission. It wasn't John. Someone else must have

John's burner phone. I want to know who that is." She dipped her head toward the people in the room. "I trust you all will have a good night. We have a lot of work to do tomorrow. Though we know Jane is Indigo, we still don't know who she was before Trinity. I believe we owe her a real name, not a code name." She smiled. "Good night."

Jane's gaze followed Charlie up the stairs. As she passed Gus, Jane captured his glance.

Gus held out his hand. He didn't give a damn what the others thought. He wanted Jane to know he was there to protect her.

She placed her hand in his.

He chuckled as he started up the steps out of the basement. "You're not going to argue?"

"I'm too tired to care what anyone thinks." She let him hold her hand all the way up the stairs to the third floor.

Inside the suite, Gus didn't even push the sofa up against the door. He left it in the middle of the room.

Jane's brow twisted. "Do you *want* me to make a break for it? Or are you showing me that you trust me to stay?"

"Like you, I'm tired. I don't think either one of us is leaving this suite until morning." He drew her into his arms and tipped her chin up. "And if you feel like you need to run, by all means. But I, for one, would rather you stayed."

At his words, warmth spread through her body. "And the others?"

"I can't speak for them, but Charlie likes you," Gus

said. "And she's the boss." He bent to brush his lips across her forehead. "I'm sorry you had to go through everything you did."

"I don't need anyone's pity," she protested. At the same time, she liked what his lips were doing to her face and wished he would drop a little lower to claim hers.

"So, what do I call you?" Gus swept his lips along her left cheek to capture her earlobe between his teeth.

"Not Indigo. I'm done with Trinity."

"What about Trinity being like the mob? Once you're in, you can never leave."

She snorted. "Oh, I'm sure I can leave…in a body bag."

He pressed a finger to her lips. "Don't."

She looked up into his eyes. "Trinity plays for keeps. As much as I'd like to think I can start over with a new identity and new life, until Trinity is eradicated, and the leader is jailed or killed, I will never be free."

"You don't know what can happen." He bent to claim her lips in what should have been a long, toe-curling kiss. When he brought his head up, he frowned down at her. "Something wrong?"

"You deserve better," she said.

"You're right. So, kiss me again."

When he lowered his head to do just that, she put her hand between his mouth and hers. "Why get mixed up with someone like me when you can have your choice of available, uncomplicated women?"

"I think I'm attracted to complicated." Again, he tried to kiss her.

She pressed her hands against his chest. "You're making it hard for me to resist."

"Then don't." He kissed the tip of her nose. "Unless you don't want to make love with me. In that case tell me now and I'll walk away." He waited for her to do that.

Jane hesitated. He was a good man. She was tainted with a questionable past. He deserved so much better.

Gus dropped his hands to his sides. "I don't want to pressure you into anything you don't want to do."

Knowing it might be the last time she had a chance to be with Gus, Jane didn't want to miss this opportunity. No longer able to fight the desire, she grabbed both sides of his face between the palms of her hands. "Oh, shut up and make love to me."

GUS GATHERED HER in an embrace and pulled her close. "Demanding female, aren't you?" Every part of his body had lit on fire the moment they walked through the door of the suite.

Yes, they'd learned Jane was the assassin Indigo. He should be keeping his distance and watching her even more closely than ever before. But he couldn't resist her. She was strong, determined and sexy as hell. Everything about her screamed *lethal*, yet Gus couldn't fight what was happening inside himself.

He'd never met a woman like Jane. She'd been through so much, and emerged fighting. They had so much more in common than he could have originally guessed. They both were from similar backgrounds, having lost their parents when they were young. They had been through tough combat training and both seen action, killed people and been shot at on more than one occasion.

Post-traumatic stress disorder was a way of life. One they dealt with on a daily basis from all they'd lived through.

From what he'd learned about her in the very short time he'd known Jane, she wanted roots, a place to call home and a family to welcome her there. She'd fit in easily with the team and taken to Charlie's hospitality. He understood that feeling.

For years, Gus thought himself immune to the desire to marry, to have a family of his own. His family was his team. He'd convinced himself it was enough.

Now, with Jane in his arms, he realized he wanted so much more. But why this woman? She wasn't kidding when she said she was complicated. A known assassin, she would find it hard to start over. Being a part of Trinity would make it even harder.

At that moment, all of those thoughts were pushed to the back of his mind as he held Jane in his arms, kissing her and feeling her warm body against his.

She was who he wanted. No matter how hard it would be to extricate her from the tentacles of the Trinity Syndicate, he would do it.

He bent and scooped her up into his arms.

Jane frowned. "Aren't you afraid you'll rip the stitches in your arm?"

Gus shook his head. "I'm more afraid that if I don't get a move on, you'll wise up and change your mind."

She brushed her lips across his. "Not a chance."

Gus carried her into the bedroom and let her slide down his body until her feet touched the ground. Then he backed her up until she bumped into the bed.

"Before we go any further, I want to be perfectly clear. You're all in on this, right?"

She frowned, tipping her head to the side slightly. "I told you to shut up and make love to me. What part of that confused you?"

"Nothing. It's just that I watched you take down two guys in under a minute. I want to be sure you're not going to do the same to me." He winked.

Jane's eyebrows rose. "Is that so?"

He nodded and bent to nuzzle her neck. "You never know when a woman's going to kick your butt."

"You are so right." Jane grabbed the front of his shirt, spun around and pushed him backward.

Gus landed on the bed, bringing Jane with him. She landed on top of him with a grunt.

"You didn't have to get all tough on me," Gus said. "I was working my way to this exact position. If you wanted me to move faster, all you had to do was say so."

"You talk too much, marine." Jane lowered her mouth to his, stemming the flow of words from his lips.

"Mmm." She moaned. "This is more like it."

He cupped the back of her head and pulled her closer against him. "Agreed." Then as quickly as she'd toppled him into the bed, he flipped her onto her back and kissed her more fiercely. "I've wanted to do that since I saw you standing in that ballroom in that black dress."

"A stranger? You wanted to kiss a woman you didn't trust?"

"I felt something I hadn't felt in a long time." He looked up at her. "No…that's not right. I felt something I'd never felt before." Gus cupped her face in his hand. "You made me feel. My heart was pumping, my blood flowing hot and fast through my veins. I think that's why I noticed you in the first place. You looked amazing in that dress with your long black hair hanging down around your shoulders."

"I've never had a man talk to me the way you do."

"Then you've never had a man as intrigued as I am." He kissed a path from her earlobe along the side of her jaw to capture her mouth in a searing kiss. "You make me burn inside," he murmured.

She chuckled. "That doesn't sound comfortable."

"There's nothing comfortable about the way I feel about you. I want you so much it hurts."

"Then what are you waiting on?"

"I want you to be sure this is what you want," he said and trailed his lips down the length of her throat to the pulse beating wildly at the base.

"It is what I want. You. Me. Let's make love like there will be no tomorrow. We don't know what's going to happen. We can have tonight at the very least."

She entwined her hands behind the back of his neck and pulled him down to kiss her.

He leaned up on his elbows and stared down into her face. "Why are you so damned beautiful?"

She blinked up at him. "For an assassin?"

Gus frowned. "I didn't say that." He brushed a strand of her hair back behind her ear. "The combination of black hair, smooth skin and brown-black eyes give you an air of mystery I would think most men couldn't resist."

"Apparently, you're the only one who couldn't resist. Most men don't look twice at me."

"Oh, darlin', that's where you're wrong. You are stunningly attractive. I couldn't take my eyes off you at the gala."

"Because you were worried I was going to kill or kidnap Charlie." She shook her head. "I'm just a woman with a load of personal baggage that will make it hard for any man to get close to."

"But you're letting me close," he reminded her.

"Only because I know it won't last. As soon as everyone else figures out that I'm an assassin, one of a couple things could happen."

"Oh really?" He cocked an eyebrow. "What?"

"I'll be hauled off to jail for murder."

"Who will turn you in?" He pressed a kiss to her temple.

"The CIA knows I'm an assassin. When they find me, they'll arrest me, toss me in jail and throw away the key."

Gus captured her earlobe between his teeth and nibbled gently. "I didn't hear Mack or Snow say anything about the evidence that you killed anyone."

"It would only be a matter of time until someone figured it out," she said.

"They haven't so far," Gus said. "What else have you got?"

"Trinity will come after me and make my life miserable until they finally off me with a bullet to the head."

Gus swept his lips across her cheekbone and hovered over her mouth. "Maybe. But I'm not ready to let them through to do the job."

Jane leaned in and brushed her mouth across his. "You might not have a choice. They have a tendency to wait until their victims are convinced they aren't really going to come after them. That's when they strike, swift and deadly. Now, are you done talking, because I can think of better things to do in bed."

Gus kissed a path from her lips over her chin and down the long, sweet length of her neck. "You're right. There are a lot better things to do than talk about Trinity and the CIA." He reached the hollow near her collarbone and paused with his mouth to explore her lower regions with his hands.

He slipped his palm over her thigh and upward to capture her hip and pull her up against his growing erection. Holy hell, he was on fire.

No longer able to resist, he pushed the hem of her shirt up over her torso.

Jane raised her arms and let him tug it over her head.

He tossed it aside and dropped his head, pressing his lips to the swells of her breasts. She smelled of roses or some kind of flowers. He didn't know, but he liked it and tasted her skin with the tip of his tongue. Then he hooked the straps of her bra in his fingers and dragged them down over her shoulders.

Her brow furrowed and she reached behind her, undoing the clasp in the back, freeing herself from the lacy confines.

Pushing it aside he feasted his gaze on her rosy nipples, puckered tightly into pretty little nubs.

Jane clasped her hands behind his head and brought him down to take them into his mouth where he rolled the tight little buttons around with his teeth.

Her back arched off the bed and a low moan left her lips. She gripped the fabric of his shirt and pulled, dragging it over his head.

Restraint flew out the window. Gus stood, took Jane's hand and stood her on her feet. Within seconds, the rest of their clothes ended up on the floor. They stood before each other, naked.

Blood rushed through Gus's veins, pushing adrenaline and desire throughout his body. He wasn't sure what tomorrow would bring, but tonight, she was his.

JANE CUPPED GUS's cheek in her hand and leaned up on her toes to press her lips to his. "I don't know what will happen in the future, but we have now. Let's not waste the time we have."

He wrapped his arms around her waist and dragged her body against his. "I was just thinking the same thing." Gus touched the top of her head with his lips and then pressed kisses to each eyelid.

The pressure was so soft, it took her breath away. With her breasts pressed to the hard muscles of his chest and his erection nudging against her belly, she couldn't think past what he was doing to her. She wanted so much more, but she wanted more to explore every part of his body. When he started to back her into the side of the bed, she shook her head. "Not yet."

Gus groaned. "You're killing me, assassin."

She chuckled. "I've only just begun." Kiss by kiss, she worked her way from his chin, down his neck to the hard ridge of his collarbone. Her fingers traced a path downward, stopping to lightly pinch his hard, brown nipples. She replaced her fingers with her lips, rolling the little buds between her teeth.

Jane inhaled the scent of him, all woodsy and musky male. She wanted to remember that scent for when he wasn't there.

Slowly, she moved downward, dropping to her knees, nipping his skin and licking a path down his torso to the hair at the juncture of his thighs.

Gus threaded his hands into her hair and pulled her closer.

She took him into her mouth, licking the tip of his erection. Then she gripped his buttocks in both palms and pulled him into her.

He sucked in a deep breath and held it, his body stiff, his fingers digging into her scalp.

Jane moved him back out and back in, establishing a slow, sensuous pace, taking him all the way in, until he bumped against the back of her throat. She liked how he tasted, how big he was and how quickly he settled into the rhythm. But she liked even more how much power she had over him. How she turned him on by just being with him.

His thrusts grew faster and she held tight, determined to bring him all the way.

Gus stopped suddenly and pulled free of her mouth, dragged her to her feet and kissed her hard. "I want you where I am."

"I'm almost there," she whispered, her voice ragged, her breathing coming fast.

He shook his head. "You're not even close." He lifted her and laid her on the bed, her legs dangling over the side. Then he parted her thighs and bent down to capture her mouth in a long, satisfying kiss. "You taste of me. You don't know how sexy that is."

She moaned. "I have a good idea. Please, don't take too long. I'm hot all over and I want you inside me."

"Soon," he said and started his assault on her senses, by kissing a path from her chin to the base of her throat where the pulse beat fast. He moved to take one of her breasts in his mouth, sucking hard, tonguing her nipple until she arched off the bed, a moan sounding from deep inside. "Please."

"Soon," he repeated. His hands moved lower, cupping her sex in his palm.

Jane's breath caught in her throat and hitched when he pressed a finger into her channel. "Yes!"

He chuckled. "Like that?"

"Yes," she repeated.

His mouth moved over her belly and downward to the puff of curls covering her sex. He parted her folds and slipped his tongue over that nubbin of flesh packed with a million nerves all firing at once.

Jane gripped his hair in her hands and held him there, urging him to take more.

He did, tonguing her there until she writhed against him. "I can't take much more. Please."

He sucked her between his teeth and flicked her with his tongue until she rocketed over the edge.

Jane tensed, her body tingling from the point of contact all the way out to the tips of her fingers. She rode the wave of her release all the way to the very end, finally dropping back to the bed. Then she dragged him by the hair up her body.

"I need you. Inside me. Now," she said, her voice sounding like a runner having completed a marathon.

Gus scooted her up onto the bed, parted her legs with his knee and slid between them, his erection pressing against her entrance. "Now you're ready."

She smiled up at him. "Oh, yes."

He slid in, filling her channel with his wide girth, pressing in slowly.

Impatient to have all of him, Jane gripped his buttocks and slammed him home.

Gus stayed deep, letting her adjust to his size. Then he slid out, and back in, establishing a rhythm as old as time.

Jane dug her heels into the mattress and lifted up, meeting him thrust for thrust.

His pace increased until he was pumping in and out, again and again. One last thrust and he buried himself deep inside her, his shaft throbbing, his face tight.

Then he collapsed on top of her, took her in his arms and rolled them onto their sides, retaining the connection. He held her close, kissing the top of her head.

"You're amazing," he whispered against her hair.

"I don't want this night to end," she said.

"Me either."

Jane lay in the warmth of his arms long into the night, memorizing each breath he took, wanting to remember everything about this man and their short time together. Tomorrow would come all too soon.

Chapter Twelve

Gus lay awake long into the wee hours of the morning, sexually sated, physically content and wishing the night could go on forever. He wished he could have protected Jane from everything the world had thrown her way. Losing her parents had been bad enough. He knew the pain of loss and the homesickness and terror of leaving everything you ever knew behind you to go into foster care.

But to be taken even from foster care into the harsh reality of a terrorist training camp…

His arm tightened around her. If only he could protect her from how the world would treat her should they discover all she'd done as a trained assassin. He'd bet she'd chafe at his need to protect. She was more than capable of defending herself. If it came down to it, she'd drop out of sight and start a new life somewhere else. More than likely, she'd be on the run from Trinity for the rest of her existence. Organizations like Trinity didn't let their disciples walk away. If they wanted to leave, they were carried away in body bags, as she'd already pointed out.

Like John Halverson, Gus wanted to put a stop to Trinity. Once and for all.

John had made a start at identifying the key players, but he didn't get far. Code names weren't enough. They needed real names, addresses, locations of the handlers to reach the head of the snake. Cut off the head and the snake would die.

Until they found the key players, Jane would remain a target. She would not be at peace unless one of two things happened. The asp was captured…or Jane died.

Though Gus hadn't known Jane for long, he felt a connection that transcended time. They'd suffered similar events and survived. They'd not only survived, they'd grown stronger and more powerful through their adversity.

Gus admired Jane's passionate nature. Not only did she display it in bed, but she displayed it in her willingness to disobey orders to save young girls who had no one else to defend them. She was zealous about her belief that they should live free of their captors.

Sometime in the early morning hours, Gus slept, retaining his hold on the woman who was quickly capturing his heart.

A loud knock on the suite door jerked him out of a dreamless sleep and into an upright position.

The knocking continued.

Gus leaped out of bed and ran naked across the floor to the suite door.

"Gus!" Declan's voice sounded through the paneling. "You awake?"

"I am now." He opened the door a crack and peered into Declan's clean-shaven face. "What's up?"

"Get dressed and meet us in the conference room." Declan didn't give him any more information than that. And from his tone, he wanted him there ASAP.

Gus closed the door and headed for his duffel bag in the other bedroom.

"What's wrong?" Jane asked.

He turned to find her wrapped in a sheet, her hair rumpled and her brow furrowed.

Gus's heart squeezed hard in his chest. He didn't see in her the trained assassin. He saw the beautiful, vulnerable woman. He held his arms open.

She didn't hesitate but fell into them and let him hold her tight.

"Is it that bad?" she murmured against his chest.

Gus chuckled. "I have no idea. I just wanted to hold you." He kissed the top of her head. "He wants us down in the conference room ASAP. We need to get dressed."

"That might be a good idea, considering we're naked." She leaned back and kissed his prickly chin.

"I don't think he meant for me to take time to shave."

"I'm not complaining," she said and kissed his stubbled chin again.

Gus heaved a heavy sigh. "As much as I'd love to blow off Declan, we'd better get moving."

Jane stepped away, dropped the sheet and walked back to the bedroom. "I'll be ready in less than a minute."

With a growl at her blatant temptation, Gus turned back to his duffel bag and pulled out jeans and a T-shirt. He had both on and was shoving his feet into his boots when Jane appeared in his doorway, dressed, her hair neatly brushed and shoes on her feet.

"I don't know any other woman who is that quick to get ready."

"We learned to be fast or be hit."

Gus's fists clenched. He wished he could find the people who'd been Jane's so-called instructors and beat them to a pulp for what they'd done to Jane and their other conscripted assassins.

Moments later, they were descending into the basement conference room where Declan, Cole, Jonah, Charlie and Grace stood around the bank of monitors.

"What's going on?" Gus asked.

"Cole got a tip we need to follow up on." Declan nodded toward one of the monitors with a picture of several men in suits entering a hotel.

"I got an encoded message from the Dark Web early this morning while I was surfing for more information about the bombing in Syria that Jane was involved in." He clicked the keyboard and brought up the words.

Trinity's next mark.

Gus shook his head. "What's that supposed to mean?"

"The message was accompanied with a link to images on the DC news station." Cole pointed to the monitor where the suited men were entering a hotel.

The caption beneath the image read *Inquiry into Shayat Airbase Bombing Continues.*

"Isn't that the Willard hotel?" Charlie asked.

Cole nodded. "They're using the conference center in the hotel to conduct the preliminary hearings."

"What kind of security are they employing?" Gus asked.

"A mix of Homeland Security personnel and rent-a-cops." Cole's lip curled. "Apparently, they don't expect it to be a big deal, since it's a preliminary hearing."

"Anyone could access the hotel during the meeting," Declan pointed out.

Charlie tapped a finger to her chin. "They'll probably have the meeting rooms cordoned off, but the rest of the hotel will still be open to guests."

"Do you think you'd recognize any of your fellow assassins if you saw them?" Declan asked Jane.

She shrugged. "Only if they came up through the training with me. And even then, we also trained in disguising ourselves."

A soft ding sounded from the computer.

Cole leaned over the keyboard and clicked a few keys.

Another message popped up.

For more information report to HI HQ, J. Halverson's office.

Charlie gasped. "What the hell? Ask him why."

Cole keyed in the question mark and lifted his hands off the keyboard, waiting.

A full two minutes passed, and no response came.

"I assume HI HQ is the Halverson International building," Declan said.

Charlie nodded, her face pale. "I know it's not John, but if not him, who would have sent that message?"

Cole shook his head. "That's the power of the Dark Web. If you don't want anyone to know who's sending the messages, you can get around the traceability."

"Do you think it's a setup?" Gus asked.

"Halverson International has pretty tight security," Charlie insisted.

"Security can be bypassed," Declan reminded her.

"But we have to go," Charlie insisted. "If this request has anything to do with stopping Trinity from hitting their next mark, we have to respond."

"Then we go." Declan lifted his cell phone to his ear and called Mack. He explained the situation to him. "Get Snow and Mustang on the horn and let them know we're meeting at the Halverson International building as soon as you can get there." He ended the call and nodded toward Jane. "What are we going to do with you?"

Jane's lips twisted. "I'd have booted me off the estate a long time ago."

"Yeah, but we kind of like the way you operate," Declan said. "Minus the assassin thing. Besides, now that you're getting your memory back, you might come in handy identifying fellow Trinity operatives."

Jane nodded. "I'll help in any way I can. However, once we complete training, we're separated from other operatives, so we don't know each other. We don't even see the faces of our handlers. All we have is a cell phone to communicate assignments. Otherwise we're on our own."

"How did you travel in and out of the country?" Declan asked.

"With each assignment, we were given the proper identification documents we'd need. Forged, of course."

"Who gave you the documents?" Gus asked.

"My handler gave me mine," Jane said.

"Could you pick him out in a lineup?" Declan asked. "If Cole finds some shots of Trinity people, do you think you would recognize him?"

Jane shook her head. "Like I said, they never let us see them. Mine always met me in a dark alley with a hat that shadowed his entire face. The only thing I'd have to go on is his voice. That's why it was so hard for Mr. Halverson to fill in the blanks on the chain of command. They guard the levels carefully. I think some are in high-level government positions. I've heard of operatives being killed who learned who their handlers were."

"Sweet heaven, Jane. If it was that dangerous, why did you agree to help John find yours?" Charlie asked.

Jane's jaw firmed. "I didn't want to be a part of an organization that killed innocent women and children."

Grace touched a hand to her lips. "They did that?"

"One of the operatives had a family. To punish him, they murdered his wife and child, in front of him. Then they killed him." Jane's gaze went to Gus.

"They sent out a video of what they'd done to all the operatives as a warning. That happened right before John approached me with his request."

"That's awful," Grace whispered.

"All the more reason for me to leave now before they think you all are important to me," Jane said. "I don't want what happened to that man's wife and child to happen to you."

Gus's gut clenched. Jane would have to die for Trinity to leave her alone. He couldn't let that happen. There had to be another way. He wasn't ready to let go of this amazing woman he'd just found.

JANE WAS SURPRISED Charlie wanted her to come with them to Halverson International Headquarters. She suspected it was that *keeping the enemy close* mind-set. She was glad she could accompany them. In a way, she felt responsible for what Trinity was doing. Having been a part of the organization for so long, she'd done things she wished she hadn't. She'd rationalized about the men she'd killed. They'd been bad, having murdered innocent people. Taking them out had been a blessing to others who might have been their next targets.

The rest of the team met up with Charlie and the group from the estate in the garage and went through security and straight up to John Halverson's office.

Margaret met them again at the elevator, a smile on her face. "I'm so glad you came in today. There's an envelope for you. I thought I might have to bring it out to your house."

Charlie patted the woman's arm. "That's not necessary. Just let me know about things and I'll come to the office."

"Yes, ma'am." She handed her the envelope and looked to the others. "Can I get you something to drink?"

The woman reminded Jane of every grandmother she'd ever seen on television. Not that she appeared that old, but that she wanted to help and please the people she considered family or friends.

"No, thank you, Margaret," Declan said for the group.

"We'll be in John's office and we're not to be disturbed," Charlie said, leading the way into the corner office, the envelope in her hand.

Once they were all inside the office, Charlie looked around. "Now what? Are you certain your contact on the Dark Web said we should meet here? Was there a time associated?"

Jane wandered around the office, looking for clues and finding none. She stopped by the floor-to-ceiling windows and stared out at the capitol. The sun was shining, and people were moving about on the streets, happily unaware of the terrorists among them.

Cole lifted his hands, palms upward. "You know as much as I do. We were supposed to get here ASAP."

Gus nodded toward the envelope in Charlie's hand. "What's in the envelope? Maybe it's a message from the Dark Web contact."

Charlie tore open the small white envelope and

withdrew a piece of paper. She looked down at it and frowned. "This makes no sense."

She handed the paper to Declan.

The team leader read it aloud. *"Look to the symbol that embodies the strength and stability of our founding father and all shall be revealed."*

The words were typed neatly and centered on the page.

Charlie stared down at the note and shook her head. "What does it mean?"

Jane looked out the window at the skyline. She could barely see the Reflection Pool or the dome of the Capitol Building. The Washington Monument towered over the rest of the buildings, reaching its four-sided obelisk into the blue sky, a testament to the strength and stability of the founding father for which it was named.

Jane's pulse clamored in her veins. "The Washington Monument."

Gus crossed the floor to stand beside her. "What did you say?"

"Read the note again," Jane said, her excitement building.

Declan read aloud again. *"Look to the symbol that embodies the strength and stability of our founding father and all shall be revealed."*

"And who was considered our founding father?" Jane asked, her eyes narrowing as she stared at the towering obelisk.

"George Washington," Charlie answered, stopping to stand beside Jane. "Do you think the note is referring to the Washington Monument?" She stared at the tower. "I don't see anything revealing about it."

"Should we go down there and look?" Declan asked.

"Why don't you look through the telescope?" Gus suggested.

Since Charlie was the closest to the shiny brass telescope, she pressed her eye to the viewfinder and peered through the lens. "I don't see anything different," she murmured.

The whooshing sound of movement made Jane look up.

Blackout shades slid down to cover the floor-to-ceiling windows.

"What the hell?" Gus exclaimed. "Did someone hit a switch?"

"I didn't," Declan said.

"Me, either," Mack added, holding up his hands.

"Something made those shades come down." Charlie backed away from the telescope.

A click and a rumble behind her made Jane turn back to the room's interior. A huge sheet of the wood-paneled wall slid to the side, revealing an array of computer monitors. The one in the center blinked to life, displaying an image of John Halverson.

Jane and Charlie both gasped at the same time.

"I know that face," Jane whispered.

John Halverson gave a sad smile. "Hey, Charlie. If you're viewing this message, I must be gone."

Charlie pressed a hand to her chest; tears welled in her eyes and slid down her cheeks. "Oh, John."

"I had the telescope set up with an optical scanner to read your eyes only. All the security measures I put in place in this room were for a reason. I realized a little too late that what I was getting into could have repercussions that impacted you. I should have told you about it and prepared you for my potential demise."

While John had been talking, Gus grabbed the executive chair from behind the desk and pushed it over to where Charlie stood in front of the video monitor.

She didn't move until Gus touched her shoulder and urged her to sit. Charlie sank into the chair, a soft sob escaping her lips.

"I'd first run across the Trinity Syndicate when I was working a special project with the CIA. I'm sorry, dear. I knew you didn't want me to get involved in dangerous activities but I couldn't stand by and do nothing when there was an organization out there preying on children and young people, turning them into killing machines for hire and to disrupt the world political arena. I know how much you had wanted children of our own. When that didn't happen, I knew you would have wanted to help other children, like Kate Sanders." John's face disappeared and a photo image of a young girl appeared. She had long, black silky hair and dark brown eyes.

Gus stepped closer. "Is that…?"

"That's Jane," Declan declared.

Gus looked from the image to Jane and back.

John's voice continued. "Kate Sanders's parents died in a plane wreck. With no other family who could take her, she was relegated to foster care. Within days of placing her in a home, she disappeared. The missing children foundation posted her photo on milk cartons, posters, Amber Alerts and the news. She was never found. Until I witnessed a Trinity assassination of a Saudi prince who'd just raped a young girl in a tawdry bordello in New York City."

Jane remembered.

Everything. From the horror of learning she'd lost her parents to the daily beatings during training with Trinity, to when she'd met John Halverson who wanted only to stop Trinity from making monsters out of children.

She was one of Trinity's monsters.

An arm came up around her waist.

She turned to Gus. He didn't say a word, just held her.

"Now that I'm gone," John's voice continued, "you will have a decision to make."

Charlie gave another little sob.

"I never wanted you to be involved in tracking down the handlers and leaders of Trinity. It's dangerous business. You must choose whether to destroy the information I've gathered or pass it on to the FBI or CIA and let them pick up where I left off. I never wanted you to be caught in the repercussions of what I was doing.

"I'm sorry I've left you alone. I know how much you hated it when I was gone. Know this, though, I love you with all my heart."

The video ended and the monitor turned dark.

"When did you say John passed?" Jane asked.

"Four months ago," Charlie said, her voice broken and choked with emotion.

"I was in touch with John via text less than two months ago," Jane whispered. "How can that be?"

"I couldn't let his work die with him," a voice said from a corner of the room.

Jane spun to see Margaret, John's executive assistant, standing near the doorway.

Jane frowned. "You sent me the texts about getting the general out of Shayrat?"

Margaret nodded. "I've worked with John on this project from the beginning. I knew as much, sometimes more than he did. I'm as committed to the downfall of Trinity Syndicate as he was."

"I wish he would have told me," Charlie said.

"He wanted to but felt like he didn't have enough data to be useful. And he wanted to keep you safe. He knew code names of the people in key positions of leadership, but not who the people were behind the codes. When he was murdered, I stepped in where he left off, gathering information. I haven't gotten much further. I'd hoped Indigo would lead to a breakthrough."

"But I failed," Jane said.

"I'm just glad you're alive. I shouldn't have asked you to play the role of a double agent trying to get the Russian general you were supposed to assassinate out of harm's way. Once you did that, I knew I had to find a way to make you disappear. When you failed to go through with your assigned assassinations, Trinity would target you for extermination."

Jane closed her eyes and forced herself to relive that day in Syria, the memories coming back in a collage of images. "The Trinity agent who killed the general came after me." She pinched the bridge of her nose as remembered pain throbbed at the base of her skull. "He knocked me out and left me locked in a building that was supposed to be part of the US airstrike on Shayrat Airbase. I should have died in the attack. Instead, Russians who were working with the Syrian rebels found me and took me to an alternate location to interrogate me."

Gus's arm tightened around her.

"I never learned the identity of my handler. With Trinity, you didn't question, you performed. If you knew too much, it was certain death." She met Margaret's gaze.

"Then why did you agree to help John?" Charlie asked.

Jane's lips twisted. "I was tired of the killing, even though the people Trinity had me go after weren't model citizens, like the Saudi crown prince. I didn't want the syndicate to keep training kids to be like me. And I wanted out."

"And I'm still working on how to get you out and how to keep you safe," Margaret said, looking at Charlie, "as I know John would have wanted. I only bring you in on this now because you've already uncovered so much."

Jane snorted. "By now, you must realize the only way out of Trinity is death."

"No," Gus said. "I refuse to accept that."

"They know I've defected," Jane said. "The attack on the freeway was the first attempt at damage control. There will be others until they tie up this loose end."

"You are not a loose end," Margaret said. "John had a lot of faith in you. I failed you when I sent you in to get the general out."

"What was so important about the general?" Charlie asked. "And how did you get involved with him?"

"John had been working with the CIA in his effort to track down Trinity leaders. The CIA asked for help in return. I picked up where John left off with Indigo. The CIA learned of a leak in military intelligence. Information was getting to the Russians about our military operations. The CIA wanted to know who was leaking that information. The Russian was the CIA's plant. He was there when the Russians received word to evacuate Shayrat. Someone warned them about the pending US strike. The general's cover had been compromised. The CIA wanted to get him out. Indigo was there. She'd sent a message to John that she'd been tasked with the general's assassination, not knowing John had been murdered. The CIA had tapped into the burner phone she used to keep in touch with John. They knew what I knew and asked me to intervene to save the general." Margaret held out her hands, palms up. "I took over when John passed but I need help. I need Declan's Defenders. And I need them now."

"You're my link on the Dark Web, aren't you?" Cole asked.

Margaret nodded. "And I have a situation I need your help to resolve."

"Why didn't you go to the CIA or FBI?" Charlie asked.

"I don't know who to trust anymore. I'm beginning to think Trinity has tentacles in the government. Their leadership might be entrenched somewhere in the CIA, FBI or State Department. I think that's why Indigo's mission to extract the general failed. Someone knew from the inside that she'd defected and sent someone out to make sure the general died as well as Indigo. But that's not why I brought you here." She glanced down at the watch on her wrist. "In three hours, there is a preliminary hearing concerning the bombing at Shayrat. My contacts on the Dark Web indicate there will be an attack on the people in that hearing. They are to spare no one and make it look like a random terrorist attack by ISIS, not a precision execution staged by Trinity."

"What do you want us to do?" Jane asked, knowing before the woman responded.

Margaret's gaze swept the room, pausing to connect with each person, one by one, before she answered. "We need to stop the attack."

Chapter Thirteen

Three hours hadn't been much time to organize, arm and plan their defense.

The hearing had been set up at a posh hotel's conference room center.

Cole had hacked into the hotel's database and secured a reservation for Mr. and Mrs. Walsh arriving that day for a one-night stay. Gus and Jane would enter the hotel with their luggage containing the weapons the team would need to combat the threat.

Cole would man the communications van parked on the street, tap into the hotel's internal security cameras and direct those inside with what he saw.

Mack and Snow would enter the hotel as electric technicians there to fix a problem with a faulty circuit. Cole had already hacked into the hotel's systems to generate the work order.

Mustang and Declan had found their way inside earlier by sneaking into the back of a delivery van, delivering hotel staff uniforms. They'd snagged a couple of janitor coveralls and slipped through the loading dock entrance into the hotel's laundry facility. From there, they'd work their way inward to the conference center.

Each member of the team and Jane had been equipped with state-of-the-art communications devices John Halverson had stashed in a hidden storeroom in his office. The communications van, according to Margaret, had been a special project he'd been working on before he passed.

Cole had jumped in, booted the computers, updated their software and connected all of the headsets to his dashboard. He was positioned less than a block away from the hotel in a pay-to-park lot.

Gus, dressed in black trousers and a long-sleeve button-down dark shirt, stared across the backseat of the rented limousine at Jane.

She wore a sleek black jumpsuit with a black patent-leather belt cinched around her narrow waist. Charlie had loaned her the outfit, a broad-brimmed black-and-white hat and large dark sunglasses.

Jane had swept her silky black hair high up on her head and tucked it into the hat, exposing her long, sexy neck. In the matching black patent-leather pumps, she looked like a stunning DC socialite.

"What?" she said.

Gus hadn't realized he'd been staring until then. "What what?"

"Do I look all right for the part?" she asked, brushing away an imaginary speck from her pant leg.

"You look amazing," Gus said. "I only hope the Trinity operatives don't recognize you."

"In this outfit, I don't see how they can." Jane's

lips twisted. "I don't think I've ever worn anything this fancy."

"All we have to do is get in, set up and then slip down to the lobby. If Trinity is planning a coup by storming the entrance, we'll be the first line of defense with the security guards that will be in place for the hearing."

"And if they plan on a subtler attack, we can watch for infiltration, one at a time."

"Right." He reached for her hand. "I would have preferred for you to stay back with Charlie. You've been through enough already." When she started to frown, he held up his other hand. "I know you're perfectly capable of taking care of yourself. I've just never worked a mission with someone like you."

One side of her mouth curled in a half smile. "An assassin?"

"No. A woman I find myself deeply attracted to." He shook his head. "It must be the male gene. Every protective instinct in me is screaming for me to shield you from harm."

Jane's brow dipped lower. "Gus, you can't operate that way. You have to treat me like one of your team. You have to know I've got your back just as much as you have mine. You can't be thinking about protecting me when you have a job to do."

He nodded and squeezed her hand. "My mind tells me that, but my heart is freaking out."

She captured his cheeks between her palms and stared into his face, her dark eyes so intense. "Focus, marine." Then she kissed him hard, her mouth taking his by storm.

He pulled her close in the back of the limousine and deepened the kiss until they were both breathless.

The limousine pulled up in front of the hotel and came to a stop.

Jane stared once more into Gus's eyes.

He wanted to kiss her again, but knew the time had come. "Ready?"

She nodded.

He touched the communication headset in his hear. "Cole?"

"Gotcha," Cole said into the earbud communications device in Gus's ear. "Indigo?"

"That's Jane, to you," Jane answered.

Cole chuckled. "I stand corrected. Everyone set?"

Declan, Mustang, Mack, Snow and Arnold all reported in.

"It's game time," Declan said.

Arnold opened the door and held it for Jane.

She slid her legs out the door and let Arnold pull her to her feet.

Gus got out behind her and waited while Arnold unloaded the suitcase filled with the disassembled parts of the weapons they might need if the assault happened as indicated on the Dark Web.

Placing one hand on the small of her back, the other on the handle of the rollaway suitcase, Gus walked with Jane into the hotel. The limousine left the covered entrance and drove away. Arnold would park it in the pay-to-park lot near where Cole had positioned the van. He'd be Cole's eyes around the van and backup for the team inside if the going got tough.

Security guards stopped Gus on the way into the hotel. He showed his identification.

Jane patted her body and looked up at the guards with a grimace. "Oh, dear, I left my purse in the limousine."

"We'll notify the limousine company when we get inside." Gus pointed to the clipboard the security guard held with the names of the guests due to arrive. "That's us there, Mr. and Mrs. Walsh." He prayed the guard wouldn't insist on inspecting the contents of the case. The disassembled weapons were tucked into hidden compartments, but a smart guard would notice the case was bigger than the interior showed, and heavier than the few items displayed inside.

The guard put a check beside Gus's name, nodded and stepped aside, allowing them to enter the lobby.

A number of men wearing business suits stood around, talking in small groups.

Margaret had done her homework and shown them pictures of some of the people who would be attending the preliminary hearing.

Gus recognized a few of the men. "The delegates are here," he said softly.

"All is quiet in the hallways and at the entrances," Cole reported.

Gus and Jane walked to the front desk and registered. A few minutes later, they were in the elevator on their way up to their third-floor room.

"Delegates are making their way to the conference center," Cole reported.

"Almost to our room," Gus said.

They emerged from the elevator and walked to the room, waved the key card over the locking mechanism and they were in.

Gus quickly laid the case on the bed, unzipped it and unfolded it.

While he opened the hidden compartment on one side, Jane uncovered the other side. They quickly assembled the weapons in time for a knock on the door.

Gus checked through the peephole and then opened the door to Declan and Mustang dressed in janitor uniforms.

Wordlessly, Jane supplied them with handguns and several magazines of ammunition.

They tucked the guns in their pockets and exited, headed down the stairwells toward the second floor where the conference rooms were located.

A moment later, Snow and Mack arrived wearing the electrician uniforms.

"Wish I had a submachine gun," Snow lamented.

"Kind of hard to hide one," Gus said and handed Snow several magazines of ammo.

"Let's hope this doesn't get too ugly," Mack said. "There are a lot of guests in the hotel today besides the delegates for the hearing."

"The conference room doors have been closed, all delegates inside," Cole reported into their ears.

"Let's get this show on the road," Snow said. He and Mack left the room and headed down to the opposite end of the hallway where Declan and Mustang had gone and descended the stairwell.

Gus watched until they disappeared and then turned back to Jane. "Ready?"

"Almost." She strapped on a shoulder holster and tucked a handgun in the pocket. Then she slipped on the jacket Charlie had loaned her to go with the black jumpsuit. She pulled the pant leg of her suit up and checked the strap of the scabbard holding the knife she'd chosen to carry. Then she lifted the other pant leg and patted the spare magazine strapped there.

Gus smiled. "All I have to say is that I'm glad you're on our side."

She dropped the pant leg and straightened, her eyes sparkling. "You should be." Then she stepped up to him, planted a kiss on his lips and said, "I'm ready."

He grabbed her around the waist, his hand bumping against the gun beneath her jacket. It didn't deter him from pulling her close and kissing her harder. Then he set her away from him and muttered, "Focus."

"That's right. We have to focus."

Gus opened the door and stepped into the hallway, checking left and right before he held out his hand to Jane.

She placed her fingers in his palm and walked with him to the elevator.

Once inside, Gus pushed the button and waited for the doors to slide shut.

As they closed, Cole's voice sounded in his ear.

"We have movement in the hallway from the direction of the kitchen." His voice was tight, urgent.

The elevator door closed all the way and the car started down.

An explosion rocked the building.

The elevator shuddered to a stop and the lights blinked out.

"Damn." Gus pulled his cell phone out of his pocket and turned on the flashlight application. "We're trapped in the elevator. What's going on out there?"

"Can't tell," Cole replied. "The security cameras blinked off. Wait—they're back on and the hallways are lit with emergency lights. It's a lot harder to see anything with them."

"Where are the guys who were coming from the kitchen?"

"Hold on…" Cole said. "There. They're climbing the east stairwell to the second floor. They appear to be carrying automatic weapons."

"Should have brought a submachine gun," Snow said into Gus's ear.

"You guys will have to start the party without us. We're stuck in the elevator. But not for long." Gus laid his phone on the ground, the flashlight pointing up. Then he reached up and pushed on the panel above his head, shoving it to the side.

"Need a boost?" Jane laced her fingers and cupped her hands.

Gus stepped into Jane's palms and pulled himself up through the narrow opening into the elevator shaft. The elevator had stopped five feet below the third floor. If they could open the doors on the third floor, they could get out.

He leaned over the trap door and looked down at Jane's face gazing up at him. "Give me your hand."

She reached up and clasped his hand in hers.

He pulled her up through the hole until she could grasp the edges of the opening and drag herself the rest of the way through. Her hat had been knocked off and her hair spilled out of the pins and down her back. She'd tossed the sunglasses in the dark. This was the woman Gus was growing to love and admire. Not the socialite in the fancy clothing, but the kick-ass female who could take a man down with her hands and her skills.

Together, they dragged the elevator doors open to the third floor.

The hallway was empty, the only illumination that of the emergency lighting and the exits signs.

Gus pulled himself up and out the elevator doors, then reached down and helped Jane up to stand beside him.

No sooner were they on their feet than they were running for the stairwell.

"We're out and moving," Gus reported. "Heading down the west stairwell."

"Beware," Cole said. "More men, heavily armed, are heading up from the ground floor to the second floor. You might converge at the same time."

"Got it," Gus said.

"Looks like they have the conference room on lockdown," Cole added.

Cole pulled the handgun from the shoulder holster beneath his suit jacket and ran down the stairs.

Below him, he could hear the clumping sound of boots coming up the stairs from below.

Halfway down to the second floor, Gus paused on the landing and waited for Jane to catch up. *Ready.* He mouthed the word.

She gave one brief nod.

They descended quietly, clinging to the wall as they rounded to the landing onto the second floor.

Two men, carrying semiautomatic rifles, charged up the stairs only a few steps from the top. They wore black clothes, black ski masks and no police markings on the tactical vests they had strapped on over their shirts.

When the lead man spotted Gus, he jerked his rifle up in front of him and fired.

Gus saw the move coming and backed around the corner, pushing Jane behind him. If the gunmen had been hotel guards or Department of Homeland Security, they would have identified themselves before shooting.

The bullets pounded into the wall where he'd been standing.

He ducked low and popped out around the corner at around knee level and fired, hitting the man in the chest.

The man staggered backward but didn't go down.

Figuring he must be wearing protective armor in

his tactical vest, Gus aimed lower and hit him in the knees.

The front man dropped and rolled to the side to be replaced by another.

He fired up the stairs.

Gus lay flat on the floor and returned fire.

Behind him, Jane came out from the corner and aimed at the man's head, hitting him with her first round. The man went down and didn't move.

She fired at the guy Gus had hit in the knee. He didn't move.

Gus and Jane descended the rest of the way to the second floor and pushed open the stairwell door, just enough to look down the hallway.

The sound of gunfire echoed off the walls along with the screams of people caught in the melee.

"Five shooters have made it to the doors of the conference center," Cole said. "Four more are on their way through the lobby."

Jane darted past Gus and ran down the hallway toward the conference center.

"Wait," Gus called out. "You can't go in alone."

"What's going on?" Cole demanded.

"Jane's almost to the corner. She ran ahead." Gus raced after her, close, but not close enough to cover for her. The woman had worked alone for so long, she didn't know what it meant to wait for backup.

Now she was running straight into a situation where she'd be outnumbered from the get-go.

When Jane disappeared around the corner, Gus's heart skipped several beats. He wasn't far behind her, but any distance could mean the difference between dead and alive.

Shots were fired and the blurp sound of a machine gun made Gus's blood run cold.

He burst out from around the corner to find Jane lying prone on the ground, her handgun in front of her. She fired one round after another until her magazine had emptied. When Jane dropped the magazine, and pulled the second one from the strap on her leg, Gus laid down protective fire, aiming for the man who'd taken cover in an alcove. One man had a submachine gun he aimed around the corner, firing indiscriminately.

"Declan and Mustang have the ground floor," Cole reported. "They're firing now on the men moving through the lobby. Snow and Mack made it into the conference room before the lockdown. They're protecting the doors."

"We've got the hallway in front of the conference room," Jane said.

"No, we don't," Gus disagreed. "There are five of them and two of us. And one of them is armed with a submachine gun."

"He wasn't carrying additional rounds," Jane said. "He'll blow through what he has soon. We only have to keep him from doing it in the conference room."

The hallway went silent for a moment.

When Gus took the opportunity to duck out from the corner and fire, Jane grabbed hold of his shirt and yanked him back behind cover.

The man with the submachine gun lay in the middle of the hallway, aiming low to the ground. He let loose a burst toward where Jane and Gus were positioned, the number of bullets coming at them chipped away at the corner, spewing Sheetrock dust and paint.

When the firing ceased, Gus dared to look around the corner. The man with the machine gun was gone, along with his backup.

"They're closing in on the conference room," Gus said. "I'm going forward."

Jane jumped up beside him. "Not without me."

Together, they raced after the attackers, rounded another corner and came face-to-face with the five men in black ski masks, all pointing weapons at them.

"Drop your weapons and we might let you live."

"In that case," Gus said. "No." He dove for Jane as the men opened fire.

A bullet hit his arm and one pierced his side.

Jane fell to the floor, crushed by his weight.

The doors to the conference room burst open. Declan and Mustang emerged, firing on the men attacking Jane and Gus.

From the other end of the hallway, Snow and Mack flew out of the stairwell and fired, careful not to hit Declan and Mustang.

Gus lay on top of Jane, holding her down as the others picked off the attackers one by one.

When the shooting stopped, Gus rolled to the side and checked Jane. "Hey, are you all right?" Blood pooled on the floor around them.

"I think I was hit," she said, her voice weak. She

reached out and touched near the wound on his shoulder. "I can't tell if it's my blood or yours."

Gus pushed to his feet, pain shooting through his side and arm. He didn't care. Jane had been hit.

He bent and lifted her in his arms. "We have to get you to a hospital."

She shook her head. "No. I don't have any identification. And for all I know, I'm probably on a CIA most wanted list. You can't take me to a hospital. But *you* can go. Put me down."

He shook his head. "You're going." Gus headed for the stairs.

Declan stepped in front of him. "Let me take her. You're hurt."

"No. I've got her," Gus insisted. "Get out of my way. She needs a hospital, ASAP."

Gus had just about reached the stairs when a man burst through the doorway and blocked Gus's path.

"No one leaves Trinity alive," he said and pointed a gun at Jane in Gus's arms.

Jane gasped. "I know that voice."

"You should. You worked for me," the man said in a low, menacing tone. "Since you insist on disobeying orders, Trinity has no more use for you."

Gus, with his hands full, couldn't do anything but hold Jane. If he dropped her, she'd be no better off. Her handler would redirect his aim and kill her anyway.

"Don't hurt her," Gus said. "She might die anyway."

The man shook his ski-mask-covered head. "Can't leave loose ends."

"Maybe so, but I can't let you hurt my people," a woman's voice sounded behind the man.

A shot rang out.

Gus stood for a moment fully expecting the bullet to have hit either him or Jane.

The gun slipped from the hand of the man in front of him and fell to the floor. A second later, the man toppled over, dead.

Margaret Rollins stood behind the dead man, a .45 caliber Glock in her hand. She wore dark pants, a dark shirt and had her hair pulled back in a tight ponytail.

Gus, Jane, Declan and the others all glanced her way, brows raised.

"What? Did you think I was only John's secretary?" She snorted. "Back in my prime, I worked as a field agent for the CIA. I know how to fire one of these." She nodded toward the man on the ground. "Ask him." Then she bent to pull the mask off the man's head and nodded. "I thought we had a leak in Halverson International." Quincy Phishburn lay on the ground at her feet. "And I had an inkling it was him."

"I'd love to stand here and argue but Jane needs a doctor," Gus reminded her.

"I have an ambulance on standby downstairs," Margaret said. "Let one of the others carry her down."

"I'm taking her." Gus stepped around Margaret and descended the stairs to the ground level.

Police, SWAT and emergency medical personnel filled the lobby, caring for the injured and taking statements.

Cole and Arnold had joined them as soon as the threat had been neutralized.

"Lay her down here," an EMT insisted, pointing Gus to a stretcher that had been rolled in from one of the waiting ambulances.

"Get her to a hospital before she loses too much blood," Gus insisted.

"We will. Let us stabilize her before we go too far," the EMT said. "And in the meantime, take a seat on the other stretcher. You're bleeding all over the floor."

Declan placed a hand on Gus's shoulder. "Let them stop your bleeding," he said. "You're of no use to Jane if you die."

Gus eventually stepped back and let the medical personnel work over Jane. Mack and Snow ganged up on him and forced him to take a seat on a stretcher. "Don't leave her for a moment. Trinity might have someone standing by to take her out."

"We'll stick with her," Declan said. "You're losing blood. You need to let the emergency medical team help you."

"Damn it, don't worry about me. See to Jane." Gus fought back the hazy gray fog blurring his vision. "I let her down. I didn't keep her from being shot."

"You did the best you could." Declan patted his arm. "Cole, Mustang, Mack and Snow are standing around Jane. They'll make sure she gets to the hospital and the treatment she needs. You need to go, as well."

The EMTs wheeled Jane to an ambulance first. Four of Declan's Defenders climbed into the ambulance with her. Two in the front, two in the back, making it pretty crowded inside, but reassuring Gus that she would be guarded with their lives if necessary.

"Hurry up. Get me into the ambulance," Gus shouted. "I need to get to the hospital."

Margaret appeared beside him. "I'm going with you to the hospital. I have a proposal we need to discuss. Are you going to be conscious enough to listen?"

Gus closed his eyes for a moment and then nodded, reopening them. "I'm listening. As long as we get to the hospital at the same time as they bring Jane in, I'm all ears." And as long as he didn't pass out from loss of blood.

Margaret climbed into the back of the ambulance after they loaded Gus. They shut the door and pulled out into DC traffic, sirens blaring.

After the EMT situated Gus's IV and hooked up a blood pressure cuff, he sat back and nodded to Margaret.

Margaret leaned close to Gus's ear and laid out her plan.

Chapter Fourteen

"Ashes to ashes, dust to dust," the preacher said as he presided over the memorial service and the scattering of the cremated remains. With a gloved hand, he lifted a small amount of ashes and tossed it into the small hole in the ground where a tree would be planted.

"Jane would have loved that we chose a red-leaf maple tree for her service," Charlie said, wiping a tear from her eye. "She was always so tough on the outside, but I truly believe she was soft on the inside. She only wanted to belong somewhere, to find love."

"She's in a much better place," Declan assured Charlie. "Wouldn't you agree, Gus?"

With a gloved hand, Gus scooped ashes from the urn and dropped them into the hole in the ground. "Yes. I'll miss the black-haired beauty. She taught me a lot about never giving up and always fighting for what you believe in." He stepped back and brushed the ashes from his hands. "Jane Doe, Kate Sanders, rest in peace. You were a fighter and a beautiful soul."

Grace dropped ashes into the hole and murmured, "Rest in peace, Jane."

One by one, the other members of Declan's Defenders all paid their respects to the departed by dropping dirt or ashes into the hole.

"Need help planting her tree?" Declan asked.

Gus stared at the slim sapling. "No. I've got this."

When the last person had gone on to Charlie's place, Gus settled the maple tree into the hole and filled in dirt all around the roots. Then he patted down the dirt, pressing it in with his boot until the tree stood on its own, small, proud and strong. Like Jane.

He sighed, turned and walked to the waiting limousine Charlie had offered for the occasion.

Arnold, Charlie's butler, stood by the door, his shoulders back, his face expressionless. "Ready?" he asked.

Gus nodded. "Back to Charlie's?"

Arnold nodded. "Yes, sir."

"Please, don't call me sir. I work for a living."

"Yes, sir," Arnold said. Was that a twinkle in the older man's eye?

He opened the back door of the limousine and waited while Gus slid in. Then he closed the door and took his seat behind the steering wheel.

As Gus settled back against the seat a hand slid over his leg. "Was that as strange for you as it was for me?" a smoky voice said.

He turned to the blonde beside him and gathered her into his embrace. "Whatever you do, don't make me bury you twice. Agreed?"

She stared up at him with her blue eyes so different than Jane Doe's dark brown irises and smiled. "I'll do my best to stay alive."

"So, Jasmine, what's your plan?"

"I've been talking with Grace's friend, Emily, who teaches Russian at the local university and does interpretive work on the side. I think I might have a chance at working as an interpreter."

"Are you afraid it will expose you to the people who might recognize you?"

"Not since I have the different hair. Charlie said she'd help me get a different face to go along with my new identity."

"What if I like your face the way it is?" He bent to kiss the tip of her nose.

She tipped her face and captured his mouth with hers. "I guess it all depends on how soon Trinity is brought down," she said.

"We're working on it. Now that Charlie knows what her husband was up to, she's taking it as her challenge to finish what he started."

"Sounds like Declan's Defenders will have their hands full with that task." She cupped his cheeks between her palms. "You have to be careful, though. Trinity plays for keeps. And they won't go down easily."

"I've gathered that. But as long as they're still in operation, you'll never be safe, even with your new hair, eye color and identity. The change is only buying time until we can eliminate the organization." Gus frowned, his jaw tightening. "And we will."

"Though I'll be working as an interpreter by day,

you know I'll help in every way I can. I want them stopped even more than John Halverson. Those kids they are taking deserve a better life. Not what Trinity has in store for them."

"Then let's get this mission started, Jasmine Katherine Newman. Charlie, Declan and the others are waiting for us in the conference room. And when we're done with the meeting, we have some catching up to do."

She wrapped her arms around his neck. "Are you sure your injuries are healed enough?"

"I don't care if they are or not. I haven't held you close since your 'death' and your ride to the morgue. Now that the funeral's over, I plan on catching up on lost time."

"Mmm, count me in on that plan. Beats dying any day. And I hope I never to visit another morgue until I am completely dead, not just faking it." And she kissed him, long and hard.

As his tongue swept past her teeth to caress hers, Gus vowed to take down Trinity if it was the last thing he did. This woman deserved to live a happy life, free of fear. Preferably with him. He still found it difficult to believe he'd fallen in love with an assassin. More so, that she'd fallen in love with him.

* * * * *

CORNERED AT CHRISTMAS

BARB HAN

All my love to Brandon, Jacob and Tori, my favorite people in the world.

To Babe, my hero, for being my great love and my place to call home.

To Jeff Amsden, for Phoenix.

Chapter One

The weather was warmer than usual for a late fall morning in North Texas, the heavy air loaded with the threat of a thunderstorm. Mitch Kent was gripping the handlebar of the double stroller so tightly as he stalked toward the medical plaza that his knuckles were turning white. Anger roared through him as reality sucker punched him. He'd already lost so much. A father twenty-three months ago. A wife less than that. The possibility of losing Rea, his infant daughter, gnawed away what was left of his gut.

Granted, all signs pointed toward positive news this visit for his younger and smaller twin. Life had taught Mitch how fast it could reverse and how devastating it could be when it took a wrong turn. He felt like he had about as much control as a sailboat in a hurricane. And that made him all kinds of frustrated. Mitch didn't go the helpless-victim route.

His cell buzzed in his pocket, breaking the pressure building between his shoulders that was threatening to crack him in half. He fished it out and checked the screen. It was Amber, his sister and the youngest of six Kent siblings.

"Wish I could be there with you, Mitch." She skipped over hellos.

"It's fine," he said probably a little too fast.

"*You're* not and you don't have to be," she countered, her voice strained. He appreciated the concern, just not the fuss.

"We talked about it last night when you called. You're needed at the ranch and I can handle this," he reassured her. He hoped she didn't pick up on the emptiness in those words.

There was a long pause.

"Are you sure you want to do this by yourself?" she finally asked. He didn't want to do any of it alone but life had detoured, leaving him to roll with the turns and try not to get sucked into the current.

"I haven't had two minutes of privacy since the twins were born," he said with a half laugh. That part was true enough and he tried to lighten the mood with humor. Anything to keep his thoughts from taking the headfirst dive that always left him wondering how he'd do any of this without Kimberly.

"You know what I mean." She was the last of his siblings to call before the twins' one-year checkup. Each of his brothers—Will, Devin, Nate and Jordan—had done their best to lift Mitch's mood. During the appointment, he'd learn if his younger twin, the little girl, was in the clear or headed for surgery. The thought of anyone cracking open her tiny body was a hot poker in his chest.

"I know you'd be here if you could, Amber. The ranch needs you more than I do." The Kent siblings had inherited their parents' North Texas cattle ranch nearly two years ago, following their father's death. Their mother had passed six months prior.

The one-hour drive into Fort Worth had been smooth and the twins had slept most of the way. But the two were wide-awake now and taking in the scenery as he pushed their stroller onto the center of the medical plaza. A maze of buildings surrounded them and there was a memorial fountain that was catching the twins' attention in the center of the complex. Mitch stopped in front of the three-story glass-walled structure attached to the hospital in the state-of-the-art building that contained the doctor his wife had handpicked for their babies.

"She's going to be okay, Mitch. You know that, right?" Amber said, and he could hear the concern in her voice even though she tried to mask it.

"There's every reason to hope based on the last couple of appointments," he responded. The last eleven months without Kimberly had been hell. Mitch Kent missed his wife. He missed the way her hair smelled like freshly cut lilies when she would curl into the crook of his arm every night in bed. He missed the feel of her warm body pressed to his, long into the night. The easy way they had with each other, talking until the sun came up. And he missed coming home to her smile every night after a long day of working his family's cattle ranch. Losing her had damn near shattered him.

First his mother, followed by his father. Then his wife. He'd lost so much.

Mitch realized he was still tightly gripping the stroller with his left hand. He flexed and released his fingers to get the blood flowing again.

"Those babies couldn't have asked for a better father." With five rough-and-tumble brothers, Amber was the emotional voice of the Kent brood.

"They need their mother." There were more times

than Mitch could count that he'd wished his wife was still alive. They might have dated only a few months before tying the knot, but he'd fallen hard. When a man met the woman he was supposed to spend the rest of his life with, he knew it. Hers had been cut way too short. "I'm glad they have you."

"Good. Because I'm not going anywhere. Call me Super Aunt." He could tell she was getting emotional based on the change in her tone and the lame attempt at humor.

"Sounds like a plan." He went with it.

"And don't forget Amy." She was referring to their cousin. Amber and Amy were close in age, and both were mostly sweet with wild streaks that got them in trouble from time to time. Both had hearts of gold, and he couldn't have asked for better women to be in his twins' lives.

"Call or text the minute you get word." Amber made him promise.

"I will," he said before ending the call.

Mitch would learn today if his daughter, born two minutes after his son and almost two pounds lighter, was in the clear. In the best-case scenario, the small hole in the wall that separated the two lower chambers of Rea's heart was still too small to cause any serious damage, like overworking her heart and lungs or sending blood flowing in the wrong direction. Mitch blocked out another possibility. The one that involved a lot of medical jargon, some kind of fabric patch and cracking open the center of his baby girl's chest.

The appointment last month had gone off without a hitch. The doctor had said he was encouraged by what he heard when he listened to her chest. All signs were pointing toward good news. But doing any of this without his Kimberly seemed wrong. Then again everything that had happened in the past eleven months since her devastating car crash had been all wrong.

An all-consuming fist of guilt took another punch at him for not stopping her from walking out the door that day with her car keys in hand. For the sake of his children, he pushed the unproductive emotion aside. Reliving hell didn't ease the burns.

His courtship with Kimberly might've been a whirlwind but his feelings for his wife were anything but a passing storm. He'd known her barely two months before popping the question, which had surprised him even more than his siblings. They'd gone along with the wedding without protest after meeting Kimberly and seeing the two of them together. And they'd stood by his side on that cold rainy day when he'd first heard about the crash.

Mitch rubbed the scruff on his chin and blinked his blurry eyes, forcing back the barrage of thoughts racing through him. Letting his mind run wild wouldn't bring his wife back.

Exhaustion had thrown him off today. He gave himself a mental slap to shake off the bad mood.

He needed more caffeine.

Sleep and twins went together about as well as hot sauce and ice cream, and Mitch was beginning to feel the effects of being up for most of the night with the kiddos. Both were teething, which pretty much meant drippy chins.

The sounds of his daughter's babbling floated on top of the heavy fall air. He'd insisted on naming their little girl after her mother, but Kimberly had argued against it. They'd finally agreed on Andrea if she could go by

Rea instead—Aaron and Andrea. Of course, he'd take back every disagreement if he could get back that last day with her and tell her to stay home instead of walking her out the door, handing her the car keys and telling her how much she needed a break.

Rea was growing into a talker. Mitch had no idea what the little tyke was saying, but that didn't stop his daughter from prattling on and on. Both he and Kimberly were quiet people, so he wasn't sure how his daughter had gotten the trait. Aaron was the silent one. He'd pick something up and examine it rather than chuck it across the room. Mitch had a babbler and a thinker.

Mitch thought about the labels he'd picked up in the past two years. Ranch owner. Husband. Father. *Widower.*

The worst part about being the latter—aside from the sobering fact that he'd lost the only woman he could ever love—was the cursed feeling that Kimberly was somehow still alive.

Granted, her body was never found. But Mitch's other cousin, Sheriff Zachary McWilliams, had assured him that there was no way she'd survived the accident. The car, *her* car, had been pulled out of the ravine with barely half a windshield. Based on estimates, she'd shot out of the driver's side like a cannon and ejected some twenty-five feet across the water before sinking. The official search had lasted six days. Flash floods and more severe storms had complicated the effort, and her body had most likely been swept away. Extra divers had volunteered to work on their days off once word had gotten around that Mitch Kent's wife had been involved in a terrible accident. But getting a late start because of worsening conditions had meant recovering a body was less likely.

He'd requested privacy from the media, which was something he was certain his wife would've wanted. Zach had also assured him that it would minimize the number of crackpots coming out of the woodwork, trying to get a piece of the Kent fortune. Mostly he'd done it for his wife. She'd insisted on staying out of the spotlight. The family attorney, Harley Durant, had kept the entire story limited to a blurb on the last page of the *Fort Worth Star Telegram*. Harley knew how to move mountains. He also knew how to keep a secret, and he had enough connections to back it up.

Since losing Dad and inheriting the cattle ranch with his five siblings two years ago, Mitch had been getting a good feel for running the place, and that was in large part due to Harley. So far Mitch was the only one living on the land full-time, but construction was planned or in process for the others to join him on the property with homes of their own.

It had been him and his wife living on the ranch up until now. Mitch still half expected her to walk through the front door.

He'd been told by a well-meaning aunt that he couldn't expect closure because her body had never been found. The same person had encouraged him to join a support group and find a way to move on. Mitch didn't especially believe in that mumbo jumbo. It was most likely the fact that Rea's eyes and thick black hair made her look more like her mother every day. Both twins reminded him of Kimberly. And maybe that was the reason he saw her everywhere.

Mitch pushed the babies toward the double glass doors of the three-story building attached to the east side of the hospital.

His cell buzzed in his pocket again, so he fished it out and checked the screen. Out of the corner of his eye, he caught sight of someone staring at him and a chill raced up his spine. Coming up on the anniversary of Kimberly's death must be playing tricks on him, because the woman was her height and had her figure, so his mind immediately snapped to thinking it could be her. Damn, he needed to get a grip.

Did he really think Kimberly would be at the plaza near the hospital and pediatrician's office? That was impossible. He'd buried Kimberly Kent at least mentally if not physically. Her grave was in the meadow she loved, not a hundred yards from the house, from her family.

"What's going on?" he asked his top cowhand, Lonnie Roark, aka Lone Star Lonnie.

"Found something near the base of Rushing Creek that I thought you might want to take a look at personally," Lone Star said.

"Okay. What will I see?" Mitch asked impatiently. He wasn't frustrated with Lonnie; he was aggravated with himself for imagining his dead wife in the plaza.

Curiosity got the best of him, so he turned to get a better look at the woman. She shifted her purse to her other shoulder and he could've sworn her movements mimicked Kimberly's.

It couldn't be her, though. His wife had blue-black hair the color of a cloudless night sky that cascaded down her back. This woman had short, curly hair with so much bleach that it had turned white.

For a split second he locked gazes with her. She spun around, putting her back to him and tucking her chin to her chest. That was odd and it sent a cold ripple down his back. He strained to get a better look from this distance, but she'd moved next to a sculpture of some sort. He supposed it was modern art but he never did understand what that meant. The woman glanced back at him and his gut coiled.

Or maybe it wasn't that strange and he was just overly on edge. She sidestepped, breaking his line of sight as she blocked herself with the sculpture. What was Bleached-Blonde up to?

"It's one of the herd." Lone Star hesitated, which wasn't like him and set off a firework display of warning lights inside Mitch. This day was going to hell fast.

"What's going on?" Mitch tried to stifle his annoyance. He couldn't take his eyes off the partially blocked mystery woman. His need to get a closer look to prove she wasn't Kimberly set him off. If he knew what was best, he'd walk away. Leave it alone.

So why the hell couldn't he?

"One of the heifers must've caught hold of something and it tore one of her hooves off. Thing is I've searched everywhere within a fifty-foot radius and can't find the darn thing. What's left of her leg is a mess."

"You got an opinion on what could've happened?" Mitch didn't like the sound of this and it darkened his already somber mood.

"I'd be throwing spaghetti against the wall. There's no other sign of trouble and it looks like she died from bleeding out."

Mitch winced at the slow death that would've been for her. He bit back a curse. "Any tracks leading up to her?"

"Nothing I can see."

"You were right to call," he said on a sharp sigh. The stress of the day that had barely started already wore on him.

"I know you have enough on your plate this morning, boss." The people closest to Mitch knew about Rea's condition. Lone Star was in Mitch's inner circle. Even though Mitch was the boss, he and Lonnie were long-time friends. Mitch knew most folks in town, having grown up in Jacobstown, and he and Lonnie had been schoolmates.

"This was worth the interruption. Keep her right where she is until I can get back. You were right about me wanting to see for myself. Do me a favor and keep everyone else out of the area until I can check it out." Mitch didn't like the sound of this one bit. It could involve anything from bored teens who were up to no good or acting on a dare to cultists, and Mitch wanted answers. If this was a prank gone wrong, he'd deal with it. Anger fisted his free hand. There was no excuse for making an animal suffer. "Thanks for the heads-up. Give me a call if you find any others. For now I'm assuming this is the only issue."

"Haven't found others but I have the boys counting heads," Lone Star Lonnie confirmed. "I'll keep my eyes peeled just in case."

"Let's keep the rest of the herd away from the area." Mitch figured it would be a good idea to keep them closer to the south-facing pasture.

He glanced up to see the woman had disappeared. Curiosity had him scanning the area, searching for her.

Out of the corner of his eye, he saw a streak of blond hair jutting out from the front of a hoodie. The woman wore jeans, tennis shoes and sunglasses. He did a double take to make sure it was the same person. Had she noticed that he'd been staring?

Of course she had; otherwise why put on the hoodie

that had been tied around her waist? Mitch needed to turn around and get his tail in gear so he wouldn't be late for the doctor visit.

So why couldn't he force his boots to move?

Mitch rubbed his blurry eyes before ending the call with Lone Star. All kinds of scenarios ran through his mind about the mystery woman. Could Kimberly have survived the accident but had no idea who she was? Had someone saved her from the wreckage? Been keeping her all of this time?

No, someone would've put two and two together by now.

Lack of sleep wasn't doing great things for his brain. The woman couldn't be Kimberly. His wife was dead.

For whatever reason he couldn't take his eyes off her. Curiosity? Something else? Something more primal?

An ache formed in his chest. It was wishful thinking that had him wanting to get a closer look at the blonde. He'd already calculated the odds and knew this was a losing hand. Try getting his fool heart to listen to logic.

Mitch checked his watch. Technically he was ten minutes early.

Turning the stroller toward the mystery woman, he decided to double down on his bad luck. He scanned the area and noticed a pair of men on the opposite side of the plaza, standing with their faces angled toward her. She turned her head slightly toward the men and he could see her tense up. She took a step closer to a light pole and Mitch realized she was trying to block their line of sight.

Now Mitch's curiosity really skyrocketed.

Call it the cowboy code, but he needed to know that she would be okay. The blonde seemed to be in some kind of trouble, and he didn't like the looks of the two men wearing their jacket collars upturned, reflective sunglasses and ball caps. Very little of their faces were visible and his experience had taught him that law-abiding citizens didn't hide their faces in public. Nothing about either of them said they were law enforcement, so he assumed the blonde wasn't doing anything illegal.

One of the men moved enough to see around the light pole. He had his phone out, angled toward the blonde. Was he stalking her? Was he an ex? Someone she'd rejected? More thoughts along those lines crossed his mind, and none of them sat well.

Of course, a stalker would be alone. The guy standing next to the picture taker seemed just as interested in her, and didn't that jack up more of Mitch's danger radar? Were the men targeting her?

The blonde seemed to realize something was going on. Good for her. She wouldn't be an easy mark that way.

Once again his thoughts circled back to how familiar this woman seemed. Was there any chance his wife had survived the accident but lost her memory? Could she have been walking around for the past eleven months with no idea who she was or where she came from?

It might be a stretch but he'd heard stranger things had happened.

Or did he want to see his wife again so badly that he was confusing her with a stranger? A woman who was similar in size and shape, who also seemed to be alone and in trouble? Was he grasping at any sign of hope?

There was only one way to find out.

Chapter Two

Kimberly's husband turned toward her and took a few steps in her direction. *No. No. No. Go back.*

Seeing her babies, their sweet faces, was so much harder than she'd thought it would be. The twins were one-year-old now and she'd known their first-year checkup would be around this time. It wasn't difficult to call the scheduler of the pediatrician she'd meticulously vetted to get the exact day and time.

Pain nearly crippled her but she fought against the tide of emotion. She couldn't lose control. There was too much at stake.

Life was about to spin out of control. *Again.* Seeing her twins one more time was a risk that Kimberly Kent—*correction*, Lily Grable—had had to take. The past eleven months had been excruciating, like living in a cave with no prayer of sunlight breaking through the darkness.

Life had taught Kimberly how to deal with loss early on. But nothing had prepared her for walking away from the only man she could ever love and the babies she'd only dreamed were possible. Happily-ever-after was for princesses, not orphans like Kimberly. And now she risked making all of that heartache count for nothing if Mitch recognized her. Or worse if the men watching her connected the dots to her family.

Panic seized her.

Let Mitch get a few steps closer and he would make a scene. She let herself take another look at him even though the grip around her heart from before tightened the minute she did.

Mitch looked even better than she remembered. At six foot four he'd always dwarfed her. His wide chest and ripples of muscles were visible underneath his Western shirt. Those muscled thighs… She could see wisps of his sandy-brown hair from the rim of his gray Stetson. The color of his hat would match the steel of his eyes.

Maybe she could play it cool and Mitch would stop. There was no way he could realize who she was with as much as she'd changed her appearance. *Right?* She looked at her husband from out of the corner of her eye and her stomach fell. He was too curious to give up, and that was bad.

He'd expose her, himself and the babies. She glanced toward the pair of men who'd found her. They'd seen her but had they pegged her? Did they know who she was? That was the big question.

Kimberly eased around the back of the sculpture, forcing her body to move away from Mitch when every muscle inside her wanted to run toward him instead. She breathed in the heavy Texas autumn air and tried to block out the memories of feeling safe in his arms. A storm was brewing and the humidity kicked up a few notches alongside her pulse.

Her heart pounded against her ribs at the thought she might be bringing the men who were chasing her right to her husband and children's doorstep. Whoever had killed her father and was now after her seemed ready to stop at nothing. The men wouldn't think twice about using her children or Mitch to draw her out. And even after two and a half years she had no idea what they wanted from her. All she knew was that her father had gotten himself into trouble. Beyond that she had no idea with whom or how. Her street smarts had kept her alive. She'd immediately changed her identity and gotten out of New Mexico.

But those creeps always seemed to catch up no matter how well she hid.

She'd had no choice but to disappear after giving birth, once the creeps had shown up in Jacobstown, Texas. She still had no idea what they wanted from her. Her father had left her a cryptic message to stay in the shadows until he cleaned up his mess hours before his death—a death that had been ruled an accident, but Kimberly knew better. There was no way her father would've drowned. He couldn't swim and was deathly afraid of the water, although he'd never admitted to that fear. The man had never once been out on a boat, so it made even less sense that he would've rented one, taken it out and then—what?—decided to jump off the side and swim for the first time in his life?

Guilt nipped at her. She'd known he was in trouble but she had been too involved in work at the small craft boutique and night school to stop to ask why. Her father had been acting strange for months, missing their dinner dates and not picking up his cell when she called. His behavior had been erratic and she could kick herself for not pressing him for details about why he was acting so weird. She'd honestly and naively believed that he'd tell her if something was really wrong. He'd always been her rock and she'd been able to count on him. Losing her foster mom to kidney disease had been hard on both of them. At the time she had thought that most of her dad's antics had to do with grief.

Looking back she should've seen the signs. Should've taken him more seriously. Should've been a better daughter to the man who'd taken her in when she was at her lowest point and saved her life.

"You're scaring me, Dad," she'd admitted when he'd asked her to get rid of her cell and use the new one he'd handed her.

"I'm being cautious," he'd defended. "Make your old man happy and use the phone."

"Only if you promise to tell me what this is about," she'd said.

"I will. Give me a couple of days to get it sorted out first," he'd promised.

"You're sure this isn't a big deal?" It had felt like one with the way he was acting.

"I owe someone a little money and they're blowing it out of proportion." He'd winked at her. "Nothing I can't handle. I just don't want you being bothered until I get this sorted out."

The only reason she'd left it at that was because he'd seemed embarrassed. She'd thought maybe he didn't want his creditor calling her, so she'd left it at face value.

Guilt was a face punch. If she'd pushed him for answers, he might still be alive.

When Deputy Talisman had all but accused her of foul play in order to inherit her father's business, she'd been defensive. It had become clear to her pretty quickly that she was going to be the target of his investigation. And then two men had busted into her apartment in the middle of the night. She'd barely managed to escape and had been on the run ever since.

Marrying Mitch had been done on a whim. The almost-immediate pregnancy had been a shock. And she would pay the price for those lapses in judgment for the rest of her life, which would be short if the creeps following her caught up to her.

A part of her wondered if this whole ordeal would ever be over. Could she come back to the life she'd loved with Mitch and the babies?

Reality said it would be impossible.

Her heart galloped at the sight of her husband moving toward her out of the corner of her eye, along with her sweet babies, who turned one today. Birthdays were supposed to be happy events. But being this close without being able to touch her children felt like knife jabs to her chest.

Knowing that the twins would be at the office of the pediatrician she'd meticulously vetted prior to having those two little miracles had made it far too tempting. Going anywhere near Jacobstown, Texas, or the ranch was and had been off-limits. Those were lines she knew better than to cross. No matter how much she wanted—no, needed—to see her babies again, she couldn't risk bringing the creeps she'd been running from for an exhausting two and-a-half years to their doorstep. And then there was Mitch…

Seeing him again hurt.

Leaving a question mark in her husband's mind about her death wasn't ideal—a determined man could be dangerous. And part of her wished she could've confided in him, wished he could save her. She'd been close to confessing in the days before finding out she was pregnant. She'd known he would put his life at risk and she'd needed him to focus on protecting the twins.

How stupid had she been when she'd met him to think she could ever have a normal life? A normal life with kids and a man she loved, who loved her in return more than anything else?

That kind of love had been too powerful to turn her back on and had seduced her into thinking she could disappear into obscurity in the small town where she'd been hiding.

Mitch was everything a man should be to her—strong, virile...honest. Lying to him about her identity had been even more difficult because of that. Kimberly had been lying to herself for so long that she'd all but forgotten how to be truthful anymore. And maybe that's what had drawn her to the serious rancher with the steel-colored eyes.

Falling for Mitch Kent had been the easy part. She'd done that hard. Apparently she'd knocked a few screws loose when she'd made that tumble, because she'd landed in a fantasy that said if she kept a low profile, everything in her life would magically work out. But there were a few determined men who wanted to erase her presence. By the time she'd met Mitch, she'd already been running for six months.

A part of her wished—prayed—that he would forget all about her. The other part—the selfish part—couldn't go there even hypothetically. She wanted him to remember her, to love her.

"Kimberly," he said from behind her, and there was certainty in his voice instead of a question.

Certainty would kill them all.

A glance to the right said Mitch wasn't the only one

about to close in on her. She felt like a mouse trapped in a maze.

There had to be something to use to create a distraction so she could get out of there. The air thinned, making it difficult to breathe.

A middle-aged woman wearing jeans and a light sweater walked toward her from the south with a black Lab on a leash. Kimberly bolted toward the woman and forced a smile.

"Can I pet your dog, ma'am?" she asked, pouring on the sweetness.

The woman beamed.

"Of course," she said as she went on about the dog's age and pedigree.

Kimberly dropped down to one knee before unhooking the leash in the bustling complex.

"I'm sorry," she said to the confused woman before popping to her feet. She shooed the dog. "Run!"

The black Lab darted toward the fountain as the woman gasped and then called after him.

Okay, Kimberly felt awful for doing that and wished there'd been another way to create a diversion. In the heat of the moment, that was all she could think of.

With another quick apology, Kimberly wheeled left and sprinted away from the pediatrician's building. A pair of heavy footsteps sounded from behind and she could tell by their rhythm that they were faster than her, racing closer and gaining ground.

At least Mitch would be stopped because of the stroller. Seeing those angelic round faces threatened to cripple her, but she couldn't afford to give in. She had to protect what was hers. Stuffing her feelings down deep helped her focus.

Kimberly's best chance to lose the pair of creeps catching up to her was to get lost inside the hospital behind the pediatrician's office. She knew the area and that would give her an advantage. There would be armed security and the men following her wouldn't risk making themselves the center of attention by pulling something stupid. She hoped.

At least she could draw them away from Mitch and the babies. Kimberly sprinted around another building, trying to lose the men in the maze of buildings. Her thighs burned and her lungs were starting to wheeze.

The footsteps behind her stopped. Her worst fear seized her. Were the men circling back for Mitch?

Her breath caught and her heart screamed *no.*

How stupid and selfish had she been to come here? The past eleven months had been about taking calculated risks and watching her back at every turn. She'd just led those men practically to Mitch's doorstep. Kimberly bit back a few choice words, refusing to let negativity drag her under.

With the stroller, it would be impossible for Mitch to catch up to her. She'd cleared a few buildings and had crossed over to the front of the hospital, slowing her pace to a brisk walk as she entered through the automatic glass doors.

Activity buzzed all around her, and the modern lobby looked like a coffeehouse, with tables sprinkled around and folks on their laptops. The main difference was the fact that doctors and nurses cut across the open space, making their way to restricted-access areas.

Taking a chance, Kimberly checked behind her for the men. Nothing. Her heart took a dive.

Where were they?

MITCH FLEXED AND released his hands on the grip bar of the stroller. He'd scared a woman half to death by thinking she was his dead wife. Wasn't this turning into a banner day?

He wished he'd gotten a good look at Bleached-Blonde's face before she'd put her arm up to shield it and then disappeared in the commotion after a dog got loose from its owner.

Great. Now he could add scaring strangers to the already stressful morning he was having.

Thankfully the twins were clueless. Rea happily cooed and chatted, and Aaron took everything in while sucking on a pair of his fingers.

The men who'd been eyeing the Bleached-Blonde seemed to have given up on her. They'd returned to the plaza before heading toward the parking lot. It was probably Mitch's imagination that had him thinking those two were after her. He could add paranoia to his growing list of deficiencies.

The news from Lone Star Lonnie had thrown Mitch for a loop, on top of everything else he was dealing with, and maybe he was starting to crack. That was the only explanation for why he believed that he'd just seen his dead wife. She was on his mind even more than usual today. It was time to get back to reality, including getting his babies to their appointment.

Mitch pushed the stroller through the opened double doors and then took the elevator up to the third floor. He checked in and then waited.

A few minutes later he was ushered into the blue room to wait for the doctor and find out how much his life was about to change. Again.

Good news came from the pediatrician. Rea looked

to be growing out of her heart defect. She'd have to continue to be monitored, which he'd expected, but the hole in her lower valve seemed to be closing on its own. Gratitude washed over Mitch, bringing a few stray tears to his eyes.

The drive from Fort Worth to Jacobstown gave him the chance to fill in his siblings and cousins, thanks to Bluetooth technology and his cell phone. Joyce, the twins' caregiver, met him on the driveway. She'd decorated the dining room with balloons and went to work serving lunch and cake to celebrate before taking the kiddos up for their naps.

Mitch had kissed both babies before picking up the fresh flowers he'd ordered and heading out the back door.

Joyce was a sweet woman in her late sixties who'd helped bring up Mitch, along with his siblings. She'd managed to wrangle six Kent children before retiring years ago but when she'd learned one of her "babies" was having babies, she'd insisted on returning to care for them.

Lucky for him, Kimberly had welcomed Joyce's help. The fact that she'd taken to the idea had caught him off guard at first. Kimberly had always been a private person. And that was where his luck had run out.

Sitting on the bench he'd carved out of solid wood beside the tallest oak on the property, he looked down at the marker. Kimberly Kent—loving wife and devoted mother.

She wasn't supposed to be buried there. His mind pointed out that she technically wasn't. It didn't matter. Kimberly Kent was gone.

He crossed his boots at the ankles.

When the twins were old enough, he'd bring them here to see their mother. He set the fresh flowers down—lilies. Her favorite. They reminded him of her, of her fresh-from-the-shower scent.

The wind started to pick up as a few more gray clouds rolled in, reflecting his somber mood. Rain was in the forecast, in the air, and it had been drier than a salt lick all week.

The feeling of being watched settled over him. Amber? One of his brothers? He scanned the meadow but saw nothing. Further proof that he was losing it.

The idea anyone could be in the meadow without his knowledge hit hard. Someone had been on the ranch undetected. The sheer amount of acreage owned by the Kent family made it impossible to monitor every inch. But still…

His gaze dropped to the plot of land in front of him.

"I saw you outside the pediatrician's office today," he said to the green grass over an empty grave. "Even though it couldn't have been you, I wanted her to be." He paused, choking back the emotion threatening to consume him—emotion that he'd successfully buried. "Rea's doctor visit was good. She's going to be just fine." Another pause to get his emotions in check. "I miss you, Kimberly."

Mitch cursed. Now he was talking to dirt.

He pushed up to stand as an empty feeling engulfed him, threatening to drag him under and toss him around before spitting him out again like a deadly riptide.

Pain made him feel alive after being hollow inside for months. The ache in his chest every time he took in air was the only reminder he was still breathing.

A prickly feeling ran up the back of his neck, like when someone said a cat walked over a grave.

Mitch didn't do emotions, so why the hell were his like a race car at full speed, careening out of control and toward the wall today? His baby sister's words from last year kept winding through his thoughts, drowning out logic and reason, the two things he was good at.

What if she's alive? What if she's still out there?

Mitch touched the grave marker, dragging his fingers across the smooth granite and into the grooves made by the letters of Kimberly's name.

And then he tucked his feelings down deep before texting Lone Star Lonnie that he was on his way to check out the heifer before it rained.

Walking away from his wife's grave was especially tough today. His thoughts were heavy as he made his way to the base of Rushing Creek, on the northeast side of the property.

Even though he'd prepared for the worst, the site still caught him off guard. Blood was everywhere. His heifer was on her right side in a pool of red on flat land. There was no sign of a trap that could've taken off her hoof and messed up her leg like that. She'd bled out and that would've been a slow death.

Anger roared through him as he thought about how much she'd suffered. It was inhumane to do this to an animal. Lone Star Lonnie had downplayed the situation with the heifer, Mitch thought as he stood over her.

Everything inside him felt as torn up and drained as the lifeless heifer next to him.

Whoever had done this would be brought to justice.

Chapter Three

The pitch-black night sky was a dark canopy overhead. Thick clouds smothered the moon, blocking out any possibility of light. Rain came down in sheets. The conditions were a problem. There'd be tracks. Kimberly couldn't afford to leave a trail or any sign she'd been there.

If the storm continued, there'd be no issue. Flash floods were common in this area of Texas and could wash away her hiking-boot prints. If the weather dried up, anyone could follow her based on the imprints she made.

She stepped lightly, careful to weave through the low-hanging branches rather than break them—again another way to track her movements. Being on the run had taught her to leave the smallest footprint possible. Leave a trace and someone would find her—the creeps following her had already proven that more than once. She'd racked her brain, thinking how they could've picked up her trail leading to the pediatrician's office earlier.

Kimberly cursed under her breath as tears threatened. How could she have been so careless? So stupid?

Guilt nearly impaled her.

She couldn't sit by and watch the only people she

loved get hurt because of her. She had to make this right. She prayed that she could find the right words to convince Mitch to leave with the babies and disappear.

Seeing her alive would shock her husband. And he would hate her for what she'd done to him, to their family. Not that she could blame him. Sharp stabs of pain spiked through her, because she would feel the same way if the situation was reversed.

That wouldn't stop—couldn't stop—her from doing what she needed to do.

Being on the ranch brought back other memories. Memories that punched her in the stomach. Memories of being under this same sky on a starlit evening with Mitch's arms around her, feeling like she could slay her fears and stay right there for the rest of her life. Then there were all of those Sunday-morning breakfasts in bed after passionate nights.

They'd when she'd rented a cabin on Lake Orion. On her weekly trip into town for supplies was when she'd first seen him. She'd been at the lake for a couple of days already and had worn her hair down around her face, a light cotton T-shirt and a simple pair of jeans with tennis shoes.

Mitch had come up behind her while she stood in line with her small cart filled with everything she'd need for two weeks for a single person. He didn't speak to her right away, but she turned to look at him the minute she felt the strong male presence. It seemed like every single woman in the place came over to say hello while he stood in line behind Kimberly. Mitch was handsome—no question about that—but he also had a sexual appeal that made women blush when they spoke to him. The pitch in their voices raised and it was so easy to tell they were flirting.

Kimberly thought her eyes would roll into the back of her head when one of the women nearly knocked over the media stand while she complimented his boots. There'd been so much bemusement in his voice—a deep voice that trailed down the sensitive skin of her neck and wrapped around her—when he thanked the woman that Kimberly had almost laughed out loud. The ladies had been so sickeningly sweet that Kimberly wanted to throw up.

Her reaction must've been written all over her face when she turned to get another look at the all-male presence stirring up all of the commotion behind her. Yeah, she'd been rubbernecking but she couldn't help herself. She had only a couple of weeks to be in town and she needed to see what all the fuss was about.

The second she turned and got a good look, she realized her mistake. Her cheeks flamed, her throat dried and a thousand birds fluttered inside her chest, leaving her to wonder, *Who is this man?*

Her hand fell slack and she dropped her wallet, spilling change all over his boots, which actually were nice. If embarrassment could kill a person, she would've dropped dead on the spot. Lucky for her, it couldn't. And the tall, muscled cowboy had dropped down to help her collect her things.

He'd been gracious and generous and all of the things she figured a cowboy code would require. But when his fingers grazed her palm as he handed over her quarters and pennies, pure electricity shot through her. Her body hummed and based on the look in his steel-gray eyes when their gazes connected, he felt the current every bit as much.

After introducing himself, he'd asked if she would have dinner with him that night.

It took a few seconds for logic to kick in and for her to remember how dangerous that would be for both of them, but it did and she refused—albeit without conviction. She thanked him for helping her, turned and was grateful she was next in line. The cashier acknowledged her with a smile as she busied herself placing her items on the motorized belt. Inside, she concentrated on trying to breathe as the cashier ran her items across the scanner.

Kimberly's pulse raced and all she could think about was getting out of there and back to the privacy of the cabin on the lake. She fumbled for the right dollar amount. Using cash was another way to stay off the grid.

The handsome cowboy had followed her to the parking lot as she loaded groceries into the plastic container she'd fixed onto the back of the dirt bike she'd bought from a seventeen-year-old boy who went by the name Smash. Based on the condition of the dirt bike, he'd earned that nickname, but she didn't care. All she'd needed was reliable transportation to get her to and from the store and something she could use for a quick escape if the need arose.

Experience had taught her to be prepared for anything and especially the pair of creeps who always seemed to be one step behind.

"You sure about dinner?" he'd asked with the kind of smile that made women go weak at the knees as he held out a fistful of coins. She knew for sure because her legs almost gave.

It had most likely been that moment of hesitation—

that too-quick smile—that had him showing up two days after she'd refused him in the lot.

The rain had been coming down in sheets on that day, too.

"What are you doing here?" she'd asked as she opened the door to find him standing on her porch, waterlogged and even more handsome than she remembered.

"I haven't stopped thinking about you for two days," he'd said, and her heart pounded so hard against her ribs, she thought they might crack. There he stood, with rain trailing down the brim of his gray Stetson. He wore a black V-neck T-shirt that, soaked with rain, outlined every one of his mass of muscles. "Tell me to leave and I will. I'll leave you alone. You have my word. Agree to have dinner with me and we can go anywhere you like."

As he stood there, with rain dripping from his tall, muscled physique, all of her willpower—and good sense—took a hike.

"Only if we stay here," she'd said. "We have to stay inside."

His face had broken into a wide smile—the same one that had seduced her willingly by the third night. And then less than two months later he'd proposed.

Tears sprang to her eyes at the memories. Walking away from Mitch Kent had been one of the most difficult things she'd ever done.

And setting foot in the house they'd once shared was going to be right up there.

MITCH RUBBED BLURRY eyes as he heard a noise come from another room for the second time. He glanced at the clock as he muttered a curse. The twins shouldn't be up for another few hours.

In a past life, he would've slept right through the small creak. Having babies had trained him to jump at the first noise. If he entered the room fast enough, sometimes he could solve the problem before the other woke up. Let it go even for a few seconds, and he'd be dealing with two fussy babies and not enough arms to hold them both. Joyce had volunteered to move into the guest room half a dozen times, but Mitch had refused every request. Her heart was in the right place; she wanted to make his life easier. But Kimberly wouldn't have wanted it that way. She might've agreed to receiving Joyce's help during the day, but she wouldn't want another person taking care of their babies overnight.

Another creak sounded and he was awake enough to hear it clearly now.

He threw off the covers and slid into the jeans on the chair next to his bed. This noise in the next room had nothing to do with the twins.

Was someone inside his house?

His hardwood floors creaked in exactly three places in the hallway. The first two had already made noise.

And now came the third. His adrenaline surged, flooding his body with heat.

Someone was walking toward his bedroom.

The twins' room was across the hall and a fleeting thought struck that someone was coming for them. But who could that be? And how in the hell did the person get past ranch security?

It took a minute for that to sink in.

Another thought struck that it could be one of his family members, but that couldn't be right, either. His brothers and sister would've called if there'd been an emergency. There was no way his cousins, Zach and

Amy, would show in the middle of the night without calling. Those would be the only people who could get past security.

Mitch double-checked his cell in case he'd silenced his phone instead of switching it to vibrate. He thought about the heifer, and for a split second he thought the butchering might've been a warning.

The doorknob turned, so he jumped into action. Whoever thought they were going to get the best of him had another thing coming.

In two seconds he stood next to the door. It opened toward him, so it would shield him as the intruder stepped inside.

This probably wasn't the time to realize his shotgun was locked in a gun cabinet, a precaution he took for the sake of his children. Even if he could get to it, it wouldn't do any good. The shells were locked in a drawer.

As the door eased open, Mitch held his breath. He had his physical size, athletic conditioning and the element of surprise on his side, and that was about it. He had no idea what could be pushing through on the other side of that door.

In that moment he regretted not arming the alarm. He'd put one in, based on his wife's insistence, but never used it now that she was gone.

Another few seconds and he'd be ready to grab whoever crossed that threshold. And he hoped like hell it was only one person.

Mitch flexed and released his fingers. He was ready.

A smallish—at least in comparison to his size—figure slipped inside. He took a step toward the intruder and grabbed whatever he could, wrapping his hands around the person's upper arms. The intruder seemed familiar but he dismissed the thought.

Until the person kicked where no man wanted a foot and he gulped for air. The intruder put their hands on top of his and then dropped to the floor, breaking his grip. This person had skills.

"Stop it and I won't hurt you," he warned through sharp intakes of air. He was still trying to regain his footing after taking a hit to the groin.

Before the intruder could scoot away completely, he had a fistful of shirt material. He took another knee in the same spot, ignoring the pain shooting up his abdomen and causing his gut to clench.

Fists flew at him until he wrangled the stranger's arms under control, but in pulling him or her close he ushered in a scent—lilies—and froze.

The intruder scooted out from underneath him.

"Whatever you do, don't turn on the light," the familiar voice warned through gasps.

"Who are you?" he asked but he already knew the answer—an answer that was a throat punch.

"It's me. Kimberly."

Chapter Four

Kimberly needed to find the right words to get her husba—Mitch motivated to get out of the house and Jacobstown until she was certain the men who'd found her had moved on. Thinking about him in terms of being her husband only crushed her heart more.

Instead she stood there, mute.

"My wife is dead," Mitch said out loud. His angry tone came off like he said the words more for himself than for her benefit. Either way, they scored a direct hit. Guilt was another punch.

All she could think to do was back away from him, slip past him and dart into the twins' nursery across the hall. She didn't flip on the light because her eyes had long ago adjusted to the darkness and she didn't want to wake the babies yet.

She knew that he followed her based on the tension she felt radiating from behind her.

Mitch's hand gripped her arm as she started toward the set of cribs nestled against the wall. Her heart nearly burst at the thought she would actually get to see them again. Hold them?

"Stop right there." Mitch's voice came out in a growl.

Reality slapped her in the face. He was about to kick

her out. She jerked her arm out of his grasp and whirled around on him.

"I know what this must look like but trust me when I say you and the babies are in danger," she said in barely more than a whisper. "If we don't get out of here right now, a pair of men will show up. And that'll be bad news for everyone."

He stood there and stared at her like he was facing down a ghost. And he was. At least in his mind.

Mitch stilled and she could tell that she was getting through to him. Angry or not, he'd always been reasonable. Even though she could tell his armor was up and she'd never truly be able to break through it again, he considered what she was saying.

"Where have you been?" he finally ground out.

"Around." As far as answers went, it was awful. But it was also true. And there was no way she was telling him her locations. It would be too easy for him to predict where she went next.

Mitch stood in an athletic stance and crossed his arms over his solid bare chest.

"Why?" There was no sign of weakness in his voice when he asked the question. No sign of long nights without her. No sign of the hurt he must've felt. His tone was steady as steel now. *He* was steady as steel. The only thing that could melt steel was a temperature of 2,500 degrees Fahrenheit, and his glare felt at least that scorching.

He deserved an explanation. There was no time to go into details. She needed to get him to safety and then she could figure out the right words. Everything had careened out of control faster than an Indy driver staring down a wall after veering off course. The wall was coming. The crash was going to be devastating. The only question was how many of the pieces she could pick up afterward.

"Please say you'll come with me and bring the babies," she begged.

"You're supposed to be dead. Explain to me why you're alive and standing in front of me." His arms crossed tighter over his chest and there was so much anger in his eyes.

"I can't right now. But I promise—"

"Not good enough." He stood there, being a stubborn mule.

"Mitch. Come on. Just listen to me," she started, but he stopped her with a hand in the air.

Frustration seethed, pouring off him in waves.

"Forgive me, but I've been talking to a headstone for the past eleven months."

Those words were daggers and robbed her of breath.

"I buried your memory and as much of you as I could along with it," he continued, unblinking.

Wind blasted the window, rattling the casing. She jumped and sucked in a sharp breath. "We need to go *now.*"

"The kids need stability. Being here will give them that." His lips thinned. "Give me one reason I should take it away from them."

He wanted answers she couldn't give. But asking him to trust her at this point would be a slap in the face.

Reluctantly, she moved into the hallway, knowing full well he'd follow. Waking the twins would create a commotion and her heart would break if she heard them cry. She also couldn't risk them drawing attention or covering up the sound of someone breaking in. Words failed her and she wanted to scream. Panic gripped her like a vise, squeezing air from her lungs.

Mitch was so close on her heels, he almost ran into her when she stopped.

"People are after me and they'll use you and the twins to draw me out. I shouldn't have shown up at the doctor's office today," she admitted, both hands out in defense.

"That *was* you?" Recognition dawned with the admission but it didn't help with his anger.

"I'm sorry, Mitch. I truly am. I made a mistake but I can't change that now. You and the babies aren't safe here."

"Why not call the sheriff?" He shrugged. Suspicion laced his tone and she completely understood why he'd feel that way even though it hurt.

"Because in my case that will do more damage than good," she admitted. The night-light plugged into the socket in the hallway cast a warm glow on his chiseled features. Again she stared into eyes of suspicion and disbelief.

"I don't know what to tell you. Sounds like you got yourself into a mess of trouble." His words came out clipped.

"It's so much worse than that. I got *you* and the *babies* in a terrible fix. There's no way out but to run. I need you to believe me, Mitch." She stared into his eyes, which had hardened toward her. Was she even getting through? Based on his stern expression and closed-off stance, the answer was *no*.

This wasn't the time to back down. "I'm serious, Mitch. Please come with me and I'll explain everything once we're out of danger. Trust me when I say men could show up anytime and they'll outnumber you. They'll bring weapons." There were times when she felt like she would always be on the run. By the time she met Mitch, she'd been running for half a year. When the man who raised her had given her a throwaway phone and insisted she try to reach him only using the cell, she'd worried that he might be getting senile.

The first few calls had gone fine. As fine as they could be with him acting so strange. He'd mumbled about putting her in danger, but he never explained when she questioned him. She didn't put too much stock into what he said. She knew full well that he was a decent man. She played along while she tried to figure out the next move. Counseling? Support group? Her thoughts moved to questions like was it safe for him to be behind a wheel? And was it okay for him to live on his own and continue to run his business? Her worries quickly shifted from thinking about taking his car keys away to realizing something was really wrong when he didn't answer her calls. Days later, the deputy had found him. He'd drowned, which was highly unlikely for a man who never went near the water. And now the men who'd killed her father were after her.

But then again gloom had always followed Kimberly. Mitch had been a light against so much darkness. Falling for him had been so easy, so effortless. He was sunshine in a world that had become pitch-black.

It was selfish of her to want to hang on to the feeling of finally basking in the sun again, a feeling she hadn't experienced in so long.

A well of resolve sprang inside her. Loving him was exactly the reason she needed to buck up and be strong right now. She'd put Mitch and the babies in danger. So *she* would get them out.

A flash of light followed by a crack of thunder split the night air.

"What do those men want from you?" he finally asked, and she realized he must've seen them earlier.

"They must've followed me to the plaza. I hadn't seen them in a few days, so I thought I was in the clear. I'm sure they saw my reaction to you and put two and two together because they disappeared when I was so close. They've never done that before," she admitted.

"They won't get past security on the ranch. They don't know the place like you do," he started and then paused. A strange look crossed his features.

"What? What is it?"

"A heifer's hoof was cut off, butchered. Any chance your men would do something like that?" he asked, and it was a genuine question.

"Like a warning?" She was already shaking her head. "No. They'd use you or the babies to draw me out. You wouldn't see them coming."

Mitch stood there, all fire and frustration. More signs she was making progress with him.

"It also proves someone can get past security," she added for good measure.

When he didn't argue, she realized she was getting closer to his agreeing to cooperate.

"I promise this will all make sense soon. Just please come with me. I don't know how much time we have before they get here," she stated as plainly as she could. Seeing the man she would always love stirred up so many emotions inside her once again. Emotions she needed to keep in check for the sake of everyone she loved. In another time and place, the two of them could have shared something very special, very real.

Where was the reboot button when it came to life?

"LOOK. I DON'T know what you have going on or what game you're playing but your problems are not my problems anymore. That all stopped when you walked out on us," Mitch said through clenched teeth. For a split second he thought maybe his wife had been in a crash and survived but lost her memory or her mind.

All hope was decimated when he heard her speak. She knew who he was. She knew that they had children together, children she hadn't once thought to check on in the last year. Those were her choices. This woman's mind was as clear as water in a mason jar.

So he stood there, examining her. Anger boiled inside him at the fact that she stood in his home without an apology for what she'd put their children through by making them live the first year of their lives without a mother.

"My wife is buried on the west lawn at the entrance to her favorite place on the ranch, the meadow," he ground out, trying and failing to keep his voice at a whisper. He refused to believe that the woman he'd fallen in love with could be so heartless.

His words were intended to deliver a physical blow.

"I—I'm sorry for that, Mi—"

"Don't apologize to me. I got exactly what I deserved. But they didn't." He nodded toward the babies' room. "Those two didn't do anything wrong."

Kimberly stood there, her gaze scanning the area. She looked scared and a little bit angry. As much as he didn't want to admit it, she also had that protective-mother look. The one that said nothing and no one would hurt her babies. And he couldn't ignore what she'd said. Someone had slipped past security and butchered one of his animals on his watch. Could they get to the babies, too?

Determination radiated off her five-foot-six-inch frame. Standing there, she was just as beautiful as he remembered. Dozens of times she'd slipped into his dreams. He'd imagine her right there next to him in bed. Or bounding through the house with that energy and light only she had.

Never once did he envision she'd return in the middle of the night with a warning. There were scenarios that had crossed his mind. The loss-of-memory one had always been prominent. Maybe because that would explain her leaving him behind, with his heart stomped on.

His dead wife standing in his hallway in the middle of the night, trying to convince him to go somewhere with him before she explained what the hell was going on, wasn't exactly topping the list of scenarios in which he'd dreamed of seeing her again.

"Please, Mitch. I know I don't deserve your trust. But believe it or not I'm here to help not hurt anyone," she pleaded one more time.

"You can't hurt me anymore. I don't care what happens to you." The words escaped before he could reel them in. It wasn't true. He did care for his kids' sake. They needed a mother. But what kind of mother disappeared? Or worse—faked her death? "Why'd you do it, Kimberly?"

"There was a reason I was so private and never wanted to be photographed or interviewed the entire time we were married, a good reason. Did you ever once think that there could've been another reason besides the flimsy excuses I gave that I just didn't like having my picture taken or that I was just a homebody?"

"What reason did I have to question you? Until today I had no idea what you were capable of. I still don't know who you are." The words had the effect he'd intended—sharp and direct—even though a twinge of guilt tried to worm its way into his heart. Mitch slammed the door on that emotion. He had nothing to feel guilty about. He wasn't the one who'd abandoned their family.

"I understand if you hate me but everything I did was out of love." She seemed to choke back a sob as determination set her features. "No one, not even you, can call me a bad mother. I put my children first."

"Here's a question..." Anger was rising like a volcano that was minutes from erupting. "Why have kids in the first place if you didn't want them?"

"Is that what you think?" Her strong facade was cracking deeper. Anger shot from her eyes, which he could see clearly now in the soft light of the hallway. She looked like she was about to spew a few choice words at him but then she must've thought twice because she blew out a breath and let her shoulders sag. Kimberly had never looked so defeated. But he meant what he said. He couldn't possibly have truly known her if she was capable of—what? Faking her own death? Ditching their family? Walking out on him without so much as a word?

"I cared."

"Actions are more important than empty words," he stated. She wasn't getting off this easily.

Another gust of wind blasted against the kids' window, and Kimberly looked like she was ready to jump out of her skin. It was clear to him that something had her spooked, but without any real answers—and she'd been dodging his questions so far—he couldn't make a decent decision. And then there were the men who had been after her earlier. He'd noticed their intent and it had brought out his protective instincts before he'd confirmed she was his supposedly dead wife.

Yet going with her on a whim seemed extreme.

"Tell me why you're running and who's after you." He decided to play along. During the time they had been together, he'd never picked up on a hint of her losing touch with reality. No matter what else he felt about her, he knew she wasn't the type for drugs or alcohol. So if she was sane and not under the influence of any substance, he probably should at least hear her out. His heart clenched at the sight of her, and being this close without answers or explanations caused his fists to tighten.

"I can't." Her gaze darted around like she expected someone to blast through a wall or window at any second.

"Why are you really here?" he asked. Surely it wasn't to save him and the twins from some unknown threat. That would mean she cared.

"I already said." She could be stubborn. He'd believed it to be sexy before. And, hell, it was now, too. Even though nothing in him wanted it to be.

"Are you sure this doesn't have anything to do with the heifer we found near the base of Rushing Creek?"

"No. These men wouldn't touch your livestock."

"Tell me who's after you." Maybe he could put the pieces together to see if there was a connection. Or maybe she could tell him something that would make the killing make sense.

"I can't." A look of something—such as frustration or fear—marred her beautiful features.

"Well, then we don't have anything else to talk about." He faced her down, not budging an inch.

"I leave here and they'll show." She glanced at the wrist on which she used to wear a watch, but there was nothing there. "It'll happen and you won't be prepared."

"You're not giving me anything to work with. I can't evaluate a threat if I don't know what it is." No way was he softening his stance. Of course he'd do anything to protect the little ones in the next room. And after her visit he planned to take extra precaution. But he wasn't convinced that leaving the ranch was in the twins' best interest.

"I'm being honest. I can't tell you who's after me or why," she said on a sharp sigh. It was more than she'd planned to say. He could tell by her tense body language.

"How do you know someone's targeting you then?"

"It has to do with Randy Bristol, my foster father, but that's all I know." Thunder clapped and it got her feet moving into the babies' room again. "I know you wouldn't put either of these two in harm's way, Mitch. Believe me when I say trouble is coming your way whether you choose to acknowledge it or not. That part's up to you, but I can't let them get to my babies."

"You lost rights to these two when you died," he fired back.

"It's pretty plain to see that I'm still here," she said.

"Not in the court's eyes," he shot back.

"Try and stop me," she dared to say.

"Take another step toward those cribs and I'll do just that. Then I'll call Zach." He referred to his cousin, the sheriff, to rattle her. "He'll arrest you, which is something you said you can't afford."

She issued a sharp grunt but stopped. "You wouldn't do that to me."

"Try me."

Chapter Five

Kimberly stared at Mitch. His set jaw and narrowed gaze challenged her. Her back was against the wall, because that look said he wasn't going anywhere until she confessed. The only progress she'd made so far was the fact that he was listening to her.

"Someone is trying to get rid of me. This is somehow related to my foster father, but I don't know how or why. He warned me, sort of cryptically right before he supposedly drowned but was really killed, and then the deputy who interviewed me strongly insinuated that I benefited the most from his death. That night someone came after me directly," Kimberly admitted, and it was like a huge weight lifted off her by being able to say those words out loud.

He looked at her like she was crazy. She couldn't exactly blame him.

"I never knew you were in the system." He paused a minute as though to let his brain click puzzle pieces into place. "You said your parents died when you were a teenager, and you had to spend high school living with a sick aunt who'd since passed away."

She shot him a look. "I'm sorry that I lied before. He

is the only father I've known. It wouldn't have helped if I'd told you the truth."

"How can you say that?" he shot back. "It seems to me that it matters a whole helluva lot that I had no idea who my wife really was and now my life is in danger."

How stupid had she been to think she could pull off a marriage and family when the creeps were never far behind? Granted she hadn't known she was marrying one of the wealthiest and most eligible bachelors in Texas at the time. His downplayed clothing, calloused hands and rugged good looks made him seem like a salt-of-the-earth type, a cowboy and not a wealthy ranch owner.

"You weren't exactly honest with me, either," she fired back. She'd been seduced by the idea that she could live on a ranch in a bunkhouse and be perfectly happy for the rest of her life.

"I thought you knew who I was," he defended.

It was her turn to balk because she was pretty damn sure he'd enjoyed meeting someone who didn't have designs on him for his family ties. "And Christmas comes in June."

Mitch stood there for what felt like half an hour but was probably less than a couple of minutes. An inappropriate shiver raced down her arms as his gaze intensified on her. The hint of appreciation in his honest gray eyes made her want things she knew better than to consider.

"You better plan on filling me in as soon as we're settled." His tone was cold enough to make her shiver. She rubbed her arms to hide her physical reaction to him—one minute hot and then the next so cold. There was more to it than she was ready to admit to herself, because thoughts of his hands doing other things to her crept into her mind. Those were useless. He was agreeing to go with her, and that's all she needed for now.

"Fine. But we need to go. They can't be far behind me and we've wasted enough time talking already. If we don't get out of here soon, it could be too late." It was her turn to fold her arms and dare him not to believe her.

He nodded.

"I'll pack up the twins." She moved to the diaper bags she'd seen sitting on top of the dresser.

"You can't. You don't know what they need." His words stabbed her in the way that hard truths often hurt. Hard truths like the fact that a dark cloud had always followed her. Hard truths like the fact that everyone she'd ever cared about hated her or was dead. Hard truths like the fact that she would never live a normal life.

"How do you know these people are after you?" He was stalling. He wasn't naive or slow. He had to know the men from this morning were hunting her.

A flash of light was followed by a crack of thunder that rattled the windows.

"I'll explain later. We gotta go *now. Please, Mitch.*" She could set her pride aside and beg for the sake of her children.

On an exhale, Mitch moved to the set of cribs.

If seeing him again was already a knife to the center of her chest, watching the normally rough-around-the-edges cowboy soften his stance as he picked up one of the twins nearly did her in. But then again Mitch had always been that perfect blend of raw masculinity and gentleness. His hands were rough as they roamed her body but she liked it that way. His hands might be rough but his touch was anything but. Thinking about all of the sensations those hands had brought about so easily sent a sensual shiver racing up her spine, tingling her nerve endings.

But her heart fell when she got a good look at her daughter's face from over his shoulder. Tears sprang to her eyes at seeing her. *Rea.* Such a beautiful baby with a round, angelic face topped off by thick curly black hair. Kimberly knew this was going to hurt. Seeing her daughter stung so much more than she thought. She was reminded of everything she'd missed. Her entire body ached.

What had she expected?

The changes in her daughter from a one-month-old infant to a one-year-old baby were staggering, and her breath caught.

"She's so big," Kimberly said so quietly that she didn't think Mitch had heard until she caught a slight nod.

"The trick is to wake her and get her changed before her brother opens his eyes." He walked over to a changing table, cradling the half-asleep baby against his bare chest. If there was something sexier than that image, Kimberly had never seen it. A dozen butterflies fluttered in her stomach. For a split second it occurred to her that the man holding that baby was *her* husband, or at least he *had* been.

As it was, Mitch wanted nothing to do with her. He was entertaining her by going along with her pleas. It was easy to see that he would never trust her again. Mitch was an honest and decent man. He didn't deserve what she'd done to him. Blaming their whirlwind affair on letting her emotions get carried away wasn't fair.

Kimberly had messed up big-time. She would pay the price for the rest of her life for that slip. Since she deserved every bit of misery that came her way, she wouldn't fight Mitch or try to convince him that she was there because she cared. And she sure as hell wouldn't let her eyes linger on the lines of his muscled back or his arm muscles while they bulged and released as he lifted their daughter and gently placed her on the changing table. Seeing him so capable with their child stirred her heart in painful ways.

Digging deep to muster whatever courage and self-discipline she had left, Kimberly forced her gaze away. Being around Mitch was exhausting. Emotions were more exhausting than anything she'd ever done physically. She'd been a runner in high school. She had no idea the same term would define her life now. Running had been an outlet for her pain. Workouts had started at five o'clock in the morning and she'd trained on her own after school sometimes, running to her job across town. At night she barely had enough energy to get through a shower before dropping into bed.

She thought about the charms she'd given her babies and moved to the top drawer of Aaron's dresser.

"What are you looking for?" Mitch asked as she dug her hand around in the last place she remembered placing Aaron's pair of silver running shoes.

It must've dawned on Mitch, because a beat later he said, "The box is on top of the dresser."

She looked up, not ready to admit how frantic she'd been fearing that he'd tossed it, along with any other memory of her. "If it had been a snake, it would've bitten me."

How many times had Mitch delivered that line to her when she'd been looking for something she'd misplaced?

"Sometimes it's hardest to see what's right under

your nose," he stated. "Rea's is in the same place on her dresser."

She located both and placed one in each diaper bag. "I'm sure I can figure out what else needs to be packed. All babies need diapers and wipes," she said in a low voice.

Before Mitch could warn her to be quiet again, the other twin stirred. Based on the sound of the wail Aaron unleashed, he had a healthy set of lungs.

Kimberly didn't debate her actions. Mothering instincts kicked in, causing her to rush to his side and scoop him into her arms. His eyes were closed as he belted out another cry. The sound nearly brought her to her knees. She hoped that maybe he would realize his mother was holding him. Her body softened, a physical reaction to holding her son that she remembered from when he was first born. He was heavy now.

For a split second her world—which had been tipped on its axis for eleven long months without her family—righted itself. There was something magical about being in the same room with Mitch and the twins, like she was a whole person again after having her soul splintered into a thousand flecks of dust.

She nearly crumbled, as her legs felt almost rubber-like, at the thought of leaving them again. A tear escaped as she stood there, doing what she thought would never be possible again, holding her child.

Before she could get too comfortable, Mitch was there, taking their son from her.

Kimberly was so lost in the moment, she hadn't realized that Mitch had placed their daughter in a carrier that hummed with vibration.

Her arms felt so cold the minute the warm baby was plucked from them.

"I can take it from here," Mitch said, clearly uncomfortable with her holding their child. But he couldn't hold both of the twins every time. At some point he was going to have to let her help.

He had a territorial look that she knew better than to argue with at the moment.

Getting to hold her child, even for a few seconds, was so much more than she'd expected to experience after her disappearance. A selfish part of her was glad she had come back. But the feeling was quickly obliterated by the fact that doing so had just put her family in danger. The reason she'd taken off in the first place was moot. All that suffering for naught if she brought the threat to their doorstep. She could only pray that she was overreacting. That the creeps chasing her hadn't put two and two together.

What are the odds? an annoying little voice in the back of her mind asked.

Pretty damn slim.

A bolt of lightning lit the room, and the sharp crack of thunder that followed said the storm was directly overhead.

Kimberly bolted into action, moving to the set of diaper bags on the dresser next to the door and grabbing a few. She rummaged through drawers, looking for clothing, and then crammed a few items in each bag.

"You know security will stop anyone from driving onto the property," Mitch stated, eyeing her as his hands worked on the diaper.

"These people won't exactly drive up to the window and ask permission."

And when another bolt of lightning crossed the sky with the accompanying crack of thunder, she added, "We have to go *now.*"

MITCH WAS STILL second-guessing his decision to load up the twins in the middle of the night and take off to nowhere with his supposed-to-be-dead wife.

Kimberly was alive. The thought hadn't really sunk in, and shock was most likely to blame.

Even so, here they were on the road with the twins.

"I need coffee," he said, pulling his SUV into the gas station on Route 25. So far they'd left the ranch without incident, despite Kimberly's dire warnings. If he didn't know her better, he'd think she was crazy. He also remembered seeing the men in the plaza who'd set his radar on edge and knew she was being honest when she said he and the twins were in danger.

Sitting in the front of the SUV, her stress level was high. Tension radiated from her. When they were married, he knew exactly what to do when she was anxious or upset. Now it hardly seemed appropriate to think about how to ease her tension. Her paranoia during their marriage made a whole lot more sense now. He didn't classify it as such while they were hitched. Things had changed.

She didn't argue but her gaze darted around the parking lot.

"You stay in the vehicle with the twins." He hesitated for a split second, but reality said she wouldn't do anything to hurt herself or the babies. If there was one thing he knew for certain about his wife—correction, about Kimberly—it was that she loved those angels sleeping in the back seat.

Car rides had been his saving grace in the early months following losing his wife.

He pushed open the driver's-side door and tried to shake the thought. Kimberly was alive. How many times had he prayed this scenario was actually true? Too many to count.

Now that it was true, there was so much confusion rattling around in his brain. Another reason he needed the caffeine boost. A small part of him wanted to believe he was still asleep, dreaming that his wife had returned. He'd had plenty of those nights in which he'd wake with a start, half expecting her to be right beside him. The smell of her shampoo—lilies—filling his lungs as he took a deep breath.

Kimberly, his wife, would forever be dead to him.

He opened the glass door leading into the gas station that doubled as a convenience store. This place had everything—and he meant *everything*—a traveler could possibly need or want, with enough cashiers to ensure no one wasted valuable road time waiting in line. The walls were covered, from the ceiling to the floor, with everything from bags of assorted nuts to sunflower seeds.

Mitch scanned the room and locked on to the coffee machine.

There were enough vehicles coming and going outside that his SUV would blend right in with the traffic and Kimberly would be safe. Changing his primary vehicle had been his wife's idea. He'd driven the same truck for most of his life, until the twins were born. Since their arrival, he needed more cab room, so driving a bigger vehicle made sense. He couldn't part with his F-150, though. It sat in his garage, reminding him of a time before life was filled with diaper bags and strollers. He wouldn't change any of it, though. Except the part about being betrayed by the person he thought had loved him.

Mitch needed caffeine. He made a beeline to the coffee machine. He wasn't the kind of guy who got really wrapped up in emotions. Being a cattle rancher was simple. Take care of the animals, and they'll return the favor.

So being anywhere near the woman sitting in his SUV brought another bout of anger flooding through him because her presence confused the hell out of him. He didn't want to feel anything for her, and yet she stirred a feeling in his chest that he'd buried deep down when he'd buried her.

He was so distracted by his thought that he overfilled his cup with black coffee, causing it to spill over onto his hand. Nothing woke a person up like burning-hot coffee on exposed skin.

Mitch shook it off, poured a little out and placed a plastic lid on his cup. He poured a second cup and pocketed a couple of packets of sugar and creamer for Kimberly. He paid and quickly took a sip of the hot liquid meant for him. It burned going down his throat in the best way possible.

Back at the SUV, Kimberly rolled down her window so he could hand her one of the cups. He gave her the condiments next, frustrated that he remembered in such detail the way she took her coffee. Two packets of sugar. One and a half packets of creamer. She stirred twice and then dipped the stirrer into her mouth to get the first taste. That was generally followed by a sigh of pleasure when she got it just right or a frown when the balance of flavor was off. Mitch liked his coffee strong and black; he didn't need any fancy fixings.

He took another sip as he rounded the front of his vehicle. His gaze stopped on a white sedan pulling in from the east entrance. It was the middle of the night but this place was hopping.

The sedan slowed to almost a crawl and an uneasy feeling settled over Mitch. What was this guy doing?

He tucked his chin to his chest and climbed into the driver's seat. "Anyone you know drive a white four-door sedan?"

Kimberly shook her head.

It was probably nothing. Mitch decided to err on the side of caution when he pulled out of his parking spot and then took off in the opposite direction that he'd intended. He glanced at his rearview mirror in time to see the sedan hesitate. Was the driver watching?

He'd know in a minute.

"Where am I taking you?" he asked.

"You're coming with me, right?" Kimberly balked.

"There's no reason for us to be together. The way I see it, if someone's after you the babies are in danger as long as you're around." Saying those words were knife jabs, but he choked his own feelings back. There was no reason to give in to nostalgia. "If the people who are after you are criminals—and it sounds like they are—you'd be better off turning yourself into a government office. The US Marshals Service comes to mind. In case you haven't heard, there's a thing called witness protection."

"I didn't see anything to report," she pushed back. "I'm not a witness."

"You'd do better with law enforcement investigating your father," he stated. She didn't seem too keen on that idea based on the sharp breath she blew out.

"If all you plan to do is drop me off somewhere, you shouldn't care what I do next," she said.

"Your actions so far have put me and the twins in danger." He didn't want to admit this, but if she was determined not to bring in law enforcement, he had no choice but to watch her. He told himself that it had nothing to do with his instincts to protect his family. He could hide out for a couple of days without putting too much strain on the ranch. The image of the butchered heifer crowded his thoughts. If he put a great security team in place, he could figure out what the hell was going on with Kimberly.

His feelings toward his wife should be dead by now.

So why did the prospect of being with her 24/7 stir up feelings he couldn't afford to allow?

Chapter Six

Mitch had been driving for an hour, heading toward New Mexico. He knew of an off-grid place near the Texas border. Keeping the twins far away from Jacobstown was his priority until he sorted this out.

Kimberly settled into the passenger seat. It would take him a minute to get used to her bleached-blond hair, but as much as he didn't want to admit it, she was still as beautiful as the day he'd met her. Anger swirled like a storm cloud forming. How could he have been so off base about a person? Pride kicked him in the gut another time.

The small highway he'd been on for the past fifteen minutes turned to farm road. Since he hadn't seen a car in the past twenty minutes, he figured it was safe to stop off for a minute to make a call.

Kimberly's slow, steady breathing as she leaned her head against the headrest said she'd drifted off. She seemed to have been fighting sleep for as long as she could before it had finally claimed her.

Since Mitch couldn't be sure he'd have cell coverage much longer, he decided to pull over and make a call to Lone Star Lonnie. His foreman would be worried, since Mitch hadn't shown for their usual 5:00 a.m. roundup.

No doubt Lone Star already realized that Mitch hadn't saddled up Phoenix. With the recent event involving the heifer, Mitch didn't want Lonnie worrying about him.

While most cattle ranchers used pickup trucks and four-wheelers to round up their heard, Mitch preferred horseback. A few of the men had made jokes about Mitch being a Renaissance man, but he knew they appreciated his nod to nostalgia. Heck, many of them had followed suit in the years since. The truth was that his father, who was a good man and an excellent rancher, believed in being close to the animals and never felt like he could get that sitting behind the wheel of a truck. Efficiency was one thing and no one could argue the tidiness of using a gas-powered vehicle. When Mitch had tried it out in his early twenties—probably more of a rebellion than anything else—he could make good arguments for the efficiency.

But now he couldn't imagine herding any other way. He loved his red gelding, Phoenix. The horse had sustained a supporting-limb laminitis injury at Lone Star Park that would have put most under. He'd risen from the ashes. With surgery and rehab—not to mention money and patience—Phoenix had pulled through the injury that most horses had to be put down for. It might've killed his racing career but he'd found a new lease on life on the ranch, and it seemed to suit him better anyway. The horse could cut faster and cleaner than a can opener.

Mitch kept the engine running while he stepped out of his SUV.

"Everything all right?" Lone Star Lonnie asked almost immediately.

"Fine. I'll be out of pocket for a few days and need you and the others to cover for me."

"Not a problem," Lonnie said on a relieved-sounding sigh. "We got you covered here. Anything else I can do?"

"Nah. Thought the twins could use a break with all that's been going on," Mitch said.

"Great news about Rea," Lonnie confirmed. Based on Lone Star's tone, Mitch figured his foreman understood that they also needed a break to honor the upcoming anniversary of Kimberly's death.

"We can all breathe easier," Mitch agreed.

"Any word from Zach on the heifer?" Lonnie asked.

"He couldn't get so much as a boot print from the area. Seems I made a mess of the scene and covered anyone else's possible tracks." Mitch didn't do blame, so he kept to himself that Lone Star Lonnie had trampled all over the crime scene.

Lone Star mumbled a couple of choice words. "I should've known better than to clomp my big feet—"

"I'm going to stop you right there. You had no idea what you were walking up to or you would've been more careful," Mitch defended.

"Easy for you to say. Did you trample all over the crime scene?" Lone Star Lonnie asked with all sincerity.

Mitch drew in a sharp breath. "No. But I had a heads-up about what I was walking into. You didn't. Comparing the two scenarios is a little like asking if an apple tastes like an orange, wouldn't you say?"

Now it was Lone Star Lonnie's turn to issue a sharp breath. "No. I didn't realize. You make a good point but I'm not ready to let myself off the hook. If not for me this case might be zipped up already."

"That's one way to look at it. It's wrong but everyone's entitled to their own opinion. I know that if you'd had any idea what that could've been, you would've walked so light you couldn't have punched through a cloud. Besides, the earth is hard. There wasn't much if anything there to work with anyway by way of a footprint. It's just wishful thinking that Zach could've found anything. Not to mention the fact that there are only so many types of boots in production if the jerk who did that was even wearing them." It was all true.

Lone Star Lonnie knew it, too, because he paused before speaking. "If you didn't call about that, what's really going on?" He paused for a few seconds before adding, "I know that tone of voice, and something's wrong. Twins okay?"

The two had been friends for a long time. Lone Star would be able to pick up on a difference in Mitch's tone.

"The two of them are fine." Mitch hesitated, hoping the right words would magically appear. "There's been a lot of stress with the doctor visit and the anniversary of...well...you know what I'm talking about—"

"I do." Lone Star Lonnie knew full well what Mitch referred to. He'd buried his wife almost a year ago. As far as Mitch was concerned, she was still dead.

"A friend of mine needed a hand and I thought it would be a good time to get away for a few days." He had no intention of committing to more than that. Being away from home for a few hours with one-year-old twins was a challenge. More than that, and Mitch would lose his mind.

"Understood. I'll take care of everything here. We'll all make sure this place runs like a well-oiled machine." Lone Star would keep his word.

"The friend I'm helping might have put the ranch in danger." Mitch wasn't sure how much he could believe of Kimberly's story so far. He also had no idea how long he could disappear with the children. Their lives had been disrupted enough without adding to it. He glanced toward the passenger's seat, wondering who in hell's name the woman occupying it really was. Damned if he hadn't been the fool who'd fallen in love with her. He remembered how timid she'd been when she first arrived in Jacobstown.

"Oh." Lonnie's tone had questions written all over it, but to his credit he didn't try to dig.

"Be careful. And keep watch at each other's back."

"Always do," Lonnie said.

"Between my friend and the heifer, I'd rather be on the ranch," Mitch said. "But I'm doing what's best for the twins right now."

"Understood. And I agree with you. If there's any danger here, the twins don't need to be around," Lonnie agreed.

With Jacobstown being a tight-knit community, Mitch couldn't risk word getting out about Kimberly. Her return from the dead would be news. Big news. And that would draw unwanted attention and visitors. No matter how many times Mitch turned it around in his head, leaving the area was the right thing to do for everyone. He remembered how quickly news had spread when Kimberly had first arrived in town. Speculation as to the mystery woman's arrival had started before her bags were unpacked. Mrs. Wilder had gone on and on about how nice it was that someone wanted to pay cash for a change instead of 3 percent of rent going to credit-card-company fees or one of those annoying new apps taking a piece of everyone's money.

Meeting Kimberly in person had taken a couple of days. Rumors were starting to spread about what she could possibly be doing at the lake house alone. Since she didn't talk to anyone and people's imaginations were often so far off base from the truth, townsfolk had decided she was either mourning a loved one or a vicious killer biding her time until she could attack. According to most that would likely happen at some point after dark or when the rest of the town slept. Hell, a few even decided she'd strike during a full moon. Imaginations had a way of getting out of control in these situations.

"Mitch." Lone Star Lonnie sounded concerned.

"Sorry." He'd dazed out with the memory, the fog of betrayal thick in his thoughts. "Be extra careful on the ranch while I'm gone and tell the others to do the same. My friend seems to think everyone in Jacobstown could be under threat—especially us."

"Because of the heifer?" Lone Star Lonnie asked, but it was more statement than question.

"Partly. She has her reasons. Reasons that I don't have the full scoop on, but until I do I'd like to operate on full alert when it comes to security. Take no chances," he warned. Mitch didn't care how unlikely the scenario was that anyone else could be targeted; he planned to warn Lone Star Lonnie and his family. "I'll be off the grid for a couple of days. I couldn't reach the others this morning. I'd like you to call a family meeting and let the others in on what's going on."

It was a big responsibility he was handing to Lone Star Lonnie, and Mitch would trust few with it. Ensuring his family was safe at all times was his number one priority.

"I'll put the word out as soon as we hang up," Lone Star Lonnie promised.

"You know how much I appreciate it," Mitch said.

"Just doing my job as your foreman and friend," Lone Star replied in a heartfelt manner. "Be safe out there."

"You know I will."

Lone Star most likely assumed that Mitch was overreacting due to the upcoming anniversary of Kimberly's death. Mitch despised lies. Even more now that Kimberly had returned and he found out he'd been living one. He'd never get his mind around how she could fake her death and walk away from him and their children.

Mitch ended the call with Lone Star and navigated onto the road.

Nearly two hours later he pulled up to a small log-style hunting cabin.

Kimberly jolted up as soon as the engine died. She grabbed her chest and glanced around with wild eyes. Fear radiated off her.

"You're safe." Mitch didn't want to be her comfort after she'd caused him so much pain. Call it ingrained cowboy code, but he couldn't stop himself from trying to help another human in need. Plus her reaction caught him off guard.

"Sorry," she said in that raspy sleepy voice that had been so damn sexy before. "I forgot where I was for a minute."

He turned and really looked at her. Too many questions flooded his mind and he didn't want to talk when the babies were so close. The twins would need to eat as soon as they woke. Mitch also couldn't trust his temper. If she said something he didn't want to hear, he might just give her a piece of his mind. Reacting in anger was something he would've done before the kids had come along. Fatherhood had given him a new perspective.

Examining her now, he couldn't help but notice the

stress cracks on her forehead and the worry deepening her dark eyes.

"Where are we?" she asked, pulling her phone out of her pocket. He didn't even think about the fact that she brought nothing with her. No purse. No backpack. Just a phone and probably cash.

Since the twins had been born, traveling light was a joke. Mitch felt like he packed up the entire house every time he walked out the front door.

"This place belongs to a buddy of mine. And you can put that thing away," he nodded toward her cell. "You won't get any reception out here."

KIMBERLY'S CHEST SQUEEZED with panic. She glanced around, trying to get her bearings. Carrying the phone she'd bought six months ago had been a tether to a world she no longer felt part of. There were no contacts in the cell, which only served to remind her just how alone she was now. She felt like she stood out without one and she figured there might come a time when she would need to call 9-1-1. "What time is it?"

"Just after seven o'clock in the morning," he supplied.

She decided to remedy at least one issue. "Put my number in your phone." She rattled off her number while he added her as a contact.

"How long was I asleep?" She rubbed blurry eyes. It wasn't like her to sleep so soundly or for this long. She hadn't done more than nap an hour or two, as best as she could, since leaving Jacobstown eleven months ago. The gravity of the current situation punched her in the gut. She'd put the three people she loved more than anything else in danger.

But how could she *not* see her family one more time?

How could she *not* see how much her children had grown? Or if her husband would be showing up to the doctor appointment with another woman. The thought was a knife stab straight to the heart.

She glanced at his ring finger and noticed that he still wore his wedding band. Again her heart squeezed. She wore hers on a necklace, where it would always be close to her heart. He'd had their initials engraved on the gold band he'd given her on the day they'd exchanged vows. The band was the most important part because it stood for infinity—exactly the amount of time he said he would love her.

Looking into his cold eyes hurt.

Her mouth started to form the words *I'm sorry.*

Before she could manage to speak, he pushed open the driver's-side door and stepped out. He leaned on the open door. "I'll make sure the place is clear before I come back for the twins. They'll wake if you try to pick them up, so sit tight until I get back."

And then the door closed softly and she plunged into that cold, dark feeling that had nearly consumed her before. Tears welled in her eyes but she refused to cry or feel sorry for herself.

Life was about choices.

She'd made the only ones she could in order to save Mitch and her children. She refused to think of either as a mistake. In fact they were the three biggest miracles she would most likely ever know, following the foster parents who'd taken her in and treated her as their own. Maybe her luck had run out. Maybe a person got only so much of it before it went up in smoke. Maybe it was too much to wish anything could last. Kimberly had learned early on that life took every wrong turn possible.

Twisting around to look at her babies, the sound of the door opening rocked her. Mitch could be stealthy.

"There's a hot shower if you need one. Turn on only the light you need." Mitch's deep timbre wrapped around her like a warm blanket, sending sensual shivers to places she knew better than to allow.

"You don't need me to help with them?" she asked. Maybe it was naive to think he would ask her to help with the babies.

"No." He didn't say that she'd done enough but the ice in his tone spoke volumes.

She exited the vehicle, walked inside and headed straight to the shower.

Ten minutes into the warm water sluicing over her, a knock sounded.

She panicked a little bit, realizing that she was naked and Mitch was only a few feet away. Feeling exposed, she grabbed the towel hanging over the shower rod. She peeked her head around the curtain only to find that the door was still closed and he couldn't see her.

"Did you want something?" she said for lack of something better.

"Do you want a cup of coffee?" he asked.

"Sure. I'll be out in a minute. I'm almost done," she said.

The door opened a crack. "I have clean clothes. I'll just put them on the sink and be out of your way."

"Mitch."

She waited for an answer.

"Yeah."

"Thank you for everything you're doing." She hoped it would be enough to express her gratitude. This was hard.

Mitch grunted something and then closed the door. Kimberly had no idea what he'd said and figured she probably didn't want to know.

By some miracle the kids were still asleep when she strolled into the living room/kitchen area of the cabin. The main areas were open, with a kitchenette next to the back door. There was one bedroom with a bathroom connected. The decor was simple. There was a couch and a three-piece, small, round wood dinette set. The bedroom consisted of a bed, a nightstand and a wardrobe. The place might not be much, but it felt like shelter against a raging storm.

"Coffee's on the counter," Mitch said. He stared at her for a minute before shaking his head and refocusing on the wood table, in front of which he was seated. The place had a rustic charm and looked like no one had been there in weeks. Months?

Kimberly walked over and gripped the plain white mug. It was simple and felt warm in her hands as she rolled it around in her palms.

"The best place to figure out what's going on is to start with your father. What can you tell me about him?" Mitch motioned toward the chair opposite him at the table.

She took a sip before joining him, sitting directly across from him.

"Randy Bristol was a good man. Whatever he got involved in couldn't have been on purpose or his fault, no matter how it looked," she said defensively.

"I'm not here to crucify anyone. I just want to know the truth so we can figure out the source of the threat. We both need to get this behind us so we can move on with our lives," he said.

Those last words hurt more than she could admit.

She wished she could tell him what all this was about. Hell, she wished she knew.

Chapter Seven

"With you and the babies safe, I'll take off at first light," Kimberly said, hoping he would accept that on the surface, but knowing deep down that the chances were slim.

"What would that accomplish exactly?" His steel-eyed stare was as blunt as his words.

"All I needed to know is that you guys were out of danger," she said with an apologetic shrug. "You said it clearly—I'm the problem."

"So, what just happened?" He issued a grunt. "*That* was your entire plan?"

She searched the room, wishing for answers, hoping they were written on a wall, while feeling the intense heat of his glare. "Um, I don't have one. I think that's pretty obvious."

"I figured that out the minute you showed up, looking desperate," he commented before taking another sip of coffee.

"I reacted to putting you and the babies in danger. None of this was supposed to happen." Her voice climbed along with her frustration levels.

Mitch didn't immediately answer. His gaze dropped to her hands and she realized she was tightly gripping the coffee mug. She also noticed that he checked her wedding finger for a band. She forced her hand to relax by willpower and flexed the fingers of her free hand a few times. There wasn't much she could do about not wearing her ring on her finger anymore. She couldn't chance it.

He twisted his around on his finger. She couldn't blame him if he regretted still wearing it no matter how much those thoughts burned a hole in her chest.

"Consider me your shadow until we put this whole situation to rest," he continued after a thoughtful pause. His stare felt like a dare to argue.

"What would that accomplish? And what changed your mind?" She balked. He seemed determined to get away from her hours ago. "You made your point clear that you want nothing to do with me."

Before she could continue her argument, he threw his hands up in the surrender position.

"Hear me out," he started and his tone had softened a notch. Nothing in her wanted to listen. His earlier comments still stung. "Until this is over for you, it sounds like it could come back on me and the kids."

She bit her lip to keep from interrupting him, because what he was saying was true. She wanted to argue, to fight his point, but dammit she couldn't. The reminder that *she* was putting her family in harm's way felt like pinchers latched onto her heart.

"There's no way I'll sleep at night knowing there could be a random threat out there that could pop up at any time for the twins. You already know that I work the ranch and can't be around the kids 24/7 to protect them. Plus I won't put Joyce is harm's way by leaving them with her even if I could tell her what's up, which I doubt you'll agree to."

Frustration nipped at Kimberly as she sat there, practically biting her tongue. She trusted Joyce with her kids, but all of their lives was a different story. Joyce was the most well-meaning person on the planet, but one slip and it could all be over.

"I can't argue your points." Even though she wanted to. It was unthinkable that she had caused so much pain to the person she cared most about. To that end, she wanted everyone to be safe and this whole nightmare to end. Two and a half years. Thirty long months on the run, never feeling settled or like she belonged. Meeting Mitch had changed that last part, but she'd always known it was only a matter of time until she'd have to leave him. Even then a dark cloud had hovered over their happiness. "What do you suggest?"

"We can't stay on the run with the babies, so I need to figure out where they can go that won't put anyone else at risk while keeping them safe." Mitch's low timbre washed over her, sending an inappropriate shiver racing up her arms, toward her heart.

"When you put it like that, it sounds impossible," she said in a low voice before taking another sip of coffee. Coffee might not save the world but at least it helped her think clearly. The thought of leaving her babies again nearly hollowed out her chest.

"I'd like to figure out a solution that doesn't disrupt their lives more than necessary," he continued.

"Would Joyce be able to go somewhere with them? Put them under lock and key?" she asked.

"My great-grandmother was from Gunner's Pass, a small town in Colorado. I could have Joyce and the twins brought there under tight security. I still have relatives in the area, so no one would ask questions if they showed up out of the blue," he said.

"Do you know how hard it is to stay completely off the grid nowadays? You'd have to make sure no one—and I mean *no one*—posts a picture of them online," she stated, feeling heat crawl up her neck at the thought of being separated from her babies once again. Heat that came with knowing that Mitch was on the right track and hating the idea at the same time. "Is that even possible in this day and age?" Her voice was rising, even though she tried to keep her temper and her panic levels in check. She especially didn't want to wake the babies sleeping in the next room. Although, a part of her wanted them awake and in her arms. She wanted nothing more than to hold them, feed them, *be* with them. Be their mother. None of that was realistic and she knew better than to wish for the impossible.

"We need to investigate what really happened to your father and why. We can't do that with the babies around. *I* can't protect them *and you* and track down the truth," Mitch stated, his voice a study in calm confidence. His ability to stay cool in every conceivable situation had always been sexy to her, and it was even more so now.

Kimberly picked up her mug and gripped it with both hands. She thought long and hard about what Mitch was saying. She flipped over the options several times but there were very few. Counterarguments felt like a balloon deflating.

"You're right," she said after a long pause. "I can't disagree with what you're saying. The twins are in more danger when they're with me."

"With us," he corrected.

The feeling of hope that enveloped her with the word

us was false at best. Mitch was a good man and that's the only reason he included himself. He was trying to make her feel better but she knew the truth. She was toxic to the people she loved, and they'd be safer without her.

"I like the idea of keeping the twins with Joyce for consistency as long as the three of them leave town and she has no idea I'm in the picture." He wasn't asking her permission, but she was grateful to be able to offer her opinion anyway. Chalk it up to cowboy code but Mitch was too much of a gentleman to cut her off. She could also see that he was an amazing father. "I'm also thinking that you're right about getting them out of Texas and keeping them out." It hurt to say that because Texas had been her sanctuary and she believed it was her children's, too. "No one will look for them in Colorado. And especially since they must realize that I'd never go back to New Mexico or anywhere near it. I'd be recognized in my hometown immediately."

"Sounds like we're in agreement," he said. "Colorado will work at least for a temporary residence. I'm planning to send top-notch security with them. It's almost the holidays and tourists will be coming and going in the town of Gunner's Pass, for skiing and the Christmas festivities. No one will suspect anything if the kids show up with their nanny, and no one will be able to trace them back to you. We'll figure out a couple of security personnel who can pose as husband and wife and fit the bill as their parents."

The thought of her children being "parented" by another couple sat like a lead fireball in her stomach. Thoughts of Mitch remarrying and giving the children another mother had shocked her out of many a night's sleep. Again, she had no right to own any of those feelings. It was her fault Mitch and the kids were in danger. So she swallowed her pride and nodded. "That's solid."

Before she could say anything else, his stare centered on her eyes.

"Are both of your parents really dead?" he asked.

"To me? Yes," she stated. He deserved to know the truth.

"Do you know where they are now?" He twisted his wedding ring around his finger again before picking up his black coffee and taking a sip.

She shrugged in answer, and when he shot her a frustrated look she added, "New Mexico, I guess."

They sat in silence as he took another sip.

"If this is going to work, you have to be up front with me." He took off his wedding ring and set it on the table.

She stared at it like it was a bomb about to detonate. Pain could cause that kind of explosion in her chest at any second at the gesture. "I am. The people who brought me into this world walked away from me and never looked back. The people I call my parents were my last foster family."

"What about sisters or brothers?" he probed.

It was so difficult to talk about her past. "I had a sister when I was young. Lost track of her within a couple years of going into the system. I have no idea if there are others. I barely remember her."

She swiped away a surprising tear, refusing to look at him.

"Her name was Rose," she continued, not sure why she felt the need to keep talking. It had been so long since she'd been honest with anyone, with herself. "My real name is Lily Grable."

If Mitch was shocked by the admission, he didn't

show it. And then it dawned on her that he would most likely suspect she'd given him a fake name. She'd had supporting documents to cover her tracks, too. Fake ID. Fake name. Fake life. With him, it had felt a little too real and a little too much like a fairy tale come true.

Betrayal scored stress lines across his forehead, resembling slash marks.

THE MORE MITCH knew about Kimb—correction, *Lily*—the better he'd be able to track down the person or persons targeting her. He was trying to get his arms around this new reality but at least this conversation was real. His life with her had been a sham, and that angered him beyond belief.

He stared at the gold band on the wooden table.

In order to help her, he had to distance himself from the pain of realizing he'd been a first-class idiot. He could look at this solely as helping someone who was lost. And the woman sitting across the table from him was the most lost person he'd ever met. Even her eyes had a lost quality to them.

It had attracted him to her in the beginning and he should've known that would come back to haunt him.

Now he wanted to punch himself for not seeing any of this coming. There'd been signs. Kimber—Lily had been the most private person he'd ever met. She'd been alone in the lake house and had seemed to want to keep it that way. Part of him could admit that he'd forced his way into her life. She'd been clear about wanting to be alone and he'd seen that as a challenge—a challenge she'd given him the green light to accept. A challenge he didn't need to rush because he saw that she wanted to be together as much as he did. He'd planned on giving her time and space to realize it, too. But then for reasons he still couldn't explain, he'd shown up at her cabin that rainy afternoon. She'd invited him to come inside her cabin and her life. The two had been inseparable after.

But still, there'd been signs.

A beautiful mystery woman staying alone in a lake house had been too much temptation. When she'd pushed him away—weak as her attempts might have been—he'd seen that as a challenge, too. He wouldn't have forced himself on anyone. A good man wasn't built that way and especially not a Kent. She'd given him enough go-ahead signs for him to realize she was into him.

And when she warned him that he'd regret it if he didn't walk away before things got too complicated, he'd realized he was already in too deep. Mitch didn't do "serious" with anyone. He took life seriously and his responsibilities at the ranch. Losing his father had intensified Mitch's serious side. Or so he'd been told by his siblings.

He had a lot of responsibilities and he didn't take the family business lightly.

Since rehashing the past was about as productive as chasing a ghost pepper with a shot of tequila, Mitch picked up his ring and pocketed it. He looked her square in the eye, ignoring the way his pulse raced every time. "Running away from a problem never made it better."

"All I know is there are two creeps who've been following me around the country," she admitted. "I've been shot at and nearly run off the road more times than I can count."

It took a minute for the shock of those words to wear off. He really thought about what she was saying. Two men against her. Don't get him wrong—she was feisty as all get out. But she was no match for men with guns. She also happened to be deathly afraid of them. She was smart and that's most likely why she was still alive. What was he missing? He remembered the pair from yesterday morning. Yes, they'd been watching her. Following her. He'd suspected they were up to no good. But he didn't see a weapon. Although, it was a crowded plaza. "These men—how far away from you have they been when they shot at you?"

"What do you mean…?" She paused and it looked like she was searching her memory. "Well, I guess they've mostly shot from a distance. No. Wait. They've been close range. There was this one time in Atlanta…" She froze like she'd just given away the combination to her vault. "I guess I've been lucky every time."

He didn't like the fact that she'd closed up. He liked the fact that she didn't wear her wedding ring even less, but he was being sentimental. The marriage had been a fraud, a hiding place. Again, frustration galled him at being played like an idiot. He gave himself a mental slap. This wasn't the time to dwell on his mistakes. "Does that seem odd to you?"

A delicate brow arched. "What do you mean?"

"Seems like they'd have to be awfully bad shots to miss you so much," he continued.

"I always assumed they wanted me dead," she admitted. Confusion drew her brows together. She wasn't following.

"There's a difference between shooting at someone and shooting to kill them. I'm guessing the men who were after your foster father would be decent shots. Even a bad shot wouldn't miss every time. Probability kicks in at some point, saying they'd hit by accident if nothing else. Seems like the creeps following you knew what they were doing, considering they've found you every time. How many times have they shot at you?"

She sat there, completely still, with her gaze unfocused like she was searching inside herself for the answer.

And then light filled her eyes. "Dozens. And you're right. They sure have missed a lot."

The corner of her mouth quirked and he could tell she had an idea, a bad one at that. "Don't even think about it, Kimb—Lily."

"How do you know what's going on in my mind?" she countered.

"There's a certain twinkle you get in your eyes when an idea sparks. It's like the first firefly of summer's in there and it lights your face. And then your mouth does that thing." He pointed to the corner of her lips. "In between a pout and a smirk. When it's a bad idea that smirk is more of a frown."

Without rationalizing his actions, he reached forward and tucked a piece of her hair behind her ear.

Damn. Damn. Damn.

Mitch pulled back as if he'd touched a hot stove and mumbled a curse word. No way was he going there again.

"Lily, you're not sacrificing yourself by turning yourself over to those creeps to keep me and the babies out of danger," he ground out.

"I'm not Lily anymore. Call me Kimberly. And if they're not trying to kill me, they must want me for something. I can find out what that is and maybe stop this whole—"

He waved her off. "I said *no*."

She issued a grunt. "You're not my boss and you don't get to tell me what to do, Mitch."

"No, but I'm still your husband and that should give me some right to talk you out of nonsense."

Now she really did shoot him a loaded look.

Damn, he wasn't trying to offend her.

"All I'm saying is that it's too dangerous and spouses have a right to warn each other." He intentionally softened his tone, unsure why he'd played the still-married card. They weren't.

She gave him another look—one that said she'd made up her mind.

Rather than debate his actions, he stood and took a step toward her. She popped to her feet in the small kitchenette and backed up until her slender hip was against the counter. He noticed that she'd lost too much weight, even though he didn't want to pay attention to those things about her. Things that made him have sympathy for her.

Sympathy or not, he couldn't let her continue down the trail of putting herself more at risk. "And then what? You go in and actually get yourself killed? Have you lost your mind?"

"Am I crazy or stupid? Say what you mean, Mitch," she said through clenched teeth.

"You really want me to speak my mind?" Heat ricocheted between them with their bodies this close. Sex had never been a problem. Neither had talking. Or at least that's what he'd believed.

He touched her arm, trying not to notice the sensual shiver that raced through him when he made contact with her.

She steadied herself for what she must've figured would be an angry spew of words.

Instead of blasting her, he leaned toward her until they were so close that he could see her pupils. But he didn't care about that. For some messed up reason he needed to inhale her flowery scent and remember that she was very much alive.

Hell, half of the time along this weird psychedelic journey, he expected to wake up next to an empty bottle of tequila. He'd welcome a hangover to the mixed-up emotions coursing through him at present. But he'd never been big on alcohol.

This close, he breathed in her unique scent—lilies and fresh-from-the-shower clean. That was her. That was Kimberly. And she was right there in front of him, after eleven long months of his chest feeling like it might cave in every time he took a breath.

Weakness had him wanting to grab hold of her and not let go.

Chapter Eight

Kimberly's hands came up to Mitch's chest, palms flat against him, and he half expected her to use them to push him away. Or hell, yell at him. To scream that he was crossing the line.

Instead she leaned her forehead against his as he dipped his head and she ran her index finger along the muscles in his chest, like she was drawing an outline that she could memorize for the next time they were separated from each other. She had to know as well as he did that this reunion wasn't going to last long, *couldn't* last long.

But this moment enveloped them both and neither seemed to have the will to fight it.

He brought his finger to her lips and traced each one. They were pink and full. Memories of how they tasted assaulted him.

Mitch didn't debate his next actions, either. He dipped his head and pressed his lips against hers.

When her lips parted and she bit his bottom lip, the air around them charged. Her body hummed with electricity as he teased her with the tip of his tongue before thrusting it inside her mouth. He dropped his hand to the nape of her neck and wrapped lean fingers around it, leaving his thumb to rest at the base. She mewled pleasure and that was all the coaxing he needed to deepen the kiss.

Her hands came up around his neck, her fingers tunneled in his hair.

Need was a lightning strike, hitting with such force that Mitch forgot where he was for a second—on the run with a near stranger. That sobering thought was the equivalent of a bucket of ice water being poured over his head.

A little voice in the back of his mind reminded him that kissing his wife was the most natural thing in the world, next to holding their children.

And that's pretty much where he knew he had to stop. Willpower was difficult to come by but he summoned up enough to pull back first.

Kimberly's beautiful eyes glittered with need, and that didn't help one bit with his self-control.

"This is a bad idea," he managed to say under his breath. His hands didn't seem to get the message because they were pulling her toward him until she was flush with his chest.

"You're right about that," she said, a little breathless. He could tell that she was trying to pluck up the courage to walk away.

It didn't help that the tiny freckle above her upper lip twinkled at him. He wanted to take it in his mouth, to taste her again. There'd been too many sleepless nights in the last eleven months in which his arms had ached to hold his wife. If someone had asked him if a body could have muscle memory for a mate and act on its own accord in mourning, he would've said hell no. That was before Kimberly. Before the wife that he loved with everything inside him had come into his life and then died.

Died.

Another sobering word. Because this close it was a little too easy to forget that the only reason she came back into his life was to save him and their children. It had nothing to do with the love he believed they'd shared.

Damn if he wasn't going soft in the brain.

Time to put the past behind and cowboy up.

"I need to check on the twins," he said, attempting to put a little space—and reality!—between him and his wife.

"Can I help?" she asked.

"I've got this covered." Shutting her down was as much for her protection as it was for his. Once this was over and she got her life back, he fully expected her to be in their children's lives. Hell, he was even happy for the twins. They'd have a mother. Having grown up with a mother who loved her children was part of the reason he counted his childhood as lucky.

The twins having to grow up without a mother was one in a long list of reasons he missed his wife.

A thought struck. Kimberly might've been his wife but what had he really known about her? Precious little, he decided as he slipped inside the dark room with the babies.

It would be easy to let the woman step back into the role of mother. But mothering wasn't like a winter coat that someone put on when it got cold outside. Being a parent was a full-time job. The best one in the world, granted, but it wasn't for the weakhearted. He'd need to figure out what this new life would look like for all of them and maybe do a little investigating into her background before he trusted her alone with the kiddos.

He could work on finding a job in town for Kimberly if she wanted to stick around Jacobstown. Fort Worth was nearby. There was a lot of work there for anyone willing and able-bodied.

Mitch stepped lightly to the carriers with the twins inside. They slept so peacefully. He'd marveled at that eleven months ago. They didn't seem to be aware of everything they'd lost when Kimberly had died.

Babies had no sense of reality. For them, he'd seen that as a good thing. But they also had no idea how much their lives were going to change now that their mother was back.

The words seemed strange in his head.

How many times had he wished for this? For his wife to come back to life?

Would he also have to tell the twins how she'd willingly disappeared from their lives?

The babies were still sleeping, so he stepped into the doorway.

"I need to get cell coverage in order to call home. Get some rest. We'll leave when it's time to put the twins down for a nap later," he said to the woman he barely knew. His heart wanted to argue that she was still the same person, but that was a lie—everything about her was a deception.

She twisted her hands and he could tell that she was nervous. She also bit her bottom lip, which meant she was about to ask a question.

"I know that I don't deserve it but is there any chance you'd allow me to feed one of the twins?" He could see that she was holding her breath, waiting for his answer. The way she cocked her head to the side also told him that she didn't expect him to agree.

Here were the facts.

Like it or not, Kimberly was their mother.

Like it or not, Kimberly was back.

Like it or not, Kimberly was going to be in all of their lives.

The twins stirred in the room behind him. Rea belted out a cry. Time to get to work, changing and then feeding the babies.

Mitch turned on his heel.

"You can take Aaron. I'll take Rea," he said in a low growl.

KIMBERLY NEVER THOUGHT she'd have the chance to see her babies again, let alone hold one in her arms. Joyful tears sprang to her eyes as she held her son. He was big and strong, much more so than she'd expected him to be. Her arms ached to hold Rea, too, but she wouldn't push her luck. Holding her son was already a gift beyond anything she'd imagined in the past eleven months.

For the first time in a long time, Kimberly felt like she was home again. She knew full well that it would be a mistake to get too comfortable. There was always something or someone a few steps behind, lurking, waiting to take away everything she cared about. Anger shot through her.

This should *not* be her life.

Self-pity was a bottomless pool she had no intention of diving into.

After tearing her gaze away from her son, she locked on to Mitch's eyes from across the table. She could see the myriad of questions burning through his mind. They would have to wait a little while longer, because she had no plans to ruin this perfect moment of feeding her baby.

It was all the little things she'd missed in the last year, even the middle-of-the-night feedings and walking around, feeling half dead for most of the day. Giving her children their baths. The sweet smell of their soft, clean skin. The way they seemed to concentrate really hard to make their eyes focus enough to see her. Had they been memorizing her, too? Had they known she was temporary?

Kimberly had poured all of the love she could into those children for that first month of their existence, wishing that it could last a lifetime. She hadn't even expected to still be alive, so holding her babies was a gift beyond measure.

Mitch's words wound back through her thoughts. Were the men trying to kidnap her rather than kill her?

If so, they must either think she saw something, knew something. Wouldn't they want to get rid of her in either case?

Unless…

It dawned on her. They thought she knew *where* something was. It's the only reason she could think of that would make them want to keep her alive. They must need her.

But what are they looking for?

She drew a frustrating blank.

Trying too hard to recall something never worked, so she focused on the angelic face of her son instead.

Those gorgeous gray eyes, so much like his father's, studied her. Did he realize that she was his mother? Did he care at this age? She'd missed so much of his life already.

Sadly, he wouldn't know any different, since she'd disappeared so early in his life. Kimberly thought about her own biological family and the mother who'd walked out on her, the anger she'd always felt toward both of her parents.

Or at least *used* to feel.

Now that she was older and had more experience, life was becoming less black-and-white. Part of her felt sympathy for her parents. Granted, the situations were totally different, but losing children had to be the worst feeling for any parent. Even for ones like hers, who'd given them up so willingly.

Of course, life was also teaching her that there were always two sides to every story.

And an inkling of guilt said that she'd given up her children willingly, as well. She wanted to argue against the thought. But could she?

How different was she really?

Her thoughts drifted to her sister, Rose. What did she look like all grown-up? Where was she? Did she still have the lucky charm that Kimberly had fastened to a string and tucked inside her sister's pocket before the pair had been separated for good. Rose had been so young that Kimberly wondered if she even remembered having an older sibling. Kimberly had fought to keep the two of them together. Wonder Sisters—they'd given themselves the name at ages six and eight. No matter how hard Kimberly tried, she couldn't recall the details of her sister's face clearly anymore.

Lily was dead. She was Kimberly now.

That part of her, like so much of her life, had disappeared.

The past didn't have to determine her future, did it?

It was time to get her life back. Because after being with her babies and the man she—once? still?—loved, she was more determined than ever to put this whole situation with the creeps to rest. The only mother and father she'd known were gone. Her biological parents had never been in her life and never would be. Things would be different without her foster dad.

Could she find Rose someday?

The thought made her heart nearly burst. She was afraid to want it. But she had two beautiful children to reclaim. For the first time she allowed herself to consider the notion that coming back might've been something besides a disaster.

Kimberly marveled at her son in her arms while he finished the bottle.

"Bottle's empty. I've got it from here." Mitch set up a blanket with some toys in the middle of the floor before taking Aaron from her. "You should get some rest while you can."

"I'll be okay." She bit back a yawn. Considering they were planning to drop the babies off later, she wanted to spend every minute she could with them.

Mitch stared at her for a long moment after he positioned their son on the blanket. He must've picked up on her stress.

"When this all settles down, you'll get time to spend with them," he said. She shouldn't allow his deep timbre to affect her. It did anyway. Being here with their children had her heart wishing they could be something more. Like a real family.

"How do we do that?" she asked, feeling like a distant aunt when it came to knowing her own children's schedule instead of the mother she should be. She *should* know the little things about her kids. She *should* be the one to put them to bed. She *should* be the one to say when it was time for them to eat.

"I don't know." He issued a sharp sigh. "But these two deserve a mother and we'll figure it out. Right now we can't focus on anything but finding the truth of what's going on. But you have my word that we will."

Kimberly didn't want to push her luck, so she acknowledged his offering with a genuine smile. The look he returned, a brief moment of tenderness, nearly stole her breath. Not wanting to look a gift horse in the mouth, she disappeared into the other room. Sleep would be impossible. But she could rest. She could do that much for the tentative partnership Mitch had offered.

Dozens of scenarios ran through Kimberly's mind as she stretched out on the bed. Was it even possible that she could build a life near Jacobstown and be with her children? Soon, they would have to be separated again. Mitch was probably setting up the handoff to his security team now. As much as her heart ached at the thought of being away from her babies, knowing she wasn't alone in finding answers filled her with something that felt a lot like hope.

A renewed sense of purpose filled her, too.

That feeling carried her off to sleep.

When he popped into the room hours later and informed her the babies were awake, fed and ready to go, she freshened up and quietly gathered her things before following him out to the SUV. Mitch had a baby carrier in each hand, so she opened the door for him without speaking—without needing to—enjoying the feeling of cooperation. Could they build on the sentiment?

The first real spark of hope for a future lit inside her chest as she climbed into the passenger's seat.

The twins made cooing noises in the back that warmed her heart.

"Where are we going?"

"To a truck stop off the highway to meet up with Isaac. He's been with us for ten years and I'd trust him with my life." Mitch navigated down the gravel path toward the road. "Tell me about Randy Bristol."

"My foster father owned a small rental-truck-and-van company," she informed him. "He rented mostly to businesses."

"The possibilities from that really get my brain going," he said.

"What could someone gain from using his trucks?" she asked.

"Don't you mean what couldn't they do?"

"My first thought is drugs," she stated.

"That's one possibility," he admitted. "I read in the news recently that laundering money was becoming an even bigger problem in the US. It would be easy to move with rental trucks."

"I don't know about criminal activity, though." She shrugged. "Wouldn't that also leave a paper trail? I mean people have to give a copy of their driver's license in order to rent one of my father's vehicles. If the truck ended up in a bust, the person who rented it would be easy to track down."

"The men following you could believe you have access to those files. When did your foster mother pass away?" he asked reverently. He could understand the pain of losing a mother, even though Kimberly had lived with Randy and Julie Bristol for only six years before graduating from high school. After that Kimberly had landed a full-time job and started community college.

She'd moved into her own apartment near campus to be close to her favorite fosters and the only couple she considered to be family.

"The day before her birthday, three and a half years ago," she said, hearing how low her voice had become.

"I'm sorry." Mitch bowed his head so slightly that she almost missed it, and she could tell that he meant those words. He would know the feeling of losing a mother. Even though Julie wasn't technically Kimberly's mother, she loved her the same.

"Losing a mother is hard." Again his voice held so much reverence.

Did that mean a little piece of him actually still cared about her feelings? About her? Or was it just his nature to be kind to someone in pain?

"What happened to the business after your father's murder?" he asked.

"I'd planned to step in for him but everything fell apart back home after the creeps showed up in the middle of the night," she admitted. "The office caught on fire. I was basically accused of destroying his life. His entire legacy went up in smoke, and since it was suspicious circumstances, insurance refused to release a check."

"What stopped you from going to the law then?" He quirked a brow. With his cousin being in law enforcement, essentially *being* the law, she could easily see why that would be his first question.

"Whoever was behind all of this did," she admitted. "I spoke to a deputy immediately following my father's death. I thought I was a witness. But the deputy looked at me, *spoke* to me, like I'd done something wrong and it was only a matter of time before he figured out how I'd pulled it all off."

"But did the investigation go anywhere?" He would already know the answer.

"No. The creeps showed up in the middle of the night and I took off," she stated.

"What did you tell the deputy in the interview?" he continued.

"I told them my father didn't like the water, didn't swim. I said it was odd that someone who was afraid of the water would rent a boat. But they had a distant relative who I'd never heard of mention that he said something about learning to fish." She blew out a frustrated breath. "I couldn't seem to get it through the deputy's thick head that even if that was true, fishing wasn't the same thing as renting a boat. My father did want to take up fishing. Said it would be relaxing to sit on a dock and cast out a line. But there was no way he'd do that in a boat. He'd be terrified and there'd be no use being out there."

"So he dismissed your concerns," he said.

"I asked for an autopsy. Coroner ruled his death an accident," she admitted.

"But then his business went up in flames and no one thinks to reopen the case?" he asked.

"Honestly, by then I was scared. My father's behavior had been off. He'd warned me and when I tried to figure out what was going on, ask a few questions, I was told to leave it alone and that he could handle it," she said.

"Did you tell the police about the cell phone he gave you?" he asked.

She shook her head. "He wasn't listening to me, so I kept a few things to myself. At that point I can't deny that I suspected my father of being involved in something illegal, and I wanted to protect his reputation. Fire Marshal said his office was claimed by an accidental fire set by hikers. Dry climate and s'mores aren't really a good mix according to them," she said.

"Did they track down the hikers?" he asked.

"Never found out who set the campfire because the evidence went up in flames and no one claimed responsibility," she said.

"Any chance your father kept some information off-site?" he asked.

"Yes, I thought the same thing but there was no way I was going back to his house after everything that happened," she admitted.

"What about your place? What are the chances that something was left there?"

"I didn't keep any of my father's work files at my apartment," she said.

"Maybe he hid something when he was visiting?" He was looking for a needle in a haystack and drawing straws at this point.

"It's possible but that's a problem." She glanced at the sleeping babies in the back seat. They slept so peacefully.

"Why's that?"

"I didn't go back to my apartment, so I have no idea where my stuff is," she said.

"You didn't keep up rent payments?"

"I wasn't trying to skip out on purpose, if that's what you mean," she countered and she could hear the defensiveness in her own voice.

He issued a sharp sigh.

"I wasn't calling you irresponsible." He grunted.

"Then why don't you just come out and say what you mean?" Frustration had her baiting him into an argument.

"Fine. I will. You let your apartment go with your belongings because you were scared if you went back someone would find you. You were mourning the loss of the only person close to you and you ran away from it all instead of sticking it out and actually working out your problems. Does that sound about right?" His heated words were knife jabs to her chest.

"Guess that sums it up as you would see it," she said defensively.

He scoffed. "I'm pretty sure the world would see it like that, too."

"Say what you mean, Mitch."

The jabs were scoring direct hits and she didn't want to hear more.

"Fine. You want the truth?"

"Go ahead," she baited.

"You need to learn that you can't outrun your problems."

Kimberly shot him an angry glare. "Neither can you."

"Spit it out." Mitch was never one to mince words.

"It doesn't matter." Kimberly folded her arms. "Nothing else matters until we figure out what happened."

And that breakthrough felt about as possible as snow in July.

Chapter Nine

The balance of the ride to the meet-up spot with Mitch's security guard was spent in silence. Kimberly sat facing the door. She sniffed back the hot tears that had threatened.

She didn't know how long they'd been driving when the turn-signal clicks broke through her sour mood.

Mitch parked and got out of the vehicle before she could apologize. She needed to stay on his good side to gain his cooperation. But something inside her called out the lie. She wanted to get along with Mitch. They'd never argued when they were together before. A little voice reminded her that she'd known their relationship would be short-lived, that she would have to leave. So every minute had been precious to her and she wasn't going to spend them fighting.

Amy's face went ghostly white when her gaze landed on Kimberly. "I know Isaac told me you were okay but, damn. Seeing you here…alive…" Her gaze bounced from Kimberly to Mitch. "What's really going on here?"

"It's a long story but I'm okay," Kimberly said.

"We're supposed to be meeting with Isaac. What are you doing here?" Mitch asked his cousin. His voice left no room for doubt that he was upset.

Amy threw her hands out, offering a wide hug to her cousin. “What kind of greeting is that?”

Her gaze didn’t leave Kimberly as shock turned to wonder.

“What’s going on?” Amy asked.

“You can’t dodge my question,” Mitch insisted as Amy wrapped Kimberly in a tight hug.

“I’m sorry I deceived everyone. There were…circumstances beyond my control,” Kimberly said to Amy.

Mitch grunted.

She regretted the conversation that put him in this mood. He was taking out his frustration on Amy and that wasn’t exactly fair.

Amy recovered her normal, easy smile and threw a soft punch at his arm, looking put out at having to explain herself. “Okay. Fine. I needed a break from school before finals, so I came home yesterday. There. Happy now? Think he’ll ask to see my Christmas shopping list now?”

Kimberly couldn’t help but smile. She’d always admired Amy’s spunk and figured it came in handy, considering she and Amber were the only females in a family full of alpha males.

“Isaac was supposed to bring a pseudo-wife, not my little cousin.” Mitch cocked an angry brow but Amy dismissed him like he was being silly.

She turned to Kimberly and said, “Hope you don’t mind that Isaac updated me.”

Kimberly’s chest squeezed with panic as her gaze zeroed in on Mitch. She’d been under the impression that the family knew very little about what was really going on.

"I had to brief Isaac. He has access to networks that we don't," Mitch said in his own defense.

"And your family could end up tangled in this mess." It was bad enough that she'd dragged Mitch and the babies into her drama.

Mitch blew out a sharp breath and the babies stirred.

Amy stepped between him and Kimberly. "It's what he does for a living. Isaac is used to dealing with dangerous people." Amy was the youngest. Her mother and Mitch's were sisters, and the family resemblance was striking. Amy was a couple of inches shorter than Kimberly. Her body was a stick with hips and she had a horse's mane for hair. It was the same honey-wheat as most of the Kents'. Hers was just as thick and gorgeous. Her personality, much like her hair, was a little bit untamed. "He'll be discreet about digging around to see if there's a legal trail."

Amy might be the youngest and the wildest but she was also wise beyond her years.

"I know Isaac is capable of doing his job." She'd give him that. "If anything happened to him, to *any* of you, because of me—"

Amy's hands were already up, waving Kimberly off like Isaac digging around in her background was just another day at the office.

Meanwhile Kimberly's throat was closing up on her.

He was Kent security and used to dealing with pretty much everything. He was also like family and would treat the situation delicately. At least she hoped. The idea of anyone digging around in her background was enough to give her night sweats. Law enforcement had used her background against her when her father had been murdered instead of going out looking for the actual murderer. Her record had cast doubt in the community's eyes and tainted those who were closest to her. She remembered hearing that one of the neighbors had all but accused her of burning down her father's office. He'd insinuated that she could've been involved in his death. A few had even stretched it to say they wouldn't be surprised if she'd poisoned her foster mother, Julie. Those hurt just as badly.

The memories felt like knives that were tearing up her insides. There'd been so much judgment. Hate.

Would Mitch look at her with those same condemning eyes as Deputy Talisman's if he knew about her past? He'd fallen in love with the person he thought she was. Would he have loved her if he'd known the real her?

The decision to leave New Mexico had been easy once it had become clear to her that someone wanted her dead. But if Mitch was on the right track about the creeps wanting her alive, she was really confused. She didn't know what she had that anyone else would want but had every intention of finding out.

"Why is Isaac still in the car?" Mitch broke into her heavy thoughts as he eyed the vehicle. His danger radar had been on full alert since leaving the cabin, his gaze constantly sweeping the road from all angles. Kimberly wasn't complaining. An extra set of eyes meant more protection for the ones she loved most. She'd take what she could get. Isaac worked security at the Kent family ranch and was clearly trusted.

"I asked him to stay in there until I smoothed things over." Amy's elbows came up as she positioned her hands on the hips of her skinny jeans. "He wasn't thrilled about it but I thought we should talk first. He told me what was going on when I intercepted your message and demanded to know what was going on."

Her gaze bounced from Kimberly to Mitch.

"When did you and Isaac start speaking to each again?" Mitch couldn't let it go, and his protectiveness over Amy was another reminder of how much he cared about his family.

"Well, he had to talk to me on a three-hour car ride here, didn't he?" Amy's eyes twinkled with her smile. Kimberly wanted to hear the story behind that spark but that would have to wait. Right now, she needed to convince Amy this job wasn't right for her.

As Kimberly opened her mouth to speak, a car crept out from behind the convenience store. The hair on the back of her neck bristled.

Touching Mitch's arm, ignoring the host of other less-appropriate impulses firing, she said, "We need to get out of here."

Confusion stamped his dark features. Mitch scanned the area and almost immediately locked on to the silver Toyota Camry that was backing up to shield a good view of the driver.

"Change of plans. Get behind the wheel of my SUV, Amy," Mitch said in almost a whisper. "Kimberly, you go with her."

Isaac's gaze was focused on Mitch, Kimberly noticed. And he seemed to be picking up on what was going down.

"Get on the highway and head south for a little while," Mitch instructed as he placed his keys in Amy's palm. It was the opposite direction of their ultimate destination in Gunner's Pass, Colorado, and Kimberly could plainly see that he was sending a mixed message to whoever might be following them.

The younger woman seemed cool under pressure, and she put on a breezy smile and hugged her older cousin. Out of the side of her mouth, she said to Kimberly, "Ready when you are."

Kimberly took in a fortifying breath. Fear assaulted her but she wasn't concerned for herself. The twins. Amy. Mitch. Isaac. They were all innocent in this mess. Anger replaced fear. She would protect the people she loved no matter what. "Let's go."

Amy made a big show of hugging Mitch goodbye. She turned to Kimberly and in a loud Southern voice said, "Ready to hit the road for our girls' trip?"

"Not sure Cancun can handle the two of us," Kimberly said as loudly as she could.

Amy glanced from Kimberly to Mitch. Amy expected them to say goodbye. Right.

She leaned in for a side hug and found herself being swept into Mitch's arms. Her breath caught as she felt that solid chest of his flush with her body. A trill of awareness followed and her chest squeezed. Mitch's actions made him seem concerned about what happened to her.

"Whatever you do..." he whispered so low she had to strain to hear him. "Don't let anything happen to those children."

"I won't," she managed to say, unwilling to admit how much she'd wanted his concern to extend to her welfare. She'd thought about the kiss they'd shared—one that couldn't happen again!—a little too much. Under normal circumstances, she might let herself dwell on any one of those things but this wasn't the time for rogue thoughts about Mitch.

He was concerned about their children. He was an amazing father. He didn't deserve any of what was happening. And neither did those two angels.

Breaking apart made her instantly aware of what her life had been like the past eleven months in the shadows. It was dark and cold. If she saw an opportunity to end this misery, she wouldn't hesitate even if it meant sacrificing herself. She told herself that she could handle anything the men did to her. But her children? Mitch? The others? She couldn't go there.

Kimberly turned toward the convenience store. How hard would it be to dart over there and give the men what they really wanted…*her*?

As if reading her mind, Mitch took her hand in his and tugged. He locked gazes. "Don't do anything crazy. The children need their mother."

The statement scored a direct hit. If anything happened to her, what would her children think? Would they know that she'd sacrificed everything to keep them safe? To make sure they lived? Or would they resent her for abandoning them?

Just like her own mother had abandoned her.

Damn. The last thought pierced her chest.

Mitch was right, so she shot him a look of acknowledgment.

Walking toward the SUV, Kimberly noticed Amy's hand trembling just a little bit as she fisted the keys.

"YOU WATCH MY family and I'll keep eyes on the sedan." Mitch slipped into the passenger seat of Isaac's black hardtop Jeep. The vehicle would be agile enough to go off the road if needed, and the engine had been doctored so it would go as fast as necessary. Given that the suspect vehicle was a silver Toyota Camry, Mitch didn't expect to need to use the souped-up engine.

"Will do, boss," Isaac responded.

The Oklahoma plates also made him think the vehicle had been stolen. But then again Oklahoma plates weren't exactly unusual in Texas. The Camry topped the list of most-stolen vehicles in the US. Apparently, Mitch had read, they were easy to steal and easy to bust up in order to sell the parts. The black market for this vehicle was vast.

Mitch fished his cell out of his pocket as the sedan eased forward and then stopped as soon as the driver would be able to get a good view of the Jeep.

Discreetly, Mitch zoomed in and snapped a picture of the license plate. He immediately texted the image to Zach. He tried to zoom in on the driver's face but the picture was too grainy to make out any features. Besides, both the driver and passenger wore hoodies and reflective sunglasses.

Zach's response came within seconds.

Checking on this ASAP.

"The SUV is turning out of the parking lot," Isaac said.

As for Isaac and Amy, Mitch suspected that the silent treatment Amy had been giving Isaac had something to do with the two of them being in a relationship. If the two were dating, they kept it on the sly. And he'd been seen spending time with someone else.

For as long as Mitch could remember, she'd acted different whenever Isaac was anywhere within earshot. Her voice raised a couple of octaves and her fingers twirled in her hair. He'd come out and asked her about it once and she'd denied having a crush on Isaac, who was eight years her senior.

"No action with the sedan," Mitch informed. "Hold on. Check that. The Camry is on the move."

Adrenaline thumped through Mitch, giving him a sudden burst of extra energy. Protective instincts kicked in and he flew out the opened door.

He jumped in front of the sedan, with his cell in hand, and snapped a pic of the pair of men inside. With the Texas sun high in the sky, the sun glinted off the windshield, making it impossible to see who was inside.

The sedan swerved in time to miss Mitch and that's when he saw the end of a small barrel sticking out of the cracked window.

He dove toward the Jeep at the same time he heard the crack of a bullet split the air.

Unsure if he'd been hit, he darted into the passenger seat before another shot could be fired.

"Go," he demanded as the sedan peeled out of the lot, hot on the trail of the SUV.

Mitch glanced left in time to see blood pulsing from Isaac's neck. He muttered a curse as guilt punched him in the gut.

"You're hit," he said to Isaac.

"I'll be fine." Isaac was already unbuckled and trading seats with Mitch. "Don't let that bastard get anywhere near the SUV."

His gun was drawn as Mitch squealed out of the parking spot, racing toward the bumper of the SUV.

Mitch put on the seat belt using one hand. "Get some pressure on that wound."

Now it was Isaac's turn to bite out a few choice words. He fumbled as he opened the glove box and pulled out a first-aid kit with one hand, while trying to keep his Glock trained on the back of the Camry with his other hand.

The Jeep bounced on the potholed service road.

"Talk to me. Tell me how you're doin'," Mitch said, unable to take his eyes off the road when he really wanted to check on his employee and friend. The Camry pushed the pace to seventy miles an hour. His stress levels weren't helped by the fact that Isaac wasn't talking. There were vehicles dotting the highway, traveling at a leisurely Saturday-afternoon pace. The speed limit was fifty-five on this stretch of road. Lower than that on the service road.

The Camry zipped around a Honda. Mitch followed, and the driver flashed high beams at him.

Yeah, I know, buddy. I'm not happy about this, either.

"Give me an update or I'll be forced to pull over," Mitch said.

"Spider bite would hurt more than this," Isaac finally said through a half grunt. It sounded like his words were coming through clenched teeth. Mitch detected the stress his friend was covering up even though he tried to come off like it was no big deal. Shock and adrenaline would keep the pain at bay temporarily.

Mitch risked a glance at Isaac. He exhaled when he saw the bleeding had been stemmed with a large quantity of gauze that was now soaked with blood. "Get out your phone and call 9-1-1."

"We've got this covered," Isaac protested.

"You're shot, bleeding and probably in shock." Mitch knew exactly what that was like. He'd been shot by illegal hunters for the first time when he was barely old enough to shave. Youth had him thinking he could push through in order to track down the responsible party. He'd overestimated his own abilities and miscalculated the men he'd tracked. Taking his injury too lightly had nearly gotten him killed.

As soon as he'd gotten close to the shooter's encampment, he'd fallen facedown from blood loss. They'd left him to die but not before getting a few kicks in. He'd come to in the hospital after his brother Will had found him.

The entire Kent and McWilliams brood had refused to give up searching until they'd found him. That was the kind of loyalty he was used to. Exactly the reason he trusted very few people besides his kin. Blood could be counted on. And after Kimberly had carved a hole in his chest, he was more resigned than ever to keep his circle closed.

"Talk to me, Isaac."

"I'm good as new, boss."

The sedan swerved in between a truck and a compact car. Kimberly and his children were a short stretch ahead and the sedan was closing in.

"I'm serious about that 9-1-1 call. Bring in the locals on this one," Mitch said with a quick glance at Isaac. Based on the amount of blood loss, Isaac wasn't in as good a shape as he claimed.

The other side of the Jeep was quiet.

"That an order?" Isaac finally asked, resignation deepening his voice.

"It's a suggestion," Mitch conceded. Was he feeling a sense of responsibility to keep Isaac safe? Alive? Hell, yes. Isaac was the only one who could determine whether or not he needed immediate medical attention.

"I'm hit. There's blood. Another day at the office for me, boss." Isaac wouldn't give up easily. It was his job to keep the Kent family safe. He also wasn't stupid, so Mitch would take another tact.

"We gotta play this right. A lot's at stake. And one or more of these cars probably made the call already based on the way this joker's driving. We call it in and we end up on the right side of the law on this."

"Or we end up detained as suspects or witnesses while this guy gets to the people who matter most to us."

Chapter Ten

Isaac made a good point about local law enforcement. Mitch didn't know anyone out here and was outside his cousin's jurisdiction. Isaac also seemed to realize his slip—he'd admitted to having feelings for Amy. Since this wasn't the time to dig deeper into the subject, Mitch filed the information away for later.

"My phone's going crazy in my pocket. Zach might have something on the plate," Mitch said.

"That's a better person to talk to if you ask me but it's your call." Isaac's reasoning was sound. Mitch would trust his judgment.

"Zach can alert locals," Mitch agreed, not daring to take his eyes off the sedan gaining on his SUV. "Put Zach on speaker when he answers."

Isaac did.

"The Camry was stolen," Zach started right in. "A family is stranded at a gas station about a half hour from where you are now."

"I figured as much. It would've been too easy to ID these jerks otherwise," Mitch said, cutting the wheel left to avoid a collision with a blue Buick. He cursed under his breath. It was wishful thinking on his part that the driver could be identified and this whole nightmare could be wrapped up in a bow before it got messy. Kimberly had secrets that put his children at risk.

Isaac already had his weapon out, ready to shoot out a tire and slow the Camry down, but there was too much traffic and he couldn't risk a stray bullet hitting innocent people.

"Where are you now?" Zach asked.

"The last sign I read was Smithtown," Mitch informed him.

Zach cursed. "That's Sheriff Bogart's jurisdiction."

"Sounds like bad news." Mitch had to veer right to snake through thickening traffic.

"Tell me everything that's going on, starting with the vehicle you're driving," Zach instructed. "I'll need to give him a complete picture."

"You need to know something, cousin," Mitch warned. "Amy's involved."

"What's my sister doing with you?" Zach had always been protective of family, but especially when it came to his little sister.

"She came with Isaac—"

"Why would she do that? What are you guys doing in Bogart's jurisdiction, where I can't help you?" Zach's voice was steady and that meant one thing: he was working hard to control his emotions.

"I had a visitor last night. I was heading out of town with the twins," Mitch admitted.

"Devin mentioned you were helping out a friend. What's that all about?" Zach asked, still with that steady investigator's tone.

"It's Kimberly," Mitch said.

"What about her?" Zach sounded confused.

"She came back last night to warn me." Mitch paused a moment to let that sink in.

"Kimberly? As in your dead wife Kimberly?" Zach normally had more tact but he was clearly reeling from the admission.

The Camry passenger took a wild shot at them.

Mitch jammed the wheel right and muttered a curse.

"Anyone hit?" Zach finally asked after a few tense seconds.

"No, sir," Isaac reported.

"I'm fine," Mitch added. He didn't like the way the Camry zipped in between cars.

Zach issued a sharp sigh. "What else do I need to know?"

Isaac relayed additional details, leaving out a crucial fact.

"What Isaac didn't tell you is that he took a bullet," Mitch added when his security detail was finished.

"I'm sending an ambulance," Zach immediately fired back.

"Not necessary," Isaac said, trying to dismiss it.

"How is he really?" Zach asked, like Isaac wasn't sitting in the passenger's seat.

Isaac grunted his dissatisfaction.

"Took a hit to the neck. Seems to have stemmed the bleeding for now but I'd feel a helluva lot better if he would agree to have it looked at," Mitch informed him.

"A piece of a bullet scraped me, mind you," Isaac interjected. "And it's not that big of a deal."

"How's Tough Guy's coloring?" Zach asked, concern quieting his voice.

"Have no idea. My eyes have been glued to the road and have to stay there," Mitch admitted.

"The only real concern we have right now is what's in front of us," Isaac said.

"Bring 'em back on Highway 30. I'll have deputies waiting at the edge of my jurisdiction and an ambulance—no arguments, Isaac," Zach said.

"We get them back safely and you won't hear a peep from me," Isaac said.

"In the meantime," Zach continued, "I'll see how much cooperation I can get from local law enforcement. The sheriff there has a reputation for being uncooperative. Get out of his county as fast as you can."

"Once we turn around we've got a good hour and a half to go before we get to Jacobstown," Mitch admitted.

"Wish you'd clued me in sooner," Zach stated.

"We're in the same boat on that one," Mitch admitted. "This has all been coming at me at a hundred miles an hour. All I know is that Kimb—*Lily Grable* is her real name, by the way. Lily has a foster father who got himself into some kind of trouble and it was big enough to create a trail leading to her. She said she has no idea what's going on and I believe her." Mitch wasn't sure why he added the last part. It seemed important for Zach to know that Mitch trusted her. At least about that.

"Kimberly's real name is Lily Grable?" Zach asked.

"She had fake papers for the wedding that were apparently good enough to fool the man who married us. You know anything about her?" Mitch asked.

"It shouldn't take much to dig around into her background," Zach stated.

"She may have gotten into some trouble in her early teens. She was bounced around in the system," Mitch warned.

"Any juvenile records will be sealed. I'm sorry to ask

this question…" Zach paused, and Mitch picked up on his cousin's hesitation.

"Go ahead." Mitch figured he knew what his cousin would ask.

"Has she kept her record clean as an adult?"

Mitch should know the answer to that. His traitorous heart said he did and that she wasn't some kind of con artist. But he'd trusted his emotions once already and that had left him with a shattered heart. "I believe so but then I thought I knew her. All I know for sure is that she's in trouble. She thinks it has something to do with her foster father's business but…"

"Get her here," Zach advised. "We can sort out the rest once she's in protective custody."

Now it was Mitch's turn to go silent. He wanted to know the truth but he didn't want to get her in trouble. Again, his heart said she wouldn't lie to him unless she felt like she had no way out.

"I'll do my best," Mitch promised.

"Until we know what we're dealing with, be careful," Zach warned.

"Always," Mitch confirmed. His children had lost their mother once. He had no intention of allowing that or anything like it to happen again. They'd been too young to understand what was going on and that had been the only grace. *Grace?* Mitch almost laughed. Nothing in his present situation fell under that category.

With the Camry taking a more aggressive stance, he had no choice but to respond in kind.

The late Saturday-afternoon traffic was thinning as they moved away from another town, but Mitch didn't like the fact that anyone else was on the road with the aggressive way he was driving. No one deserved to get caught in the middle.

The Camry started racing toward his SUV on an open stretch of highway, moving at the pace of a bullet train. He needed to cut off the Camry before it reached Kimberly, Amy and the kids.

Mitch cut the wheel left and stomped the gas pedal.

"Get Kimberly on the phone," he instructed Isaac.

THE CAMRY CAME rushing toward the back bumper of the SUV. The plates were visible in the side-view mirror. Kimberly searched for the Jeep but couldn't see any signs of it.

Amy's phone buzzed. "Can you see who that is?"

Panicked, she checked the screen. "It's Isaac."

"You should answer," Amy said.

Kimberly put the call on speaker. "Hello."

"Isaac here. How're you two doing?"

"Never better," Amy quipped and her familiarity with him brought Kimberly's stress levels down a notch. Amy's white-knuckle grip on the steering wheel belied her calmly spoken words.

"Good to hear." There was a note of relief in Isaac's voice.

Kimberly glanced at the side-view mirror again. "I lost the Jeep. Where are you guys?"

"Behind the black Dodge Ram. We're a few cars back but we got eyes on the Camry. He seems to be making a move toward you guys." He paused. "I have more bad news. We need you to turn around and we gotta get out of this county."

"Mitch?" Hearing his voice, his confirmation, would go a long way toward calming her fried nerves.

The moment of hesitation caused her heart to pound against her ribcage.

"He's right," Mitch confirmed. "There's no reason to be scared, Kimberly. I'm on the Camry and I need you headed in the opposite direction, toward Jacobstown. You hear, Amy?"

"Yes, sir," Amy confirmed.

"Don't stop or turn around. Get back to Broward County as quick as you can without being stopped. Your brother will have support waiting for you there," Mitch informed her.

Amy's grip on the steering wheel relaxed a little bit more with those words. She quirked a tiny smile and the stress cracks on the side of her eye relaxed.

"Wait a minute. You're coming, aren't you?" There was no way she was going back to Jacobstown without Mitch.

"As soon as I take care of a little problem," was all he said.

Isaac's voice came on the line. "Amy."

"Yes." Her voice perked up considerably at the sound of his. "Take the exit now."

Kimberly felt the jerk of the tires gripping the asphalt as Amy spun the wheel, cutting off a car and barely making the exit. She did, though. She swerved onto the service road and Kimberly watched as the Camry's brake lights lit up and it slowed onto the shoulder. Gravel spewed out from underneath its tires as the Jeep pulled up behind.

A shot rang out. The sound of a bullet cracking the air sent waves of panic rippling through her.

And then the SUV was fishtailing.

Amy was unfazed. She let out a resounding "Whoop!"

And then she added, "Hold tight. It's about to get interesting in here."

One of the twins stirred, letting out a small, pitiful-sounding wail. The other almost immediately followed.

"Sorry, babies," Amy said, handling the wheel like a pro and straightening out the SUV.

Her driving skills were something else.

The babies wound up to a good cry in the back seat, belting out their dissatisfaction with the situation. The same feeling of helplessness that she'd felt when she'd first brought them home assaulted her.

They were older now and she was out of practice in calming them.

"What can I do?" she asked Amy, hating how small her own voice sounded.

"Binkies. Get their Binkies in their mouths. Mitch usually has them clipped to their shirts." Amy motioned toward the back seat. "Rea's should be on a Winnie the Pooh clip."

Kimberly unbuckled, climbed over the seat and positioned herself between the car seats.

"Here it is," she said after moving the strap around in order to locate the pacifier. "It's okay, sweet girl."

Kimberly hoped that her voice was what soothed her daughter enough to calm her, but it was probably just the pacifier. Her son wasn't as agreeable. It took a little coaxing, but he finally accepted the Binky and settled back to sleep.

"They're great babies," Amy said, her voice still edged with the adrenaline shot they'd both received. "Car rides knock them out every time."

Kimberly should be the one who knew what to do instead of being wrapped in that blanket of helplessness, a feeling she hated. With the babies needing attention, she lost track of the others. “Where are Mitch and Isaac?”

Amy shrugged. “Haven’t seen them since we made the turn east. Camry’s out of sight, too.”

Kimberly had been too caught up in trying to get the babies back to sleep to notice. Being on the road with the twins made even less sense but the thought of being away from them again was an even bigger knife to the chest.

“Mitch and Isaac will be okay and especially if they don’t have to worry about us and the babies,” Amy added as though she could read Kimberly’s thoughts. “Isaac works security for a living. It’s what he does and he’s damn good at his job. My cousin has come up against some seriously bad dudes in his life. Poachers are right up there with the most dangerous scumbags, and my family knows how to handle them.”

Kimberly didn’t answer. Nothing was okay. Nothing would be okay again. She’d trusted her foster father. He was an honest man. Right? A little voice asked why he would’ve given her the phone. Why he would’ve warned her if that was true.

Was he involved in criminal activity? Was he a criminal? It was so hard to believe the man who’d taken her in, accepted her rough edges and had the patience to wait for them to smooth out was capable of doing anything wrong. Randy Bristol was the best kind of person. If he couldn’t be trusted, no one could.

Did the mirror always have two faces? Her heart argued against the idea and her instincts backed it.

But Randy was probably the first person who’d ever been truly kind to her, and her mind constantly tried to convince her that he couldn’t be a criminal.

Would she have known?

Or was she being too stubborn to see the facts right in front of her nose?

Chapter Eleven

Mitch cut the wheel right across two lanes of traffic and navigated his way onto the shoulder of the highway. The Camry was making a move toward the service road and he needed to block it before the driver traversed down the ravine. That incline was the only thing giving him a chance to catch the Camry.

As Mitch swooped around the right side of the vehicle, the passenger got off a shot. Mitch could feel the Jeep leaning heavily against its right side. It was an off-road vehicle but the roll bar reminded him Jeeps were also made for the impact that came with tipping over. Its high profile was making the tires claw to stay upright on the incline. He hoped like hell they'd dig in as the left-side nose of the Jeep pressed against the back-right bumper of the Camry.

The passenger's window went down, the end of a pistol poked out and before Mitch could react he saw that telltale flash of fire and heard the crack of a bullet.

"Windshield's bulletproof," Isaac reminded and Mitch knew that on some level. If it wasn't he'd have been hit between the eyes based on where the windshield took impact. Even so, adrenaline shot through him like a lightning bolt.

The Camry swerved, no doubt looking for a better angle to fire off another shot.

"I'll get behind him," Mitch bit out as he stomped the brake and spun the wheel to the left, practically scraping the Camry's bumper with the maneuver.

He scanned the road. The thought of an innocent person taking a stray bullet slammed into him. At least the other drivers had enough sense to give them space. Mitch was also certain there'd be a host of 9-1-1 calls and that wasn't good since they were still in Bogart's county.

"We'll slow 'em down if I can get a good aim on a tire." Isaac voiced what Mitch was thinking.

Mitch swerved left in order to give Isaac a better vantage point. The Camry did the same.

Isaac bit out a curse as he tried to keep the gauze secure against his neck and still manage a decent aim.

"Hold on." Mitch sped up alongside the driver's side of the Camry. He couldn't get a good look inside the vehicle. There'd be no description of the driver. Just a stolen vehicle. And by now a few frantic "shots fired" calls to the sheriff's office from concerned citizens.

Isaac was right. The law would detain them and the Camry could get away, leaving Kimberly and Amy defenseless. Amy had to watch her driving with the twins in the back seat.

The Camry banked right, making another move toward the embankment leading toward the service road. Mitch lost track of the SUV. The Camry caught gravel and swerved, creating an opening. "Now."

"This jerk is about to slow way down." Isaac took aim and fired a round.

The crack was loud inside the cab of the Jeep, causing Mitch's ears to ring. He shook it off and kept his focus on the silver sedan. There was no doubt about it—Mitch had to keep the Camry from following Kimberly, Amy and the kids.

As the sedan driver struggled to regain control from the fishtail, Mitch wedged the Jeep in between it and the service road. The incline was steep and gravel made it difficult for his tires to maintain purchase at high speeds.

Thankfully the silver sedan slowed.

As the Camry made another play for the shoulder, Mitch hesitated. The choice to keep going and risk Isaac's life or leave and risk Amy, Kimberly and the children was a hot poker inside his chest.

"Don't even think about it," Isaac ground out.

"What are you? A mind reader?" Mitch shot back even though Isaac was dead-on with his assessment.

"I know what's at stake, boss. Stay on the Camry." Then he added, "Please."

Under normal circumstances, Isaac wouldn't argue. This was extreme and Mitch was all too familiar with the guilt that came with letting someone get away who could do damage to the people he loved.

The sun was bright on the horizon, causing Mitch to squint in order to see clearly. Beams burst from the back windshield.

Mitch had cut off access to the service road, using the Jeep to block it. He prepared himself for another gunshot but instead the Camry's driver spun the wheel right into him, edging him off the road.

The tires of the Jeep struggled for purchase on the gravelly incline.

Before he could jam the brake, the Camry slammed into him, tipping the Jeep over and into a death roll.

Even with his seat belt securely fastened, Mitch's

body got tossed around and his brain scrambled. Everything was happening too fast but seemed to be in slow motion at the same time—an odd feeling. One he was familiar enough with to realize his mind was playing tricks on him. It was most likely the shock coupled with another jolt of adrenaline. His brain tried to wrap around the idea that he was taking a tumble. All he could think about was Kimberly, Amy and the kids.

The Jeep sounded like it was cracking in half as it rolled.

Mitch's head snapped back before a lightning bolt of pain exploded, the aftershocks bouncing around inside his skull, creating an echo-like effect before…blackness.

MITCH HEARD AN unfamiliar voice hovering over him. There was shouting—all male voices.

His brain cramped, his head felt like it would split in two and he couldn't open his eyes.

The smell of smoke filled his lungs. He coughed. His eyes and nose burned.

His eyes blurred as he tried to blink them open. Pain shot through him.

And then it dawned on him why.

The Jeep had rolled off the highway.

His first thought was of Isaac and then Kimberly, Amy and the children. His mind railed against the thought of anything happening to them.

And then blackness pulled him under again.

"HOW LONG DO the babies usually nap?" Kimberly checked the clock on the SUV's dashboard, resigned to the fact that she'd have to rely on someone else to learn the daily habits of her children. And although she'd met the entire Kent brood, cousins and all, she'd used the pregnancy as an excuse to keep to herself. She had no idea how Amy truly felt about her and especially now that everyone knew she'd deceived them.

The younger woman had always treated Kimberly with kindness. Amy was a good person. She was most likely just being polite now for her cousin's sake. The whole Kent/McWilliams clan was tight.

Now she wished she'd gotten out more, spent more time with people. To be fair she couldn't risk having her face show up on social media pages and that was a big part of the reason she'd secluded herself. A voice in the back of her head called her out for lying.

Thankfully the Kents were a private bunch but that had lulled her into thinking she and Mitch could live a quiet life together.

She'd gone to great lengths to ensure she had legitimate-looking documentation that could prove she was Kimberly Smith. She'd given herself a new identity and believed she could have a new life to go along with it. Her judgment had been off base and her heart had overruled logic when she'd met Mitch.

She'd allowed herself to get swept up in the fantasy that life would somehow turn out all right despite the fact that the one person in the world whom she'd trusted aside from her foster mother had been involved in illegal activity right under her nose. Her stubborn mind said her father couldn't have done anything wrong. He didn't have a criminal bone in his body.

By living so much of her life on her own, she'd become good at reading people for survival. One of her foster mothers was nice after two drinks but turned into a depressed wreck after the fourth. At five, her anger turned outward toward anyone who was near. Kimberly counted drinks the first six months she lived in the Monger home. After six months she could tell how much Olivia drank with one look at her eyes. She'd become adept at identifying the tipping point where the society woman became downright mean. Thankfully the house had been large enough for Kimberly to hide in a new place every few weeks. Olivia would hunt for her on the really bad nights. The clicks of high heels against wood floors still echoed in Kimberly's thoughts.

Kimberly had learned to hide well. Olivia would eventually pass out. The next afternoon when the effects of the prior evening wore off, she'd take Kimberly out for ice cream, making sure to snap plenty of pictures to show the social worker.

That and other similar experiences had taught Kimberly to read people well. At least she believed she'd become good at it. If Randy Bristol could be a criminal, anyone could.

"They're usually awake by now," Amy said in an apologetic voice. No doubt she picked up on Kimberly's melancholy tone despite her best efforts to cover it. "Car rides always put them to sleep."

"Right. You mentioned that before and so did Mitch," Kimberly said in a low voice, making a mental note. She wanted to learn all of the ins and outs of the twins' habits. And then it occurred to her that someone was missing. Mitch had said the babysitter would accompany the twins to Colorado. "Where's Joyce?"

"She was scheduled to fly in after we arrived. Mitch didn't want anyone to know the twins were away from home. News travels fast in small towns. Joyce reported to work as usual this morning so no one would be the wiser," Amy informed her.

She shouldn't be surprised that Mitch had thought of everything.

"It's been quiet. Should we try to call Mitch again?" Kimberly turned the phone over a couple of times in her hands. All contact had been broken off and she'd been waiting impatiently for Mitch or Isaac to check in.

"As much as I want to do just that, we should wait for word," Amy said.

"You're right. I know you're right. Not knowing what's going on is hard." Kimberly could only imagine what Mitch had gone through when he'd believed her to be dead. Stabs of guilt jabbed at her stomach over the pain she'd caused.

Looking back at the babies, she couldn't help but wonder if they'd be better off without her in their lives. She seemed to bring pain and sadness to the ones she loved.

"Thank you for being so nice to me after—"

"Don't give it a thought," Amy interrupted.

"Not many people would be willing to pitch in let alone risk their life after what happened, knowing that I lied to them," Kimberly continued, wiping away a stray tear and wondering why the waterworks were springing now? She'd gone eleven months dry as a draught in a Texas summer and it seemed that the floodgates were cracking since she'd returned to the area.

Seeing her babies—and her husband—again had caused the weakness. Distance had made it easier to block everything out, to stuff her emotions down so deep she could get through the day. Feeling dead to the world was an improvement over loneliness and loss.

"I know your situation is...*complicated.* I won't pretend to understand it all. But sticking together, covering each other's backs—it's what family does." The words spoken with such conviction cracked a little more of the casing around Kimberly's heart.

Every last one of them had been part of her family. "I'm sorry for…putting everyone at risk. I was trying to protect the people I love but made a mess instead."

"We all make mistakes," Amy said with a half shrug, like putting Mitch and the children in danger ranked right up there with forgetting to pay the electric bill.

"Mitch won't forgive me," Kimberly confided. "And you shouldn't, either."

"As for me, who said I forgave you?" Amy asked with a wink. She was trying to lighten the mood. She really was wise beyond her years.

"When it comes to Mitch, he'll get over this in time," she conceded. There was so much confidence in her tone.

Could it be that easy? There was no way he could accept what she'd done, but if there was even a chance that he'd accept her as an acquaintance—could she dare hope for something more, like a partner in raising their children?—she'd be overjoyed.

She flashed a smile at Amy.

"It's nice of you to say that but he won't." Under normal circumstances, maybe Mitch could forgive family for an error in judgment. He'd view what she'd done as flat-out betrayal. And he'd be right. There was no mistaking the look in his eyes every time he looked at her now. Well, *almost* every time. There'd been something else leading up to the moment he'd kissed her.

She thought about that kiss, that moment between

them that he'd shut down before feelings could spiral out of control.

They'd "been there, done that" dozens of times. A welcome-home kiss heated up until clothes were in a pile on the floor and they were tangled in the sheets. The memory caused her heart to squeeze. He was right to pull back before they slipped down that path again.

She would've stopped it herself if she hadn't been so caught up in what was happening between them, in the all-consuming, all-too-familiar heat that simmered between them until that one spark ignited an out-of-control flame.

Reality struck her again.

How much time did Kimberly have? Was there even a remote possibility that she could go to jail for her foster father's actions?

The deputy who'd interviewed her had made it clear that he couldn't wait to find evidence linking her to the investigation. If she landed in jail she wouldn't want her children to grow up knowing they had a mother who was behind bars. They would be better off believing that she was dead.

"Hey, it's all going to work out," Amy reassured.

"How do you know what I'm thinking?" Kimberly said, grateful for the attempt to make her feel better.

"You got quiet. Mitch does the same thing. Gets all inside his head with worry and stops talking to everyone," Amy stated.

"I noticed that about him, too." It felt good to remember.

She just hoped that Mitch wasn't lying in a ditch somewhere with Isaac, paying for her foster father's sins. She wasn't sure why she felt the need to confess to Amy. Maybe it was the younger woman's kindness and understanding. She had a down-to-earth quality that belied the money she'd grown up having.

"There's a mess with my father. I really don't know what he got himself into," Kimberly admitted. "He was a good man. I mean, look, he took me in when no one wanted me. I'd already been bounced around in the system. Some bad things happened to me and my younger sister before they split us up. Losing her is probably what made me lose hope in humanity."

"I'm sorry for your loss." Amy's voice held so much reverence. "That couldn't have been easy on either of you. She was all you had left. And none of that was your fault."

"It sure feels like it was," Kimberly admitted.

"You were kids," Amy said with so much sympathy, tears sprang to Kimberly's eyes.

She sniffed them back and faked a cough to cover a sob.

"Getting in trouble with the law was a choice I made, though," she said.

Amy sat quiet with a steady grip on the steering wheel.

"What did you do?"

"It was mostly petty crime, stealing. At first I did it to keep from starving but then I took what I wanted. Candy bars. I'd slip into the movies when people were coming out," Kimberly said.

Amy inclined her head and even though she never broke focus with the road, there was a lot of sympathy and acceptance radiating from her. "No wonder you wanted to keep to yourself when you first showed up."

As much as Kimberly appreciated the kind gesture,

the woman wasn't hearing her. "I'm telling you that there's something broken in me that causes me to hurt people. I take what I want and leave."

It wasn't accurate to the letter but it was close enough to call.

"I hear what you're saying," Amy said after a thoughtful pause. "You might be able to convince yourself that story's true. And that's fine. But I see a strong person who has survived more than any one person should have to endure. That makes you a hero in my book, not a criminal."

Those words, that acceptance, brought out another sob in Kimberly.

"But those things I took. I didn't need them to survive," Kimberly continued, shame a tightrope around her neck, cutting off her oxygen.

"How old were you when this happened?" Amy asked.

The question threw Kimberly off guard. "Eleven, twelve. I don't exactly remember. Old enough to know better."

"When I was twelve I took a candy bar from Tom's Grocer just to see if I could get away with it. Does that make me a criminal?" Amy asked.

"Well, no. You were just being a kid," Kimberly admitted.

"Exactly. I was a good kid by most accounts. I had a good family. My brother went on to become sheriff. I knew right from wrong but I was testing the boundaries," she said. "Let me ask you this. The candy that you stole—you enjoy eating it?"

"Made me sick. I couldn't finish half of one bar," Kimberly said. "Threw the whole lot in a dumpster."

"But there was nothing wrong with the chocolate or any of the other ingredients. The bar wasn't past the expiration," she said.

Kimberly cocked a brow. She couldn't see where this was headed. "It was fresh."

"And have you eaten candy since then without getting sick?" Amy pressed.

"Of course."

"Then it would seem the action made you sick. Not the candy bar. Same thing happened to me. I couldn't enjoy what I'd stolen. I had two bites and wanted to vomit. Had to throw the rest of it away," she said. "I was too embarrassed to admit it to my family or to the owner, Tom. He goes way back with my family. He'd always been good to me. Gave me a summer job. That weighed heavy on my mind for a long time. When I got old enough to start babysitting for relatives, I learned that kids do all kinds of things while they're figuring out who they are. Stealing that candy bar taught me that I'm not a thief. As much as I can't take any of it back, I'm not sure I would if I could. I learned a valuable lesson about myself that day."

Kimberly allowed herself a small smile. She couldn't argue against Amy's logic. It made perfect sense. Her heart leaped at the thought that her actions could be forgiven so easily. She'd always been so hard on herself, she'd never once considered absolving herself of her crimes. A small part of her had believed she'd gotten what she deserved with Olivia and the others. "I guess if I'd really thought about it, I would've come to the same conclusion."

"Which proves you're not a bad person now and you weren't then, either."

Looking at the back seat, at her babies, she wasn't ready to let herself off the hook. She didn't deserve to.

And she was certain that Mitch wouldn't see it the same way. Speaking of whom, where was he and why hadn't he reached out?

Chapter Twelve

"Any word?" Kimberly asked Deputy Hanson as soon as Amy pulled the SUV alongside his in the parking lot of the Dairy Dip. They'd made it to Broward County and the sight of a law enforcement officer on their side was a welcome reprieve. Until Kimberly remembered that her real name was out there and she had no idea if she was wanted for questioning in New Mexico.

"Sheriff wants to fill you in himself," he responded. He was in his early thirties with black hair and brown eyes. He worked out and Kimberly remembered that he liked to talk about his CrossFit training. He wore reflective sunglasses and she didn't like the fact that she couldn't see his eyes.

Did Zach plan to arrest her?

"That can't be good," Kimberly said to Amy.

"They're alive, right?" Amy's voice trembled.

The deputy nodded and she blew out the breath she'd been holding.

"Follow me and I'll get us there in no time," Hanson said, shooting a look of apology before turning on his lights and siren.

The escort got them to the sheriff's office in less than

half an hour. The sirens woke the babies, who cried on and off during the entire ride.

Amy shot a look toward Kimberly as though steeling her resolve. "Let's get these guys changed and fed. I can take Aaron."

Kimberly hopped out of the seat and opened the back door to her daughter, grateful to have this time with her children. The thought that she might be sent away for years sat heavily on her chest as she fumbled with the car seat buckle.

"Like this," Amy said, demonstrating the release valve.

She mimicked her and was holding her daughter within a few seconds. "Thank you."

Amy gave a quick nod. "I got the diaper bag."

Deputy Hanson was already next to Kimberly, ready to escort the women and children into the sheriff's office. Kimberly wondered if his being nice was an act. On second thought, she realized he was being especially nice to Amy. He apparently hadn't gotten the memo that she had feelings for Isaac, which also probably meant that Zach wasn't aware, either.

Once inside she half expected to be arrested.

Instead Zach greeted her with a bear hug after an equally hearty greeting with his baby sister.

Marybeth, his administrative assistant, was on her feet and circling around her desk as soon as she saw Kimberly. The middle-aged single mother had always been so kind to Kimberly. Another stab of guilt penetrated her armor.

"Good to see you, Kimberly," Marybeth said, offering a hug.

Kimberly accepted the kindness.

"Can I help with one of the babies?" Marybeth asked as her phone rang. She shot a look toward Kimberly and held her hands up. "Go on ahead. We're waiting on an important call."

Did that mean there was no word on Mitch and Isaac?

"You don't know how happy I am to see both of you," Zach said, taking Kimberly's arm and ushering her into his office.

One look at Kimberly and he seemed to realize there was no way she was handing over her baby, so he didn't ask.

Amy followed them into his office as the babies fussed.

"Go ahead and take care of the little ones," he instructed. "I'll wait."

Amy went to work, placing Aaron on the sofa and patting the spot next to him.

Kimberly took Amy's suggestion and gently placed Rea next to her brother. The little girl looked up into her mother's eyes and Kimberly felt her heart melt. Rea had the saddest little pout when she wound up to cry. She was heavier than Kimberly had expected.

Babies really did grow fast.

She quickly worked on changing Rea's diaper, hoping to hear news that Mitch and Isaac were all right.

"We can listen and take care of the kids," Kimberly urged with a pleading look.

"Mitch and Isaac are in custody," Zach informed her.

Kimberly gasped. "What did they do wrong?"

"They're safe and that's the most important part," Zach cautioned.

"Agreed." Kimberly shot a worried look toward Amy, who returned it in kind.

Joyce padded in, holding a tray with jars of baby food, along with sippy cups.

Kimberly braced for the older woman to say something mean to her—heck, give her a dirty look. Instead she set the tray down on the coffee table and then hugged her.

"I've missed you so much. It's so good to see you." Joyce used her wrist to wipe away a tear.

The emotions radiating from her children's caregiver were genuine. *She* was genuine. And Kimberly was grateful that such a loving woman had been helping out with the kids in her absence.

"Thank you for everything you've done for my family," Kimberly said to the older woman, and she meant every word.

Joyce acknowledged her with the warmest smile. "I have their favorite foods warmed. I'd be happy to help feed them while you speak to Zach. Or we can set up in the break room if you'd like privacy for grown-up talk."

If she was about to be arrested she certainly didn't want her children seeing that. But she had to believe Zach wouldn't do that in front of the children. He was a good sheriff and an even better man.

Kimberly must've given Joyce a panicked look that reflected exactly how she felt about being apart from her children even for a few minutes, because Joyce immediately proposed a different option.

"Or I could give you a hand right here," she offered.

Zach was already to his feet, calling out to Marybeth for assistance. He'd glanced at his phone more than once; the call he was expecting mustn't have come through.

Once the babies were happily being fed on the sofa,

Zach motioned for Kimberly and Amy to follow him to his desk off to the right-hand side of his office.

He focused a sympathetic look on his sister. "Isaac's in the hospital. He's in surgery to remove a bullet fragment from his neck. I'm waiting for word on his prognosis."

Amy gasped. Her hand came up to her throat like she was trying to stop herself from having a panic attack.

"What happened?" A sob escaped but then she immediately took in a breath, looking like she was reining in her emotions.

"A bullet fragment lodged in his neck, beneath his jaw. He lost enough blood to worry the EMT on the scene," he said before his gaze shifted to Kimberly. "There was an accident."

A gasp escaped before she could suppress it. Her first thought was that the children didn't deserve to lose the only parent they'd known. Mitch was an amazing father. "But he's okay, right?" She searched for any signs of mourning in Zach's eyes. Was that why he wasn't arresting her? He couldn't take both parents away from Rea and Aaron?

Nothing could happen to Mitch. She shook off the thought and refocused.

"How bad is it?"

"Physically, he'll be fine. He has a couple of bruised ribs from the seat belt, which saved both of their lives," Zach said, but there was a note of worry in his voice.

"But?"

"The local sheriff put him under arrest," he said on a sharp sigh.

Amy started pacing. "That's crazy. Why on earth would he do that?"

"It should never have happened but witnesses claimed they were shooting weapons and driving in a manner that endangered others." Zach's hands came up in the surrender position. "I'm waiting for a call back from the governor's office. He owes me a favor and I'm asking that both men be released into my custody. Of course, we'll have to wait until Isaac gets out of surgery before he can be transported nearby."

"What are the chances any of that will happen?" Amy hurled back angry words, quickly reining in her temper when her brother started to respond. "I'm sorry. I shouldn't take my frustration out on you."

"We're all fuming about this," Zach responded and there was no return anger in his voice.

He gave a reassuring look to his sister. He also seemed to realize there was more going on between Isaac and Amy than concern for a friend.

"I'm doing everything in my power to bring him home, Amy," Zach comforted. "If I have to drive there myself and pick him up, I will."

"I know," Amy said. "Between Isaac in surgery and Mitch in jail, I feel like I'm in a nightmare and can't wake up."

Welcome to Kimberly's life, she thought. Seeing the interaction between brother and sister made her think about her sister and how much she missed her.

Tracking her down now that she was old enough for the file to be unsealed would be next to impossible if Rose didn't want to be found.

But this wasn't the time to dwell on her loss. Her losses were racking up and she refused to allow anything to happen to Mitch because of her. Their children needed him. He was the stable one between the two of them.

She had a past that seemed like it would always catch up to her no matter how much she tried to outpace it.

"What about me?" she plucked up enough courage to ask Zach. Bad news was like old fish—it would only smell worse with time. If she was going to be arrested, she wanted to be prepared. "You've looked into my background by now."

"I have." He gave an apologetic look.

"Whatever's in her file can't possibly represent who she is as a person," Amy defended, and Kimberly's heart swelled at the kindness.

Joyce shouted an "Amen" from where she sat on the floor, feeding the babies.

"I realize that," Zach said and his tone sounded offended.

"Glad you do," Joyce interjected. "Any one of us could vouch for her character."

The love and acceptance in the room was beyond anything Kimberly had felt with anyone else but Randy and Julie Bristol.

Grateful tears streamed from her eyes before she could get hold of her emotions. She wiped away a few tears. "You can't know how much all of this means to me."

Kimberly's ringtone sounded. She palmed her cell and immediately checked the screen.

"It's Mitch."

On instinct she spun around to face the corner and lowered her voice when she said, "Hello."

"Where are you?" There was so much concern in Mitch's voice and she wanted it to be for her. He was most likely worried about the babies, which was fair, even though her heart decided to go rogue and wish for the impossible.

"With your cousin at Zach's office. We're all fine. But what happened to you? Zach said you were in an accident." Her words spilled out.

"The Camry knocked the Jeep off the road. We took a spill down the ravine," he said quietly. "A few concerned citizens contacted the local sheriff. Camry driver and his passenger got away. I couldn't leave Isaac on the side of the road and go after them."

"What about Isaac?" she asked. A small sigh of relief slipped out at hearing Mitch's voice and knowing he was alive. She quickly turned to a nervously waiting audience and said, "Mitch is okay."

"By the time the EMTs arrived, Isaac had lost consciousness." She could hear the heaviness in his voice.

"But Isaac's going to be all right, isn't he?" she asked.

"They separated us. He went to the hospital and I'm in lockup," he admitted. "A deputy walked in and handed me my phone. I don't know what's going on and planned to call Zach next to see if he knew."

There was noise in the background and then she heard a male voice.

"Time to go, Kent."

The line went dead.

Chapter Thirteen

"Mitch is fine," Zach said for the fourth time in the past hour. He'd done a little more digging, called in a favor and found out that Isaac was being treated at Broward County General Hospital. They had been waiting for news all night, and finally learned that Isaac was out of surgery and in stable condition, and Zach had been working on getting him transferred to nearby Dawson Memorial Hospital.

Kimberly crossed the room again, making sure to keep a calm demeanor as the babies happily played with their toys in the corner, blissfully unaware of the day's events.

She noticed that Aaron liked objects of all kinds and pretty much everything went in his mouth. Rea wasn't much different except she seemed to delight in books of all sizes and shapes.

Her daughter especially seemed to love one about animals that had fur-like substance on the dog page and other touchy-feely animals. She cooed in delight and chatted in baby talk as she patted a page. Being with her children gave Kimberly strength and focus. She was starting to see a life with them in some way. She had no idea what that might look like just yet but she had to figure out a way to be with them again.

Life without her family made her feel like she was dead already.

Zach's desk phone rang. Marybeth's voice came over his intercom.

"It's Deputy Talisman from Hatch, New Mexico," she said.

Fear struck like stray voltage. Why would he be calling? How would he know where she was?

Zach glanced at Kimberly before walking over and picking up the phone.

After a perfunctory greeting, he said, "Would you mind repeating the name one more time?"

Kimberly prepared herself for what would come next, the same look of condemnation she'd experienced growing up. The judgment. The rejection.

She steeled herself against the pain that would come because she cared what the Kent and McWilliams families thought about her. Her gaze bounced from the door to the twins.

Amy must've been watching because she came over and sat down, taking Kimberly's hand in hers for comfort.

Zach said, "I see," a few times into the receiver.

Every time he spoke, the knot inside Kimberly's stomach tightened. Her fate was sealed and it frustrated her that everything in her life could be taken away again with the click of handcuffs.

Everything but her mind and her willpower, a little voice inside her said. Give up hope and she might as well be dead.

Zach ended the call and she took in a sharp breath.

Instead of talking, he leaned back in his chair. His gaze fixed on a spot on the opposite wall.

"What is it?" Amy asked. "What did the deputy say?"

"I'm pretty certain that I was just threatened," Zach admitted. There was a mix of surprise and anger in his voice.

"Threatened?" Amy repeated, like there was no way it could be true.

"I should probably be shocked," Kimberly said. She wasn't. "You know who I am." Although, in her mind she'd left the past behind and was Kimberly Kent, not Lily Grable. "The question is what are you going to do about it?"

"About you?" he asked. "Nothing. I told Talisman that I haven't seen you. But I have every intention of doing something about him." He turned to face Kimberly. "Tell me what happened in Hatch."

She filled him in on the way she'd been interrogated by Talisman following her foster father's murder.

"I've been in trouble with the law before." She was prepared for judgment and was surprised when she got sympathy instead. "For the record, I was a kid acting out. I'm not that person anymore. Although, there are people who would say a leopard never changes its spots."

Amy patted her hand. "It's brave of you to admit your mistakes to us."

Kimberly's heart nearly burst. She'd experienced that kind of acceptance only with the Bristols.

"You're family," Zach said. "You're one of us now. And a leopard's spots do change from adolescence to adulthood."

Those beautiful words sounded so natural coming out

of his mouth. It convinced her that he believed them as much as she wanted to.

But she didn't want to put him in a bad position. "I know you can't harbor a fugitive."

"The deputy said that you skipped out of town before he could complete an investigation. All he said was that he'd like to talk to you if you showed up in town," Zach said. "He hasn't issued a warrant and was careful not to give away too much information."

"I don't understand the threat," Amy interjected.

"He said that I should be careful with this case. That it was complicated and could come back on me otherwise," he stated. "Those were his exact words."

What did that mean for Mitch and Isaac?

Before she could mount another plea for Zach to make another call to Sheriff Bogart, Mitch's athletic frame filled the doorway. She didn't think about her next actions; she just ran to him. He caught her in his arms and held her tightly against his chest.

For a long moment there were no words. Her eyes welled with tears—a surprising well had sprung in the last hour she'd spent waiting for news about Mitch.

Mitch tipped her chin up.

"It's okay. I'm here." That strong male voice of his reverberated down her neck, arms and spine.

"I was scared something had happen to you." She blinked away the tears blurring her vision and zeroed in on a large piece of gauze taped to his forehead. "What happened?"

"It's a scrape. Treated and released at the scene of the accident." His voice, his confidence, was so reassuring. She'd been a mess since this whole ordeal had begun and she wanted to wrap herself in a blanket of his confidence that everything would magically work out. It was a childish fantasy. "The Jeep rolled and I took a hit from Isaac's toolbox that got knocked loose."

Mitch shifted gears, focusing on Zach. "Any word on Isaac?"

"He's at Broward County General in stable condition," Zach informed him. "I'm working on a transfer."

Mitch kept his arms around Kimberly. He didn't seem to mind the quizzical glances from Amy and Zach. Joyce sat on the floor, playing with the children, and Zach invited Mitch to sit down.

He held tightly to Kimberly as he made his way over to the leather sofa. He made an attempt to bend down to comfort Rea but he winced with the movement and Kimberly realized he was downplaying his injuries.

"I can get her for you," Kimberly offered.

Mitch nodded as he eased onto the sofa. He was most likely still shaken up, and nothing more. He'd be fine once he knew Isaac was headed home.

"A deputy drove me over. I would've called to let you know we were on the way but he kept my cell until he parked out front. Marybeth signed the paperwork and then shooed him away the minute I'd been handed over. I'm technically in protective custody, pending a grand-jury investigation into the case," Mitch said as he locked gazes with Zach. "Thank you for getting me out of there."

"The charges won't stick. Sheriff Bogart should've dropped them altogether." Zack shook his head. "He's being a mule."

"That reminds me. I owe a call to Harley," Mitch said and Kimberly recognized the family attorney's name.

"He'll see to it Bogart focuses on finding the bad guys

instead of wasting his time with me," Mitch continued. "A name came up. Ever hear of anyone called Baxter?"

Everyone's gaze shot to Kimberly.

"Never heard the name before." She shrugged.

"I got a partial description of the men in the Camry when I overheard a deputy talking."

Kimberly had never gotten close enough to the men chasing her for an accurate description. Her heart hammered her ribs.

Zach perked up at the news.

The thought of putting faces to the male figures frightened her.

"One of the males has light blond hair. He was described as being short." But then Mitch would most likely already know that since he'd seen him at the medical plaza. "Maybe five feet eight inches. He's built like a male gymnast according to witness accounts. The other one is a couple of inches taller but definitely shorter than six-feet tall. He has black hair and a runner's build. Both are being considered armed and dangerous—obviously. The sheriff informed his deputy that he's about to put out a bulletin that both are wanted for fleeing the scene of an accident. Both were wearing aviator sunglasses and hoodies. Similar to when I saw them in the plaza."

"What plaza?" Zach asked.

Mitch brought his cousin up-to-date.

The descriptions weren't much more than they already knew. She stared blankly at the wall.

"You've never seen the men before they started following you?" Zach asked, striking his keyboard with decisive finger strokes.

"No," she responded. "Wish I knew who they were.

My father didn't say anything about new people hanging around, either."

"Fair enough." Zach paused. "Nothing about the descriptions strikes a familiar chord? Nor does the name Baxter?"

"No. I doubt there's any trace of this guy. He wiped out my father's business with a fire, no doubt to cover any documentation of their business transactions," she informed him.

"People use fires to cover tracks. They also use them to cover crimes," Zach stated.

"I do feel like my foster father's truck-rental business is key. I mean why burn it down otherwise in either case," Kimberly said. Without a criminal case pending there was no way for Zach to get more information. No agency cared about her foster father's death.

"I haven't gotten any bulletins in the system," Zach said.

"Do you think Bogart's involved?" she asked.

"Based on his reputation, he's not playing both sides of the law. He could be scared, though," Zach admitted.

That made two of them, she thought.

"Tell me more about your parents. What kind of people were they?" Zach questioned. He had to know it was a dead end but she appreciated the effort he was making. And he was most likely just killing time while he waited for a hit in the system.

"Mom was incredible. She volunteered at my school when I came to live with them. She'd been working full-time on Dad's business and said it was a nice change to have something else to focus on. She said I was good company even though we both knew it was a lie when I first came to live with them. Dad was a rock. He was always lending someone his personal vehicle if they didn't have money to pay for one of his rentals. Mom used to say he had a heart of gold. She was right." It was nice to refer to him as Dad again, like she'd begun calling him junior year of high school. She'd bought him one of those super-cheesy #1 Dad coffee mugs from her part-time job selling pretzels at a kiosk in the mall. He'd teared up when he opened the present. Then he'd surprised her by asking if she'd like to call him by that name instead of Randy. She'd shocked herself by saying she would. They'd both had a good cry that Christmas morning. Her foster mother, Julie, had joined in, wrapping both of them in a warm embrace. It was then that their family seemed to click. Life seemed easier and Kimberly felt like she belonged somewhere for the first time in her life. Tears streamed down her cheeks at the memories. When she shook off the reverie and looked up, everyone in the room had become intensely interested on what was in front of them or in their lap.

She cleared her throat, swiped at a few stray tears and continued, "They put up with me and acted like my antics were no trouble."

"What kind of antics?" Zach asked but there was no judgment in his voice like she'd expected to hear.

"Flunking a history test so hard it should've been embarrassing after my mom had spent the entire night studying with me." Kimberly looked toward the window that bathed the room in sunlight. "I expected her to lose her temper with me after that. Maybe grab a switch from outside like so many others had. I knew that material inside and out." She paused. "All she did when I walked through the back door after school was hug me, hand me a bowl of chocolate ice cream and tell me I'd get the hang of taking tests."

"Sounds like an amazing woman," Mitch said with so much reverence, goose bumps raised on Kimberly's arms.

"She was. The best." Kimberly had to suppress a sob. She could admit to still getting emotional about her mother's death. Kidney disease had been a slow, painful way to go. A woman who was so…*good*…didn't deserve to die like that.

Kimberly's being there by her mother's side as she left the world was the only consolation. The two had held hands until her mother's had gone slack.

"I didn't stop there. I guess I wanted to prove by that point that I was as unlovable as I felt," she admitted.

"It's normal for teens to test the boundaries," Zach said. "With your background, I'm surprised your behavior didn't get a whole lot worse."

"It did." Admitting this next part—the part about being a criminal—hurt. But the family had been so kind to her and they deserved to know everything at this point. "I broke into a neighbor's barn with a guy I'd been sneaking out to see. He seemed so tough, like he could handle anything. He'd made a trip to juvie and I thought he could teach me how to live in the real world and show the Bristols there was no saving me. Mark coaxed me into taking a couple drinks of beer. At least, that's what I thought it was. Turns out he'd laced it with that popular date-rape drug. Thankfully the owner came home and caught him before he could follow through on…"

Kimberly looked down, trying to get a handle on her emotions.

"…his *plans*."

"How old were you when this happened?" Mitch asked. His voice was a low rumble of anger.

"Fifteen," she answered. "My fosters pleaded for leniency and the judge must've been feeling good that day because he let me off with time served after my arrest and three years of probation. He wouldn't have had to do anything, though. I was so freaked out by the whole experience when I realized that Mark could've done anything he wanted to me. I never wanted to be that vulnerable again." She glanced at Mitch. "Which is the reason I didn't want champagne on our wedding day. I can't stand alcohol."

"You could've told me before, Kimberly," he said and his voice was soft this time. "I would've understood."

She needed to change the subject or she might get lost in that same sense of comfort that had caused her to make so many mistakes in her life recently. Even with the Bristols she'd never felt the sense of home that she did when she was with Mitch. He was her true north. But letting herself get lost in that feeling again would be a mistake. Even if her current situation could be cleared up—which she highly doubted would happen with her still being alive—what would happen next? Something had always come along to mess up the scarce few good situations in her life.

She also needed to change the subject before she got wrapped up in the warm sensations that would cloud her judgment when the time came to split again.

"Why would Sheriff Bogart suspect you had anything to do with what was going on?" Kimberly asked Mitch, picking up Rea and moving to the sofa. She set the baby in between her and Mitch. The feeling of being a family overwhelmed her. It all seemed so natural. The three of them sitting on the sofa together. But it wouldn't last; it *couldn't* last.

Mitch and Zach exchanged knowing glances. What was that all about?

"Mr. Clean would be jealous of your spotless criminal record," she added.

"Not important." Mitch glanced at her so quickly, she almost didn't catch it.

And then it dawned on her why.

"It's because of me, isn't it?" she asked. "He suspects you because of my criminal background."

"It doesn't matter," he said, focusing on Rea. Her daughter was innocent and beautiful and full of potential.

Birds of a feather, she thought. Mitch was most likely arrested because of his association with her. Her reputation would damage her innocent children's lives. They'd be better off never knowing her than to be hemmed into that same box as she'd been her whole life and *would* be for her entire existence.

"That's not fair to you. You had no idea what was going on. That's part of why I never told you anything. Exactly so you would never be put in this position." She reminded herself to calm down for Rea's and Aaron's sakes. Her past would follow her for the rest of her life, tainting everyone around her. When word got out about her faking her death and her involvement with this Baxter person—whoever he turned out to be—her children would be labeled, too. Anger churned through her. It wasn't fair. People made mistakes. Why was it so hard to shuck the past and start fresh?

"I'm sorry," she whispered.

"No need to apologize," he said quickly. "It is what it is."

That might be true. But her presence dragged down the good Kent family name—a name she wanted her children to be proud of precisely because of the one she'd been given.

The name Grable was most often associated with unemployment, get-rich-quick scams and deceit.

No matter how right it felt to be with Mitch and their children in the moment, Kimberly's background would always be an albatross around their necks.

If she stuck around.

Chapter Fourteen

"We have to get the babies to a safe place and get out of here," Kimberly said in a whisper to Mitch. He was confused by the changes in her. When he'd first arrived she'd practically thrown herself into his arms. Now she was keeping her distance.

She was suddenly acting strange toward him, sending mixed signals. He couldn't ask her what was going on outright. She seemed too aware of everyone else in the room. Her occasional longing look toward one of the babies had him concerned. He was thankful she seemed to want to include him in the plans she was cooking up. Mitch wondered if the others in the room were picking up on her increasing anxiety.

"Or we could let the law do its job and find out who murdered your foster father," he said quietly.

"How did it feel to be interrogated like a common criminal?" she responded.

"It wasn't a trip to the State Fair but that *is* part of a law-enforcement investigation. At times innocent people have to put up with being inconvenienced while the investigator gets to the bottom of what's really going on." Based on her reaction so far, it seemed like there was more to the question than she was letting on. "Why?"

"Long story," she said a little too defensively. So there was something to his suspicion.

Since she seemed determined to shut him out, he decided to bring up the subject again later.

"Think Zach's finding anything?" she asked, her hands twisted together.

"We'll know soon enough." On closer examination she looked wiped out. Dark circles cradled her brown eyes. She looked like she'd spent the last couple of hours on the edge of her seat and her exhaustion was starting to show.

Mitch took her hand in his to reassure her, ignoring the frissons of heat the contact produced. "We'll sort this mess out and I'll be right here until the end."

Kimberly sat there, still, for a long moment. Was he getting through? She had so many layers of defense built up. So much more than when he'd first met her.

"You shouldn't make promises that you can't keep," she said after a thoughtful pause. "And now I've put everyone in danger. I shouldn't be here."

Then she stood up and crossed the room without looking back.

Zach walked over to Mitch.

"She'll come around," Zach said, taking a seat next to his cousin.

To what?

What would she be coming around to? Joint custody? Friendship? Something more? Trust was big in Mitch's book and she'd obliterated theirs.

She'd had her reasons and, he could admit, most of them had to do with him and their children. Put in her shoes, would he have done the same thing?

No, he wouldn't. But then he'd grown up with a huge

support network and more people who had his back than he could count.

What had she grown up with?

Parents who weren't fit and had abandoned her before she was old enough to fend for herself. Heartache from losing the only sister she'd ever known and had tried to protect. Then there was a string of people who'd let her down in the years when she needed stability the most. There'd been others who'd taken advantage of her and used her as a workhorse, abused her. She'd been through hell and back when he'd had the love and support of five siblings, two cousins and two of the best parents a kid could hope for.

Had life been easy for the Kents?

Hell no. They suffered the same as everybody else. People they loved died just like everyone else. They experienced the world as everyone did—heartaches and happiness.

They'd been brought up to know the value of a hard day's work, that money bought food and other necessities—not necessarily happiness—and that they could always count on one another when life handed them hard times.

He examined Kimberly and wondered if she'd ever be able to break down the walls she'd constructed to protect herself.

Then again what exactly was he offering her?

"Jordan called to see if I'd heard from you," Zach said.

"I need to call home and let the rest of my brothers know I'm all right," Mitch conceded. He'd been wrapped up in trying to figure out what was going on and hadn't checked in with any of his brothers. Of course, everyone would be worried by now. He could kick himself for not thinking about his family. His heart wanted to argue that his family was right here in the room with him. And that part was true. Kimberly was the mother of his children. She would always be connected to him. Family.

Thinking of the ranch brought up the issue of the heifer.

"Have you made any progress on the investigation at the ranch?" he asked his cousin.

Zach shook his head. "My first thought was teenagers playing a cruel prank."

"They'd have to be pretty damn twisted to think that was funny."

"Or on something that distorted reality," Zach agreed.

"Jacobstown's never had a drug problem." Mitch arched a brow.

"Not prior to this, if that's what we're dealing with," Zach stated.

"But that's not what you think now?"

"Town's in an uproar. Social media has been going crazy with speculation. Everything from high teenagers passing through from Fort Worth to a cult traveling in the area," Zach admitted. "There's no shortage of speculation on who or what might've been involved. A few have pointed toward an illegal trapper."

"I'm guessing you're not refuting the claim," Mitch said.

"No. I'd rather folks go down that trail than some of the others, which have them ready to break out pitchforks and take shifts guarding Main Street," Zach said with an eye roll.

"People can get carried away," Mitch agreed.

"Thing is the only tracks leading up to the heifer belong to you and Lone Star," Zach continued.

"Seems strange that you couldn't find anything else," Mitch said.

"I did. I found marks leading away from the scene," Zach stated.

"What kind of *marks*?"

"Like a tree limb being used to brush over someone's tracks." Zach ground his back teeth. "Might be nothing. Old. There's evidence teenagers have been slipping onto your property to hike."

"Nothing new there," Mitch said, but his mind was flipping over possibilities.

"Everyone's on guard right now. At the very least they're seeing this as a bad omen," Zach informed him.

"Could've been an illegal trapper," Mitch said after a thoughtful pause. That area was his brother's responsibility. "Will checks the fences on that side of the property. Maybe he was near and spooked the guy who then covered his tracks as he bailed."

"I'll keep my eyes peeled the same," Zach mentioned.

"We'll keep on the extra security we hired just in case there's foul play," Mitch said.

"Good idea."

Zach informed Mitch of his offer to take the babies, along with Joyce, to his house.

"Is Kimberly aware?" Mitch asked. It should be strange to include someone else in the decision-making process when it came to his children. It wasn't.

"Yes. She wanted to ask your opinion about it," Zach answered.

Amy came over and sat next to Mitch.

"Kimberly okay?" she asked before correcting herself. "Never mind that question. How could anyone be sane under the circumstances?"

He nodded in agreement.

"I just spoke to Isaac," she said, and he could tell she was trying to keep her tone as even as possible. Her eyes were brighter, though. She chanced a glance toward her brother. "He's going to be released from the hospital and into my brother's custody tomorrow."

"He should probably stay at my place while he heals," Zach offered.

"Knowing Isaac, he has an opinion on the matter," Mitch said. He shot an apologetic look in Amy's direction. "He's been seen around town with Hailey Jepson. She might want to weigh in, too."

Amy needed to know, but Mitch didn't like being the one to give her the heads-up about Isaac's personal business. It was better she hear the news from family, though.

Aaron fussed, throwing the toy that had been keeping him occupied.

"I'll go help Kimberly," Amy said. She couldn't get to her feet fast enough after Mitch's revelation. Again, he hated to be the one to inform her but he didn't want her to think she had another chance with Isaac if she didn't. Mitch had it on good authority Isaac was seeing Hailey now. He had no idea how serious the relationship was. He'd been out of the loop on most issues since inheriting the ranch and losing Kimberly. But Amy deserved to know what she was up against.

One thing was certain.

Relationships were tricky as hell.

Speaking of which, Kimberly was on her way over to Mitch and Zach.

She stopped in front of Mitch.

"What do you think about the babies staying with your cousin temporarily?" she asked.

"He'll take care of them. Make sure they're safe," Mitch stated.

Zach nodded.

"Then how about you and me get out of here." She made a show of yawning. "I'm beat and I can't think straight anymore. I just had another cup of coffee and I could've been drinking water for the effect it had. I need to grab a couple hours of sleep. What about you?"

It was pretty obvious to Mitch, and most likely Zach, that she was making the move she'd been in the corner contemplating for the past hour.

"I can use a few hours of shut-eye," he admitted, curious as to where she was planning to go with this. There was a corrupt deputy in Hatch. He was pretty damn sure of that. How far up the chain did the deception go?

Mitch had a feeling they'd figure it out soon enough because Kimberly had that focused look in her eye.

"Then, let's take off."

KIMBERLY PINCHED THE bridge of her nose to stem the raging headache threatening to crack her skull in half. The plan to leave the babies in Zach's care and get away from Jacobstown was solid. The borrowed truck from his cousin Zach wasn't as comfortable as the SUV but should keep them both under the radar. She leaned her head against the headrest and started counting exit signs. "Do you think the babies will do okay without you there? You've been the steady force in their lives."

"The whole family plans to check in with them. Joyce will be there 24/7. They'll be surrounded by people who love them," Mitch said.

"It's not the same as having you there," she countered. The idea that her babies had so many wonderful people to depend on warmed her inside and out. No matter how much she wanted to be the one who put her kids to bed every night, she realized that might not be possible. Not if Baxter got what he wanted. It was clear that he wanted something from her. What would happen if he got it? She doubted a criminal would let her live long enough to be a witness no matter how much she pleaded.

"There'll be no shortage of folks to fuss over them." His tone was certain while she was churning like a blender inside.

"Will they be able to sleep somewhere besides their own beds?" she asked, picking up her cell and then turning it over and over in her hands. She couldn't risk having photos of them on her phone in case those jerks got to her. She'd envied all the mothers she'd come across in the past eleven months with prominent pictures of their children as their wallpaper. In conversation, which she'd avoided as much as possible, she'd had to lie about having babies of her own.

Since she was on the run and her heart belonged to Mitch anyway, dating had been out of the question. *Everything* about a normal life was out of bounds in the life she'd been living.

"You saw them in the SUV. They'll do fine at Zach's," he said and there was a hint of sympathy in his voice.

Snapping them into their child seats in Zach's personal vehicle had caused her heart to beat in painful stabs. The air had thinned. She couldn't breathe. She'd blame it on the humidity thickening the air but all the threatening clouds had cleared up after a brief shower and it had been sunny ever since.

"If you say so." She had no personal experience to draw on with the twins when it came to their sleep schedules. The last time she'd put them to bed they woke every four to six hours to feed.

They'd be safe at Zach's, a little voice in the back of her head reassured. At least she could count on that much.

"Mind if we change the subject?" Mitch asked, and she appreciated his thoughtfulness.

"Go ahead."

"What do you really think happened with your dad?" he asked. "Deep down."

"Gut level?" she asked.

"Yes. What do your instincts tell you?" he pressed.

"I can't prove it, but I know he wouldn't do anything illegal or immoral. The man once drove an hour in one of his rentals to buy a refrigeration system so he could deliver food to a town that had been hit hard by layoffs, all of which came out of his pocket. If a store clerk accidentally gave him too much change or forgot to charge for an item, he'd turn around and go back. I mean, seriously, he'd turn around for fifty cents so the cashier would balance all right at the end of the night. So whatever was going on I'm thinking that he couldn't have really known about it," she informed him. "He could've been mixed up in a crime accidentally or seen something he shouldn't have. In which case no one should be looking at me."

"Unless they're thinking the same thing and figuring you might've gotten him involved in some kind of trouble," he reasoned. His point was valid.

"I might've made mistakes as a kid but it shouldn't be difficult for an investigator to figure out that my life has been clean since junior year of high school," she said a little defensively. No matter how well she'd been living her life since then it was still hard to talk about the person she'd been. Thinking back to the manner in which the investigator had grilled her made even more sense. "Disappearing most likely didn't help matters."

"We already know there hasn't been a warrant issued for your arrest. We have a name. Baxter. And Zach is knee-deep in the investigation," Mitch offered.

"Which means more people are in jeopardy because of me," she said on a sharp sigh.

"People are in jeopardy because of a criminal," Mitch interjected. "My cousin deals with bad people on a daily basis. He knows how to handle himself."

At least he knew to be careful and take the threat seriously.

Mitch shot a quick look of apology before focusing on the stretch of highway ahead. "Did he and your mother take in other foster kids?"

"None that I know of. I never asked and there weren't any pictures around," she said. "Seems like there would have been some evidence."

"Sounds like the kind of guy who'd give the shirt off his back if someone needed it," Mitch said.

"He was." She thought about the young guy who'd shown up at the back door on her last visit to her father's office. "Maybe this all had to do with someone my father was trying to help." Was it wishful thinking? Or had he crossed the line? The more she thought about the man Randy Bristol had been the less him being a criminal made sense. "There was this guy. I never really got a good look at his face or maybe I just wasn't really paying attention. He was in his late teens, maybe early twenties. Thin. He had long hair that he kept in a messy braid. Think I heard my dad call him Tonto once. Have no idea what it meant."

"Do you remember the name of your caseworker when you were in the system?" he asked.

"Absolutely. Old Train-wreck Turner. I got lucky with the Bristols. Train-wreck placed me in some nightmare homes before them. She didn't care where I ended up." She glanced at him in time to see his fist tighten around the steering wheel.

"She still live in the area where you grew up?"

"It's possible." She shrugged. "Been a long time since I've been home, and I lost contact with her the minute I turned eighteen."

"I'm guessing that was on purpose," he stated.

"Didn't see a point keeping in touch with someone I couldn't trust or stand," she admitted.

"Take my phone out of the cup holder and text her name to Zach if you don't mind," he said.

She palmed his cell and entered the password he'd supplied, noticing that he'd changed it from her birthday to the twins'.

Everything else on the home screen looked the same as the last time she'd used his phone, so it was easy to navigate.

Zach replied almost immediately to the text with a thumbs-up icon and a promise to get back to them ASAP.

"He's on it, but I doubt she'll be any help. She was pretty old and has most likely retired since then."

"Let's hope for an address by morning," Mitch said. Then he added, "Might want to tell him about Tonto."

"Okay." It was most likely nothing but it couldn't

hurt. She entered everything she could recall about Tonto. "Done."

Another thumbs-up icon popped onto the screen.

Mitch took the next exit and then followed GPS on his phone to the nearest cash-based motel.

After parking on the opposite-side lot and doing a quick check-in that required no ID, she followed him into room number six. The external door leading straight to the east-facing parking lot wasn't ideal from a security standpoint but paying in cash was more important since it didn't leave a digital trail.

The room was typical for the price. Two well-used mattresses topping a pair of full-size beds were separated by a small nightstand. There was a lamp, notepad and pen, and landline telephone sitting on top. If Kimberly had to bet, there'd be a Bible in the drawer.

"Shower's in the back." Mitch pointed to the only place it could be.

Ten minutes later she came out wearing a towel. Mitch handed her a toothbrush and toothpaste, which was manna from heaven at this point.

"Do I want to ask where you got these?" She made eyes at him.

"It's okay. They're fine. Came from camping supplies in the trunk of the SUV," he said.

She must've scrubbed her teeth for five minutes.

"There's a clean T-shirt on the bed. It's mine but you're welcome to it," he practically growled as he passed her and his low rumble of a voice sent sensual skitters across her skin. She recognized that tone, and intense, hungry, passionate sex usually followed.

Suddenly aware of just how little material covered her, she gripped the knot on her towel to secure it.

An exhale of relief followed as he kept walking, because being this close to the only man she'd given her heart to was its own hell. Add the sexual chemistry that constantly pinged between them and it was draining to keep fighting what her body deemed as the most natural thing.

As she walked past him, he caught her arm. She stopped and faced him.

"Where'd you go last year?" There was so much emotion present in his eyes. A mix of hurt, anger and something else…something much more primal simmered between them. *Hunger.*

Letting the chemistry between them rule would be a huge mistake and yet her feet were planted.

"We should get some sleep." The words sounded hollow even to her.

She couldn't.

"Kimberly." That one word was spoken so loaded with emotion that her breath caught.

Heat ricocheted between them as they stood this close, barely more than a foot apart. Where his fingers touched her forearm, tingles of uncapped sexual energy pulsed.

"It's better for both of us if I don't say where I've been hiding out."

"Why? Because you plan to disappear again when it gets tough? Use those same places to hide?"

She turned her face away, not wanting to look at him. "Maybe."

"On our wedding day, did you mean those vows or were they just empty words to you?" No emotion was present in his voice now and she couldn't read him when she glanced up.

She should lie. Tell him what he seemed to need to hear. That it was all a fake and she'd never loved him.

She couldn't.

"Yes."

"Then why didn't you trust me enough to tell me the truth?" he asked.

"Because you would've gone all cowboy code on me and tried to fix my problems," she shot back, feeling anger rise in her chest.

"Isn't that what married people do? Face down trouble together? Stick by each other's side?"

"Yes. But—"

"Never mind." There was so much finality in those words. "Get some sleep."

Kimberly wished there was some way to tell him she was sorry for the past, a way that didn't feel like an insult to his pride.

She couldn't.

So she stood on tiptoe, wrapped her arms around his neck and kissed him.

Mitch pulled back. His eyes were closed. His mental debate was written across the stress cracks on his forehead.

"I'm not trying to cause more pain," she said in a low voice. "I just missed this. I missed you so much I didn't think I could breathe. And I'm tired of fighting against what my body wants when you're anywhere near me."

"We cross that line and I can't undo that," he said, pressing his forehead to hers.

"Do you want me, Mitch?" She tugged the knot on the towel free and let the cotton material drop to the floor.

Standing there, naked, in front of the man her body craved should feel awkward. She should be embarrassed about her body like she'd always been before Mitch. But this was Mitch. He was her husband. And though a piece of paper had declared her dead, she was very much alive. Very much a woman. Very much reacting to the sexy male standing in front of her.

"That's not the right question to ask." His warm breath sensitized her skin. He brought his hands up to her hips, where they rested on either side of her body. Contact sent currents of heat coursing through her body, seeking an outlet.

"Then, what is?"

Chapter Fifteen

Mitch trailed his fingers up the sides of Kimberly's hips in a lazy *S* curve. He took in a sharp shot of air before he ran his flat palm against her belly—the place that had given him two beautiful children. She had more curves since giving birth and her skin was milky-soft perfection. *She* was perfection.

Kimberly's hands went to the snap of his jeans. His hands joined hers and a few seconds later his jeans joined her towel on the floor. He shrugged out of his T-shirt next and then she helped him take off his boxers.

"I thought I'd lost you for good," he said, hearing the huskiness in his own voice.

"I'm here, Mitch." The sound of his name rolling off her tongue was the sweetest damn sound he'd heard. Hell, he should be angry right now. He couldn't be if he tried. His feelings ran too deep. He'd missed her too much.

There she was, standing right in front of him.

Consequences be damned—he couldn't let himself care about the fallout from doing one of the most basic human needs—making love to his wife.

Mitch took a step toward her. He took her hands in his and braided their fingers.

A beat later, she pressed her body to his. Their hands broke apart but made immediate contact with skin. Her flat palm went against his chest, her fingers running along the ridges of his pecs.

One of his hands found her chin and lifted it to better angle her mouth toward his. He took his sweet time kissing her even though his body cried out with urgency. He had no plans to rush this moment. He'd waited too long, wanted it too much. There were split seconds where he thought this couldn't be real, *she* couldn't be real.

Mitch wrapped his hands around her waist and pulled her body flush with his. Skin-to-skin contact caused his erection to strain. Urgency escalated but he was a disciplined man. Or so he thought until her hands tunneled through his hair and her sweet tongue darted inside his mouth.

He needed to think about something else besides the soft feel of her creamy skin and her quickening breath that matched his own. No way was he allowing this to be over before he could really get started.

An attempt to focus on the paperwork that needed to be done at the ranch when he returned lasted two seconds. *Way to crush being in control, Mitch.*

He trailed his fingers along her soft curves until he palmed her nipples. They pebbled with contact. He rolled them around between his thumb and forefinger and then swallowed her sounds of pleasure.

Kisses intensified. Hands searched. Pleasure mounted.

Kimberly opened her eyes, caught his stare and then said, "Make love to me, Mitch."

He picked her up and she wrapped her legs around

his midsection. He carried her the couple of steps to the bed before setting her down and dropping to his knees.

Before he could locate a condom, she'd wrapped her fingers around his shaft and was guiding him inside her. "We better hold on a second."

He didn't want to stop this but had to.

After fishing an old condom out of his wallet, he returned a few seconds later and she helped roll it down his shaft. She bucked her hips—she was ready for him—until he reached deep inside her. Her eyes were wild with passion when she looked up at him. He drove himself inside her, hard and fast, as he gripped both sides of her hips, digging his fingers into her sexy round bottom. She moaned and rocked harder on his erection, driving him to the brink.

His mouth found hers and his tongue slid inside her mouth, searching for the sweet honey there.

He tightened his arms around her beautiful body and bucked deeper inside her sex. She matched him stride for stride.

Urgency built, demanding release.

Mitch slowed his pacing for a second, trying to gain control, but it was useless with his wife in his arms, bodies melting together as her internal muscles quivered around his stiff erection.

Her breathing quickened and she bucked harder and faster until their bodies were a frenzy of electric impulses.

He detonated a few seconds after he was certain that her body was drained.

Instead of relaxing, she rode a second wave with him as his body exploded with sexual impulses.

She pulled him down on top of her as they caught their breath.

Quietly, in barely a whisper, he said into her ear, "I never stopped loving you, Kimberly."

KIMBERLY JOLTED AWAKE out of deep sleep. It took a second to get her bearings. She realized that she was in a motel room an hour from the New Mexico border.

Rolling onto her side, she felt around the bed. The room was dark. No doubt the blackout curtains were still drawn but she had no idea what time it was.

Mitch was gone.

Reaching out, her hand landed on an object. It crinkled. Paper? She reached onto the nightstand next to the bed and located her phone.

Using the flashlight app, she picked up the note.

Be right back. M

The door burst open, causing her to jump.

Mitch hustled inside, locking the door behind him and flipping on the light. "Time to get up. We gotta go."

"What is it?" she asked, already to her feet and gripping her phone so hard that she noticed her knuckles had gone white.

"Baxter's creeps are here."

She muttered a curse as she jumped into action, throwing on clothes and gathering what little supplies they had as she tossed them into the backpack.

"What are we going to do?" she asked.

"Get out of here alive." He ate up the space between them in a couple of strides, took the backpack from her and shouldered it.

He took her hand—and this wasn't the time to think about where they stood romantically, but it did flash across her mind—and gave a quick squeeze. Her heart practically danced from the look in his eye when he made eye contact with her. Things had changed. She didn't know what that meant yet but it was a sign things were moving in the right direction between them.

"How do you plan to do that?" she whispered.

"They found our vehicle, but not us," he stated.

"So they're on the opposite side of the parking lot?"

He nodded as he opened the door and led her outside. The sun was breaking against the horizon and during this time of year that meant it had to be around 7:00 a.m.

There was a Denny's restaurant next door to the motel and a crossroad to the highway.

"We get out of sight long enough for the area to clear and we get the vehicle back. Or we make a new plan." He nodded toward a cluster of warehouse-looking buildings across the road. "For now our best chance is to find a place to get out of sight before they figure out which room we've been in."

The sound of a window breaking crashed through the quiet morning, save for the occasional car on the highway whooshing by. They could hear the noise but could not see the road.

With the creeps closing in Kimberly was grateful the babies were safe with Zach and Amy and nowhere near the motel. A thought struck that if anything went down, both of their parents could be dead. She crouched down low—trying to squash any such possibility—as Mitch did and followed him across the road toward the row of buildings, unsure what frightened her more—the thought of dying or living without her family.

Nothing could happen to either one of them. The twins deserved to grow up with both parents.

"Mitch," Kimberly said as they cleared the road and got closer to the cluster of buildings. "I'm truly sorry for everything I've put you through. Loving you was the most selfish thing I've ever done."

"Loving someone else isn't selfish," he countered, and she was surprised at how quickly he'd responded.

"It is for me. I've done nothing but hurt you and I must've known on some level that I would," she said.

He didn't answer right away as they rounded the corner of a building and he stood upright.

Mitch spun around, looped his hands around her waist and tugged her toward him. He captured her lips with his. When he'd kissed her so thoroughly that her knees almost buckled he pulled back and said, "You tried to warn me. I didn't want to hear you. You brought me back to life, made me feel something deeper than I've ever felt before. If anyone's to blame, it's me. You told me there was no room in your life for me, and I took advantage of the fact that you wanted this as much as I did."

"You couldn't have known about...*this*." She waved her arm toward the motel.

"No. But I've never felt more alive than when I'm with you. I just don't know what that means when all this is over. I'm questioning how I could let my feelings run out of control with someone I never really knew in the first place." Mitch had grown up in Jacobstown and lived on the family ranch his whole life. She could see where falling for a stranger would throw him off. But those last words were daggers to her heart because she felt like she knew him. It was odd, really, but she felt like they'd had this deep connection from day one. The kind that made her feel like she knew him at the most intimate level even though he was right that they didn't know basic facts about each other, like family medical history. But then again she didn't know her parents' medical history, either. Mitch would know his. His parents had been the bedrock of the community. From everything she knew they had been decent, upstanding people who'd loved their children.

"We should find a place to hunker down until the coast is clear," Mitch finally said.

He managed to find an unlocked vehicle and they slipped into the cab of the pickup. He closed and locked the door behind them before opening a small box underneath the dashboard.

"What are you doing?" she asked.

"Checking to see if I can hot-wire this thing if there's no other option," he admitted. He played around with something she couldn't quite see before he repositioned himself to cover her.

It was light outside. If anyone came near the truck they'd see one or both of them. But this was the best they had to work with at the moment. There were steel doors on the warehouses with similar-looking loading docks. None would be easy to break in to.

"I'm sorry that I lied to you about my parents," she said in a low voice. "I was embarrassed to admit that I don't really know who they are. All I was ever told was that I was left in that parking lot and when no one claimed me and my sister, we were dumped into the system. I was seven years old. Now, I have no idea where they are or what they're doing. I don't even know if they're alive. I don't want to care either way but I guess I'm curious about my past. Where I come from. My caseworker tried to keep my sister and I together for as long as possible, or so she said. But when one of my foster dads knocked my little sister into the wall for chewing her food too loudly I lost it."

"That couldn't have gone well for you," he said and his voice was steady, unreadable.

"He said I was violent and they believed him over me. His wife lied to my caseworker, saying that I'd become too hard to handle but that Rose was still okay. She never cried. Not when one of them was listening. I heard her at night when the lights were turned out. She'd sniffle for hours. Sometimes I'd crawl into her bed but that was dangerous because I got in trouble if I didn't stick to my own. And some nights, I'd be so tired that I'd fall asleep. Those lead to bad days," she said. All those memories bearing down on her like heavy weights pressing against her chest made it hard to breathe.

"No child should be treated that way," he said. His voice was low but there was palpable anger in it. "Did you ever ask about your parents?"

"No. What would be the use? They didn't want me." She heard the hurt in her own voice even though she'd spent years building up walls that made it impossible to feel when she thought about her past.

"History, for one," he said. "The truth, for another."

"I know everything I need to about them. They rejected me." A few tears welled in her eyes but she refused to let them fall.

"How can you be certain?" he asked.

"Because they left me behind at a strip mall with my sister. They took off and didn't look back. They just left me and my sister and that was it." She heard the defensiveness in her tone.

Mitch got quiet, like he did when he was angry.

"I'm sorry you went through that, Kimberly. You deserved better."

She kept her voice low so he wouldn't hear.

"That's where you're wrong. *You* deserved better."

Chapter Sixteen

Mitch heard voices. The men were coming. He silently cursed for not thinking to bring his shotgun. He'd kept all of his weapons locked up since the babies had arrived for safety's sake.

"Hey, Ron," one of the men said. "They have to be here somewhere. We're not leaving without her."

"The spotter's sure it was them?" Ron responded.

"Bet his mother's life on it," the other creep said.

"Baxter's none too thrilled she's gotten away this long," Ron said.

Spotter? Rental vans and trucks. A picture was emerging that caused Mitch to grind his back teeth in anger. Those elements added up to human traffickers. Hatch, New Mexico, being situated near the Mexican border, was the perfect gateway.

Based on the picture Kimberly portrayed of her foster father, he didn't seem the type to be involved in a human-trafficking ring—a ring that could be paying the local sheriff's deputy to look the other way. Pinning their crime on an innocent woman could provide cover. Tonto might've provided transportation, and that's where Randy Bristol came in. Maybe the kid came asking for a favor, pretended to be in trouble. Then again maybe he'd gotten in over his head and Bristol was trying to dig him out.

Mitch would share his suspicions with Zach as soon as he and Kimberly were in the clear.

A truck door opened and closed. Then another. They were checking the trucks first.

"Climb over here on my side," Mitch instructed. He had to get her out of there. Hell, get them both out of there. This was a no-win situation. He searched around for a spare key.

It was wishful thinking and a waste of time.

Mitch risked a glance at the side-view mirror.

The man on his side had a pistol, so he assumed the other one did, too. The half dozen trucks in between wouldn't take long for the creeps to clear. They moved quickly, methodically checking the cab of each truck.

Mitch cranked the window down, thankful these older models didn't have automatic buttons, which would require starting the engine and, therefore, a key.

"They want me. Let them take me," Kimberly said, hoisting up her phone. "I can put on GPS and you can regroup and find me before anything happens. You said yourself that they aren't trying to kill me. It'll give you time."

"Not a chance. We have another option," he said.

"Mitch. Listen to reason. They don't need you, which means they'll shoot to kill," she continued.

She made a good point.

But there was no way Mitch would willingly allow her to give herself up to save him.

He couldn't let the men get any closer.

There had to be a better plan.

"Promise me that you'll try to get away," he said.

She didn't respond.

"Kimberly. Promise me."

Another beat of silence passed before she finally said, "I promise."

"Good. I'll create a diversion and I need you to run like hell around the side of the warehouse." He fished keys from his pocket and handed them to her. "If you make it to the truck before me, don't wait."

"Mitch—"

"There's no time to argue. I'll be fine. They want you and there's no reason to kill me," he said but he knew they'd take the shot in a heartbeat. He hoped they were bad shots. Either way he had every intention of making it home to his children. "If we get separated, get out of here and make contact as soon as you're clear."

"I will if you will," she committed.

"Deal." Now all he had to do was get them both out of there alive.

"What's the plan?" She popped her head up and checked her side. "My guy's getting close. He's two trucks back."

"No matter what I say in the next thirty seconds, stay right here and keep your head down." Mitch opened the door and hopped out before she could put up an argument. He slammed the door shut behind him, glanced at his guy and then darted toward the warehouse.

"Run, Kimberly. Get out of there. They found us. Go," he shouted as he ran. He darted around the side of the building, praying she'd stay put.

The crack of a bullet split the air.

His heart thudded.

He paused long enough to listen for footsteps. Heard

them. The *clomp-clomp* of two sets of boots meant both men were on his tail.

He checked the window for an alarm system. Found one. The blinking light near the office door was a welcome relief.

He picked up a rock and slammed it against the glass of the door. The small pane shattered, bringing an ear-piercing alarm to life.

Soon police would descend on the cluster of warehouses. They'd anticipate a threat.

Mitch listened for the footsteps but couldn't pick up the sound over the shrieking alarm. The men should've rounded the corner by now.

Which meant they'd most likely doubled back to Kimberly.

He muttered a curse as he turned back and pushed his legs as fast as they could go. As he rounded the corner, he slammed into an object full force.

After he was knocked off his feet, he immediately popped back up.

He leaned against the building to regain his balance as blood dripped down his face. His brain scrambled for a split second but he forced clarity.

Diving into the knees of his attacker, he knocked the guy off balance. The guy had a runner's build. The Runner proved his strength with a jab to Mitch's gut, followed by a knee to his groin.

Mitch had control of the guy's gun hand. Being shot at point-blank range wasn't in the plan today.

The Runner bucked, knocking Mitch off balance. The next thing Mitch knew he was facedown, eating gravel. The move knocked the gun loose. It scraped against concrete as it spun out of reach.

Mitch tried to twist around but was blocked. This guy was using Mitch's considerable size against him, beating him to the punch.

That was about to change.

Mitch spun one way and then shifted to the opposite direction. He slammed his fist into the Runner's jaw as he tumbled sideways.

The move gained Mitch enough of an advantage to climb on top of his opponent. Police sirens—a welcome relief—sounded.

He scanned the parking lot for Kimberly. The distraction gave the Runner an opportunity to land a punch hard enough to snap Mitch's head back. He spit blood as he tightened his thighs to a viselike grip and pinned the Runner's right arm underneath Mitch's left knee.

Tires squealed to a stop on the cruiser. The driver's door flew open and the business end of a gun was pointed at Mitch.

"Get your hands up," the officer shouted in the authoritative voice he'd heard Zach use with suspects.

Mitch threw his hands in the air and shouted, "There's a weapon ten feet from us on the ground. This man tried to shoot me and I defended myself."

The Runner struggled.

"I want both of your hands in the air. Now!"

As soon as Mitch lightened his grip, the Runner made a move.

"He's not going to cooperate and I'm not dying out here. Tell me what you want me to do," Mitch ground out as he pinned the Runner down again.

Another cruiser blasted in beside the first.

"Freeze." The cop moved closer, weapon leading the way.

"I can't. Not until this guy stops fighting," Mitch countered. "My name is Mitch Kent. My cousin is the sheriff of Broward County."

That seemed to satisfy the officer as he moved toward the weapon on the ground. He kicked it out of the way.

The second officer, gun aimed directly at the Runner now, came up alongside Mitch. He holstered his weapon and palmed zip cuffs.

Mitch got a good angle with his thighs on the Runner and then held his hands up. "This man shot at me and my wife. She's in a truck, waiting for me. There's another man."

When he put two and two together his heart fisted.

The second guy was nowhere to be seen.

That meant one thing.

He had Kimberly.

MITCH WAS AT the sheriff's office when he really wanted to be out searching for Kimberly. The truck had been empty, just as he'd feared. It had been half an hour since the parking-lot incident, and the Runner wasn't talking.

The only shred of hope he could hold on to was the knowledge that Baxter had wanted her alive.

Another fifteen minutes and the plane carrying Zach would land at the private airstrip ten minutes away from Sheriff Anderson's office.

Every minute lost while sitting in an office, doing nothing, was excruciating.

To be fair, the sheriff had every available man hunting for Kimberly.

The Runner had been identified as Ron Sawyer. He had a well-known association with Paul Baxter. Baxter ran one the larger human-trafficking rings in the south-west. There was an obvious connection to Randy Bristol's van-and-truck-rental business but like Kimberly had pointed out, her father's industry was heavily regulated. Even so, a man who'd give his shirt off his back would find a way to help someone in need—and that person in need was Tonto.

Mitch's cell buzzed in his pocket. He prayed that it would be Kimberly, letting him know that she was safe somewhere. It was unrealistic. The truck was still in the parking lot when he and the deputies had checked.

Zach's name popped up on the screen.

"Hello," Mitch answered.

"I have news." That Zach didn't prep him one way or the other sat heavily on Mitch's chest.

"Go ahead." He paced.

"The name Kimberly supplied came back with a hit. Tonto, otherwise known as Kenny Tonornato by his given name, is dead."

"How'd it happen?"

"He was tossed out of the back of a vehicle on a road leading to the Mescalero Reservation, which is not a far drive from Hatch," Zach informed him. "His wrists and ankles were bound…" Zach hesitated. The news was about to get worse. "There was a bullet wound in between his eyes. He was shot at point-blank range with a 9 millimeter."

Mitch muttered a string of curse words.

"He was a good kid who'd had it rough. Neighbors of the family reported that he was trying to work odd jobs in order to raise enough money to bring his grandmother across the border. She needed medical help. His mother was worrying herself sick." Zach paused.

"The pieces aren't hard to put together from there.

He was getting desperate to help his mother, so he went to the person who could get the job done and bring his grandmother to the States," Mitch said. "Baxter."

"Only, that kind of help comes at a price. He tells the kid to get a truck," Zach continued.

"And the only person he knows with one big enough is Randy Bristol," Mitch said. "Who also has a heart to match."

"Which explains why a decent man would willingly lend out a truck to a known criminal," Zach stated. "Because he thought he was lending it to Tonto. When he put two and two together he thought he could find a way out, thus the warnings to Kimberly."

Kimberly needed to know that the man she knew and loved as her father wasn't a criminal. Mitch wasn't sure why that was so important to him but it was.

"I thought you should know what we found," Zach said.

"Thank you doesn't begin to cover my gratitude," Mitch stated.

"It's what family does for each other. You'd do the same if the shoe was on the other foot." Zach was dead on. "Speaking of which, those bogus charges against you and Isaac have been dropped."

"As they should have been." Mitch was never more grateful for family than he was right now. Between his brothers, sister and cousins there was always someone who had his back. He returned the favor, too. There was a sense of belonging in that.

What did Kimberly have?

There had been two people she trusted before the age of eighteen. Both were gone. One was murdered.

She'd held steadfastly to her belief in her foster father's innocence no matter how much evidence mounted against him.

If Randy Bristol was guilty it was because of his kind heart. She'd said herself that he'd give the shirt off his back to someone in need. Tonto was a young kid, barely of age, who needed a helping hand. A man like Bristol wouldn't have let him down—that was the kind of man Mitch hoped he was. He could see himself tripping over the same wire. There must have been some paper trail in the rental agreements that could lead authorities to Baxter.

He sure as hell had no intention of disappointing Kimberly.

Mitch glanced at the clock.

An hour had passed since he'd last seen her, with no word on her whereabouts.

Chapter Seventeen

Kimberly's head hurt to the tune of feeling like someone had run a pitchfork through it, stabbing her multiple times.

Pain shot through her skull as she opened her eyes. A thumping noise pounded in her ears. She could count each beat of her heart.

"Sleeping Beauty's awake." Her gaze zeroed in on the quiet voice in the corner of the small dark room.

Sweat dripped off her nose as she tried to reposition herself to get a better look. Her wrists were bound together. She angled her body and quickly realized the same was true of her ankles.

She scanned the small space for Mitch. And then for the other creep when she couldn't find her husband.

It was just the two of them.

For now.

He'd obviously just alerted someone to the fact that she was conscious. She tried to memorize her surroundings so she could lead law enforcement back when she broke away from this creep. Her eyes strained to see in the dim light.

"Who are you?" she asked. He knew she was awake so there was no point in trying to pretend otherwise.

Maybe she could get some information from the creep who was built like a male gymnast. His hair was black as night. The reflective sunglasses he wore most likely covered brown eyes. He wore jeans and a collared shirt, and the underarms were stained with rings of sweat.

He sat in a fold-up chair. His frame blocked something… *What?*

She noticed the creep's hip holster, too, with a handgun in it. She had no idea what kind it was and wished she'd taken Mitch up on one of his offers to teach her to shoot a gun. She knew enough to realize that there was a safety mechanism that had to be flipped before the gun would fire. If she got close enough to him to take it, she would need to remember that.

Memorizing details about the creep caused hope to blossom that she might make it out of there alive.

Baxter wanted something from her. Is that who he'd called?

"Do you have a family?" she asked, hoping to get him to speak to her. He'd ended the call without another word and set his phone in his lap. He leaned toward her, clasped both of his hands together and rested his elbows on his knees.

The creep was chewing a mouthful of tobacco. He leaned to the left and spit.

Kimberly felt the hard concrete against her body. Each movement hurt, so she must've racked up some bruises on the way down.

Her mouth was dry, making it difficult to swallow. Dust was everywhere and the building couldn't be bigger than ten by twelve feet. A shed? The red clay on the creep's boots said she was in West Texas or New Mexico—most likely the latter.

Was she back in her hometown? A chill raced down her back.

Where was Mitch?

Panic nearly doubled her over at thinking anything could've happened to him.

The heat gripped her, making it difficult to breathe with all of the dusty clay filling her lungs when she tried to make a move.

This place reminded her of home. The dry air. The heat. If they weren't in New Mexico, they were close.

"Sit tight," the creep said. He had overly tanned skin—orange? Did he wear too much self-tanner? His face could only be described as squatty. Much like the rest of him—tree-trunk arms with a thick middle and not a lot of height. He looked strong. The man could bench-press Arnold Schwarzenegger.

The last thing she remembered was being dragged across the parking lot, with a viselike grip secured around her waist, before she was struck with something hard on top of her head. A rock? The butt of a gun? His free hand had covered her mouth so she couldn't scream for help as he toted her across the parking lot and away from Mitch.

She had the headache to prove she'd received a serious blow.

"Where's your friend?" she asked when she got no response from her other questions.

"In hell with your boyfriend," he shot back.

Kimberly's lungs almost seized but she covered her reaction with a blank face. Mitch had to be alive. The twins needed him. His family needed him. *She* needed him.

"Tell me where I am and why I'm here," she said.

He issued a grunt.

"You telling me that you have no idea?" he asked, his voice incredulous.

"Would I ask if I did?" She wished she could reel in the sarcasm as soon as the insulting words left her mouth.

Luckily he didn't seem offended. That or he didn't realize he was being insulted. Either way she wouldn't look a gift horse in the mouth. She wasn't sure if she should tip her hand and let the creep know she knew about Baxter.

She could throw out another name and see what response came.

"Is Tonto involved in this—whatever *this* is?" she asked.

"Not anymore."

Her heart pitched. From what she could tell, Tonto wasn't out of his teens yet. He wasn't much more than a kid. And the creep's grin said all she needed to know about what had happened.

"So you killed him. For what? I don't have any money. My father wasn't a wealthy man," she said, trying to hold back tears at the senseless loss of life.

"Tonto was stupid," he said. The smug smile said he'd most likely done the dirty work himself.

"Stupid people drive past me on the highway every day. Doesn't mean they should die."

"No one refuses a job from the boss." There was disdain in his voice.

"I doubt we're talking about a legitimate business," she countered. At least she had him speaking to her. "Maybe he wasn't a criminal."

"You're right about that. He was too weak—"

"To what?" she interrupted. "Hurt innocent people?"

"No one asked him to hurt anyone." He balked. "The kid would've slept with the light on the rest of his life if he had to walk one day in my shoes."

"Then what was the job?" she prodded.

"To give you up," he said like he was reading a cereal-box label. *Twenty-six grams of sugar. Zero carbohydrates. Kill a kid.*

Her breath caught.

"What do you mean by that?" she regained composure before he could see how much hearing those words hurt. Were they true? He could be playing her. Trying to throw her off track.

"He wouldn't tell us where you'd run off to hide." He sneered. Spit.

Everything inside her wanted to break free of her bindings and hurt this soulless creep.

For the sake of her children, she would play it as cool as she could.

The door swung open, causing beams of sunlight to bathe the room. She blinked against the sudden burst of light, trying to make out the male silhouette moving toward her. She prayed that Mitch would walk in behind the guy.

When the door slammed shut, she could see again after blinking her eyes a few times.

"It's about time we finally meet." A man with tight-cut hair that was graying at the temples strolled in like he was walking into the lobby of the Four Seasons Hotel.

"Baxter." It was more of a statement than a question.

"There's no need to be so formal. You can call me Paul." He wore dress slacks and an expensive-looking collared shirt. The material was fine—maybe silk. He seemed too—she didn't know—clean-cut to be a criminal. Too well dressed to get his hands dirty. But then again he most likely had lackeys, like the creep, for that.

Another thought struck. This one lodged a knot in her stomach.

Would a criminal let her see his face or give out details like his first name if he planned to let her live?

The voice of reason in the back of her head shouted a resounding *no.*

Her heart hammered her ribs at thinking about her babies. The twins…and Mitch would have to live without her if this man had his way.

If she had to die today, she wanted her children to know she'd gone out fighting…fighting for them…fighting to stay alive so they could be a family even if that meant shared custody and every other Christmas spent together. Her heart wished for more, for Mitch, for a family. But that was wishful thinking.

Now that she'd had a taste of being with them again there was no way she could go back to being on the run alone.

In being face-to-face with the man she was sure had killed her father and ruined her life, she expected to hate him, to want to lash out. And part of her did. But another side to her—the side Randy and Julie had influenced—felt something she didn't expect to feel, compassion.

Was she frustrated? Yes.

Did she feel a sense of loss? Yes.

Did she hate Paul Baxter? No.

Instead she felt pity. The man standing in front of her was a coldhearted shell. She couldn't hate him no matter how much a part of her wanted to. She saw a little piece of herself inside his cold blue eyes—eyes that the world had hardened. And she wondered if she hadn't met the Bristols would she have gone down a different path?

A man like Baxter would only ever live half a life. He'd never know the best gifts in life—true love, kindness and forgiveness. And she was beginning to see the first step to healing was to learn to forgive herself.

A man like Baxter would only know hate and revenge.

A man who lived on the rim of society, preying on innocent people, would need two eyes in the back of his head for the rest of his life because someone would always want to rise up and take him out in order to replace him.

The world he lived in was violent and brutal.

She was even more grateful for the gift of her foster parents. They'd taught her how to reach deep inside herself to become a better person. They'd forgiven her mistakes—a lesson she was still learning. They'd taught her the meaning of real love.

In doing so, they'd given her a life. They were the reason she could open up to Mitch and let love inside. Real love. And if she survived this…nightmare…she would work as hard as she needed to in order to deserve his trust again.

"Whatever it is that you think I have, you're going to be sadly disappointed," she told him. "You destroyed my father's business. I have no money. I've got nothing a man like you would want."

Baxter motioned for the creep sitting in the chair to move out of his way.

As the man stood up and shoved his chair to one side, a metal container came into view—a safe. More than that, her father's safe. She'd forgotten about the small safe he'd had tucked away in a specially built filing cabinet in his office. He'd shown it to her the day after her eighteenth birthday. No wonder she'd forgotten it existed—that was seven years ago.

"Open it," Baxter demanded.

"I can't. I don't know how. Never seen it before in my life," she lied.

The expensive leather of his shoe caught the side of her cheek with full force as he kicked her. She let out a cry—a weakness she immediately quelled—as her head snapped back. She felt the cool trickle of blood. Her jaw felt like it was going to explode from pain.

"Are you trying to play me?" Like a shark circling its prey, Baxter walked a ring around her, each step quicker than the last. He reminded her of a prizefighter in the ring, working up to his next punch. "You and I both know Tonto gave your father photos and statements implicating me and my men. I'm not leaving here without the evidence."

She let her body go limp on the concrete and then curled into a ball to protect her vital organs.

"You better get to work," he demanded. "Figure it out."

"I can't," she admitted, holding her breath to steel herself for the next blow.

It didn't come but she didn't dare look up or speak again. She'd read an article about grizzly bears while waiting for a bus once. It stated that if one came charging toward a human, the best possibility for survival was to curl up in a ball and play dead. That's exactly what she did, figuring it couldn't hurt.

A moment later she felt herself being jerked up to

sitting position. She curled her arms around her bent knees, hugging them to her chest.

"I'm not lying. I can't help you. Why don't you just use a sledgehammer?" she said. She knew the combination at one time but that was years ago.

"It wouldn't work. Not a sledgehammer or explosives. Not with this kind of safe," he said. "Now do what you're told. Open it."

She held up her bound wrists, figuring she had no choice but to go along with what he said until she figured out a plan B.

"How long have I been here?" she asked.

Baxter nodded toward the creep.

He looked at his wristwatch. "You slept around eleven hours."

That explained the hunger pangs. She'd been starved as a child at one of her foster homes. Mrs. Saint had used starvation tactics as punishment if the carpets hadn't been vacuumed when she got home from bridge club.

Eleven hours. That would make this Monday. Afternoon. Her brain cramped at trying to think. She was still woozy and more than a little bit nauseous.

Creep walked toward her with an opened blade from a pocketknife.

She sucked in a burst of air when he ran the blade alongside her cheek with a sneer.

"Just get it over with if you're going to kill me," she said through clenched teeth.

"Quit messing with her. Let's see what she knows, Landry," Baxter interjected.

"I haven't seen this thing since I was eighteen years old," she said. "I'm sure my father has changed the combination since then."

"Now we're getting somewhere," Baxter said, acknowledging that she'd just modified her recollection.

Again, he would only give her information if he planned to make sure she'd never sit across from him in a witness box. She thought about Tonto and her heart seized.

The creep sliced through the masking tape binding her wrists.

She motioned toward her ankles.

"I die and you'll go to prison for the rest of your life for the murder. Law enforcement is looking for me. They know who you are and that you've been chasing me around the country," she said to Baxter, looking him straight in the eye. She figured that she might as well play her cards, considering she had precious few.

"Are you threatening me?" He laughed but then his face twisted into a sneer. He nodded to the creep.

The creep picked up a backpack before sliding on a pair of plastic gloves. He pulled a rope with a hangman's knot tied to it. He tugged at the noose.

Baxter took a menacing step toward her. "It's terrible what happened to that girl from Hatch. It was her turbulent upbringing that caused her to turn on the two people who'd rescued her from the system. The only people who loved her and provided her with a home, food and clothing, according to interested neighbors."

Baxter let out a wicked-sounding squeal. The man was psycho.

"No one will believe you. I loved Randy and Julie Bristol. People will testify to that effect," she countered.

"No one's saying that you didn't love your foster parents. It's precisely your love for them and subsequent betrayal that caused the guilt to drive you crazy. You couldn't live with yourself anymore. So…pity really… you hung yourself." Baxter physically punctuated his sentence by pretending to place the noose around his neck and pulling. He let his eyes bulge and stuck his tongue out, mimicking a dead person hanging from a rope.

He walked to her, stopping in front of her and then ran his finger along her jawline.

"A shame to waste such a pretty girl."

"You can't make me put that thing around my neck." She breathed steady breaths to hold on to tendrils of what little calm she could.

"That's where you're wrong," Baxter said. "I can do anything I want."

Deputy Talisman.

"Law enforcement knows that you have a deputy in your pocket. The FBI is being brought in to investigate Talisman," she lied. She had no idea how it would work and prayed that Baxter had none, either.

The look that flashed across his face was priceless.

She tried to work the bindings on her feet as discreetly as possible. At least her hands were free. Was there any way she could get to her feet and charge toward the creep? Have a go at his weapon?

Her legs were numb and she couldn't remember the last time she felt anything other than prickly sensations on her feet. Without blood circulation she didn't stand much of a chance of carrying out her plan.

The thought that her twins might find a news story someday that said their mother had taken her own life heated her blood to boiling.

In the shed, it was two against one, and she already

knew the creep was strong. She'd picked up a few martial-arts skills but they were mostly defensive maneuvers.

Baxter grabbed her by the back of her hair and pulled her off the ground a few inches. Her hands came up and grabbed hold of his hands.

She used momentum to twist her body around while gripping his hands and land a kick to his groin. He grunted.

"Bitch," Baxter screamed.

He doubled over. She rolled onto her back and thrust her feet toward his head.

Chapter Eighteen

"So, let me make sure I'm understanding this correctly…" Mitch was done being patient. He and Zach had been riding shotgun in separate cruisers with well-meaning deputies for—he glanced at the clock—eleven hours straight.

The most productive thing about their meeting up at the gas station so far was the caffeine. Mitch had downed his first cup and was on his second. Adrenaline was wearing thin and he needed the boost. "We're no closer to figuring out where she could be, and all we're planning to do about it is drive around some more and hope we stumble across Baxter or where his goons may have taken Kimberly?"

"Everyone in the county is looking for her. Hell, everyone in the state," Zach stated. "You have a small fleet of airplanes in the air. If you can think of a better course of action, I'd like to hear it."

His cousin was just as frustrated as he was. Mitch could tell based on the stress cracks on his forehead.

There was no sign of Kimberly. No sightings. Deputy Talisman was being interrogated. So far, to no avail.

Her cell phone had been dumped on the side of the

highway outside El Paso. She had to be right under their noses and they were missing it.

"You're the one with law-enforcement experience. What does your gut tell you?" Mitch asked his cousin. He wasn't trying to frustrate Zach; he just wanted Kimberly home safely where she belonged.

"That she's here and we're missing something," he said.

"Is she still alive? Wait. Don't answer that." Mitch changed his mind. He didn't want to hear statistics. She *had* to be alive. He couldn't accept another outcome. "We're looking for a needle in a haystack."

"I know it seems that way," Zach began.

Mitch issued a sharp sigh. Eleven hours had passed. He checked his watch. Eleven hours and fifteen minutes to be exact. He couldn't allow himself to go to a place in his mind where this ended badly. There was too much left unsaid between him and Kimberly, dammit.

Deputy Bright walked up to the pair. He glanced at Mitch. "Ready?"

Mitch nodded before thanking the man. It couldn't be much fun for him to have Mitch riding along for his twelve-hour shift. Speaking of which, a shift change would come up soon. Mitch wondered how long the sheriff would be able to allocate his resources to one case without any leads.

It was a short walk to the cruiser.

As he gripped the handle, Zach called out.

Mitch turned in time to see Zach waving him over. His cell was to his ear. A knot twisted in his gut as he hightailed it over to his cousin.

"Where is that?" Zach asked the caller as he made eye contact with Mitch. The call was on speaker and

Deputy Stillwater nodded. Stillwater was tall, dark in complexion and had an athletic build. He wore a white Stetson and reflective sunglasses. He had a serious expression and looked like the kind of guy who wouldn't put up with a lot of flak.

"I know that location," Stillwater said. "It used to be named Shoots but it's been closed a few years."

"He's sure?" Zach said into the receiver after a nod of acknowledgment to the deputy.

"We've already sent people to watch Baxter's home and other known hangouts. There's been no activity, sir," the female voice assured. "We're out of ideas. Talisman started talking a few minutes ago. I ran out of the room to call you."

No activity at Baxter's local haunts for hours on end sounded odd even to a civilian. But Talisman's giving up the location could be a trap. Even if Baxter was there, he could've been alerted.

Not that Mitch and Zach had another option.

"We're on our way," Zach confirmed with a look toward Stillwater. The deputy nodded.

Deputy Bright was already making tracks to his vehicle. Mitch took off running to catch up.

Hope was a slippery slope, so he wouldn't go down that path just yet.

"Where are we going and how far away is Shoots?" he asked Bright.

"About twenty minutes," Bright replied, pushing buttons to turn on the lights and siren. Wheels spewed gravel as they peeled out of the parking lot. "We'll go dark as soon as we get closer."

Mitch had a feeling this was going to be the longest twenty minutes of his life.

Five minutes out, Bright darkened the lights and turned off the siren. A ride that was supposed to take twenty minutes took sixteen at the speeds he traveled.

He and Bright were the first to arrive to the location, almost immediately followed by Zach and Stillwater. The place was still set up as an outdoor shooting range.

Mitch shouldered the door open. He recognized a couple of trap fields and more than double that in skeet fields.

"Hold on," Bright said. "I need you to stay in the vehicle."

As much as Mitch had no plans to get in the way of law enforcement, he couldn't sit idly by.

"I won't interfere," he promised.

Bright issued a sharp sigh. "Sir, I can't allow—"

Stillwater and Zach were already out of their vehicle.

"I take full responsibility for him," Zach said.

"With all due respect you're out of your jurisdiction, Sheriff," Bright said. "Protocol's in place for a reason."

"I'd like to offer my assistance as backup. I'm a sworn peace officer and you need all the help you can get," Zach continued.

Time was wasting.

"We can't afford to lose another minute. We'll stay right here. Just find her and bring her back alive," Mitch said.

Stillwater called for backup. He and Bright had their weapons out, sweeping from side to side as they moved, methodically clearing obstacles and small makeshift buildings.

"So we just stand here?" Mitch asked Zach.

A plane flew overhead. And then another.

"We need to find cover. Standing out here like this,

we're an easy target. Baxter or one of his men could come out from behind one of these obstacles, shooting," Zach said.

"How do we know he's here?" Mitch asked, following Zach around a barricade, where they crouched low. The sun was high in the sky, heat bearing down on them.

"I overhead a report that two vehicles were parked near a shed on the property," Zach answered.

"This person say anything about seeing her?" Mitch asked.

Zach shook his head. Mitch didn't want to think about the fact that this could be a wild-goose chase. That Kimberly could have been murdered hours ago and left in a ditch along the highway or, like Tonto, tossed out of the back of a vehicle…

His cousin had his phone out and he was studying a map. "Follow me."

"Where to?" Zach was too smart to get them mixed up in friendly fire.

"We need to locate the vehicles. If things go sour Baxter will use his SUV to flee the scene."

Smart.

Zach pulled out his Glock and led the way with it.

"You have a spare one of those?" Mitch didn't like the idea of being the only one showing up to the party unarmed.

"This didn't come from me." Zach reached down to his ankle holster and retrieved a pistol.

Mitch accepted the offering, thanked him and then followed his cousin.

Beads of sweat rolled down Mitch's face in the dry, blistering New Mexico heat as they progressed toward the location.

Rapid shots fired, crackling like fireworks, freezing them in their tracks. Both dropped to the ground and then rolled onto their stomachs.

"Stay low," Zach whispered as they belly crawled toward an expensive-looking white SUV. Parked next to it was a late-model king-cab pickup truck. "They come out this way and we've got 'em."

Mitch knew enough about gun safety to realize he needed to put a solid barrier between the two of them and whoever came at them. He scanned the area and located a three-and-a-half-foot-tall concrete wall. It was approximately five feet wide. No doubt another tool meant for training Baxter's lackeys.

A small measure of hope tried to take root at the fact that the men hadn't been shooting Kimberly to kill. But then again all that really said was they needed her for something.

Once they got it, she'd most likely be tossed aside just like Tonto.

Again, Mitch couldn't allow the possibility to take seed in his thoughts. In order to push ahead he had to be convinced that she was still alive.

More bullets split the air. Zach muttered a few choice words as he palmed his cell. He fired off a text asking for an update from the sheriff and then stared at the screen.

He muttered another curse.

"We can't go in blind," Zach said. "We could end up hurting more than helping."

"I can't imagine how that could be possible," Mitch countered. A shot of adrenaline made it even harder to sit back and wait. Do nothing. The sound of blood rushing in his ears matched the *thump-thump-thump* of his heartbeat. The only good news so far was that Baxter was on-site.

Mitch didn't want to consider the possibility that Kimberly had been taken somewhere else. All signs pointed to her being here.

"This is hell for me, too," Zach admitted. He glanced at his screen again. "Nothing yet. It'll come."

Those last two words sounded more like hope than promise.

And then Zach's phone vibrated.

He put it on speaker and turned the volume down so low that Mitch could scarcely hear.

"I have two men down on the scene. ETA for backup is twenty-three minutes," Sheriff Knell said, sounding solemn. "Do not engage with the suspect. I repeat. Do not engage."

Zach's expression wore the stress cracks of a seasoned soldier returning from battle. Mitch had spent enough time around law enforcement to realize no one wanted to leave men down if they could help.

"What are the numbers?" Zach asked.

"Two men holed up in a shed," Sheriff Knell reported.

"Any signs of a female victim?"

"My officers have no idea if anyone else is inside that shed." The sheriff's voice was heavy.

Zach thanked his colleague and ended the call. He stared at Mitch. "You heard the man. We have no idea if she's in there."

"She is." Mitch couldn't say why he knew but a sense of certainty came over him. "Why else would they shoot if they had nothing to hide?"

"There are a lot of reasons. This could be the home base of their operation," he said.

Mitch examined his cousin. He could get a read on him with one look.

"That's not what you really believe," Mitch said.

"Good men are out there, dying. I'm going in one way or another. I'm just trying to figure out a way to keep you out of this," Zach said honestly.

"Then there's no reason to waste another minute sitting here." Mitch hopped to his feet.

"First instinct will be to go to the injured men. We need to secure the perimeter first. Baxter might be on the move. Best case is that he's still in the shed, figuring out his next step." Zach shot a look.

Mitch acknowledged that was the best scenario for the injured men. Not necessarily for Kimberly.

First things first, they needed to assess the situation up close.

"I won't do anything stupid."

"Didn't think you would," Zach replied as he crouched low and proceeded toward the trail.

Mitch followed, thighs burning as they passed the final barricade that lead to an open space about the size of an acre.

The trail opened up to flat land. A ten-by-twelve shed stood toward the right-hand side of the property. A ring of man-made barricades surrounded the area, making it easy for someone to navigate an escape situation.

Everything was still and dead quiet. There was no breeze. The sun pelted him, causing sweat to roll down the sides of his face.

Mitch scanned the area for signs of the officers. Two metal barrels to his left had fresh-looking blood streaks marking them. He nudged Zach and nodded toward the barrels.

Zach followed his gaze. He rocked his head slightly. His gaze swept the perimeter. The metal door to the shed was closed. There were no windows.

On closer inspection Mitch noticed a round cutout in place of a knob. The opening was large enough to fit a barrel and for someone to see through.

His cousin was eyeing the same area.

Zach turned to Mitch and signaled that he was going to check on the deputies. Another signal from his cousin indicated that he wanted Mitch to cover him.

Zach doubled back the way they came. Smart.

Zach reappeared in Mitch's sightline at the double barrels. The next thing he saw was his cousin administering CPR from behind the barrels.

Mitch kept vigilant watch at the metal door.

It swung open and his heart cramped.

Kimberly stumbled out and took a few unsteady steps.

His heart clutched.

"Don't shoot," she pleaded, dropping to her knees.

A clean-cut man stepped behind her and forced her to stand. Her body blocked a clean shot.

From the corner of his eye, he saw Zach abandon CPR and pop to his feet, crouching low behind the barrels. He wouldn't do anything stupid.

The barrel of a gun poked out of the hole on the shed's door.

Mitch had no way to warn Zach and could only hope that his cousin could see it.

And then he realized what was about to happen.

Baxter sidestepped as the shot cracked the air.

Kimberly's eyes widened as she searched her body. A red dot flowered on her stomach. Mitch had to stop himself from going nuts, giving away his location and getting himself killed. As much as he wanted to run toward her, he realized that's exactly what the men wanted. He refused to play into their hands.

Baxter took off a second later to Mitch's right, an easier trail to his SUV.

Fighting the urge to run to Kimberly, Mitch darted after Baxter instead.

The next thing he knew, Baxter had spun around on him and drawn a weapon. Before the man could get off a shot, Mitch fired.

Gunning toward Baxter at full speed, Mitch experienced a rush of adrenaline that made it impossible for him to steady his hand, but he was close enough for the bullet to take a chunk out of the inside of Baxter's left arm.

Baxter instinctively grabbed his wound.

Mitch took another couple of steps and then dove headfirst into the man's knees, knocking him backward and causing him to lose his balance. He stumbled a step before falling. The gun in his right hand flew onto the hard, unforgiving earth a few feet away.

Baxter stretched toward the weapon but Mitch was already on top of him, connecting jabs to his jaw. Baxter's head jerked with every punch landed. Blood splattered everywhere, both from Baxter's nose and from Mitch's knuckles.

The sounds of more shots being fired behind him registered. The knot braiding Mitch's gut twisted relentlessly.

He nailed punch after punch until Baxter's body went limp underneath him.

Chapter Nineteen

The next thing Mitch knew he was being dragged off Baxter by two sets of hands that felt like vise grips around his arms.

It took a second to register that one of the voices shouting at him was his cousin's.

"Kimberly needs you," Zach said in an urgent tone.

Mitch stopped resisting and popped to his feet.

Zach stepped over Baxter's bloody frame.

"Patch him up," he said to one of the EMTs. "He's going to spend the rest of his life in jail. I want him well enough to serve his sentence for a very long lifetime."

Law enforcement had descended on the scene that was now a bustle of activity. EMTs were on the ground, working on someone—Kimberly.

Mitch bolted toward them, toward her.

"Let him through," Zach commanded, using the authoritative voice all lawmen seemed to possess.

Mitch dropped to his knees beside her as an EMT allowed passage. He was performing chest compressions on her.

An oxygen mask covered most of her face. Seeing Kimberly lying there, lifeless, Mitch couldn't breathe.

He'd lost her once. He'd never survive losing her again

and especially now that he knew the real her. Smart. Brave. Fierce.

Tears welled in his eyes. He swiped at them.

"Stay with me, Kimberly," he said, taking her by the hand. "Don't go away again. My life means nothing without you. I love you. I want you to stay here with me and our twins. Aaron and Rea need you. I need you."

There was no response from her still, breathless body.

This wasn't right. None of this was right.

Dammit.

He leaned down next to her ear.

"Can you hear me? These next words that I'm about to say never came easy to me before I met you. I love you. I need you. I'm half a man without you." He sniffed the tears that had started rolling down his nose.

And then her hand twitched.

He heard an EMT say, "She's breathing."

And another, "You're doing great. Chopper's landing. We're going to fix you right up."

The sudden bursts of wind and *chop-chop-chop* of the helicopter registered somewhere in the back of Mitch's mind.

"Sir, we're taking her to Hope Memorial Hospital. Someone will take you there to meet us," the younger EMT said.

"Take good care of her," Mitch said.

Zach was already behind him, urging him toward the parking area. He glanced back to see that law-enforcement officers had the other one of Baxter's associates facedown and cuffed.

Kimberly's nightmare was over.

His was just beginning.

For three long days, Mitch held vigil by his wife's side after surgery to remove bullet fragments from her stomach. She'd been in and out of consciousness since then. Mostly out. The nurse had told him that she wouldn't remember any of this. Her vitals were strong. She was young and healthy. All signs pointed toward a full recovery. But no one knew for certain if she'd lost too much blood. Or if she'd ever be the same after the shooting.

His family had been taking shifts to keep him company. His brothers were at a hotel with Joyce and the twins. Amy and his sister, Amber, had gone to pick up an important package at the airport.

Exhaustion was wearing thin as Mitch sipped his umpteenth cup of coffee in the last seventy-two hours.

He watched his wife sleep, occasionally offering words of reassurance. She was going to be fine. She *had* to be okay when she woke.

Mitch wasn't much of a praying man, but he wasn't afraid to admit that he'd called in a man of the cloth to pray over her. He figured it couldn't hurt.

His brothers made sure he got fresh coffee, and Joyce made him a homemade meal every day. He didn't want to insult her but he had no appetite. One of his brothers would cover for him, slipping out with a full plate and returning with an empty one.

"Come on, Kimberly," he finally said, wishing he could see those beautiful eyes of hers again.

And then Kimberly coughed. Her eyes opened. She blinked a few times as her eyes adjusted to the sunlight bathing the room.

"I can close the blinds," Mitch offered. His heart galloped.

Her eyes found him and his chest squeezed. There was nothing left of him to protect. The past seventy-two hours of not knowing if she'd ever wake had hollowed him out. Every encouraging sign that she was recovering meant nothing if he couldn't share his life with her.

"It's okay," she rasped.

She seemed to realize he was holding her hand. Her other one came up and searched around her neck.

"Are you looking for this?" He pulled her wedding ring still attached to a string out of his pocket. The nurse had given it to him for safekeeping before wheeling her into surgery.

Her eyes lit up when she saw the gold band. "Yes."

"I can get the nurse." He placed the makeshift necklace into her palm.

"No. Not yet. What happened?" She glanced around, looking a little scared.

"You're recovering from surgery," he said. "Baxter and his cronies are locked away. It's over. You're safe now."

Relief crossed her tense features.

"What day is it?" She tried to sit up.

"Hold on. Doc says you have to take it easy." He picked up a remote and placed it in her hand.

"I liked holding your hand better," she admitted and her cheeks flushed. It was the first sign of color in her face.

"You have no idea how happy it makes me to hear that."

"What time is it?" she asked, raising her bed to an upright position. Her voice cracked when she spoke.

Mitch checked his phone. "Four thirty."

He scooted the tray table next to her and brought a cup of water to her lips.

She took a sip. "That's good. My throat is so dry."

Hearing her voice and seeing her sit up were about the best things he'd ever experienced after fearing that he'd lost her.

"It's Thursday," he stated.

A look of confusion drew her brows together before she started counting on her fingers.

"I've been here for three days?"

"Surgery went well and you've been sleeping a lot," he said.

"Have you been here this whole time?" She didn't hide her shock at the revelation.

"Yes. And I'll be here for the rest of your life if you say the word." He dropped down beside her bed, took her hand in his and rested it against his forehead. He feared he'd overwhelm her with his next words but his heart was about to burst if he didn't say them. So he lifted his chin to look directly at her. "I love you, Kimberly. And I want my wife back home where she belongs, where *you* belong. What do you think? Will you come home with me?"

Tears streamed down her cheeks and she smiled the biggest smile he'd ever seen.

"I love you, Mitch. I can't wait to come home."

He stood up and pressed a tender kiss to her lips.

"How soon can I get out of here?" she asked. The spark in her eyes had returned.

A soft knock sounded at the door.

"Come in," Mitch said.

Zach peeked around the half-opened door. "Is this a good time?"

"Yes," Kimberly said with another smile.

Mitch and Zach exchanged bear hugs before Zach moved to Kimberly's side.

She motioned for Mitch to sit on the edge of the bed, which he did.

"I remember a couple of deputies being shot at. Are they here?" she asked.

Mitch hadn't had time to give her the bad news.

Zach tucked his chin to his chest in reverence. "We lost one. The other has been treated and released."

"Zach couldn't save them both," Mitch added. His cousin had done everything he could. Stillwater had survived because of Zach's quick thinking.

"I'm so sorry," Kimberly said.

Mitch had set up a fund to take care of Bright's parents. The loss of the young deputy had hit the community hard. Mitch had also set up a college scholarship fund in Bright's name in order to honor his memory.

"Baxter and his men will do hard time," Zach reassured. "It won't bring him back or take away the pain you've suffered. But justice will be served. Talisman will spend the rest of his life behind bars, too. He started talking as soon as he realized he was in a no-win situation."

"And did he say how my father was involved in all of this?" she asked.

"Tonto was desperate to get his sick grandmother across the border, where she could get medical care. He was introduced to Baxter, who promised to help if Tonto could get access to a van," Zach informed her. "That's when Tonto went to your father, who agreed to help. But then—"

"My father figured out the partnership between Deputy Talisman and Paul Baxter," she said on a sharp sigh.

"He had proof in the safe," Zach continued.

"That's what he was really talking about," she said.

Mitch's cell vibrated. He checked the screen and turned to Zach. "Mind keeping her company for a second?"

"Not at all." Zach took the seat next to Kimberly. "We can't replace the Bristols. I know you loved them very much. But you have family to lean on now. You'll never be alone again."

Mitch heard Kimberly sniff back tears as he stepped into the hallway.

The trio of women coming toward him wore the second biggest smiles he'd seen all day.

The one in the middle's resemblance to his wife caused him to perform a double take. Her hair was more brown than black—Kimberly's original color—and her nose was slightly bigger. But he didn't need an introduction.

"She doesn't know you're here," he said to Rose.

"I can't wait to see her. It's been so long," the younger version of Kimberly had tearstained cheeks. And when he really looked at them, so did Amy and Amber.

He thanked them both for delivering the "package" that had taken Isaac exactly six hours to track down. He'd been begging for work to do since he'd been released from the hospital and the incident with the heifer seemed to be isolated.

The first conversation had lasted three hours. Rose had wanted to know everything about her older sister.

"I have goose bumps," Rose admitted. "I've thought about her every day for more years than I care to count."

"Well, then let's not keep you waiting any longer," Mitch said.

He stepped inside the door and then stepped to the side.

"There's someone here to see you," he said to Kimberly.

"The babies?" She perked up.

They would come a little later after being fed dinner. "Not exactly."

He nodded to Rose, who rushed in and to Kimberly's side.

Kimberly gasped and her hand covered her mouth. "It can't be. Is it really you?"

"It's me. Your little sister."

"You're okay," Kimberly said, throwing out her arms.

"Yeah." Rose seemed surprised. "I always had you with me to protect me."

She pulled out the charm on a string that Kimberly had given her before she'd been hauled off to a new home.

Tears streamed down Kimberly's cheeks as she pulled her sister into a hug.

Mitch took a back seat, chatting with his cousins and sister until the nurse came in, followed shortly by the doctor. The news was good. Kimberly was healing well and could leave the hospital in a couple of days.

The early evening hours flew by. Rose and Kimberly seemed to catch up on years in the span of a few hours.

A nurse came in and cleared everyone out, saying they could return once Kimberly ate her dinner and had a bath.

Mitch wrangled a spot in the chair next to his wife. Nothing and no one was going to keep the two of them apart again, and the nurse seemed to realize this as she excused herself to let Kimberly eat in peace. She promised to return in half an hour to help Kimberly bathe.

When the room was quiet and it was just the two of them again, Kimberly leaned toward Mitch.

"First you gave me love and then a family. Now my sister." Tears fell and he thumbed them away for her. "I'm a leaky faucet. But I just want to say that I can't imagine spending my life with a better man. I love you, Mitch Kent."

"The day we met is the day I found home," he said. "I'm ready to put the past behind us and start forever as a real family. No more hiding. No secrets. Just the two of us and our babies."

Kimberly wiped away more of those tears. "I love you. And I can't wait to go home."

* * * * *